THE GENTLEMAN

A ROMANCE OF THE SEA

ALFRED OLLIVANT

1st WORLD
LIBRARY
Literary Society

The Gentleman

Alfred Ollivant

© 1st World Library – Literary Society, 2004
PO Box 2211
Fairfield, IA 52556
www.1stworldlibrary.org
First Edition

LCCN: 2004195191

Softcover ISBN: 1-4218-0101-9
Hardcover ISBN: 1-4218-0001-2
eBook ISBN: 1-4218-0201-5

Purchase *"The Gentleman"*
as a traditional bound book at:
www.1stWorldLibrary.org/purchase.asp?ISBN=1-4218-0101-9

The Gentleman
contributed by Tim, Ed & Rodney
in support of
1st World Library Literary Society

TO

THE NAVY

CONTENTS

BOOK I - THE LITTLE TREMENDOUS

I - THE DEATH OF BLACK DIAMOND

II - MAGNIFICENT ARRY

III - UNDER THE CLIFF

BOOK II - BEACHY HEAD

I - THE GAP GANG

II - THE MAN ON THE CLIFF

III - ABERCROMBY'S BLACK COCK

IV - THE GARRISON

V - THE BOARDING OF THE PRIVATEER

BOOK III - FORT FLINT

I - BESIEGED

II - THE SALLY

III - THE SHADOW OF THE WOMAN

IV - THE GENTLEMAN'S LAST CARD

V - THE FORLORN HOPE

BOOK IV - NELSON

I - H.M.S. *MEDUSA*

II - KNAPP'S STORY

III - THE WISH AT EVENING

The introductory poem appeared originally in the *Pall Mall Magazine*, and is re-published by permission of the Editor.

OUR SEA

The Sea! the Sea!
Our own home-land, the Sea!
'Tis, as it always was, and still, please God, will be,
When we are gone,
Our own,
Possessing it for Thee,
Ours, ours, and ours alone,
The Anglo-Saxon Sea.

The stripped, moon-shining, naked-bosomed Sea.

No jerry-building here;
No scenes that once were dear
Beneath man's tawdry touch to disappear;
Always the same, the Sea,
Th' unstable-steadfast Sea.
'Tis, as it always was, and still, please God, will be,
When we are gone,
Our own,
Vice-regents under Thee,
Ours, ours, and ours alone,
The Anglo-Saxon Sea.

The mighty-furrowed, moody-minded Sea.

New suns and moons arise;
Perish old dynasties;
For ever rise and die the centuries;
Only remains the Sea,
Our right of way, the Sea.
'Tis, as it always was, and still, phase God, will be,
When we are gone,
Our own,
Our heritage from Thee,
Ours, ours, and ours alone,
The Anglo-Saxon Sea.

Our good, grey, faithful, Saxon-loving Sea.

Alfred Ollivant

JULY 1805

"Succeed, and you command the Irish Expedition," said the squat fellow.

"My Emperor!" replied the tall cavalry-man, saluted, and clanked away in the gloom.

*   *   *   *   *

A sweet evening, very fresh, the tide crashing at the foot of the cliff.

In the twilight, above Boulogne, a man was standing, hands behind him.

The moon lay on the water, making a broad white road that led from his feet across the flowing darkness West.

The dusk was falling. About him the earth grew dark; above him all was purity and pale stars.

Only the tumble of the tide, white-lipped on the beach beneath, stirred the silence; while one little dodging ship, black in the wake of the moon, told of some dare-devil British sloop, bluffing the batteries upon the cliff.

The rustle of the water beneath, its crashing rhythm and hiss as of breath intaken swiftly, soothed him. He fell into a waking dream.

It seemed to his wide eyes that the sea rose, heavenward as a wall; its foot set in foam, its summit on a level with his face. Against it a silver ladder leaned. He had but to mount that ladder to pluck the island-jewel, the desire of his heart these many years.

He reached a hand into the night as though to realise his wish; and even as he did so, the sloop barked.

A mortar hard by boomed; the sea splashed; the sloop scudded seaward, laughing; and the dreamer awoke.

Behind him, hutted on the cliffs, lay the Army of England: [Footnote: The Army of England was Napoleon's name for the Army of Invasion.] such a sword, now two years a-tempering, as even he, the Great Swordsman, had never wielded.

Beneath him in the dimming basin huddled 3000 gun-vessels, waiting their call.

Before him, across the moon-white waste, under the North star, lay that stubborn little land of Bibles and evening bells, of smoky cities, and hedge-rows fragrant with dog-rose and honeysuckle, of apple-cheeked children, greedy fighting-men, and still-eyed women who became the mothers of indomitable seamen - that storm-beaten land which for so long now, turn he where he would, had risen before him, Angel of the Flaming Sword, and waved him back.

Between him and it ran a narrow lane of sea, the moon-road white across it: so narrow he could almost leap it; so broad that now after years of trying he was

Alfred Ollivant

baffled still.

Could his Admirals only stop the Westward end of that narrow lane for six hours, that he and his two-hundred-thousand might take the moon-road unmolested, he was Master of the World.

But - they could not.

In his hand, fiercely crumpled, lay the despatch that told him Villeneuve was back in Vigo, shepherded home again.

And by whom?

That little one-eyed one-armed seaman, who for ten years now had stood between him and his destiny.

One man, the man of Aboukir Bay. [Footnote: On August 1, 1798, Nelson destroyed the French fleet in Aboukir Bay at the Battle of the Nile.]

BOOK I

THE LITTLE TREMENDOUS

I - THE DEATH OF BLACK DIAMOND

CHAPTER I

THE MAN ON THE GREY

The man on the grey was in a hurry.

The stab of his backward heels; the shake and swirl of his bridle-hand; the flog of his arm in time with the horse's stride, told their own tale.

A huge fellow, his face was red and round as a November sun. Hat and wig were gone; and his once white neck-cloth was soaked with blood.

He came over the crest of the Downs at a lurching gallop; down the ragged rut-worn lane, the dusty convolvuluses glimmering up at him in the dusk; past the squat-spired Church in the high Churchyard among the sycamores; down the rough and twisted Highstreet of Newhaven in the chill of that August evening, as no man had ever come before.

A bevy of smoke-dimmed men in the bar of the

Bridge, discussing in awed whispers last night's affair of the Revenue cutter off Darby's Hole, hushed suddenly at the clatter and rushed out as he stormed past. He paid no heed. Those staring eyes saw nothing but the brown street sliding under him, a pair of sweating ears, a flapping mane, and before him a tumble of old roofs; while beyond in the harbour, the spars of a sloop of war pricked the evening.

Clear of the little town huddling on the hillside, he drove along the bank of the slow green river, flogging still.

One thing was clear: the grey was dead-beat.

He was roaring like a furnace, and straight as a rail from tail to muzzle. Black and white with sweat, he jerked along at a terrible toppling stagger. Only those vice-like legs and hands plucking, plucking, kept body and soul together.

Where the river widened, and the sea gleamed misty across the harbour-mouth, as though he knew his mission was fulfilled, up went his head, and he fell in thundering ruin.

Where he fell he lay, lank-necked.

The tail twitched once; the body trembled; the great heart broke.

　　　　　Alfred Ollivant

CHAPTER II

THE GALLOPING GENT

I

A boat had just put off from the bank, a tall lad steering. The great red horseman, strangely active for so huge a man, flung himself clear of his horse, snatched a pistol from a holster, and came floundering down the cobbled river-bank, his coat-tails floating.

"Put back, sir!" he bellowed in husky fury. "Put back, my God! or I'll fire."

He was standing, the water to his tops, with heaving shoulders.

"Don't shout; don't shoot; and don't swear," replied a voice, pure as a lady's. "And perhaps I'll oblige."

The boy edged the boat into the bank. The huge fellow, in too great a hurry to wait, floundered out, clutched her by the stern, and scrambled in.

"My God, sir!" he panted, thrusting a dripping face into the boy's. "D'you know who you're a-talking to? - I'm a ridin-officer on Government business."

"And d'you know who *you're* a-talkin to?" replied the boy, cold as the other was hot. "I'm a King's officer on King's business. Remove your face, please. Sit down. And don't shake so, or you'll spill us. - I'm a midshipman going aboard my ship."

"Then you're just in time for warm work, Mr. Milkshipman," panted the other.

He bumped down on the thwart opposite the waterman, and thrust at the oars.

"Row, man, row!" he urged. "The Gallopin Gent's got through."

II

The colour of apple-blossom, coming and going in the lad's cheek, died away, and left him pale.

He was a splendid stripling, sun in his hair, sun in his eyes; with something of the lank grace of the fawn about him.

The face was fine almost to haggardness; with long chin, delicate nose, and eager eyes, very shy.

The boy had broken through the chrysalis of childhood, and not yet emerged into the fighting male. There was no down on his chin; the radiance of his cheek was yet undimmed. The soul, rosy behind its clouds, still tinged them with dawn-lights.

He was a Boy, sparkling Boy; Boy at the age when he is Woman, and Woman at her best, the playfellow, the tease, the inspiration; free of limb, as yet untrammelled of mind; with passionate hatreds and heroic adorations.

He was steering now, his eyes on the battered topsails in the mists before him; and in those eyes a glitter of swords. Had his mother or Gwen been there, they could have told from that frosty calm, those jealous-drooping lids, that Master Boy meant mischief.

And so it was.

This fat fellow with the heaving shoulders on the thwart before him, this chap with the crease across his bald neck, and the black sweat trickling from his hair, had insulted him.

As woman, he was bent upon revenge; as man, he would go warily, striking only to strike home.

"That was a fine horse you flogged to death," he began tranquilly, trailing his fingers in the dead green waters.

"Yes, sir," panted the other, thrusting at the oars. "I don't spare spur when I'm ridin agin the French. I'm a man, and an Englishman - not a pink-faced, girl-eyed booby togged out in a cocked hat and a tin dagger, calling meself a King's officer."

"I guessed that you were not one of us," replied the boy delicately. "Your manners are too distinguished. But tell me a little more about your ride. You seemed in rather a hurry. I take it you were riding for a drink."

The great man swung round. His whole life seemed to

have stopped short, and now hung behind his eyes - an appalling shadow.

For one swift moment the boy thought he would be struck.

Then the big man spoke; and his voice was measured and very still.

"If you think I burst the gamest eart that ever beat in an orse's ide for a drink, why then, sir," with crushing simplicity, "you think wrong."

He resumed his rowing, and continued with the same surprising dignity.

"I bred that orse; I broke that orse; I loved that orse."

The tide of the boy's being set back with a shock.

"O!" he cried. "O ... I didn't mean ... I really...."

"That's all right, sir," came the other's smothered voice. "I know you didn't."

He swallowed, and his face grew rigid. Then a light broke all about it.

"But there!" with husky pride. "He won't bear me no grudge - will you, old man?" with a hoarse burst of tenderness, flinging his arm towards the bank, where the dead horse's girths glimmered still in the dusk. "He know'd I wouldn't have asked it of him, only I had to. That's my old orse! that's my Robin! - Never asked no questions. Just took and died and did his duty without the talkin. Maybe some of us might learn a bit

　　　　Alfred Ollivant

from him."

Taking a great bandana from his pocket, he blew his nose like the report of a pistol.

"A'ter all," he said, with touching solemnity, "he died for his country, did my Robin - same as Abercromby at Alexandrya."

III

Behind them on the hill a clock struck eight.

The riding-officer held up his hand.

"Ark!" he cried. "It was going seven in Ditchling as I pelted down the Beacon. Gallop! gallop! gallop! There's ne'er another orse in England could ha done it, with big Jerry Ram bumpin on his back all the way; danged if there be!"

He thumped his knee.

"King George ought to know on it! He died for him. Fair lay down to it, belly all along the ground. Might ha know'd he was on the King's business, and the Gentleman with two minutes' start streakin away for Birling Gap like a bullet from the bow."

"Aw, he'll be out again than?" drawled the waterman, sleepy and Sussex.

"Out again!" shouted Big Jerry, and clapping the

handkerchief to his ear, thrust it beneath the other's eye of mildew. "What's that? - blood, ain't it? - whose? - mine. - How? - The Gentleman."

"You'll ha met him than, I expagt?" cooed the waterman in his cautious way.

"He met me more like," replied Big Jerry with the grim humour of the whole-hearted man, who gives hard knocks and takes them all in good part.

"Not but what we was expectin him, you'll understand."

"You knaw'd he was comin than surely?" came the waterman's slow musical voice.

"Know'd it!" roared the other. "O course we know'd it. Why's the *Kite* been layin in Cuckmere Haven since night afore last? - why was the Gap Gang strung out all the way from Furrel Beacon to Beachy Head all day yesterday? - Why was Black Diamond mouchin round in Lewes this morning? - Why? - why? - why?"

"Why?" asked the boy, breathless.

"Because the Gallopin Gent was comin down with despatches for Boney, and they were keepin the road for him. That's why," screamed the big man, bumping up and down in his excitement.

"Only question was which way. Ye see it's most in general all ways at once with him. Up and down, day and night, all over Sussex, these weeks past. No stoppin him; no coppin him; no nothin him. Always the same chap - gentleman, mighty gay, bit o red

Alfred Ollivant

riband in his button-hole, and blood chestnut with a white blaze between his knees. Always the same tale - gave em the go-by somehow. No sayin where or when - only just when you're least expectin him, then you can make sure of him. And when you are ready for him, seems he's readier for you."

He mopped his forehead, the laughing puckers gathering about his eyes.

"Look at us this evenin. There we was ridin easy up the Beacon, me and the orse-patrol - *lookin for him*. Just as we tops the brow who pops over the wall like a swallow but the Gentleman himself on his chestnut?"

He threw back his head and chuckled.

"There! - I can't ardly elp laughin. The cheek o the chap!"

"Did he run?" asked the boy, all eyes.

"Run!" snorted the riding-officer. "No run about *im*.... Rode at us like a rigiment of cavalry, swinging his sword, and laughin fit to bust himself.... Half the boys bolted - and I don't know as I blame them: they swear he's old Nick. Dick Halkett, old Job, and me, we stood it.... Bang he rides at old Job and bowls him over a buster; runs young Dick through the body; slops me over the pate a good un; and steals away down the hill, waving his hand and crying - 'Adoo! adoo! adoo! remember me!' - as if we was likely to forget him!"

The big man mopped his bloody ear with a quizzical grin.

"I know'd it was no good follerin. Nothing foaled o mortal mare can collar that chestnut, once she's away. So I bangs my hat down, catches the old orse by the ead, and rams him down the hill for Newhaven."

He began to push at the oars again.

"For there's two roads to Birling Gap, my lad: one by land, and one by sea. We've missed him by land. Now we'll see what the Jack-tars can do."

IV

The boy said nothing. His eyes were on his ship, dim above him in the mist.

She was in rags and tatters: so much he could see, and little else. Yet to him she seemed to glow in the dusk. He saw her through blurred eyes in a cloud of glory, and his heart thrilled to her.

She was his ship; that ship of which he had dreamed ever since he could dream, this boy born to the sea.

And was he not proud of her?

Shivering like a lover, he brought up alongside; and as he did so he thrust out a hand to feel the wooden ribs which covered that heart of valour.

For was she not the little *Tremendous*, of whom the heroic tales were told!

Alfred Ollivant

CHAPTER III

THE GUNNER OF THE SLOOP

Swiftly and silently the *Tremendous* spread her wings in the dusk.

The riding-officer was going over the side.

"Good luck, sir!" he said. "Make a cop; and Pitt'll thank you on his knees."

For all answer the block-of-granite little man by the wheel turned his back.

"Cut the cable!" he barked. "Set studdin-sails alow and aloft! Inboard side-lights! Boniface, take a party of small-arm men forrad, and keep a sharp look-out!"

Before the riding-officer had dropped into the dinghy, the *Tremendous* began to slap the water, shaking out ragged topsails as she slid out of the harbour, a misty rain shrouding her.

"There's a row-boat coming up astern, sir," ventured the boy - "rowing like mad."

"I have ears, sir, and I'm usin em," snapped the other, and stumped forward, leaning heavily on a stick, thick and surly as himself.

They were the first words he had spoken to the lad, this block-of-granite little man, across whose knees his father had died at St. Vincent; and the boy did not find them encouraging.

> "Send im victoriush,
> Appee and gloriush,
> Long to reign o er - i - ush,
> Goshave -

"Uncle George!" bawled a bibulous voice. "Row, ye devil, row! - or I'll split y'up, and chuck y'overboard."

A boat pelted up under the counter of the sloop. The singer rose suddenly, clutched at a man-rope, and came swinging up the side.

The light of the binnacle-lamp fell upon him.

He was a tall fellow, with bushy black whiskers, a long tallowy nose that in some old-time battle had been broken, and eyes with a wild wet gleam in them. Now he sheered up against the bulwark, waving riotously.

"Three cheers for the lirrel *Tremendous*! Ooray! ray! ray! - We're alf our ship's company short. There's only old Ding-dong left on the quar'er-deck. I'm drunk as David's sow. And we're off to cur out the Grand Armee. Ooray! ray! ray!" and he fell hiccoughing away into foolish laughter.

"Hadn't you better go below?" said a pure treble at his side. "You're beastly drunk."

The man pulled himself together, and stared through the gloom.

"Lumme!" he whispered. "A tottie! - a tottie for Lushy!... Lemme cuddle ye, darlin, *do*."

"I'm a midshipman," said the boy briefly. "Shut up; and behave yourself."

The man tried to stand up, and swept off his hat.

"Ow de do, sir? Ow de do? By all means ow de do? Lemme introjuice you all round. I'm Mr. Lanyon, commonly called Lushy, because? one? me failins: Gunner aboard this packet by rights, and Actin Fust Lieutenant by the grace o God - there bein no one else to act, see? This ere," he continued, smacking the bulwark, "is His - Majesty's - ship - *Tremendous*, well known and respected between the Lizard and the Nore. Not lookin her sauciest just now, I grant you: shrouds tore to tatters, mizzen spliced, bowsprit splintered, plugged fore and aft, and alf her weather bulwark carried away. But that's *ex tempore*, as the sayin is. We only put in at dawn to refit, and land wounded."

"Where's she been?" asked the boy.

"Been!" cried the other with rollicking laughter. "That's a good un. Ere's a kid ain't eard where we been. Been!" the sudden thunder in his voice. "Why, in Boulong Arbour among Boney's craft. H'in and h'out, under Nap's nose. Stormed the Arbour Battery; set the gun-vessels afire; and came out under their guns, colours at the truck, and the bosun's boy in the mizzenchains singin -

O it's a snug little island,
A right little tight little island."

He clutched the boy's shoulder, and thrust flaming eyes into his.

"Old man's got a game leg since Camperdown. Fust Lieutenant led the landin party - Mr. Wrot. Dessay you've heard tell of him. Dry Wrot, they called him. Tubby little bloke, all belly and big voice. Fine chap to fight, though, be God - only so thirsty, same as me. He took it in the tummy, crawlin through the embrasure - hand-grenade, I fancies. I was next man on the ladder." He was marching up and down, his hands swinging, seeming to smoulder almost in the gloom.

"Pretty work in the battery, be God, as ever I see! - One time we was bungin round-shot at each other across the casement, like marbles. Give the Mossoos their due they fought like eroes; but not like h'us, sir! not like h'us!"

He strode up and down, breathing flame.

"Ah, you should ha seen us. I were in me glory. A bloody massacree, that's what it were. Bloody massacree. Enough to make a blessed saint weep for joy. Pommesoul it were."

He turned in his stride, and the lamp showed the tears dribbling down his face.

"And when we'd mushed up the blanky caboodlum: spiked the guns; sent the gunners to glory; and blow'd up the battery, who led the boys out?"

He stopped dead.

"Old Lush! - Lushy, the Gunner, Gorblessim!" swelling his chest, and patting it. "And why? - because there wasn't a quarter-deck officer, not so much as a middy or mate, left to do it."

He resumed his strut with fighting hands.

"That's our sort aboard the *Tremendous*, sir. We're the halleloojah lads to fight. And what we are, old Ding-dong made us."

"Who's old Ding-dong?" asked the boy, breathlessly.

The Gunner shot a finger at the block-of-granite figure forward.

"That's the man as won the battle o the Nile," he whispered with husky magnificence. "And ere's the man that elped him."

He bowed with wide hands. Drunk as he was there was yet a dilapidated splendour about the fellow as about an historic ruin. The boy felt it through his disgust.

"I thought Nelson did a bit," he said.

"Nelson did much; I did more; *e* did most," with a wave forward. "Why!" shouting now. "Who was it led the line inside the shoal - creepin it, leadsman in the chains, soundin all the way? - We *Thunderers*, the *Goliath* treadin mighty jealous on our heels. And who commanded the *Thunderer*? - Old Ding-dong. And what did he get for it?"

He smacked a hand down on the boy's shoulder.

"Broke him, sir! - broke him back to a sloop o war! - old Ding-dong, the damdest, darndest, don't-care-a-cursest old sea-dog as ever set his teeth in a French line o battle ship, and wouldn't let go, though they fired double-shotted broadsides down his throat."

"But why did they break him?" gasped the boy. "It doesn't sound like Nelson."

The other smacked his long nose with a finger mysteriously.

"I don't know what you mean," said the boy, short and sharp.

"Ah, and just as well you don't," replied the other loftily. "Some day, Sonny, you'll know all there is to know and a leetle bit more - same as me. Plenty time first though. If you've done suckin it's more'n you look."

He began to march again.

"Yes, sir: he'd ha hoisted his broad pendant afore this, would old Ding-dong, pit-boy and powder-monkey and all, only for that. And as I'd ha gone h'up with him as he went h'up, so I goes down with him when he goes down. I know'd old Ding-dong. He was the man for me. Talk o fightin! - Dicky Keats, Ned Berry, the Honourayble Blackwood: good men all and gluttons at it! - but for the real old style stuff, ammer-and-tongs, fight to a finish, takin punishment and givin it, there ain't a seaman afloat as'll touch our old man."

He spat over the side.

"Yes, sir, when he went, I went along, and never regretted it - never. We've seen more sport aboard this blame little packet than the rest of the Fleet together. Clear'd the Channel, be God, we ave! - prowlin up and down, snow and blow, fog and shine, like a rampin champin lion. Why, sir, we've fought a first-rate from Portland Bill to Dead Man's Bay - this blame little boat you could sail in a babby's bath! *Took her too!* and towed her into Falmouth Roads, all standin, like a kid leadin its mother by the and. Talk o Cochrane and the *Speedy*! - Gor blime! - what's he alongside us?"

He steadied suddenly.

"Ush! ere comes the old man."

The boy could hear the stump of a stick on the deck.

"What's he wearin?" whispered the other, peering. "You can most always tell the lay he's on by that. Pea-jacket means boat-work, cuttins out, fire-ships, landin parties, and the like. If it's old blue frock and yaller waistcoat, then it's lay em aboard and say your prayers. And if it's cocked hat and chewin a quid, then it's elp you God: for your time's come."

"You're a disgrace to the Service, Mr. Lanyon," came a curt voice.

"And you're a credit to it, sir," was the hearty retort.

"Go below."

"And just sposin I won't," answered the drunkard -

"only sposin, mind! - just for the sake of argyment, d'ye see? - what then?"

"Irons."

The drunkard folded his arms.

"And might I make so bold, Commander Ardin," he began elaborately, "to ask who'll fight your guns, your Actin Fust in irons; and besides yourself ne'er another officer on the quar'er-deck - only this ere squab."

"I'll fight em myself if needs be. Go below, d'ye hear?"

The Gunner stumbled away, roaring laughter.

"Sail the blurry ship; fight the blurry ship; sink the blurry ship; and go to ell in the blurry ship. That's old Ding-dong."

Alfred Ollivant

CHAPTER IV

OLD DING-DONG

"They call you Kit?"

The boy started.

His name, his pet name that he had not heard for days, on the lips of this block-of-granite little man, who had only spoken so far to snub him.

"Mother does, sir - and Gwen."

There was silence; only the water talking beneath the ship's bows, as she took the open sea and began to swing to it.

"Your father was my friend," continued the voice, less harsh now. "I was a pit-boy; he was a gentleman: we was friends."

The voice was gruff again.

"Ran away to sea same night - he from the Hall; me from the pit-mouth. Met under the old oak on the green.

"'Ready, Bill?' says he.

"'Right, sir,' says I.

"'Then forge ahead.'

"And forge ahead it was, and never parted, till the Lord saw good to come atween us for the time bein at St. Vincent."

The voice in the darkness ceased and began again.

"Quiberon Bay was our first. Fifty-nine that were. I was powder-monkey on the *Royal George*; he was Hawke's orderly midshipman. St. Vincent our last. And a God's plenty in between. One time Dutchmen; one time Dons; and most all the time the French. Yes, sir," with quiet gusto, "reck'n we saw all the best that was goin in our time, and not a bad time neether - for them as like it, that's to say: seamen and such."

He was silent for a time, chewing his memories.

And what memories they were! - Had he not sailed under Boscawen in the fifties, when that old sea-dog stood between England and Invasion? Had he not lived to see Napoleon's Eagles brooding over the cliffs of France, intent on the same enterprise? - And between the two, what men, what deeds? - Hawke smashing Conflans in a hurricane; Rodney, gloriously alone, fighting his ship against a fleet; Duncan hammering the Dutch; Sam Hood, Jack Jervis, Nelson, Cuddie Collingwood; and all that grim array of big-beaked, bloody-fisted fighting men who for fifty years had held the narrow seas against all comers.

"D'you remember your father?"

The old man brooded over the boy. In a dumb and misty way he was puzzling out one of life's mysteries - this long stripling with the eyes sprung somehow from that other long stripling with the eyes, whom he had followed from the pit-mouth fifty years since.

"I just remember him coming into the nursery with mother and a candle the night before he sailed the last time, sir, to join Lord Howe."

"Ah," mused the old man, "that'd be a week afoor the First o June; and nigh three years afoor he died."

He paused again, rummaging in his memory.

"He was Post-Captain at St. Vincent; I was his First - aboord the old *Terrible*, 74.... You'll ha heard all about *that* tale. [Footnote: Sir John Jervis crushed the Spanish fleet off Cape St. Vincent in 1797. In this action the Spanish fleet was in two divisions. In order to prevent a junction between them Nelson drew out of the British line and single-handed attacked the Spanish weather-division, including the Spanish flag-ship and five other sail of the line. See Mahan's "Life of Nelson."]

"'Plucky chap, Nelson,' says the Captain, as he tumbles to the little man's game. 'Wear ship, and a'ter him.' So we hauls out? the line, us and the *Culloden* - Tom Troubridge - and pushes up, all sail set, to help him.

"By then we got alongside, the *Captain* - Nelson's ship she were - was a sheer hulk. As we pass her, your father leans over the rail.

"'Well done, *Captain*,' says he, liftin his hat.

"Nelson blinks his one eye up - I can see him now.

"'That you, Kit?' he pipes through his nose that way of is'n. 'You've got it all your own way now. I'm a wreck. Good luck, *Terrible*.'

"So on we goes bang atween two Spanish Fust-rates - hundud and twenty guns apiece. Had em all to ourselves, and asked no better.

"'Just your style, Bill,' says the Captain. He was pacing up and down the lee of the poop with me. 'Pretty work, ain't it?'

"'Too pretty to last, sir,' says I; as our fore-mast went by the board.

"Just then up runs the carpenter's mate all of a sweat.

"'Well, Michael,' says the Captain, 'what is it to-day?'

"'Goin down with a run, sir,' pants old Chips. 'Twenty foot? water in her well.'

"The Captain turns to me.

"'Where's the nearest land, Willum?' says he, with that twinkle of is'n. Always called me Willum, when he meant mischief, did the Captain.

"'Why, sir,' says I, 'the bottom, I reck'n.'

"'Wrong again,' says he. 'That's the nearest land to me,' and he points at the *Santy Maria*, Don Somebody Somethin's Flag-ship. 'Hard a-starboard, if you please, Mr. Hardin,' says he. 'I'm a-goin to land.'

"So I luffs up alongside, and fell aboard Er Oliness - like a mighty great mountain above us she was, all poop, and galleries, and Armada fittins.

"When our bow scraped her quarter,

"'Anybody for the shore!' pipes the Captain; and he jumps into her main-chain....

"Ah, but you should ha heard the men cheer!"

The old man paused, breathing deep.

"Ten minutes a'terwards he was dying acrost my knees on the spar-deck of the Don.

"'Has she struck, Bill?' he whispers, coughing....

"'The three decker's struck, sir,' says I, 'and the four-decker's strikin.'

"He shuts his eyes.

"'Then I can depart in peace,' he sighs. 'Tell Marjory I done my duty.'

"And he up and died."

There was a cough in the darkness.

"So I calls a cutter away, and rowed aboord the *San Josef*, the men blubberin like a pack o babbies, to break it to Nelson. Like twins, them two, Nelson and your father: that like, ye see!

"Well, there was the Commodore on the Don's

quarter-deck, Berry beside him, the Spanish Captain afoor him, and behind him a British Jack-Tar tuckin the Spaniards' swords under his arm like so many umberellas.

"I breaks it to him short and straight.

"'Captain Caryll's compliments, sir,' says I. 'And he's dead.'

"Nelson claps his hands to his face as though I'd struck him. Then he falls on my neck afoor em all - Dons too.

"'O Ding-dong!' says he. 'I loved him.' - Just like that. 'I loved him....'

"Yes, that was Nelson all through: one alf woman, t'other alf hero.

"Then he pulls himself together.

"'But there!' he says. 'He lived like an English gentleman; and he died like a British seaman. May I go that way when my time comes.' And he sweeps off his cocked hat as though it might ha been to the King, and -

"'God bless Kit Caryll,' says he."

The old man blew his nose in the darkness.

"Yes, sir," he continued, "that was your father and my friend," and then suddenly gruff -

"D'you mean takin a'ter him?"

"I mean to try, sir," said the boy huskily.

In the darkness a hand gripped his.

CHAPTER V

REUBEN BONIFACE'S STORY

I

Clear of the harbour, the boy's hat blew overboard.

He tasted his lips, and found them salt.

Never at sea before, yet somehow it was all strangely familiar, and strangely dear.

The feel of the ship, alive beneath his feet; the lift, the plunge, the swaying rhythm of the bows; the roll of the masts against a patch of stars - there was music in them all; a music that stirred his heart; the music of inherited Memory.

The sea was in his blood; and his blood began to sing to it. Old voices from the Past, that Past which is still the Present, woke within him. Old memories, borne down the ages upon the dark river of race life, haunted him dimly. Old and terrible experiences - murders and mutinies; distresses on rafts; thirsts and screaming madnesses; naked men howling on hen-coops under waste skies, sea-birds wailing desolately overhead; great ships, man-forsaken, God-forgotten, wallowing blindly amid green mountains that flowed and foamed upon them - shadows in shoals, they rose, glimmered, and were gone in the twilight waters of returning consciousness.

Sea-wolves in beaked ships from the Baltic; pirate-adventurers who had sailed and sacked under the Conqueror; pioneers of new-found lands: blood of his blood, and brain of his brain, they lived again, roused from centuries of sleep by the stir and whiff and secret business of the dark waters.

The mystery of it thrilled the boy: the blind night, the moving waters, the wind in his hair, the crash of spray upon the deck - old friends all, he recognised them as such, and found them beautifully familiar.

He was flowing down the River of Eternal Life and one with it. He was: he had been: he always would be. There was no Death, no Time. Life was One and Everlasting.

His nostrils wide, renewing old impressions, he walked forward, proud and self-composed.

True son of the sea, yet he knew himself her master. She was his woman, to be loved and lorded over. He found himself brooding over her dark beauty with the stern pride of possession. Manhood was rushing in on him: its passions, its power, its splendid cruelties. He began to tingle to them.

They had not met, it seemed, to know each other, these two world-old friends, for half a generation. Now once more they came together, heart to heart, man to woman, loving faithfully as ever.

II

The wind freshened. The sloop began to feel the sea and swing to it. She was a dark and secret ship: not a light save for the glare of the binnacle-lamp; the only sound the creak of a block, the mutter of canvas, and the chatter of waters.

It was a dirty night, a wet mist blowing landward. There was no moon; only here and there a star pierced the cloud-drift.

The boy groped his way forward.

In the bows a dark lantern on the deck shone on a group of sea-boots.

"Pretty night for our work, sir," came a cheery voice. "Might ha been made for us."

"Where are we?" asked the boy.

"Yon's Seaford Head, sir," as a great white dimness thrust out of the mist towards them. "We're layin along close inshore. See that glimmer forrad on the port-bow? - Ah, it's gone again! That's the Seven Sisters. And between the last o them and Beachy Head lays Birling Gap. And somewhere there or thereabouts, we'll make our cop, if a cop it's to be."

"Who is it we're after?"

"Lugger *Kite*, sir - Black Diamond's craft....

"Funny thing fortune, sir," the man continued after a

pause. "Never know how it's going to take you till you're took. Little thing sims to sway it. At one day's time there warn't a smarter seaman afloat than Bert Diamond. Might ha rose to the quarter-deck - just the sort; got a way with him and that. Only one fault, sir - the sailor's failin."

"What's that?"

"Too lovin by fur...."

"It's generally always his one fault capsizes a man," the seaman continued. "And so it were with poor old Bert - he warn't Black at that time o day, yo'll understand."

"What's the rights o that yarn, Reube?" grumbled a deep voice.

"I ca'ant rightly tall ye because I don't justly knaw, Abe. They said this here Mr. Lucy - Love-me Lucy they called him in the ward-room - got messin about a'ter Diamond's gal. But anyways there it were. Diamond struck him - struck his officer."

"What happened?"

"Why, sir; flogged round the Fleet."

A man spat noisily on the deck.

"Maybe you've never seen a man flogged round the Fleet?"

"Never."

"Then heaven help you never may, sir. I'd liefer fight a

gun in the waist through farty Fleet-actions, than see one man go through that - wouldn't you, Abe?"

"Ay, that I would," grumbled the deep voice.

"Ah; and so'd we all," came a windy chorus.

There was a stamping of feet: then the story-teller went on,

"I stood by the gang-way when he came up the side, a blanket across his shoulders.

"'Ullo, Reube,' says he....

"That were all.... I said nawthing.... I saw his face....

"When he came out o the sick-bay three months a'terwards, with his kit to go ashore - he was dismissed the Service, yo'll understand, sir - I was on deck.... He limped across, and shook hands with me out o them all.... We'd been like brothers, him and me.... Then he went down the side and never a word.... Just as his head was on a level with the deck, he stops. Good-bye all,' says he, with a laugh I never heard him laugh before. 'The British Navy ain't eard the last o Black Diamond.'... And nor we had, by thunder."

III

The *Tremendous* thrashed into a swell. A spout of foam flung up, and crashed down on the deck. When the last hiss of it had died away, Boniface took up his tale.

"That was 99 - after Acre. I was away nigh on six years, middlin busy too. We'd the lot atop on us one time or t'other - French, Roossians, Dons, Dutch, Swedes, Danes, and all; and Nap to thank for em....

"Last Spring I come home to find Black Diamond cock o the Gap Gang, and better fear'd nor Boney's self in East Sussex. That'd be a day or two after they'd done Mr. Lucy."

"What was that?"

"Why, sir, Mr. Lucy, he was Coast-guard Officer of this district. One day his grey cob cantered into Lewes alone - no Mr. Lucy. Two night a'terwards a keeper chap found his body in Abbot's Wood....

"They'd crucified him to a tree, and flogged him to the bone; then stuck an ace o diamonds on to his back, and on it

Returned with thanks."

"And that warn't all," grumbled the deep voice.

"That it warn't," came the windy chorus. "Never is with them."

"But who'd done it?" cried the boy.

"Gap Gang, sir."

"Who are they?"

"Why, sir, Birling Gap Gang it should be by rights. That's where they mostly lay rough when they're this side. And it suits them to-rights - that lonely, you see: just naked hills, cliffs, badgers, foxes, and the like. - And such a crew! God help the man or maid crosses their hawse. Fear neither God nor Devil."

"Only Black Diamond," grumbled the deep voice. "Meek as milk with him."

There was a grim chuckle all round.

"Are they smugglers?" asked the boy.

"Call emselves smugglers," replied Reuben. "But they ain't the gentlemen proper. For it's mighty little smuggling they do. Maybe run a cargo every now and then to keep in with the folk on the hill - East-dean and Friston way. But they're after bigger game, I allow."

"What's that?"

"Despatch-running for Little Boney, sir."

IV

The boy waited. There was more to come, he felt; and he was right.

In a minute Diamond's old ship-mate resumed his tale.

"Last July, I was on furlough at Alfriston. One evening I went for a bit of a stroll on the hill. Up there, under the sky, top o Snap Hill, was a look-out chap with a telescope. I knaw'd his back, and the high way with his head at first onset. It was Black Diamond.

"'Hullo, Bert,' says I, coming up behind.

"Round he jumps, terrible dark.

"I'd hardly ha know'd him - toff'd out quite the officer, bits of epaulettes, waxed moustachers, pistol and all. I'd never ha beleft it!

"'That Reube?' says he, at last, starin properly.

"'That's me, sir,' says I.

"His face cleared; and he shoved his pistol back.

"'Excuse me, Reube,' says he. 'Every man that wears that uniform is unfriends with me, with one exception - and that's yourself,' and he took my hand.

"'It's nice to look into a pair of eyes can look back at you,' he goes on, very quiet, pumping my hand. 'How are you, old mate? - We're quite strangers.'

"'I'm tidy middlin, thank-you, sir,' says I: must keep on a-sirrin him somehow. 'How's things going with you?'

"'Why,' says he, with that terrible great laugh of his, 'like God Almighty - slow but sure.'

"'Nice crowd you've got together by all accounts, sir,' says I.

"'All picked men,' says he, mighty grim. 'But drop your

voice if you're going to talk about the darlings: I've a dozen of em in the goss handy by. There's not a man sails aboard the *Kite* but swings in chains, if he's copp'd. Makes em wonderful nippy at a pinch,' says he, with that little smile o his. 'You wouldn't believe.'

"' Yes,' I says. 'Reg'lar man o war style aboard the *Kite*, they do say. Trice em up, and flog em, if everything ain't just so.'

"'That's so,' says he. 'Duchess could eat her dinner off my deck - has, too.'

"'Only wonder is they stick it,' says I.

"'Ah,' he says, 'they're my *men*, not my *mates*, see? - This ain't a free-tradin show. We ain't partners, I pay em.'

"I looked him straight in the face.

"'And who pays you, old pal?' says I - 'if you'll excuse the question.'

"'The Emperor,' says he, calm as you please. 'Nice feller, too.'

"I stared a bit.

"'Knaw him then?' says I.

"'Supp'd with him night afore last,' says he, matter-of-fact like; and I knaw'd he warn't lying - 'Me and the Emperor and another gentleman.' He began to laugh. 'Rare sport he was too, the gentleman! Hear him sauce the Emperor!' Then he takes a sweeping look through

Alfred Ollivant

his glass. 'Ye see we've a little bit o business forrard, me and him and the Emperor.'

"Well, sir, I was gettin my monkey up, as you may allow. Here'd I been tow-rowin up and down the high seas at tenpence a day these six years past, doin my little bit to spoil Boney's game; and here was this chap - dismissed with ignominy, mind! - toff'd out like a dandy Admiral, flashin his French rings and sham Emperors in my face.

"Still I aren't no mug. So cardingly,

"'What's it all about, Bert?' says I, confidential-like.

"He didn't answer: kep on all the while a-squintin through the glass towards the Forest.

"'You a blockade-man, [Footnote: The blockade-men were coast-guards.] Reube?' says he at last.

"'No,' says I, 'I'm a liberty-man from the *Tremendous*.'

"'Ah,' says he, queer and quiet. 'I'm glad to hear that, Reube. Mighty glad you're not a blockade-man.'

"'Why for?' says I, innocent-like.

"'Why,' says he, "tain't healthy for blockade-chaps in these parts just now.... You heard o poor Mr. Lucy?'

"'Yes, surely,' I says, pretty spiteful - 'dirty business and all.'

"He dropped the glass.

"'What's that?' says he, short-like.

"So cardingly I told him *all* about it.

"'That's my friend Fat George,' says he between his teeth.

"'I suppose it's news to you,' I sneers.

"He looks me in the eyes properly.

"'This is the first I've heard of it,' says he. 'Struth it is! No,' he says, 'I gave him what he gave me, no more, and no less - five hundred, *crossed*; while I lay among the blue-bells and counted em out for him, same as he done for me. And when it was over - "And now," I says, "to show you I'm a Christian, I'll leave the boys to put you out of your pain; and that's more than ever you done for *me*." And I strolled away. They must ha been up to their larks a'ter I left - mucky gaol-birds!' he says. 'Funny thing they *can't* be'ave like gentlemen.'

"'Well,' I says, 'as to Mr. Lucy, he play'd it down a dog's trick on you; and you got back on him. And man to man,' I says, 'no parsons bein by, I don't say no to that. But if it comes to selling your country for money - '

"He swings round all black and white and lightning.

"'Money!' he snarls. 'Steady, Reube.'

"'What then?' says I.

"'Ah,' says he, drawing his breath like a cat swearin. 'As I just told you, I'm a Christian; and I don't forget.'

"Talk o bitter!

"'Well,' I says, 'if it's revenge you're a'ter, sims to me you've had a belly-ful.'

"'Ah, I ain't begun yet,' says he, breathing slow. 'That's my little private account. There's the system to settle yet.'

"'What!' says I, coming closer. 'So you're going to fix up the British Navy next?'

"'Goin to try,' says he, rollin out that tarrible great laugh of his - 'God helpin me.'

"That was a bit *too* much.

"'Well, I'm a sailor myself,' says I, 'and an Englishman. So, mind yourself!' And I goes for him blind.

"He never budge: just blew his whistle; and a dozen of em sprang out o nowhere.

"'Unclasp his little arms,' says Diamond. 'He thinks I'm his lady-bird.'

"Just then a whistle sounded rithe away acrost the Weald. Another nearer took it up, and another - like partridges callin on a summer's evening.

"'Here he comes,' says Diamond, glass to his eye. 'Reube,' says he, 'there's things good kids such as you are best not seein. Boys, take him to the top o Deepdene, and give him a tilt down. Gently does it,' says he. 'He's an honester man nor any o you.'

"So cardingly they march me away.

"But I hadn't gone above a dozen steps, when I heard him comin a'ter me.

"'Reube,' says he, kind o shy-like, 'I suppose you won't shake with an old ship-mate?'

"'No,' says I, 'I don't shake with no - traitors.'

"He drops his hand.

"'Ah, well,' says he, 'think the best you can o me. You're much the man I'd ha been, if God had been gooder to me. Good-bye, Reube,' says he. 'All the luck.'

"And somehow he seemed a bit o choky; and somehow I felt the same myself.

"So cardingly they march me away to the top o the coombe, where it's steep as a ship's side, and gave me a shove.

"Down I sprawls, rolly-bowly, anyhow all among the jumping hares, and brought up in the shadows at the bottom.

"And as I was feeling to see if my head still set on my shoulders, a chap on horse-back comes cantering up the shoulder of the coombe above me, black against the light....

"That was the first o this here Gentleman all the talk's on...."

V

The mist was blowing by in huge white puffs like the breath of a giant.

"That was the beginning," continued Reuben. "It warn't the end though not by no means. Many's the time since then them words of his about the blockade-chaps, and his queer way o sayin em's come back to me."

"Why?" asked the boy.

"Why, sir? - why, indeed? - Two days later a patrol was found at the foot o the Devil's Chimney, heads bashed in. Blow'd over o course! - Week a'terwards petty officer found drowned in dew-pond top o Warren Hill. Accident o course! - Next day common seaman hung in his own braces Jevington Holt. Suicide o course! And so it's been going on ever since - blockade-men murdered; blockade-men missin; blockade-men washed ashore - until last night."

"What then?"

"Ain't you heard, sir?" aghast. "Last night - eleven o'clock - full moon - clear as crystal - Diamond laid the *Kite* aboard the Revenue cutter off Darby's Hole."

"Well?" breathlessly.

"Ah, well indeed, sir! - No one'll ever knaw the rights o that yarn. Only one chap o the crew o the *Curlew* left alive to tell the tale - poor Alf Huggett here alongside o me. Stove in a water-butt and hid in it - didn't you, Alf?"

There was a waiting silence.

"It's broke him up surely, sir," whispered Reuben. "And I don't wonder. Saw enough through that bung-hole to keep him thinking for the rest of his life."

"Fat George!" shivered a thin voice. "Fat George!"

"Ah!" came the windy chorus. "Him and old Toadie!"

"Anyways there it be!" continued Reuben. "At noon to-day the *Curlew* drifted up against Seaford jetty, yards hung with her own crew, like carcasses in a butcher's shop."

"Brutes!" gasped the boy. "But what's the meaning of it all?"

Reuben shrugged till his oil-skins crackled.

"No sayin, sir. Summat's up; summat big. Diamond wanted the coast cleared; and he's cleared it - by thunder he has! Swep it up bald as the back o my hand."

The mist blew away faint and thin. Through it the bowed crest-line of a cliff loomed up to larboard.

"There's the last o the Seven Sisters!" said Reuben. "Birling Gap's just here along." He moved among his men. "Stations, boys. It's here or hereabouts...."

"Hush!" whispered Kit.

Alfred Ollivant

CHAPTER VI

THE LUGGER KITE

I

"D'you hear anything, sir?"

The boy made no reply, listening, listening.

Had he made a mistake? - was it only the swish of waters under the keel? ... No!

"There! there, in front!"

This time there was no mistaking it - the noise of a boat's bow smashing into seas.

Reuben brought his fist down with a thump.

"To the tick!"

Just then the cloud-drift parted. Through tatters of mist the moon shone down.

II

Bowling out on the top of the tide came a lugger, the foam at her foot.

She was black in the moon, and barely a cable's length away.

"That her?" asked the gruff voice of the old Commander.

"That's the *Kite*, sir," answered Reuben. "Know her luff anywheres. Foots it like a witch, and handles like a lady. A boy could sail her; and she'll carry farty at a pinch."

The old Commander watched her across the glimmering waters.

"Means havin it," he said with a grunt half of admiration, half of satisfaction.

"Ah, that's Diamond, sir!" answered the other. "God A'mighty couldn't stop him once he's set."

The old Commander measured the lessening distance between him and his prey.

"I shall keep as I go," he said deliberately. "Reck'n he'll do the same. We oughter meet. But if he should scrape through, why let him have it nice and hearty as he goes under my bows."

"Ay, ay, sir."

He stumped aft; while the men rammed down their sou-westers.

III

"I'll lay I bag Fat George in the belly," said one, spitting leisurely, as he fingered his musket.

"I'll lay you don't then," retorted another.

"I'll lay you couldn't miss it," chipped in a wag.

There was a rumble of laughter, quickly hushed.

The boy among them sniggered, to vindicate his courage.

How brave they were! and what beasts! They made him sick, and filled him with admiration. He should like to be like that - to feel nothing; to see nothing; to loll up against the side and spit about, and make bad jokes, a minute before he took the life of a brother man. That was fine: that was manhood. One day, please God, he would be the same.

He peeped at the lugger. She was holding on, hard-driven, a long-boat with high-cocked nose tearing astern.

The big ship was bearing down on her like a hawk on a sparrow. It was bullying but O! was it not glorious? The old thrill, the thrill of thrills, incomparable, made him tremble. He was manhunting once more.

"He'll carry the sticks out of her," muttered one of the men. "Crackin along all sail - capsize or no."

"He may crack along," said another. "He's done. Black Diamond's done."

The sea flopped in the moon. Here and there a gathering swell hissed into foam. The *Tremendous* scarcely felt it; but the lugger lay over on her side, seams dripping, and thrashed furiously along.

Her crew, squatting along the weather gunwale, turned bowed and shining backs to the sloop.

Only the man at the tiller had seen her; and he made no sign.

The moon was on his face, black and white and bearded; and his eyes on the sloop.

"Calm chap!" whispered one.

"Plucky meat," replied another. "Guts like a lion on him."

"Which is Black Diamond?" asked the boy.

"Him at the tiller, sir - moon on his face. He's seen us. 'Tothers ain't - not yet."

The *Tremendous* crashed into a sea. The aftmost man on the lugger's gunwale turned.

He saw the Avenger towering over him, dark wings spread, snow-drifts spurting before her.

Alfred Ollivant

An awful horror convulsed his face.

"King's ship!" came a ghastly-screaming treble. "Put back, Diamond!"

The man at the tiller never stirred. One lightning arm flashed forward.

"Down, George!" came a voice of thunder. "I'm going through."

There was a flash in the moon; the smothered crack of a pistol; and a furious tumble of men aft.

"Gor! they're knifin him!"

"Their own skipper!"

"That's the Gap Gang!" rose in a groaning chorus from the bows of the sloop.

IV

Splash followed splash.

The crew of the lugger were jumping for the long-boat.

The moon shone down mildly on savage waters, and a tumult of men.

All about the boat was a fury of fighting. Some were in it, some in the water. Those within were slashing at the hands of those scrambling in.

Every man was for himself, and every man against his neighbour. They fought like beasts, beasts who could blaspheme.

Sin seen naked! Sin and its consequences!

Death-screams; bellowed blasphemies; howls for mercy rose as from the pit.

"No room! - It's me, Joe! - Too many aboard! - Knife the - ! - I'm done! - Elp us up! - Don't, George!"

Out of the torment of howls, oaths, prayers, came again the ghastly-screaming treble.

"Cut the painter!"

A boy, the last on the lugger, afraid before to trust the water, jumped now.

"Don't leave Jacky!" spluttered the thin boy's voice, tearful and terrified; as the little shaven head bobbed up by the boat.

"Ands off!" screamed the treble. "We're sinkin a'ready. What, you little -! then ave it! ave it! ave it!"

A shrill squeal and then again that ghastly-screaming treble -

"Row, ye -, row!"

Silence; tumbling waters; and the moon, sick with horror, darkened suddenly.

CHAPTER VII

THE MAN IN THE LUGGER

I

The lugger came bowling on, one man in her stern.

"Diamond's bested em!" rose in a roar from the *Tremendous*.

And so it seemed.

The *Kite* was making straight for the sloop, plunging giddily, as though wounded.

"All hands aloft!" roared old Ding-dong. "Back tops'ls!"

There was a scamper of feet along the deck; and up the shrouds a scurry of dark figures. Above was ordered bustle; from the deck a sounding voice ruled all, as God rules the world.

"Canst use a pistol, lad?"

The words, swift as hail, smote Kit's ear.

"I don't know, sir," babbled the boy, sick with excitement.

A minute back Hell had yawned, and he had peeped in. He was still aghast.

"Then find oot!" fierce as a sword. "Joomp into t'mizzen-chains, and pick off yon chap at the helm, as he cooms under ma counter."

He thrust a pistol into the boy's hands.

How limp the lad felt beside this masterful old man!

In another moment he was standing in the chains, the dark and giddy waters swirling beneath him. The blood thumped in his temples.

Was it to be his St. Vincent? his chance?

The lugger came tearing up. He could hear the swish of the waters, white at her foot; he could see the wet sail, the bucketing bows, the fore-deck awash. She would pass bang beneath his feet. He could see no man at the helm - only the jumping bowsprit, the thrashing foot, and that huge lug-sail, bellying over the water.

Suddenly his mind flamed. In the white glare of it he saw the thing to do, and had done it, before cold reason could check him.

He jumped.

The boat and giddy waters rose up to meet him. He fell as on to a mattress, full of wind. It was the lug-sail he had struck. Down it he sprawled to the deck, there to find himself upon his hands and knees, something soft beneath him.

One man was in the boat; and that man was staring him in the face.

There was no mistaking him. He was black, with diamond eyes. The moon was on his face; and about his lips a queer snarling smile.

Kit expected him to pounce; yet he did not, lolling back in the stern-sheets, very much at his ease. The tiller under his arm wobbled, and he wobbled with it. In spite of those staring eyes of his, there was a dreadful unsteadiness about the man. Was he wounded? - was he drunk?

Somehow the boy was not very much afraid. It was all too dream-like. He heard his heart thundering far-away on the remotest shores of being. He heard his own voice speaking, and was surprised at it - how steady it was, and how small!

It was saying,

"I'm a King's officer. That's a King's ship. There are about a thousand men on board. It's all no go. D'you give in?"

The man grinned sardonically. Then his head fell forward. He lurched horribly. The tiller slipped from under his arm. The lugger fell away, and lay on the water like a wounded bird.

Then Kit understood.

Black Diamond was dead.

II

The boy's mind relaxed like a burst bladder.

He began to laugh.

Where was he?

Alone on the deep with a dead man.

Well, well. It was not for the first time surely. A ghost, long-laid, walked again. A sudden lightning had flashed upon his past. In it he had seen and *remembered*. Something of a forgotten self floated to the surface. In turmoil, his Eternal Mind had thrown up on the sea of Time a memory from its imperishable hoard.

Slowly he recollected himself, and looked about him.

He was kneeling on something soft, and his hands were warm and slimy. He looked down, and jerked back with a scream.

He was kneeling on a dead man, and his hands were crimson.

A gust caught the lugger: she staggered forward with a flap and swing of her boom. Her master, her mate, was dead; and the spirit had gone out of her.

No time for the horrors! he must be doing.

In a moment he was at work with his dirk. The great lug came down with a rattle.

Forward under the boom, he cut the sheet of the jib. It fluttered furiously, streaming lee-ward. Then he stumbled aft.

The murdered helmsman still lolled in drunken stupor, smiling inscrutably.

Astern the sloop lay with tall clothed masts, swaying, a phantom on the troubled waters.

A boat had put off from her, and was bucking towards him.

"Lugger ahoy!" came a windy voice across the water. "Is that you, sir? - all well?"

"I'm all right," cried the boy, and was ashamed to find his voice cracked with emotion.

The boat bumped alongside. Reuben Boniface's face popped up over the side.

"Plucky thing, sir!" he cried, bobbing with the boat; then seeing the man at the tiller - "Ah, Bert! a fair cop."

"He's dead," said the boy with a sob.

"Dead!" cried the other, thrusting forward. "By thunder! so he is. Boys, Black Diamond's dead!" He took the dead man by the hand. "Poor old mate!" he continued in hushed voice. "Fancy that now. Diamond dead!"

Another head bobbed up.

"Did you kill him, sir?" asked an awed voice.

"No, I didn't. I think it was this man. He killed Black Diamond; and Black Diamond killed him back."

His heart was swollen almost to bursting.

A row of heads now bobbed all along the side, staring at the dead man. It awed them, this lay-figure with the dreadful stillness brooding about it, rocking with the rock of the sea. They spoke of it with lowered voices reverently.

"Funny thing - him so quiet. Don't seem nat'ral like."

"Warn't like that ten minutes since."

"That Black Diamond! - and can't lift his own hand now!"

"Ah, makes a change, Death, don't it?"

"One thing sure," ended a philosopher. "Like it or not - sooner or later - in this world we all gets our desarts."

So these solemn children, big of the sea, brooded over the Great Mystery. Here *they* were in the dark, the night blind about them, the old sea roaming round; and here was *It*. Dimly they tried to apprehend *It*. Somehow *It* made them feel strangely small, and somehow strangely great.

Reuben was still pumping the dead man's hand up and down, the tears coursing down his face.

"Poor old mate!" he kept saying. "He'd not ha been the same if things had been different - would you, old mate? - I wish I'd ha shook hands with you now, I do."

A shuddering voice spoke from the boat. It was the broken blockade-man.

"Ow much is he dead?" he asked.

"Why, dead as dirt," replied a matter-of-fact fellow, chewing his pig-tail phlegmatically.

"Sure he ain't learying?" came the voice of the man with the shivers.

"You fear'd on him still, Alf?" asked one curiously.

"Fear'd on him? - No, I ain't fear'd on him!" came a ghastly titter. "Got no cause, ave I?"

"He won't urt you," replied the other, soothingly. "He's dead all right - ain't you, Diamond? - You can tweak his nose, see? - and then go ome, and tell the gals what you done. Tweak Black Diamond by the conk!"

"You let him be!" growled Reuben. "Time was you'd ha crawled to him. Now any snotty little toad can make game on him."

Kit looked up at the rising voices.

A fellow had seized Diamond by the nose, plucking back his head.

The dead man's mouth gaped. Into the cavern of it shone the moon.

"One moment!" cried the boy; and hating himself, he thrust a finger and thumb into the opening, and plucked out the thing which gleamed within.

It was a cut-glass scent-bottle.

CHAPTER VIII

THE SCENT-BOTTLE

I

They came under the counter of the sloop, the boat towing the lugger, and Black Diamond dead, the moon upon him.

A face, tallowy-nosed and black-whiskered, was leaning over the side.

"Say! was there a tall chap on a blood chestnut aboard?" asked a slushy voice. "Andshomish feller - might be own brother to me. If so, pass him up the side, there's a good biy. There's £1,000 on his head."

Kit went up the side, his heart beating high.

"Anything?" asked the old Commander shortly.

"Yes, sir."

He surrendered his treasure-trove.

"What! this all?" sniffed the old man, fingering the scent-bottle contemptuously - "gal's fal-lal."

He stumped below.

The boy's heart was white-hot with indignation.

This then was his thanks!

Somebody tickled him under the arms.

"You're in the old man's good books, Sonny," said a hilarious voice. "Wha d'you think he said when you plumped overboard?"

"I don't know. What?"

"'Nelson might ha done that,' says the old man - Bible-truth, he did." And he shook out loose coils of laughter.

The compliment was so staggering that it humbled the boy.

A minute since he could have stabbed that old man with the stiff knee. Now he could have kissed him.

"No! did he *really*?" he gasped.

The Gunner clutched the boy with one arm, and tilting his chin, looked down at the uplifted face.

"There *is* a look o the little man about the kid," he said - "kind o gal-like look - all eyes, and spirit, and long chin. Funny thing! - I've always noticed the best biys to fight are them as got most gal about em."

The purser's steward tripped up.

"Mr. Caryll, sir, Commander Harding desires to see you in his cabin."

"Told you, Sonny," crowed the Gunner. "It's to give you a certificate for valour, and a drop o brandy on a lump o sugar."

II

A purser's glim lit the cabin, bare save for a solitary print upon the bulk-head.

Facing it stood the old Commander, broad as a wall, his hands behind him, and the scent-bottle, unstoppered now, in one of them.

Kit recognised the face on the wall at once. It was Nelson's.

"That you, Mr. Caryll?"

"Yes, sir."

"Can ye read French?"

"A little, sir."

"Then what ye make o this?"

He thrust a hand behind him, never turning.

Kit took from it a tiny roll of tissue paper, and unfolded it.

"Shall I begin, sir?... It's headed *Merton, [Footnote: Merton was at this time the seat of Lady Hamilton.] 17th, 2 a.m.*, and goes on - " he translated, stumbling -

Everything is going beautifully. There is only one man for England to-day; and for him there is only one woman. She is the absolute master of her N., and he of Barham and the Board. The Victory *is due to-morrow. She expects him here on Monday, and will do all. The original plan holds good. He will be off Beachy Head Thursday. The* Medusa, 44.

A.F.

Keep the frigate cruising. I am off to Dover at dawn to square up there. Diamond calls for me at the old rendezvous on Wednesday, and puts me on board the frigate that I may be in at the death *as our friends this side say.*

The boy lifted dark eyes.

"It looks like a -"

The other cut him short.

"In our Service, sir, the Captain speaks when he's the mind; the First Lieutenant all the time; and the midshipmen - *never.*"

He snapped fierce jaws.

"What date, d'ye say?"

"Seventeenth."

"Seventeenth, *sir*.... That's to-day, ain't it?"

The old man grunted.

"Started this morning - sharp work."

"He was riding a thorough-bred ... sir."

"What's a furrow-bred?... plough-oss?"

"Plough-horse!" sparkling scorn. "It's the best sort of horse going."

"What if it be? - I'm a sea-man myself - not a postboy.... How d'ye know he was ridin a what-d'ye-call-it?"

"He always does."

"Who does?"

"The man they call the Gentleman - the Galloping Gentleman."

"Who told you?"

"I picked it up, listening to the riding-officer."

The old man cocked an eye over his shoulder at the boy.

"I keep on a-listinin for that *sir*," he said. "Reck'n I'm hard o hearin."

He resumed his study of the face on the bulk-head. A long while he gazed: then smacked one fist into the other.

"That gal!" he muttered. "I always know'd how it'd be," and turned at last.

Taking the paper from the boy, he packed it into the scent-bottle.

"When I've laid this here in Nelson's hands," he said deliberately, "I'll be ready to say what your father said aboord the Don."

A curious smile made kindly wrinkles about his eyes: it was half mischievous, half wistful: the smile of a child about to gratify an innocent spite, long cherished.

Then he shoved the bottle into his breast-pocket, and looked up. The light fell on his face; and for the first time Kit saw his Captain fairly.

Square shoulders; square face; square chin; a square brow, strangely white above the terra-cotta-coloured lower face; and blue eyes that looked squarely into yours. All square, body and soul. A true man, and a born fighter, the blue and white riband for St. Vincent at his breast.

"When you joomped aboord the lugger, was you scared?" he asked curtly.

The boy looked him in the eyes.

"Yes, sir."

The old man's hand lay for a moment on his shoulder.

"So'd I ha been," he said, and went out, nodding.

III

On deck the dawn glimmered faintly.

On their lee, high in the heaven, a glowing smother hung in the dark over a snaky brood, darting red tongues hither and thither.

"What's that?" growled old Ding-dong.

"The chaps as got away in the long-boat, sir. Set a light to the gorse on Beachy Head. Signal. An old game o their'n."

The old man swung about.

As he looked, a blue light spurted seaward, and another answered it.

"Thought so," he muttered. "Burning flares."

Then he turned again.

"Bout ship!" he barked. "Make your course for Newhaven. Send a look-out man aloft. And clear for action."

II - MAGNIFICENT ARRY

CHAPTER IX

THE TWO PRIVATEERS

I

A roll of thunder woke Kit.

Starting up on his elbows he looked about him.

Where was he?

Yesterday he had waked in the blue room at the White Cellar, the sparrows chirping under the eaves, the smiling chamber-maid at the door saying, "Half-past seven, sir," and the rumble of the Lewes coach in the yard beneath.

It was an altogether different rumble that he heard now. He had never heard it before; yet how well he knew it.

It was the roll of the drum, beating to quarters.

Across the sea a bugle answered it.

Alfred Ollivant

The boy thrust his head out of the port.

All about him lay a shining floor of sea, gently undulating and six cable lengths away, bearing down upon the sloop, a black ship flying the tricolour.

Across the bulk-head a sudden roaring voice boomed out an order.

There was the scuffle and scamper of naked feet; the noise of tackle running, shot trundling along the deck, and the roll of guns.

Then all was silence but for the thumping of his heart, and the slop of the water about her sides as the little *Tremendous* footed it into her last fight.

II

Kit rushed on deck.

The sloop, stripped to her topsails, was stirring the water faintly.

Only one man was on deck - old Ding-dong, conning the ship himself bareheaded.

He was in a worn frock-coat, and faded yellow kerseymere waistcoat, stained with soup and tar; and the hands on the wheel wore grimy kid gloves.

There was such a dinginess about the old man's garments, and such a dignity about his face, that Kit almost laughed to see him.

Last night the old Commander might have been a Channel pilot, in his rough sea-jacket and sea-boots. Today he was a King's officer, fighting a King's ship; and no mistaking it.

There was a change in his face too: something subtle, almost spiritual, that the boy could feel although he could not define it. In fact the explanation was very simple. Old Ding-dong was going into action, and had brushed his hair first as was his invariable custom.

"Morn, Mr. Caryll," said the old man, never taking his eyes off his topsails. "I was just going to send for you. You'll be my orderly midshipman. We're in for a little bit o business. See them two?" He jerked his head across the water.

Then Kit saw for the first time that two black monsters were sliding down upon them over the shining waters, side by side. The nearer was close on the larboard bow of the sloop; the other, on the same tack, lay on her consort's far quarter. Their bows hardly rippled the water as they stole forward. They seemed to flow with the flowing sea rather than sail. Phantom-ships, they might have been creatures of the night, surprised by day.

The boy could see nobody aboard. Save for the flapping of the tricolours, and the occasional creak of a spar, they were still as death. The silence and terror of their coming sickened the lad.

The voice of the old Commander, gruff and everyday at his elbow, reassured him.

Alfred Ollivant

"Privateers," he growled - "old friends both. This'n's the *Cock-ot*. Happen you've heard tell of her. That'n's the *Cock-it*. Sister-ships. And 'ot and 'it they'll be afoor long if I can make em so."

He spun the wheel discreetly.

"At dawn I found em atween me and Newhaven. So I went about; I wasn't on the fightin lay - half my ship's company short, and this here in my pocket for Nelson." He tapped his breast.

"Thought I'd run for Dover. I was hardly off on that tack when I found her" - with a backward jerk of his head - "athwart-hawse me."

Kit turned and saw a third ship, very tall, a league in their wake.

"Forty-four gun frigate," continued the old Commander. "Must ha given somebody the slip. But what she's doin here along o them two pints beats me."

"They must have been waiting to escort the lugger," ventured the boy.

"Happen so," said the other phlegmatically. "Well, they've got her now - the husk, that is: I've kep the kernel," tapping his breast-pocket once again. "I didn't want all three a-top o me at the first onset, so I cut the lugger adrift, and set her bowling, helm lashd. As I reckoned, the frigate stopped to pick her up. She won't be alongside for three hours yet.... As to them two, we've been dodging about all morning, but I reck'n we're about there now - just about. So-o-o!"

There was a roar and a huge splash beneath the stern of the *Tremendous*. A cold avalanche sluiced the boy. He staggered blindly back, something crashing on the deck about him.

"O!" he cried, and opened his eyes faintly, expecting to find himself smothered with blood.

It was water, not blood, that was dripping from him.

The boy looked up in fear.

Old Ding-dong drenched too, the water trickling down his nose, still nursed his ship tender as a mother.

There was not the ghost of a smile on his face, no curl of contempt about his mouth.

Kit thanked him inwardly. After all the rough old fellow was a gentleman.

"Trying the distance with a bow-chaser," said the old man imperturbably. "I'd have a lick back, only I can't spare no men for the deck carronades. All below with Lanyon."

The tip of his tongue shot out, and made the journey of his lips, cat-like. From behind that grim and weathered visage peeped the child, arch, mischievous, infinitely cunning.

"Master Mouche, he *reckons* I'm going to cross his bows and rake him," he whispered. "He *reckons* I'll keep my course to sarve his consort the same. He *reckons* to come up under my starn and rake me fore and aft, while his consort wears ship and pounds me with her broadside. That's his little game. 'Tain't mine though, ye know, Mr. Caryll - 'tain't mine." He rolled a blue eye on the boy; and in that eye, twinkling cunning, bubbled the delight of a child about to play a practical joke on an elder.

So unexpected was the effect, and so tickling - this grim old veteran revealing in himself the Eternal Child who hides behind us all - that the Frenchmen at their guns, hearing in the silence the sudden ripple of a boy's laughter, whispered among themselves that the Englishman had a woman aboard.

III

The breeze was very light and fast falling away. Old Ding-dong kept one eye on his topsails, and one on his foe, sliding towards him across the water.

"Like the Shadow o Death a'most, ain't she?" said the old man in hushed voice - "so still-like and stealy." He dropped a kind eye on the boy's face. "Makes ye think first time, don't it? - I mind Quiberon. Guts feel fainty like."

He renewed his watch. The twinkle had left his eyes. He had withdrawn deep down into himself. Somewhere in the centre of that square body sat his mind, alert, cat-like, about to pounce.

The shadow of the *Cocotte* fell across the sea nearly to their feet. The wind breathed on the waters, dulling them. The languid topsails swelled faintly.

The old man spun the wheel. The *Tremendous* swung towards her enemy.

Delicately across the glittering floor the two ships drew towards each other, wary as panthers about to fight.

There was dead silence, alow and aloft. Only the tricolour at the enemy's fore flapped insolently; and the red-cross flag, at the mizzen gaff of the sloop, licked out a long tongue and taunted back.

"That's Mouche at the wheel," grunted the old Commander - "her skipper. A fine fighter, but treecherous like em all.... Funny thing no one on deck only him. Swarmin with men too, I'll lay."

The French skipper too was at the wheel: a dapper little personage, black-a-vised, with fierce moustachios and eye-tufts.

He wore a huge tricorne, and vast tawdry epaulettes.

"How do you, sair?" he called, all bows and smiles and teeth, as the two ships came within biscuit-toss. "Vair please to meet you once more."

"Queer lingo, ain't it?" muttered old Ding-dong. "All spit and gargle. Comes from eatin all them frogs, I reck'n. Stick in their throats or summat."

He raised his voice.

"Same to you and many on em," he growled. "I ain't seen that dirty phiz o your'n in the Channel since our little bit of a tiff off the Casquets last May. I yeard tell

Alfred Ollivant

you was in the West Indies conwalescin a'ter an attack o de *Tremendous!*" He chuckled at his joke.

The Frenchman shrugged and smiled.

"So I wass, sair, a while back. And now here - on express pisness; the Emperor's pisness."

"What's up?" asked the Englishman bluffly. "Tired o waitin to wop Nelson? Goin to embark the Armee o England straight off?"

"Not yet," replied the other, showing his teeth. "All in goot time, my Captain. This first - this pit of pisness I do for my Emperor."

"Seems to me that Emperor o your'n must be put to the push if he's druv to gettin a mucky little pirit like you to do his business," grumbled the other.

The Frenchman waved the insult aside with utmost good humour.

"He send for me across the seas. 'I need my leetle Albairt,' he says. 'Come queegly.' So I spread my wings and come. And *La Coquette* she slip out from Rochefort. And *La Guerrière*" - with a backward jerk - "from Brest. Like swallows in April we flock to the rendezvous - to meet the Queen of Hearts, is it not?"

He bowed low, hand to his bosom.

"And now you've come, sure I ope you'll stay," rumbled the grim old seaman. "The trouble with you's always been your despart hurry to get away."

"This time we stay," replied the Frenchman with a smirk - "all three, for ever, if need be."

"We'll do our best to make you at ome, sir," grunted the Englishman; and turning to Kit -

"Slip below and tell Mr. Lanyon to begin to talk when we're locked fast - and not afoor."

Alfred Ollivant

CHAPTER X

THE MAIN-DECK

Kit scampered below.

The main-deck was clear as a room before a ball: bulkheads up; hammocks slung. But for the sand on it, you might have danced there.

How big and sweet and clean it looked! - like the loft at home, where he and Gwen and the black cat's kittens played on wet days.

But there was something other than the black cat's kittens to think about now.

The sunshine poured in through the ports on the sleek guns crouching ready. On the breech of one somebody had scrawled in chalk -

God is Love. Hear me preach it:

on others obscene mottoes, texts, and lines from patriotic songs.

About each gun clustered her crew, naked to the waist, black handkerchieves bound about their foreheads. All had solemn puckers about the brows; some were silent, some ghastly-joking in whispers, and one, face averted, was obviously praying.

Up and down the sanded deck between the guns, picking his teeth, strutted a tall and faded splendour.

His cocked hat was a-rake; his kid gloves white as his skipper's were dingy; his whiskers, purple with dye newly applied, puffed out on cheeks touched with rouge.

Could this dilapidated dandy, so alert, so nonchalant, be the drunkard of last night? -

Yes. That tallowy nose, those eyes with the wild gleam in them, could not be mistaken. It was Lushy Lanyon.

Somehow he had scraped up a First Lieutenant's uniform: bright blue coat with long tails; white waist-coat, knee breeches, and stockings; black hat cock-aded, worn athwart-ships; and sword slung from a shoulder belt. And the wonder was that it fitted and became him.

The boy gave his message.

The Gunner bowed ceremoniously.

"Be so good as to give Commander Ardin my compliments, and say I don't pull a lanyard till I can see through her ports."

The other's formal politeness stirred the boy almost to laughter; yet somehow the faded splendour of the man touched him too.

It was as when a great light seeks to shine through smoked glass. Last night he had seen only the sodden body; now he beheld the soul, shining dimly, it is true, but shining still through its sullied habitation. The call to action had set it burning. It illuminated the blurred face, notable still. In his youth the man must have been extraordinarily handsome. Even now he was a noble ruin.

"Ah, you may stare, Mr. Caryll," said the Gunner, reading the other's thoughts. "It was Lushy Lanyon last night; this morning it's *Me*!"

He swelled his chest, and stalked down the deck between his guns, shooting his cuffs.

"Yes, sir. A fight's meat and drink to me. It pulls me together, and makes me remember who I am." He threw back his head - "Magnificent Arry, the man that's played more avock with earts in his day than any other seaman afloat.... It's the whiskers done it," he added simply.

The two men in him were at war: the high and mighty fighting-man and the confidential toper. Each came bobbing out in turns.

"And if you should want to see a main-deck fought as a main-deck should be fought, why, sir, be good enough to take a seat."

He kicked a powder-monkey off his box, and offered it with a bow.

"Can't," said Kit, turning. "No time. See you again later."

The other stooped and peered out of a port.

"Doobious, I should say," he replied, picking his teeth. "Vairy doobious. Ah! -"

A great black shadow stole across the port. Its effect on the Gunner was miraculous. He shot up like a flame. He was dark; he was terrible; there was something of the majesty of Satan about the man. Some huge sea of life seemed to lift him above himself, and land him among the giants.

"Stand by the starboard battery!" he roared.

Alfred Ollivant

CHAPTER XI

COMMODORE MOUCHE

Kit ran up the ladder out of that bellowing Inferno.

The *Tremendous* and her enemy lay side by side with locked spars; the *Coquette* becalmed beyond.

Then Kit understood the ruse of that wary old fighter, his Commander. Old Ding-dong had placed the *Cocotte* as a bulwark between him and her consort. As he had foreseen, the wind, falling away this hour past, had dropped to nothing now. The *Coquette* could not bring a gun into action.

Four hundred yards away, she might have been as many miles for all the assistance she could render her sister-ship.

As the boy came up, the old Commander was leaning against the wheel, bending towards his knee, and breathing hard.

There was a dark and peevish look about his face; and a trickle of red was running down his white knee-breeches.

"Tell ye 'taint etiquette to have men in your tops only

in general actions and duels atween ships of the line," he was saying in slow and painful voice, very querulous. "In all my fifty years' experience o sea fightin, I never see sich a thing afoor, never! Dirty trick I call it."

The little Frenchman across the narrow lane of water dividing the ships, chattered excuses, all sympathy and shrugged shoulders.

"Ah, I so grieve. Pain! pain! terrible, n'est-ce-pas? - But what would you, my Captain? - It is no fault of mine. The Emperor's orders. 'I trust you, my Commodore,' says he. 'Coûte que coûte.'

"Emperor! about as much a h'Emperor as you are Commodore! And you're welcome to tell him so with my compliments," snorted the old man.

He threw his eye aloft.

"Mr. Caryll, take a party o small-arm men aloft, and clear them sneakin blay-guards out of her tops. Else they'll be boardin by the yards."

The boy rushed away.

Beneath his feet the deck staggered and shook. On the lower-deck of the *Tremendous* hell had broken loose, in flame and smoke and horrible bellowings. The little ship was racked. In her agony she quivered from truck to keel.

Suddenly the spars of the *Cocotte* above him began to crackle and blaze. Plip-plop-plank! the bullets smacked all about him. He was under fire and he didn't like it.

He wanted to dodge under the bulwark and lie there; but he daren't. So he ran breathlessly, skipping as a bullet spanked the deck at his feet.

They were in the enemy's main-top, swarms of them, tiny figures, crowding along the spars, grinning at him, he thought.

How on earth with a handful of men, climbing up the rigging under a pelting fire, he would ever clear that lot out!...

Even as he wondered the enemy's main-mast seemed to become alive. It swayed; it shook; it almost danced; the taut shrouds sagged.

At first the boy thought that horror had turned his brain, and he was going mad. He stopped dead and gazed.

Yes, it was coming down, coming towards him, towering, tremendous, like a falling spire.

It came in jerks, tearing its way with a snapping of stays and crashing of spars. Figures, like black birds, seemed to detach themselves, and flop through the air. They were men, thrown clear, and falling with floating coat-tails as they revolved.

One fell with an appalling bump on the deck of the sloop hard by the wheel, a man in a red coat, bear-skinn'd and gaitered. He did not stir, kneeling, his hands before him, head bowed, in attitude of adoration. A sudden pool of scarlet seemed to spurt out of the deck and island him.

Kit, his work accomplished for him, ran back to the wheel.

"Reck'n that's the chap as got me," said old Ding-dong, nodding at the dead man with a certain grim friendliness. "A red-coat, d'ye see? - Now what's the meanin o that? - I never yeard tell of a privateer carrying regulars afoor."

The old man was leaning against the wheel. His brow was puckered; and there was a tense, breathless air about his face. It came to the boy with a shock of surprise that a man hard-hit makes just the same sort of face as a man who has got one on the funny bone at cricket.

"Are you hurt?" he asked anxiously.

"Nay, I'm none hurt, but I am hit. They've took fifty years doin it, but they've done it at last. It was yon chap with the bashed skull. Haul him alongside o me, wilta? I'll set on him - ease my old stumps!"

He lowered himself.

"I'll larn him shoot me," he said, arranging himself comfortably on his corpse.

Kit giggled. Somehow this old man with the twinkle in his eye made him feel at home among these screaming horrors.

"Lucky shot o Lanyon's," continued old Ding-dong. "There's a lot o luck in fightin; and good job for us too. Luck's the favour o God. He always favours us. We're straight, ye see."

He peered through the eddying smoke-drift.

"That there top-hamper o their'n makes a tidy bridge atween ships. Now if they was to tumble to that, reckon they'd boord - and we'd be about done."

Kit looked round.

The enemy's main-top had fallen across the deck of the sloop.

The lightning that is genius flashed in the boy's mind.

In a second he was across the self-fashioned draw-bridge between the two ships and on to the deck of the Frenchman. It was deserted save for the dead men, red-coats all, flung from the falling top, and sprawling broadcast everywhere. Even Mouche had disappeared.

Beneath him on the lower deck was the same bellowing Inferno as on the *Tremendous*. He felt the privateer stagger and rend to a broadside of the sloop, as though her bowels were being torn out. He rushed to a hatchway belching smoke. In the pit below he could see dim figures flitting about, and could hear the howls of those in torment. Deafened, blinded, dizzied, he slammed the hatch upon them, clamping it down. Swiftly he passed from hatchway to hatchway, making all fast.

With dancing heart, he ran back to the bridge.

As he did so a whimpering voice stayed him.

"O mon enfant!"

The French skipper was lying abaft the binnacle, a yard across his lower body.

There was no make-believe about him now, no mockery. He was naked man, stripped of his tinsel, and laid bare to the soul by the inexorable Master, Pain. Across his chin, as though to mock him, lay his false moustachios.

"Tuez-moi!" he whimpered hoarsely. "Tuez-moi!"

"I can't!" gasped Kit - "not in cold blood!"

The lad was face to face with one of the most appalling of God's mysteries, and was unhinged by it. Gwen with the toothache had been nothing to this.

The agonised man rolled his head from side to side.

"Sainte Mere de Dieu, intercédez pour moi!" he wailed.

Again that lightning flashed in the boy's mind.

The man's silver-mounted pistol lay on the deck beside him. He thrust it into the other's hand.

"Here, sir!"

The man clutched it, as one dying in a desert may clutch the flagon of water that means life to him.

The head ceased its dreadful weaving.

"Petit ange! petit Anglais!" he whispered, and tried to smile.

Kit ran for his bridge. Halfway across it, he heard a crack, and looked back.

He could not see the French skipper; but what he could see made his heart sick.

Boats, crammed to the teeth, were putting away from the *Coquette*. Black and scurrying, they tore across the water towards him, like rats racing for blood.

CHAPTER XII

BOARDERS

I

Kit rushed madly aft.

"Here they come, sir!" he screamed.

Old Ding-dong sat propped on his corpse, shaving a quid of tobacco.

"Who come?"

"The boats, sir - boarding."

"That's the game, is it?"

He shut his jack-knife deliberately, and arranged his plug in the corner of his jaw.

"Fetch me that ere boardin-pike. Now give me a hike up. Then nip below and pass the word to Mr. Lanyon."

As Kit turned, he heard the rip of the first boat under the counter of the sloop and a sharp command in French, sounding strange and terrible in his ears.

Alfred Ollivant

Furiously he sped along the deck. As he bundled down the ladder, he caught a glimpse of the old Commander, braced against the bulwarks, and spitting into his hands.

The boy dropped into hell.

Down there was no order. All was howling chaos. Each gun-captain fought his own gun, regardless of the rest. Billows of smoke drifted to and fro; shadowy forms flitted; guns bounded and bellowed; here and there a red glare lit the fog.

Through the shattering roar of the guns, the rendings of planks, the scream of round-shot, came the voices of men, dim-seen. Jokes, blasphemies, prayers, groans, issued in nightmare medley from that death-fog.

"Chri', kill me! - My God, I sweats! - Pore old Jake's got it!"

On mid-deck a shadow was pirouetting madly. Suddenly it collapsed; and the boy saw it ended at the neck.

A dim figure lolled against an overturned gun. As the lad gazed, it pointed to a puddle beside it.

"That's me," it said with slow and solemn interest.

The boy trod on something in the smoke. A bloody wraith, spread-eagled upon the deck, raised tired eyes to his.

"That's all right, sir," came a whisper. "Don't make no odds. I got all I want."

A hand out of the mist clutched his ankle.

"Stop this racket," gasped a voice, querulous and tearful. "I ain't well." A stump flapped in his face.

A ghost, sitting up against the side close by, began to titter.

"Once I was mother's darling. Mightn't think it to see me now."

A shot, screeching past the boy's nose, took his breath away. He staggered back, and brought up against a gun-captain, his shoulders to the breech of the gun.

The man turned with a grin. It was the Gunner, naked to the waist, and smoke-grimed.

"Sweet mess, ain't it?" he coughed. "How d'ye like your first smell o powder, sir?"

"They're boarding!" panted Kit. "Quick!"

The man leapt up.

"Boardin!" he roared. "Board *ME!* I'll give em board."

He snatched up a chain-shot, and raced down the deck.

"Up aloft the lot o you!" he howled. "Heaven waits ye there!"

II

As he flamed through the smoke-drift, the crew caught fire from him.

Behind him in roaring flood they poured - black men and bloody, snatching each the weapon nearest to hand.

An aweful joy seemed beating up through mists in their faces. Time and Eternity warred within them. Man, the creature, hideously afraid for his flesh, strove with Man, the Creator, impregnable in his immortality.

Kit, swept off his feet, was borne along with the flood. The fury of enthusiasm, which the splendid drunkard had roused in the hearts of his men, had seized him too.

His body was aflame; and his veins ran fire. Now for the first time he knew what it was to be alive - Life spurting from his finger-tips, making madness in his blood, issuing riotously from his lips. He sang; he yelled; he laughed, battering at the lunatic in front. He caught the blasphemies of his battle-fellows, and echoed them shrilly and with joy. The light in his comrades' eyes revealed to him deeps of being undreamed of before. His spirit was pouring through his flesh, making glory as it went.

Uplifted as a lover, the wine of War drowned his senses. In the glory of doing he had no thought for the thing done. His was the midsummer madness of slaying. In that singing moment how should he remember the bleak and shuddering autumn of pain inevitably to follow? - the winter of clammy death? - the March-wind voices of distant women wailing their mates?

"Jam, ain't it?" yelled a man in his ear, as they raced up the ladder.

"Glory! glory!" sang the boy, beside himself with passion.

III

Aft and alone stood the old Commander, a dead man at his feet.

Another swarmed over the side. The old Commander's boarding-pike met him fair in the face. Back the fellow went into darkness and death.

"Good old Ding-dong!" came the Gunner's rollicking bellow, as he stormed up on deck, swinging his chain-shot like a battle-axe. "That's your sort! - bash em! blast em! - disembowl the - Turks!"

Behind him, out of the smoke, poured the men, red-hot and roaring, like lava spewed up from the bowels of a volcano.

A stream of boarders, trickling over the bulwarks, raced across the deck to meet them.

"Love and War! O my God, ain't they glory?" howled the Gunner, and plunged into the opposing flood.

One man he felled with his chain-shot; then flung it aside.

"Naked does it!" he roared, and swept up a boarder in his arms. "Ow, the luscious little armful! no good kickin, duckie! You've got to ave it!" He rushed to the side, hugging his man, and screaming fearful laughter.

"Love me and forgive me, pretty tartie!" he roared, and smashed his burthen down over the side.

The fellow crashed into a ladder of boarders, swarming up one behind the other. Back they hurled into the boats, a hurricane of men, one on top of t'other. The boat rocked, crumpled up, and sank.

The tears were rolling down the Gunner's face.

"Quenched their little ardour!" he bellowed, leaping on to the bulwark. "That's the style below there, boys! Go it, ye cripples! Give em the little *Tremendous*!"

Beneath him the sea was black with boats. From the port-holes of the main-deck the wounded were leaning out, hailing round-shot down into the boats.

"Plug em! ply em!" roared the Gunner. "Red ot shot - cannister - case! anything ye like only give em slaughter for eaven's sweet sake!"

He was back in the thick of it, raving up and down the deck, sowing death broadcast, his great voice every-where.

Not a man on board but seemed to have caught something of his heroic fury. The purser's steward, primmest of Methodists, who was said to pass his time in action converting the cook, came tripping out of the galley, a black-jack of boiling water in his hand.

"Glory for you!" he screamed, and flung the contents in the face of a boarder.

"There's the proper Christian!" gasped the Gunner, slammed up against the main-mast. "Propagate the Gospel ow ye can! - bilin bilge! - buckets o filth! - spit in his face if ye can't do no better."

A tall Frenchman pistoled the little steward.

The ship's cook, a flabby great flat-footed man, all in white, and snorting strangely, bundled up with a poll-axe, and cleft the Frenchman's skull.

"It a chap your own size!" he yelled, and felled from behind, went down himself.

IV

Up and down the deck the battle raged: here a scrimmage; there a single fight; men at hand-grips; men hurling round-shot. They swayed, they staggered about in each other's arms; they shocked, parted, came together again. Dead men lay in the scuppers; wounded men crawled the deck; and up and down among them the living reeled. One man, turned cur, crouched under the bulwark with ghastly face uplifted, and met his death, whimpering. Another, strangely quiet amid the dance of devils, stood against the foremast, nursing a broken arm. Nobody heeded him. They were too busy.

To Kit a sudden madness seemed to have possessed the world. The deck danced before him. He was bumped; he was battered; he was hurled to and fro - a twig in a torrent.

All was dreadful; all was dizzy. Strange faces with appalling eyes rose before him; men breathing terribly flitted past. There was a smell of blood and sweat in his nostrils; a sound of panting and blasphemies in his ears.

This then was a battle - not much like the stories! All the same he wished they wouldn't tread on his toes so.

Blindly the boy slashed about him. Whether he killed them, or they killed him, he hardly knew, and didn't greatly care. A sort of instinct told him the men to stab at - the dirty beasts in shirts who showed their teeth. The naked men were his own lot.

Once he heard a voice beside him.

"Go it, little un! you're almost a man!"

Then the Gunner staggered by, all black eyes and straining face, his arms about a huge boarder, his teeth deep in the fellow's shoulder.

"Rip this -'s backside up!" came a gurgling voice.

His hand went up automatically; automatically his dirk came down. A mountain fell on top of him....

As he crept out a voice panted hard by,

"Old man's down."

Dizzily he saw the old Commander sprawling to a fall, a man on top of him. The boy heard him grunt as he fell. That grunt angered him.

"I'm coming, sir!" he cried, and ran wrathfully with bloody dirk. *"Beast!"* he yelled. *"Leave him alone!"*

There was no need for him to cry.

The old man had done his own work from underneath with the jack-knife. Out poked his badger-grey head from under his man, much as the boy had often seen a ferret from beneath the body of a disembowelled rabbit.

"So fur so good," grunted the old man, crawling out on hands and knees, the scent-bottle between his teeth. "How's things forrad?"

Forward the deck was all but clear.

The remnant of the boarders, jammed up in the bows, were being hammered to death. A last fellow in a red night-cap, swarming out on the bowsprit, plumped into the sea.

The Gunner leapt on to the bulwark.

"Cleared, be God! alow and aloft!" he roared, swinging his chain-shot about his head. "Ats off all! -

God save h'our gracious King."

A bandaged head poked out of the hatchway.

Alfred Ollivant

"They're swarmin in through the port-holes!" came a husky scream.

Old Ding-dong lifted on his elbows.

"Leave the quarter-deck to me and the boy!" he roared. "Clear the main-deck."

"Ay, ay, sir," answered the Gunner, racing for the ladder. "Back to hell, the leetle beetches!"

The old man looked up.

"Any more for us, Mr. Caryll?"

A boat swept under the stern.

"Here's another of them, sir!"

The boy staggered to the side. A grappling iron swung from beneath almost struck him in the face.

He seized the cook's poll-axe, and hacked away at the bulwark. Then he put his shoulder to a carronade and shoved.

"H'all together eave!" whispered the dying cook, and lent a feeble hand.

Over went the carronade with spinning wheels. It caught the boat fair amidships, and broke it up like matchwood.

The boy leaned over. Beneath him in the green and sucking waters amid a litter of wreckage one or two heads showed, swimming faintly.

Pale and panting, he turned.

"I think that's the last, sir," languidly.

The old Commander removed the plug from his mouth.

"There's two things go to make a British seaman," he growled - "guts and gumption. Maybe you've got both, as your father had afoor you. We're like to see e'er the day's out."

He wiped his jack-knife on his breeches, and began to carve his plug again.

"Now run below and see how things are going with Mr. Lanyon."

The boy went. His passion had long passed. He was sick and weary. Head and heart ached.

With shaking knees, he tottered below. Had a party of jabbering Frenchmen met him, he wouldn't have minded. He was too spent.

But no.

All below was calm now and silence; smoke-drift and dying men.

The Gunner was standing at an open port, directing operations.

His passion too had passed. The giant-hero of a few minutes' back seemed almost small now. And a strange figure he made.

The sweat had coursed through the rouge on his cheeks; and the dye on his whiskers had run, dripping on to neck and shoulders. He was naked still, save for his trousers, but wearing his cocked hat a-rake.

The man at his side heaved a French corpse through the port.

"That's the lot," said the Gunner, picking his teeth, and turned with black and grinning face to the boy.

"Well, sir, what d'ye think? me? - earty fighter, ain't I?"

CHAPTER XIII

AFTER THE FIGHT

I

All was very still on the deck of the *Tremendous*; and those quiet men lolling in the sun added to the hush.

They sprawled about in all attitudes - on their faces, on their backs, in each other's arms, as though snoozing. And the snoring noise that came from one or two of them enhanced the illusion. Only the blank unwinking eyes of those upon their backs, the expression of the upturned faces, and the wet red stuff smeared everywhere, showed that they were not holiday picnickers.

Aft by the binnacle a man sat up against the side watching with appalling solemnity the blood pat-pat-patting down from a wound in his side. He dabbed a finger in the mess, and scrawled his name on the deck,

Tom Bleach. R.I.P.

"Tom Bleach - Remember Im Please," he repeated, nodding his head with portentous gravity.

A white and crimson huddle beside him groaned.

Alfred Ollivant

The man of letters frowned at it.

"How d'ye feel, cookie?" he asked.

"Mortal queer," whispered the dying man.

"It do feel queer, dyin," admitted the other solemnly.

A French officer close by opened glazed eyes.

"I too I die," he announced. "What then will I do?"

"Why, pray God forgive you bein French," growled old Ding-dong, propped against the wheel. "That's your worst crime."

II

The boy came up from below, deathly pale, the wind lifting his hair. He crossed to the old Commander, reeling faintly among the dead as he came.

"Lanyon alive?"

"Yes, sir. All well below," in thin and ghostly voice.

The old man nodded satisfaction.

"Starry fighter, ain't he? - Wonderful gift that way. Don't know as I ever saw his ekal at a pinch."

He looked up at the lad, swaying above him.

"Feel funny?"

The boy did not reply, leaning against the side, a far-away look in his eyes.

Then he burst into tears.

"There, there!" said the old man soothingly. "Sure to come a bit okkud-like first start-off. It's been a nasty beginning for you too - messy fightin, I call it. Look at my quarter-deck! More like a slaughter-house nor a King's ship."

He mopped at his leg.

"And all the shore-goin folk on their knees in Church all the time! - Funny to think on, ain't it?"

III

The Gunner came up the ladder.

A sack was cast about his naked shoulders; his cocked hat was on the back of his head; and a tooth-pick between his lips.

He strolled to the side.

Beneath him the *Cocotte*, smoking like a damped furnace, the blood trickling from between her seams, was settling fast.

"Got her bellyful all snug," said the Gunner

complacently, picking his teeth.

He strolled off to old Ding-dong, propped on his corpse beside the wheel.

"Well, sir, you play a pretty stick with a handspike still! - how's yerself?"

"Tidy," grunted the veteran. "How fur's yon frigate yet? I can't see over the side, settin on my little sofia."

"Within random shot, sir. She's got a slant of wind, and is crowding all sail to get alongside."

"Then we'd best be sturrin. How are we ridin?"

The Gunner looked over the side.

"Why, middlin deep, sir."

"Then cut the boats away, and the anchors. Stave in the water-casks. Heave all spare shot and tackle overboard - we need nowt but the boards we stand on and the guns we fight; and make what sail you can on her.... I shall bear away for the shore. Don't mean bein took at my time o life."

IV

A breeze light as a lady's kiss smote the water. The topsails of the sloop began to fill and flutter.

Deep in the water as a barge, she drew away from her

floundering antagonist. As she did so, the privateer, as though loth to let her depart unsaluted, barked a sullen farewell.

A roar of triumph from the *Coquette*, clearing now on the port-bow and a fainter shout from the frigate to starboard, told their own tale.

The mizzen, struck twenty foot above the deck, came down with a crash. With it fell the red-cross flag, and the faces of the crew.

"Hand me that striped petticut!" roared the Gunner, pointing to the tricolour lying entangled in the ruins of the privateer's main-top on the deck of the sloop. "I want to blow me nose."

He leaped on to the bulwark, flag in hand; and staying himself by the shroud, blew his nose boisterously on the enemy's colours.

The crew, busy clearing the wreckage of the mizzen, roared delight.

The Gunner jumped down, and spread the flag over the old Commander's feet as he lay.

"There's the first on em, sir. There's two more to follow."

"Make it so," said the old man grimly.

He was chewing a quid, and a battered cocked hat tilted over his eyes.

Alfred Ollivant

V

The Gunner marched away, eyes to his right, eyes to his left. And as he marched, he swept off his cocked hat.

"Chaps," he called to the remnant of the crew gathered grimy about the after-hatch. "I thank my God for this booriful sight. Frenchman to port!" shooting his left arm. "Frenchman to starboard!" shooting his right. "Frenchman astarn!" with a backward toss. "And God A'mighty aloft. What more can a Christian ask?"

A shot from the frigate splashed under the bows of the sloop, sluicing her deck.

"There she spouts!" roared the Gunner, and clapping on his hat ran, kicking his heels behind him. "Come along, the baby-boys! - the last fight o the little *Tremendous* - and the best."

III - UNDER THE CLIFF

CHAPTER XIV

SUNDAY EVENING

It was evening.

The little *Tremendous* lay under the cliff, pounding gently, gently, on a reef. Her back was broken, she had a heavy list to starboard, and her bulwark was awash.

The mainmast had gone by the board. The quarterdeck carronades, loosed from their moorings, sprawled in the wash of the water, a dead man floating amongst them. The deck was a tangle of wreckage and bloody sails. From a splintered stump, more like a shaving-brush than a mast, the red-cross flag still flapped.

Astern of her, in the deep water, lay her enemies in smoking ruins. The privateer, her foretop in flames, was dishevelled as a virago after a street fight; while great white clouds puffing out of the frigate's quarter-gallery told that she was afire.

The sea wallowed about the sloop, green and sleek and greedy. There was scarcely a ruffle on the water; only a huge slow heaving, as of some monster breathing deeply, and licking its lips before an orgie.

Alfred Ollivant

Firing had long ceased.

Kit, squatting, his back against the mizzen-stump, was coming to with splitting head.

All through that golden summer afternoon the sloop had drifted shoreward, privateer and frigate hammering her from either side. Towards evening, her last shot spent, the frigate boarded. The Gunner, hoarse as a crow, bloody as a beefsteak, had brought up the weary remnant of the crew to repel the attack, Kit aiding him manfully.

Men had been dancing idiotically about the boy; he had heard the Gunner's raucous voice close in his ear,

"Gad, you're a game un!" and had run at a nightmare man with goggle eyes.

Then something had happened.

Now all was calm and sunset peace, and dew on the deck among the blood stains.

And how beautiful it was, this strange twilight quiet, after the howl and torment of battle!

Warily the boy opened eyes and ears. He was not dead then, not even wounded, only horribly parched, and how his head ached!

Before him the cliff fell sheer and blank - a white curtain dropped from heaven.

Over it sea-gulls floated on dream-wings. While from some remote Down village, church bells swung out the old song -

Come to Christ,
Come to Christ,
Come, dear children, come to Christ.

The boy, lying on the bloody deck, his feet cushioned on a dead man, listened with closed eyes to the old call.

Last Sunday at that hour, the blackbirds hopping on the lawn without, the swifts screaming above, he and mother and Gwen had been singing hymns together in the schoolroom - rather chokily indeed, for it was his last Sunday at home.

All that was ages and ages ago. He had lived and died a hundred times since then.

Now....

There by the wheel, in a puddle of his own blood, lay old Ding-dong, grey and ghastly. His eyes were closed; his cocked hat with a rakish forward tilt sat on his nose. He lay with shoulders hunched, his legs spread helplessly along the deck before him, stubborn chin digging into the breast of his frock-coat.

One grim fist was frozen to the shattered wheel; the other, grimmer still, clutched the scent-bottle.

Alfred Ollivant

CHAPTER XV

THE VOICE FROM THE POWDER-MAGAZINE

I

A bosun's whistle sounded.

On hands and knees the lad crept along the tilted deck past the old Commander.

"That you, Mr. Caryll?" came a husky voice. "I canna see over plain."

The old man had not moved, but one eye had opened and was glaring up from under the eaves of his cocked hat.

"Yes, sir."

"Are they coomin?"

Kit threw a glance seaward.

"The frigate's piped her boats away, sir."

The old man's head, still forward on his breast, did not move; he did not seem to breathe. All of him was dead save that little eye, cocking up at the lad from under the tilted hat.

"Canst walk?"

"Yes, sir. I'm not wounded, only stunned."

"Then run below to Mr. Lanyon, and tell him to bide my whistle."

"Where is he, sir?"

"Where he ought to be," growled the old man - "powder-magazine o coorse."

The eye closed: the little ray of soul, still haunting the body, seemed quenched for ever; but it was not.

"And bring along a brace o round-shot when ye coom back, wilta?" came the painful voice out of the deeps.

II

Kit slid down the companion ladder.

The lower deck was half awash, and foul with smoke. There was a stink of dead men, bilge, and powder.

But what a change from when he was last here!

Then sights so ghastly that he dared not recall them: screams of torn men, rending of torn planks; howling terrors on every side, shattering his head, bursting his

Alfred Ollivant

heart, dissipating his mind.

Now silence everywhere, beautiful silence, the silence of Death.

And those leaping devils with the hoarse throats, who had barked themselves red-hot then, were strangely hushed now. Loosed from their moorings, they huddled, together beneath him half under water, like so many great black beasts, cowed, it seemed, almost ashamed; here a huge breech showing, there a blunt snout, and again a thrusting trunnion.

As he crawled along in the gloom among blackened corpses he thanked God for the stillness. It was comforting to him as water in the desert to a man dying. He drank it in gulps.

A sound in the darkness and silence stopped him.

Out of the deeps a shuddering voice rose up to him, mumbling a Litany of the dead,

> "Lord ha mercy on me a sinner -
> Lord ha mercy on me a sinner -
> Lord ha mercy on me a sinner."

The boy crept to the forehatch and peered down.

One tiny yellow star flickered in the pitch blackness beneath.

"Mr. Lanyon!" His voice was frightened of itself. "Is that you?"

The Litany ceased. Some one cleared his throat.

"That's me, sir," came a voice from the pit. "I'm back where I belong - in her bow'ls."

The Gunner was squatting in a powder barrel, a lighted purser's glim between his teeth, and a pistol in one hand. Kit caught the glimmer of naked shoulders, the wet gleam of eyes, and the shine of sweat on a face black as a sweep's.

"I was ummin all the bawdy bits I know to keep me company," called up a voice husky as a ghost's and cheery as a robin's: "It's lonesome-like kickin your heels in the dark against the powder bar'l you're goin to ell in next minute. Not that it's ell I mind. Ell's all right once you're there. It's the gettin there's the trouble - the messin about and waitin and that."

"You won't have to wait long now," replied Kit in a voice so still and solemn that he hardly recognised it himself. Nothing was very real to him. Even the words he uttered were not his own: they were machine-made somehow.

"They'll be alongside in a minute. Commander Harding says you're to wait for his whistle. Then -"

"Amen. So be it. God save the King."

The Gunner dropped his voice to a whisper, rolling up his eyes.'

"Say, Sonny, are you afraid?"

"No. I can't take anything in."

"Nor'm I; and ain't got no cause neether," came the

voice from the darkness, defiant almost to truculence. "I only ad but the two talents - lovin and fightin; and they can't say I've id eether o them up in a napkin. They can't chuck that in me face."

He spat philosophically between his thighs.

"On'y one thing I wish," he continued confidentially. "I wish all the totties was settin atop o that clift to see Magnificent Arry go aloft. Ah, you mightn't think it to see me now, Mr. Caryll, squattin mother-naked in this bar'l, but I been a terror in me time. Sich a way with em and all!"

"You might think about something more decent just now," said the boy coldly. "Good-bye. I'm afraid you haven't lived a very good life."

As the boy groped his way back, the parched voice pursued him from the nether hell.

"My respects to the old man. We seen a tidy bit together, him and me; but reck'n this last little bust-up bangs the lot. I'd ha gone through a world without women for its sweet sake, blest if I wouldn't.... And now," came the voice in a sort of chant, "avin lived like a blanky King I'm goin to die like a blanky cro. Arry the Magnificent always and for h'ever!"

CHAPTER XVI

MAGNIFICENT ARRY GOES ALOFT

Old Ding-Dong lay as the boy had left him.

"Got them round-shot?" hoarsely.

"Yes, sir."

"Stuff em in my tails then."

The boy obeyed.

"Ah, that's better," sighed the old man comfortably. "No fear I shall break adrift o my moorings." He slipped the scent-bottle into his breast-pocket and patted it. "She'll lay snug along o me, she will."

He closed his eyes.

Kit, kneeling at his side, held a pannikin to his lips.

"Water, sir. Will you have a drop?"

"Nay, thank ee, ma lad. I'll bide till t'other side. Shan't be long now."

Kit drank greedily. He could hear the oars of the

Alfred Ollivant

approaching boat; he had at the most some two minutes of life, but O! the delight of that draught.

A hand grasped his.

"Mr. Caryll," said the old Commander in strange and formal voice, "I've sent for you upon the quarter-deck to thank you for your gallantry in your first action, which is also, I fear, your last.... Can you swim?"

"Yes, sir."

"Well, then, slip overboard, if you've a mind, and make shift for yourself."

"No, sir, thank you. I'll stand by the ship."

The old man grunted satisfaction.

"Then say your prayers."

He put the whistle between his teeth.

The flag he had kept flying, nailed to the splintered mizzen, curled languidly above his head.

The old mail, dying in its shadow, eyed it with silent content.

"Are they coomin, Mr. Caryll?"

"Yes, sir - near now."

"Lay low," whispered the old man, "and we'll bag the lot, God helpin us."

The sound of oars ceased. Out of the silence a voice hailed.

"Any one alife on board?"

Old Ding-dong hearkened, his cocked hat far over his eyes.

That look of the Eternal Child, arch and mischievous, played among the wrinkles about his eyes.

"Cuckoo!" he muttered. "Cuckoo!"

Kit giggled.

He knew the ship was about to be blown up; but he didn't take much interest in it himself. It didn't seem to affect him. Somehow he was so far away. All that was happening was happening in a dream-world of which he was a spectator only. True he felt a vague discomfort at the heart; but he knew that in a minute he should wake up - to find mother's eyes smiling into his, and her laughing voice saying,

"My dear boy, what *have* you been dreaming about?"

The boats were drawing nearer again, wary as hunters drawing on a dying lion.

Old Ding-dong heard them, and smiled.

The little *Tremendous* was a sheer hulk; her back was broken; her crew were dead - and still they feared her!

The old seaman's heart warmed within him. That one

sweet moment paid him generously for fifty years of toil, of battle, of chagrin.

And as though thrilling to the emotion of the man who had loved her for so long, the little ship trembled as she settled deeper.

The old man patted the deck.

"There! it wonna urt you, my dear," he said soothingly. "Too suddint."

A tricorne rose over the bulwark.

An officer cast his eyes up and down the deck, swift and alert as a bird.

"Anybody alife on board?" he repeated, and in the vast silence his voice came small and very shrill.

He clambered over the bulwark, and came up the steep deck monkey-wise.

At the foot of the mizzen he paused.

Kit, crouching in a heap close by, noticed his boots, old, split across the toe, dingy white socks showing through. He found himself wondering whether the man had corns.

Clinging to the stump the Frenchman drew his sword, and looked up at the red-cross flag flapping sullen defiance overhead.

"Dans le nom de l'Empereur!" he cried pompously.

A whistle, swift as the arrow of death, pierced him to the heart.

Alfred Ollivant

CHAPTER XVII

THE GRAVE OF THE LITTLE *Tremendous*

I

A roar drowned the boy's senses, sweeping his mind away on a mountainous billow of sound.

Earth and sea were a bubble beneath his feet, swelling and sailing; and he was walking on the bubble, and toppling backwards as he walked.

He felt himself smiling in a foolish way. There was no pain then about dying, he thought with a pleased and remote surprise - only this silly smiling content.

Things hit him outside. He was aware of them; but they did not hurt. His body was wood, dull to sensation. He himself was within somewhere, snug and safe. He had heard the parson at home talk about eternal life. Now he knew what the man meant. To be alive yet above pain, to be dead yet dimly comfortable - that was the heavenly life. It was very curious, and not half bad.

And - he had been there before. When and where, he could not recollect. But all was friendly, all familiar.

Suddenly there came a change, and for the worse. A great wet cloud swamped him. The light went out. All about him was cold, and dark, and clinging. Was this the grave and gate of Death?

He shuddered, and yet was not greatly afraid.

Everything was so far away, on the circumference of being, as it were; and he at the centre, safe and warm, was mildly interested - little more.

Somehow he knew he was in the sea, walking dream-waters; whether conscious, or unconscious, in the spirit or out of it, he knew not, and didn't greatly care.

Grotesque yet beautiful impressions of things familiar flitted across his mind. He saw his mother in a cocked hat; Cuddie Collingwood, his pet canary, strutting the maindeck and picking his teeth; and Gwen with a tarred pigtail, her brawny bosom tattooed with dancing-girls.

She was making faces at him, the faces that none but Gwen could make; and he was about to shoot his tongue back brotherly, when there came another change, terrible this time.

There was a singing in his ears; a sense of suffocation and appalling impotence. He was rushing back to the world of sense and pain - in time, no doubt, to die, when he thought he was through that trouble. Just his luck!

He was throttled, battling, distraught. About him was the rush and smother of waters. A secret power clutched him about the waist and tugged him back. For the first time in his life he felt the aweful and inexorable grip of Necessity; and his heart screamed.

Then with a bob and a gasp, he was up; the water in his nostrils; and his hands clinging to a spar.

II

About him was a fog of smoke, and the throes of water in torment, sucking, spewing, pouncing.

Then a great swell, roaring into foam, lifted him. He was swung out of the stinging smother, away from the shock and battle of waters, out and out under the calm sky.

Beneath him a sheer white wall rose. There was no top to it, and no bottom. He could have screamed. It was so huge, so blank, so incomprehensible. It fell from heaven. Was it the skirt of God?

Then he saw the dark crest miles overhead, and knew it for a cliff. He was right beneath it, and swinging towards it.

Suddenly he became aware of a badger-grey head bobbing beside him on the spar.

"Hullo, sir!" he gasped.

A voice spluttered,

"Pockets sprung a leak! - tailor! ruffian!"

A great following swell lifted them.

"Hold fast, sir!" called Kit. "This'll throw us up."

The swell drove forward, toppling to a fall; curled, and crashed down.

Kit found himself on hands and knees, banged, dripping, dizzy, in a hiss and turmoil of waters. The backward sweep of the waves almost carried him with it. But his hands were in the shingle up to the wrist, anchoring him. The body of water passed him. A thousand tresses of foam reminding him of his Granny's hair swept across his fingers.

He looked up. He was kneeling on a tiny strip of beach at the foot of the cliff. On his left sprawled the old Commander. His knees, cocked by the receding wave, swayed and toppled now; the legs wooden and dreadful as a dummy's.

Kit crawled towards him.

"Are you hurt, sir?"

The old man answered nothing. His eyes were shut, his arms wide. He lay upon his back on the wet and running shingle, his white knee-breeches sodden and rusty with blood, the square chin heavenward.

Another of those sleek green monsters stole towards them out of the smoke.

In an agony the lad tried to drag the old man back under the cliff. He might as well have attempted to lift a cask of lead.

"O, what shall I do?" wailed the boy to heaven.

"Why, cut and run," answered the voice from earth.

Then the wave was on them, swooping, worrying, white-toothed.

Kit did his best. Kneeling behind the old man, he heaved him into a sitting position, and propped him there, as the tumult of waters sluiced about them. Over the limp legs, up the great chest, the wave swept greedily; but the badger-grey head stayed above the flood.

Then the water withdrew, blind and baffled.

Kit lowered the grey head.

"Thank ee," grunted the old man, and seemed to sleep.

Kit made no answer. He was watching the sea with dreadful anxiety. Was it coming up? Was it going down? Were there to be more of those smothering floods? If so, they were lost. He knew he could not lift again that leaden old man.

No. The worst was over. A lesser wave swept towards them. It tossed those wooden legs, dreadfully sporting with them, and fled, snarling.

The boy bent with thankful heart.

"That's all, sir. It won't come again. It's the swell made by the explosion - not the tide."

"Ah," said the other sleepily; and opened his eyes.

Seaward hung a huge toad-stool of smoke. Out of the heart of it came the clash and cry of torn waters. All else was still, save for the scream of disturbed sea-birds.

Through the frayed and drifting edge of the smoke could be seen the frigate and the spars of the privateer; and sticking out of the water, a jagged mizzen - all that was left of the little *Tremendous*.

As his eye fell on the splintered stump the old Commander lifted a hand to his forehead.

"Plucky little packet," he muttered. "Plucky little packet."

Alfred Ollivant

CHAPTER XVIII

OLD DING-DONG'S REVENGE

Old Ding-dong lay at the foot of the cliff among the chalk boulders, his limp white legs glimmering in the twilight.

To Kit, kneeling at his side, it seemed that only the old man's slow blinking eyelids were alive. The horror of it thrilled the boy, and woke the woman in him. He was not repelled; he was drawn closer.

Taking off his coat, he rolled it, sopping as it was, and stuffed it beneath the other's head.

Propped so, the old man lay in the falling gloom, head quaintly cocked, and chin crushed down on his chest.

"Are you comfortable, sir?"

"Comforubble as a man can be that canna feel," the other grunted. "My back's bruk. I'm dyin uppuds."

Stealthily the boy took the old man's hand in his. A faint tightening of the clay-cold fingers surprised him.

The dusk was falling fast. At their feet the sea still crashed uneasily. Above them the cliff showed white.

Under the moon one red star sparkled. From out of the smoke they could hear the sound of oars and voices. Boats were searching amid the wreckage.

"Ay, you may sarch," muttered the grim old man. "It's little you'll find but your own carpses."

He rolled his head round. Kit marked the shine of his eyes, the blink of pale lids, and the glimmer of his face.

"Look in ma breast-pocket. It's there."

The boy's scared fingers travelled over the other's sodden coat. It was like searching a drowned man.

"Yes, sir. Here it is."

"Hod it oop."

The boy held the scent-bottle before the other's eyes. The old man gazed at it, licking his lips.

Then he rolled his eyes up to the boy's.

"Kit Caryll," came the squeezed voice suddenly, "are you your father's son?"

"I hope so, sir."

There was a thrilling silence.

"Then take charge."

Slowly the boy received the trust into his soul.

Alfred Ollivant

"Very good, sir."

He slipped the scent-bottle into his pocket.

"It's all in there," continued the ghastly voice. "It's a plot, see? - to kidnap Nelson. There's a gal in it - o coorse. Thinks she can twiddle the A'mighty round her thumb because her face ain't spotty. Lay that in Nelson's hands - and we'll see."

The dusk was falling fast; the sea stilled; a breathing calm was everywhere.

"This here's Beachy Head. Birling Gap's yonder - where there's a last glimmer yet. Don't go that road. Soon as the tide's down, round the Head, and climb t'other side. It falls away there. Make for Lewes along the top o the Downs. There's a camp o soldiers there. Soldiers ain't much account, but they'll serve to see you through to Merton. And once there, and that in Nelson's hands - I ain't died in vain."

The hoarse voice grew hoarser.

"And mind! trust no one; don't go anigh farm, cottage, or village. It's an enemy's land all this side o Lewes. Gap Gang country, the folk call it. They're all in it - up to the neck."

"I'll do my best, sir," said the boy, licking up his tears.

"And not a bad best eether, as I know," came the squeezed voice. "And when you've won through to Nelson, as win through it's my firm faith you will - and laid that there in his hand" - his voice came in pants, and pauses, and with little runs - "tell him I sarved him all I was able and give him - my kind dooty - old Ding-dong's dooty."

There was a gasping silence.

"That's my revenge. He'll understand."

CHAPTER XIX

OLD DING-DONG HOMEWARD-BOUND

The light was ebbing fast, and old Ding-dong with it.

All was silence and a few pale stars.

The old seaman began to wander.

Scenes near, scenes far, drifted across his fading mind. Now he was a tiny lad babbling in broadest dialect to his mother at the washing-tub; now he was a pit boy yelling at Susannah, the one-eyed pit pony; anon he was on the spar-deck of the Don, holding by the hand the father of the boy who now held his.

Then there came a silence, and out of it the words, clean and quiet:

"I'm the old man Nelson never forgave for doin of his dooty."

His brain seemed to clear. He began to tell a story half to himself, half to the stars - the story of the incident of his life.

"A'ter the Nile [Footnote: It was after the battle of the Nile, on his return to Naples, that Nelson succumbed to the fascination of Lady Hamilton.] it were - when we got back to Naples. Things got bad, very bad. At last Tom Troubridge wrote to him - I saw the letter. Tom and he'd been very thick - till then. Things got worse. It was in the papers and all. Somebody had to tackle him. Nobody durst - only old Ding-dong."

The wind gathered round to listen. A few curious stars pricked the darkness above. The old man's voice was gaining strength as he went on.

"So I goes aboord the *Vanguard*, and there in his own state-room I says the thing that had to be said and I says it straight."

Kit was listening intently. The strange blurred voice coming to his out of the darkness moved him to his deeps.

"Ooop joomps Nelson, raving mad. 'My God, Hardin!' he screams - 'Ger off o my ship! - *Ger off o my ship! GER OFF O MY SHIP!*'

"'Pardon, my lord,' says I. 'I've done my dooty as a man, though I may have exceeded it as a sailor!'

"He called me a blanky pit boy.

"'A pit boy I was, my lord,' says I, 'and not ashamed on it; and powder-monkey to Hawke afoor your lordship was born. For nigh on fifty years I've touched the King's pay, and ate the King's salt. I'm the Father o this fleet, and all for the Service, as the sayin is. And I can't stand by and see the first officer in the British Navy lowerin himself in the eyes of Europe without a word.'"

The darkness hushed; the moon stared; the stars crept closer.

"He struck me. Nelson struck me in the mug. I wiped the blood away with my cuff. 'That's not the Nelson I know, my lord,' says I, and stumps out. And I never seen him from that day to this."

The boy could hear the old man's breath fluttering in the darkness.

"He was mad, ye see. She'd gone to his head; and she's stayed there ever since. Mad - as a man. As a sailor he's still Nelson - the first seaman afloat, ever was, or will be."

There was a thrill in the fading voice; a thrill of devotion to the man who had destroyed him.

"So he broke me, Nelson did, and I don't blame him: discipline is discipline, all said. Told the Admiralty they could choose between him and me - between Lord Nelson of the Nile, that is, and old Ding-dong, who'd climbed to the quarter-deck through the hawse-holes.... So they chose."

The sea rustled; the night was sprinkled with stars.

"But I've paid him now," ended the old man comfortably. "Reck'n I've paid him now."

Kit had heard the tale with puzzled but passionate interest.

"What was it all about, sir?" he asked at last in awed voice.

"Why; what it's always about," grunted the other. "One o them gals."

He coughed faintly.

"Thank the Lord there's been nobbut one woman in ma life, and that's the one a man can't help.

"What did I want with a pack? - trashy wives?... Nay. Fear God; fight to a finish; and steer clear o them gals - that's been old Ding-dong's rule o life: and it's the whole duty of a British seaman."

The old man's hand stirred in the boy's.

"In ma breech-pocket you'll find a Noo Testament and the Articles o War - all my readin these forty year; and all a sailor needs. Take em and study em. It'll pay you. Happen they run a bit athwart here and there; but that makes no odds, if you keep your head. There's always light enough to steer by if your heart's right. 'Christ's my compass,' your father'd say. 'He don't deviate.'"

The old man lay back, his eyes shut, the light on his uplifted face.

About him was stillness, hushed waters, and the moon a silver bubble.

In the quiet cove, beneath the quiet stars, after sixty years of storm, his soul was slipping away into the Great Quiet.

"I like layin here," came the ghostly voice. "So calm-like a'ter the trouble."

The cold fingers grew stiff; the eyes closed.

Kit laid a hand on the old man's forehead, and stroked his hair.

"I'm a-coomin," came a tiny chuckle as of a sleepy child - "Billy's coomin."

Seaward something flapped.

The boy turned.

At first he thought the Angel of Death was hovering over the white waters on sable wings.

Then he recognised what he saw for the flag on the splintered mizzen of the *Tremendous* saluting solemnly the dying seaman.

Old Ding-dong saw it too.

He raised his head. The moonlight was on his face, and the hand in Kit's quivered.

"Them's my colours," he whispered. "I never struck em."

BOOK II

BEACHY HEAD

I - THE GAP GANG

CHAPTER XX

THE LAST OF A BRITISH SEAMAN

I

The dawn-wind blowing chilly on the boy's skin roused him.

All night he had slept like a child far from the world and its terrible distresses. The weary body had brought peace to the worn mind. The two had merged in sleep, neither demanding aught of the other except to feed and to refresh.

He was coming to himself with a sore throat and a shiver.

His bed was hard; the bed-clothes had slipped off. He tried to pull them round him. His groping hand found nothing but impossible lumps, and stuff that trickled between his fingers. Why was he naked? where was

144   Alfred Ollivant

his night-shirt? and what was this small hard thing he clutched in his hand?

With a puzzled frown he opened his eyes.

Overhead rose a dim white wall, a thin curtain swaying before it. At first he took it for the white-washed wall of his attic at home, the lace-curtains at the head of the bed blowing in the wind. Then a slow-winged shadow, passing between him and the ceiling with puling cry, startled him to the truth.

The memories surged back on him. He knew.

That white wall sheer above him was the cliff; that swaying curtain was the mist; that passing shadow a sea-bird. The hard something he was clutching so jealously was the scent-bottle; this still thing at his side was -

The thought stabbed him awake. He sat up with a start.

About him drifted a white and waving mist. It shrouded him, chilly as a winding-sheet. There was no shore, no sea - only a hiss and rustle in the silence; and this still thing at his feet.

"Sir!" he gasped.

The still thing did not answer him.

The body leapt to his feet. He was alone; alone for ever in a blank universe where nothing was - but the still thing!

A sodden heap of clothes caught his eye. Last night; he

had doffed them, dripping as they were, and slept naked beside *that,* his head pillowed on a chalk boulder. The huddle of clothes, sprawling there so unconcerned, comforted him. *They* weren't afraid: *they* took it calmly enough. Hang it! he was as good a man as they.

And after all the old man was dead; and so long as he stayed dead the boy didn't mind. It was the chance of his coming to life again, of his stirring, winking an eye-lid, speaking, that he feared.

At length he dared to look at the old man's face. A sand-fly was crawling on his nose. The boy sighed. He wasn't quite alone then: the fly was there, and the fly was alive. His courage returned to him with a leap. He flicked the fly off with joyful indignation. They knew no reverence, these beastly little beasts! The old man lay upon his back, a rusty stream running down his white shorts. The salt had dried in scurfy ridges on hair and face. His head had slipped off Kit's coat; the little tail of neat-tied hair peeped from beneath; the eyes, wide-open, stared skyward.

Kit closed them; and the action cost him more than all his valours of the day before. Almost he expected to hear the old man's harsh voice - "Now then!"

The deed done, it seemed to the boy as if his action had eased the dead man. The look of strain on the set and yellowing face passed. The old man was tired: he had done with the world; he would shut his eyes for ever on it. The kind wrinkles, deep-puckered about his mouth, seemed to gather into a smile.

Lying there with set mouth, and stubborn chin, in

Alfred Ollivant

death, as in life, he was old Ding-dong still.

II

Kit could not bury the old man: he had no tools. He could not stay with him: time pressed. What he could, he did with the tenderness of a woman, and the respect of a midshipman for the bravest of the brave.

He arranged the body orderly, straightening the legs and pulling down the coat.

As he did so, he felt something bulky in the flaps. He looked. It was a little old leather-bound New Testament, sea-soaked; and between the leaves of it the Articles of War.

The book fell open at the fly-leaf. On it three names were written, each in a different hand.

Horatio Nelson,
Christopher Caryll,
William Harding.

A bracket bound the three, and opposite the bracket, in the same hand as the first name, the words,

England and Duty.

The date was a week before St. Vincent.

The fly-leaf turned. On the back of it, in the great vague hand of a peasant-woman, rheumatic-ridden,

bili from mother
Xmas 1755
be a good boy.

Kit read the inscription with full throat. In his chest,
awaiting him at the Bridge at Newhaven, there was
such another book, with such another inscription, from
such another mother - given him the night before his
setting out on his life's voyage, she sitting on his bed
with rather a rainy smile.

The old man had left him that little sea-worn book with
his last breath; but he could not take it, perhaps the last
gift from mother to son. It had seen the old man
through his life; in it were to be found the Fighting
Instructions which had led him on through fifty years
of battle to the last great Victory; in death the two
should not be divided.

He laid the book on the old man's breast, and his sword
beside him, as he remembered his mother had done
when Uncle Jacko Gordon died.

What more could he do?

It seemed an ill thing to desert the old man; to leave
him alone among the sea-birds. Yet he must.

Putting his arm round the other, he raised his head;
then thrust a boulder between the dead man's shoulders
to prop him.

A moment he knelt beside the old Commander with
closed eyes. Then he bent and kissed the chill
forehead.

Alfred Ollivant

"Good-bye, sir," he said in breaking voice, and rising to his feet saluted.

III

Old Ding-dong was left alone: his back against the white cliffs for which he had lived and died; his head with a skyward cock; his gaze seaward to where, when the mists rose with the morning, he would see the Colours of his Country waving above those waters that he, and his peers, had made hers for ever.

The old man asked no more.

Tired now, he wished to be alone with his sword, his Bible, and his memories.

CHAPTER XXI

KIT STARTS ON HIS MISSION

The boy blew his nose, and set off along the foot of the cliff, the scent-bottle in his hand.

Beneath the chalk boulders that strewed the bottom of the cliff, weird in the white gloom, a band of shingle ran like a road before him. He took it, the shingle crunching beneath his feet.

The tide was rising: he could hear its stealthy rustle beneath him. He must reach the Head and round it before the water; and how far off the ultimate point might be, he did not know, and could not see.

Once round it, if he had understood the old man aright, the cliffs fell away. There he would climb them; and he hoped to be on the top of the Downs before the mist rolled away and the frigate, were she still lying off the wreck, could send boats to search the beach.

He was very hungry; but his heart soared. Youth, the great healer, had done its work. Already the terrors of that fierce yesterday, the tendernesses of that solemn night, were far away.

He laboured on as rapidly as the backward drag of the

shingle would permit; at every stride clutching the scent-bottle to make sure of it.

His was a tremendous mission.

Yet surely it was not for the first time he had set out on such an errand? alone, journeying through perilous lands, the fate of the world on his shoulders. No, no, no. Somewhere, somewhen.... He had forgotten; yet somehow he remembered.

Well, he had won through then: he must have - else he would not be here now. Yet not in this little life, these fifteen years of home-experience. Death then, perhaps a thousand deaths, must have intervened between him - and him. Such a strange mystery! - What was the answer to it? - Was death a sham? was there no such thing? - did He, the real He, go on for ever not merely in heaven, as the parsons affirmed, but on earth? was this life of his One, One reiterated, One to Everlasting, a tide ebbing and flowing between the night of Time and the day of Eternity? these recurring deaths only barriers blocking off terms of his Eternal Self?

Digging his toes into the shingle, he marched on, his heart strangely uplifted, the sense of his immortality strong on him.

And besides, the darkness and danger lay behind. Discretion, sharp eyes, and a nimble pair of feet should do the rest. Above all, his experience of the last thirty-six hours had given him confidence, the mother of success. He began to be aware of his own power. Action had revealed him to himself. Responsibility now confirmed him. The boy was merging in the man with extraordinary swiftness. There was in his soul an aweful joy, the joy of dawn, the dawn of holy manhood.

Rejoicing in his newly found strength, he laboured on gallantly. With luck, he would be in Lewes before the coach left; in London before night; and at Merton before Nelson sat down to breakfast to-morrow morning.

His, his, his, to save Nelson!

And O, mother? would not her heart be proud?

The mist grew thin before him, as though lace curtain after lace curtain was being swept back by unseen hand. The sun, the colour of a shilling, and as round, glimmered above the horizon. At his feet he could distinguish the sea silvery-twinkling; and not a hundred yards away the Head, bluff as a wall, loomed before him.

His heart leapt.... Hurrah!... Once round that....

He began to run with noisy feet.

A shadow stooping on the edge of the tide sprang up.

"*Hell*!" came a sudden scream.

Alfred Ollivant

CHAPTER XXII

FAT GEORGE & CO.

Kit's heart brought up with an appalling jerk.

He dropped behind a boulder.

A filthy little scarecrow of a man, trousers rolled about his knee, was standing in the sea, holding some one by the hand not ten yards away.

In the mist Kit thought at first that he was paddling with a child. Then he saw his mistake. The scarecrow was holding a bare arm by the hand. That arm thrust up horribly from the water: the body to which it belonged was beneath the surface. Between his dirty teeth the man held a knife. His business was obvious. He was spoiling the dead.

A huge fellow with a tawny beard spread fan-like on his chest strolled round the Head, a musket beneath his arm.

"What, Dingy! got the jumps aboard again?" he growled.

"I thart I yeard a chap a-walkin," trembled the scarecrow.

He let the dead man's hand flop into the water.

"Plenty o chaps - not much walkin," chirped a voice of one unseen.

A treble laugh greeted the sally.

Round the Head a boat came paddling.

In it was a man fat as a sow, and not unlike one. Honey-coloured ringlets hung down to his neck. He had slits for eyes, and the great face, dough-like, was set in an ogreish smile.

Kit saw before him in the flesh the worst of the nightmare imaginings of his nursery days. He began to dither like a monkey in the presence of a snake. There was a horror of the unnatural about the man that turned him faint. Here was Mammon, Mammon in the flesh; and so close that the boy could smell him.

"Belike it's Black Diamond come after you, Jow!" wheezed the fat man - "to pay you for what you done to him night afore last." The shrill voice, squeezing from that vat-like carcass, added to the terror of the man.

"'Twarn't me, I tall you!" screamed the scarecrow.

"It were you, Fat George; and now you're for puttin it on me."

The fat man backwatered in-shore; the smile set and horrible on his face.

"None o that, my lad, if you please," he husked - "that's

Alfred Ollivant

to say if you're wishful to stay friends with George - ole George, who don't forget."

Dingy Joe began to whimper.

"I suppose it were me flashed my knife on the Gentleman too?"

The fat man leaned on his oars.

"Now," he said with manly frankness, "that *were* me. Every man answers for his own work in this gang, and none needn't go short. I faced the Gentleman plucky, didn't I, Bandy?"

"You faced him plucky from behind," chirped the voice of the man unseen.

Hoarse laughter from behind the Head told that the shaft had gone home.

Fat George held a deprecating hand to heaven.

"Now ear k to that, my God!" he squeaked. "I risk my blessed neck for em. I'm the only man o the lot got the guts to stand up to him. I tells him straight, I says - 'We've lost our leader and our lugger in your service, my lord,' says I, 'and now you got to - well square it.'"

"'- well square it!'" snorted the giant. "That's a pretty way to talk to a gentleman, ain't it?"

Fat George pointed a derisive finger at him.

"Can't forget he was a gamekeeper!" he tittered. "Touch his at and all, didn't you, Red Beard?"

"And wish I'd never stopped touchin it!" shouted the giant. "Blasted young fool that I were! - Thought I'd take a short cut to fortune, same as the rest. - And where's it landed me?"

He swept his hand around.

"Heark to Red Beard!" giggled Fat George. "Quite the Methody man, ain't he?"

A gust of passion darkened the giant's face. He surged through the water towards the boat.

"- well square it!" he foamed. "I'll - well square *you*, you lump o lard with the heart of a maggot!" He stopped, steadying down to a fierce scorn.

"And he would ha - well squared it only for you messin about with that blasted knife o your'n be'ind him."

"He would ha - well squared it only for you knockin the blasted knife up!" shrilled the fat man. "That's the best *you* can do. Pretty set for a man to be 'sociated with."

He bent over his hand; his locks fell about his face; and he rocked to and fro like a weeping woman.

The sound of angry voices brought others trooping round the Head. Some slopped along in the water, others trailed along the edge. The eyes of all were down, hunting for prey.

Kit, watching them with shuddering heart, recalled that passage in his mother's favourite Sunday book where

Christian, at the mouth of Hell, heard a company of fiends coming to meet him.

He found himself envying Christian. An honest fiend was an honest fiend; but these were men! It was their humanity, the sense of his kinship with them, that seemed to make his heart collapse.

And their names!

Toadie, the squat brute, with the front teeth; Whitey, the albino, peering and prying; One-eye, Humpy, Bandy and the rest - all labelled like dogs from some physical deformity.

Once and for all they slew in the boy's mind the Romance of Crime. Now he understood what the old Book meant about the Wages of Sin. Death indeed; death in life. He read it in their faces. Yes; it was all true. These men *had* done evil, and they *had* come forth unto the Resurrection of Damnation.

And not so very long ago he had wished to be one such! - a highwayman, a smuggler, a gentlemanly villain of some sort, very devil-may-care and gallant, robbing the rich, helping the poor, waving a scented handkerchief to the ladies as he rode to Tyburn, debonair to the last.

Now he was face to face with criminals in real life. And what was their distinguishing feature? - *Filth*.

They had not shaved for days, nor washed for years. The stink of them blew off the clean sea towards him. It seemed to his imagination that the water curdled with disgust as the brutes slushed through it.

A phrase of his laughing mother's occurred to him - *no soap, no soul.* True too.

He would have given all he had for a look at one clean-fleshed, clear-eyed Englishman, smelling of earth and honest tobacco.

"Listen to im!" grumbled Red Beard. "Might be Cock o the Gang the way he carries on."

The fat man tossed back his locks.

"All mighty fine!" he shrilled. "But if you'd follow'd me, where'd you be now? - why back in Boulon. And cause you didn't, where are you? - why hung up on a dead foul leeshore: Diamond dead, lugger gone, the hue-and-cry up after you -"

"And our only ope in eaven," chimed in Bandy of the chirpy voice.

"And how'd stickin the Gentleman elp us?" grumbled the brutal Toadie. "I'd stuck him fast enough if I'd twigged that!"

Fat George leaned forward.

"What's the reward out agin him? - Thousand guineas, ain't it?"

"Go on! - We'd never ha took him alive. You know his hackle."

"Ah!" interposed the fat man, "but what d'ye think his corpse'd ha been worth to the British Government? him *and* the papers on him, to say nothin o pickins for pore men, what nobody needn't know nothin about - them rings, that pin, and the bundle o notes in his tail-pocket." He combed his fingers through his locks. "What'd that ha been worth? I'll tell you." He wagged a fat finger. "A free pardon to h'every man h'all round, a free pass back to Boulon -"

"And the thanks o Parlyment for what we done to the crew o the *Curlew*!" piped Bandy.

"It's God's truth, I'm talkin!" screamed the fat man. "And there's the man what stood between you and it!" He flung a fat hand at Red Beard.

The giant turned.

"What, sell him!" he drawled. "Sell the man that made you; that trusted you; that never turned his back on a rat yet - much less a pal." He spat into the sea curling at his feet. "What was it old Diamond says? - 'We're all - traitors,' says he, poor old horse; 'but we are men, only Fat George. And he's a - sow without a soul.'"

A murmur of approval ran round.

"You're right, Red Beard."

"The Genelman were a genelman."

"That he were!" came a chorus from the maingy crew.

"Gentleman!" put in Bandy. "He were better. He were a - lord. I ought to know seein I rode for one - afore my misfortune."

The boat had drifted sea-ward, the fat man giving an

occasional sly dig.

Suddenly he flung back into the oars.

"Ave it your own way," he sang out. "Ole George ain't good enough for you, I see. I'll say good-day."

The giant jerked his musket to his shoulder.

"Come in!" he thundered. "Or I'll plug a hole through that great paunch o your'n."

The fat man saw himself covered. He paddled back, grinning ghastly.

"Avast there, Red Beard!" he tittered. "You're that asty. Can't you take a little joke?"

"I can take one o your little jokes about as easy as you can take one o my little bullets in the belly," rumbled the giant. "Come in now. Get out o that boat. You'd sell us as you sold the Gentleman. That bit o wood's all that stands atween us and Kingdom Come."

"Easy all," chimed in Bandy Dick. "Only one thing's sure in our present interestin sitiwation; and that is if we don't ang together, we'll ang separate."

Alfred Ollivant

CHAPTER XXIII

THE CLIMB

I

Crouched behind the boulder, Kit listened.

Surely they must hear his heart! It was thumping so that he took his hand off the boulder before him lest it should betray him by its shaking.

Black Diamond! - Fat George! - the Gentleman!

There could be no question as to the identity of these kites. They were the Gap Gang, and in desperate plight. Their lugger was gone, and their leader dead. At sixes and sevens among themselves, they had quarrelled with the only man who might somehow have saved them. Behind them lay the gallows; before them the sea - and nothing to cross it in but the lugger's long-boat, and that water-logged.

Their condition was desperate; but what about his own?

He could not round the Head. They stood between him and his goal. Could he go back along the bay? He glanced back at the line of headlands, shimmering in the sun. The tide in places already lapped the foot of the cliff. And even as he pondered, a chill something startled his feet. He looked down. It was the water, stealing in upon him, quiet as a cat. He could not stay where he was. To do so was to drown.

There was but one thing for it - to climb.

He glanced up. Things were not so hopeless as he had feared. The mists were drifting seaward. He could see the dark crest of grass rimming the cliff-edge above him.

Thank heaven! - this was no longer the blank and aweful wall, hundreds of feet high and sheer as a curtain, which he had found above him last night. The cliff must have fallen away towards the point. That dark crest of grass, shivering in the wind, was not so far away; and the cliff itself was by no means sheer.

The tide was already lapping the point. The smugglers had drifted away before it. He could hear their voices on the other side. Now was his chance.

II

On tiptoe he crept off the betraying shingle, and began to climb, the scent-bottle in his mouth.

A recent fall of cliff helped him, making a ramp. Up it he went, a tiny trickle of dislodged shale dribbling away beneath his feet.

Alfred Ollivant

At the top of the fall a mat of weeds had grown. On this he stayed. The cliff arched out blue-white over him like the inside of a shell. There was no hope there.

He looked about him. On his right a narrow ledge, grass-grown, trickled darkly across the face of the cliff, inclining upwards and out of sight. It would give him foothold, and no more.

He took it tremblingly, sidling along, his face pressed close to the cliff, his hands finding finger-hold on the ridges and irregularities above his head.

The track led up and up. He dared not look down: all there was sheer now, he knew, and the sea lapping among the dead bones of the cliff. He could not look up: to have done so, he must have craned backwards; and little thing as that might seem, it would have been enough to upset his balance on that skimpy track.

Up and up he sidled to the noise of trickling chalk, his eyes glued to the white and callous cliff. His hands were damp and chill; his back set against nothingness; his long eyelashes swept the chalk-surface. He had a sense that the cliff was swelling itself to thrust him off. It was alive; it was hostile. The leer he detected in the great blank face pressed against his own roused his anger. He clung the more tenaciously because of it, snarling back. G-r-r! - it shouldn't beat him - beast!

All the same his fingers were getting tired and sore. He was whimpering as he went. The great horror was overwhelming him. He shut his mind against it: still it crept in. Head swirled: brain lost grip of body: all was dissipation.

O - o - oh!

The voice of one of the Gang rose to his ears. It steadied him; recalling all that hung on him ... old Ding-dong's trust ... Nelson ... Duty....

The track led round a corner - and ran away into nothing.

Retreat along that path or headlong death - these seemed his alternatives. Of the two the latter appeared just then least horrible, as swifter, and more certain: he had no need to look down to make sure of that.

Biting his nails, he listened to his own breathing. A tiny shell had become incrusted in the great blind face, so close to his own. Putting out his tongue, he licked it, and hardly knew he had.

Suddenly he saw his mother. She was sitting in her particular little low chair beside the fire in the Library, reading aloud a favourite passage from her favourite Sunday book, Gwen sprawling at her feet.

To go back is nothing but Death, came the familiar voice, pure and tranquil; *to go forward is fear of Death, and life everlasting beyond it. I will yet go forward.*

The book snapped softly; his mother's eyes lifted to his as she repeated,

I will yet go forward.

Alfred Ollivant

III

Yes, if there's a way!

On his right, some ten feet distant, a little table-land of grass projected from the face of the cliff - the green top of a flying buttress, as it were.

Once there he could at least lie down and recover himself. And, unless he was mistaken, the cliff above there was no longer sheer.

But how to get there? - a ten-foot jump to be attempted off one leg at a stand and sideways.

Half-way between him and the plateau a bush with feathery green plumes grew out of a crevice overhead. Those green plumes stirred deliciously in the breeze; the little stem, thick as his wrist, and reddish of hue, thrust out sturdily over the sea. It was three feet out of reach, and above him.

He scanned the distance. Without wings he certainly could not do it.

A butterfly settled on a purple sea-thistle close to his head. It poised there with fanning wings, so languid, so unconcerned. *It* didn't mind.

A bitter anger surged up in the boy's heart. It was sitting there flopping its wings out of swagger - to show it had them. He'd teach it to swagger!

He put up his thumb to crush it.

Then he remembered himself. He must be just in this that might be his last moment on earth. After all the butterfly couldn't help itself. It was made that way; and perhaps it didn't mean it. To kill it was spiteful - worthy of a girl, worthy of Gwen, as he would have told her had she been present. That would get Gwen into one of her states. His eyes twinkled, and grew haggard again.

He observed the butterfly with extraordinary intensity. Its body and wings were the colour of the sea; the undersides of the wings a silvery-brown. The face was white, with large black eyes, and long antennae. Lovely furry down clothed body, thighs, and lower wings. On the nose two tiny horns stuck up....

He would have given all he possessed to be that butterfly just then. Yet after all - could the butterfly venture for his country? - and would he if he could?

Suddenly the boy's soul broke through the darkness shrouding it, and bubbled up, a sea of twinkling, tumbling light. Standing there, clawing the cliff, death at his feet, Eternity within touch of him, he laughed.

At the crisis his humour, heaven's best gift, had saved him.

I will yet go forward.

A knob of chalk, swelling out of the side of the cliff, caught his eye. He saw it, and too wise to pause for thought, sprang. His foot touched the knob. He thrust back. As he thrust, it gave beneath him, and fell with a resounding splash into the sea.

But it had done its work; and he was swinging with one hand on the stem of the green-plumed bush....

Curiously familiar this swinging in space with fluttering heart.... Was it only in dreams?...

The splash of the falling boulder set the gulls screaming.

"There!" shrilled a voice, faint and far beneath. *"What did I tell you?"*

"Take the boat, Red Beard, and have a look."

Kit, swinging, heard the dip of oars. Another second and the boat would be round the Head, and he, hanging there, black against the white cliff, as easy to kill as a fly on a window-pane.

He reached up his left arm, swung once and again, and loosed his hold.

He flung through the air, the sea glancing sickeningly miles below, and landed on hands and knees on the green carpet.

Hallowed be Thy Name.

CHAPTER XXIV

THE CLIMB

I

"There's nowt here," called a voice from below. *"A fall of the cliff belike."*

The boat put back.

Kit stayed on hands and knees on the grass plateau, his forehead bowed to the ground in attitude of prayer.

He was sick with humility and thankfulness.

Already the boy began to have that sense which distinguishes the great man from the herd, swinging him over obstacles to others insurmountable, the sense that God is with him, and therefore he cannot fail.

A fly was buzzing somewhere near. It comforted him amazingly. It was earthy and every-day, that solid buz-z-z-z; reminding him of the kitchen at home, fat Maria kneading dough, and the smell of fly-papers. It steadied him as a feast of bread and meat steadies a man heady with long fasting.

Alfred Ollivant

Rolling over on his back, he lay flat, panting.

How good it was to feel the earth beneath him once more! Faithful old thing! she wouldn't give way beneath her child. He hammered her with his heels; he patted her with his hands; he wriggled his shoulders into her: all massive, all motherly, all good.

Turning on his side, he kissed her.

A while he lay there, arms and legs wide, eyes shut, breathing in security and peace. Angels fanned him; strong arms held him up. Yes, yes. It was all true. He *was* loved.

The sea rustled beneath him, flowing on and on. How happy it was in its work! He could have listened to it for ever. The sun, labouring too, was climbing upwards in a shroud of glory. It stared him fiercely in the face, bidding him rise and get to business.

He sat up and looked round.

It was as he had thought. He was on a flying buttress of the cliff, at his feet a floor of water, silvery-ruffled.

On his right cathedral cliffs blocked out the light. Mighty-towering, they made a white and awful gloom between him and heaven. The shadow of them darkened his heart. Crouching fly-like there, he cowered as he peered up at them. They were terrible: so stern, so white, so inexorable. Had he wronged them? - They seemed to stand over him in fearful and affronted majesty. Yet with the awe there came a pride, the pride of possession. They were his, these tremendous battlements; they were England's. With what a high and massive steadfastness they challenged France! Surely they knew themselves impregnable.

Beneath him the sea, a vast plain of silver-blue, merged in a sky white as diamonds. The one drifted, the other was still; the one sparkled, the other shone: for the rest there was no distinction, no dividing line. Each ran into the other; and all was splendid with light and life.

Below, those dark dead men still scavenged on the edge of the tide. He could have dropped a pebble on them. Dingy Joe's whine floated up to him....

"This cove's rings won't come off."

"Ain't you got a knife, then?" growled the brutal Toadie - *"talks like a Miss."*

"Say! look at this chap's lady-bird."

Bandy Dick held something aloft.

"He won't want no lady-bird no more. She'll ave to get another fancy-man."

Followed filthiest jests on women ... love.... Such love!

Pah! - Were they men? - The beasts were purer.

The boy straight from his own white home and gayhearted mother sickened as he heard.

Hell? - What need of Hell hereafter for these men, when they had plunged into it on earth?

Alfred Ollivant

The words of a greater than Bunyan rang in his ears -

Whosoever committeth sin is the servant of sin.

Servants! slaves rather; slaves of themselves.

From his perch in the high heavens the boy looked down on them as an angel may look down on souls in torment.

An aweful anger seized his heart. He longed to do God's work for Him - to avenge.

"*Vengeance is mine,*" came a voice. "*I will repay.*"

He started back, amazed.

Had he spoken? had the Lord?

The lightning words flashed down out of the heavens on the self-damned below.

Dingy Joe flung up a ghastly face, screamed, and falling on his knees in the water, began to babble about his Redeemer.

Fat George took to his heels. Furiously he splashed along, yellow locks flopping. Kit could hear him snorting as he ran. All his life the fat man had been running away from God, the Great Enemy; and still He was there. Some day He would catch him - Fat George never doubted that ... some day ... but not while he had legs.

How should he know that as he ran, God ran with him?

The others huddled together like thunder-frightened cattle. Bandy Dick cocked a scared snook, while Red Beard was man enough to loose his musket at the zenith.

"*Not yet, Governor!*" he shouted with a roaring laugh - "*not yet!*"

Fools! - they were living in the Hell they feared. Their punishment was *now*. They had long been damned. While they lived God, the Avenger, would punish them inexorably. When they died, God, the merciful Saviour, would take them and make them clean.

Death, the death they feared and fled from, would be their Salvation, as it is every man's.

II

I will yet go forward.
Kit turned to a reconsideration of his enterprise.

The top was far yet, but the cliff was no longer sheer; a precipitous slope rather, patched with grass.

On hands and knees he set out. The grass trickled down like a dark torrent from above, cutting as it were a channel between two bastions, sheer on either side of him, and naked as the moon.

Up that dark trickle he climbed, and the sun climbed with him.

The grass gave him hand-hold. The chalk was rough and shale-like. He dug knees and toes into it. There was a constant dribble of stuff away from beneath his feet, and once a little land-slide, slithering seaward.

Beneath was nothing but a shining waste, waiting for him. He rather felt than saw it: for he dared not look down. He must think of what lay above. Therein was his hope. He clung to it, as he clung to the cliff-face, desperately.

The sun blazed on his back. The sweat trickled down his face. He kept his mind to his work, and his nose to the cliff. A bee with an orange tail sucked at a purple thistle. Butterflies chased, loved, and sipped all round him. O for Gwen, and her killing-bottle!

Up and up; the sun fierce upon his back; the earth bulging beneath his nose, the splash and ripple of the sea growing fainter and more faint below.

Blue above him, blue beneath, blue in his brain, blue everywhere, save for this dull leprous white beneath his nose - blue emptiness, calling him, clutching him, waiting for him. Would it never end?

Once he looked up.

He was climbing into heaven.

The cliff bluffed up into the sky. He could see the bearded crest dark against the light. Up there a pair of kestrels floated - two living cross-bows bent above him. They were almost transparent and very still: a tremble of the wings, a turn of the broad steering tail, a motion of the blunt head, a swoop and a sway and a glint of russet back.

They had wings too! Everything in the world had wings but himself, the only one who really needed them.

Once he slipped, and hung sprawling over Eternity. The grass, tough as wire, and wound about his hands, stood his friend. He recovered foothold.

On again with battering heart. The top was not far now.

Hope began to flutter in his breast. It seemed to heave him upwards. The way grew steeper and more steep. The stream of grass, faithful so far, ended abruptly five feet below the top. Those feet were sheer, the chalk darkening to the blackness of soil, and the crest of grass making a rusty *chevaux-de-frise* at the summit.

Cautiously he crept on, his hands feeling the blank wall. Now his fingers touched the top.

He drew himself up.

His struggling toes found some sort of foot-hold. The wind blew on his wet forehead. His eyes were on a level with the summit.

He could see over.

A man was sitting by the edge.

Kit could have stroked his back.

II - THE MAN ON THE CLIFF

CHAPTER XXV

THE GENTLEMAN BOWS

I

The man was babbling French and weeping; weeping over a dead woman.

So much was clear.

His back was against the light. He wore no hat; and here and there a hair caught the sun and flashed like the sword of a fairy.

The dead girl must be lying with her head in his lap.

Unaware of anybody by, the young man poured out his heart: the dead woman was his little one, his darling of the chestnut hair, his petite pit-a-pat.

There was something so desolate about the grief of man, perched up there between sea and sky, nobody near but a floating sea-gull, that Kit almost wept to hear him.

But he had his own affairs to think about.

The man was a Frenchman: therefore an enemy.

What should he do?

As often happens, the question was decided for him.

Suddenly the projection on which his feet had found resting-place gave way.

A lurch, and he was dangling at arms' length. His toes could find no foothold. To drop even an inch or two was certain death: for he would land on a slope almost sheer; and the impetus must carry him - down - down - down....

"Sir!" he gasped.

II

A face flashed over the cliff, eagle-beaked and beautiful.

A young man knelt above him.

"Hullo!" he said in voice of quiet amusement, peering down at the boy beneath him. "May I ask what you are doing here?"

If he was a Frenchman, he spoke English without a trace of accent.

Alfred Ollivant

"Hanging on for dear life!" gurgled Kit, the scent-bottle between his teeth.

The young man broke into a ripple of boyish laughter.

"Flew so far: then the wings gave out, eh?"

He rose to his feet, and Kit saw he was wearing buck-skin breeches and top-boots.

Bending, he grasped the boy's wrists.

"One - two - and - h'up she comes!"

He staggered back, and fell with a gay laugh, the boy on top of him.

"Thank you," said Kit between his teeth. "Let go my wrists, please."

The man, lying on his back, smiled up at him.

How strong he was! how young! and how handsome!

Tears still bedewed his lashes, and his eyes had the sparkle and colour of the sword he wore at his side.

"What have you got between those nice milk-teeth of yours, Little Chap?"

"Nothing for you," stammered the boy. "That is - only eggs. I've been birds-nesting. Let go, please. I must get home. I'm late. I'll get into a row as it is."

The other loosed his wrists suddenly; a long arm swept about him; the thumb and forefinger of a hand like a steel-vice pressed his jaws asunder.

"Parrdon," said a voice, half tender, half teasing, the roll of the r for the first time betraying an alien strain.

Perforce the boy must open.

The scent-bottle rolled out upon the grass, and trundled towards the edge.

Lithe as a panther, the young man pounced and snatched it.

As he did so, Kit leapt on his back.

"Give it up or I dirk!" he panted.

For all answer the man fell back on top of him with the merriest laughter.

The boy's breath was shaken out of him. Two hands loosed his; and he was left gasping on his back.

"I say! did I hurt you?" came an anxious voice.

Kit scrambled to his feet.

"Give it up!" he cried passionately, thrusting out a hand. "It was given me. It's a trust."

"It's only eggs," the other reminded him, twinkling.

"I don't care what it is!" cried the boy. "It's mine!"

He was almost in tears, stamping his foot, much as in old days when Gwen, a born tease, had stolen his woolly bear, and refused to give it up.

The man made him feel like a baby - he, a King's officer.

"Forgive me," replied the other. "It is mine."

"Finding's keeping, I suppose!" sneered the boy, ablaze. "You take it by brute force - you steal it - and it's yours! And I daresay you call yourself a gentleman!"

"When I said it was mine," replied the other with the grave tenderness of a gentleman dealing with an angry woman, "I meant it was mine. It was given me by a lady. These are her initials on the stopper - E.H., d'you see? - If I was to surrender this bottle to you, two things would happen. My work of weeks past would be undone, and a noble woman would be hung unjustly." He put the bottle into his pocket. "And now to prove to you that it really is mine I will tell you what it contains, shall I? - A letter on tissue paper signed A. F. Is it not so?"

The flames in the boy's soul were beaten back.

"How d'you know?" sullenly.

"I wrote it."

Breathing through his nostrils, Kit eyed him.

"Then you're the Gentleman."

The young man bowed with an action that was altogether French.

CHAPTER XXVI

THE DEAD WOMAN

I

He stood bareheaded in the sun in long black riding-coat and muddied boots and breeches.

"What's that red riband in your button-hole?" asked the boy in a kind of awe.

"That! that's the Legion of Honour." He came a step forward. "Put your finger on it. That little bit of riband once lay upon the heart of Napoleon."

The boy began to tremble. That tiny square of red from which he could not take his eyes had once throbbed to the heart-beats of the Arch-enemy!

"D'you know him?"

"Little Boney!" laughing. "Yes, I know him."

The boy listened without hearing. It was all too dreamlike.

"D'you - d'you like him?"

The other chuckled.

"*Like* him? - I don't know that I exactly *like* him. You see he's not what you and I should call a gentleman. Still he serves me, so I serve him."

The boy's thumb was to his mouth, baby-like. All his anger had passed. He was gazing at the other with brooding admiration.

This was the man who had kept three counties agog these two months past!

He was an enemy, but O! he was a hero.

Strangely young too, almost a boy; tall and slight as his own sword, the grey eyes big under dark brows, the face sun-golden and lean almost to gauntness.

"How *did* you do it?" murmured the boy.

The other's eyes clouded; the lids fell.

"I could not have done it but for her," he said.

Then for the first time the boy remembered the dead woman.

II

But it was no dead woman the Gentleman was standing over now; it was a chestnut mare, the sun glistening on a coat that shone like a girl's hair. She lay along the turf with lank neck, belly exposed, and shoes flashing; strangely pathetic as a horse seen in such position always looks.

There was not a stain of sweat on her coat, not a trace of froth about her muzzle. A plain snaffle bridle lay beside her. Her head was bare and fine as a lady's; the eyes wide, the nostrils still.

Strangely like somehow, mare and man; and about both faces something of the length and strength of the eagle.

There was one marked difference. In the man life still rippled gloriously; the mare was quiet for ever.

Born to the saddle as to the sea, the boy's eye ran over her.

"What a beauty!" he gasped.

"I couldn't have attempted it but for her," replied the other quietly. "When the Emperor asked me to undertake it - 'Sire,' I said, 'if I may take my Bonnet Rouge!'... I tell you," he cried, turning almost fiercely on the boy, "I've left Merton as the first star peeped, and seen the sun rise out of the sea from here!... But I forgot...."

III

A cold shadow swept over him. Kit could feel the change - it was like passing from day to night; and it chilled the boy's heart.

Up there in the lonely stillness, sea beneath, heaven above, earth around, the two faced each other.

All the laughter had ebbed from the man's being. He was still and cold as his sword.

"D'you know what is in here?" tapping the scent-bottle.

His eyes, frosty now, seemed to bore down to the boy's soul.

Kit froze too.

"Why?"

"Because if you will give me your word that you do not know, I will let you go."

Those eyes of his were terrible.

"Will you give me your word?"

The boy was pale as ice.

Death in cold blood here on the quiet hillside - death like a pig's in a sty.... Ugh!...

"No, thank you."

"Then prepare to meet your Maker."

He turned and fiddled with a pistol, snapped it, cursed in an undertone, and thrust it back in his pocket.

Then he turned again.

The boy stood before him with dark eyes. Slight as a lily, and the colour of one, he seemed to sway in the breeze.

"Give me your word not to speak of what you know till after Thursday next - and you may go."

The boy shook his head.

"I mustn't."

The man flashed the hue of lightning.

"Then I must."

An arm swept about the boy. A hand at his waist was fumbling for his dirk.

For a second the lad struggled: then he felt himself helpless as a rabbit in a python's grip, and lay back quite still.

Once face to face with God, his heart calmed strangely.

There was a horrible breathing in his ear.

A face, all eyes, was bending over him.

"*My God! how like a girl he is*!" came a far whisper.

"Go on, please, and don't insult me," gurgled the boy. And as he said it, his mind flashed back to Gwen: Gwen with her pride of sex, standing before him, fists closed, challenging him to fight - "cad!"

"What are you chuckling about?"

"Gwen - my sister.... She thinks a girl's as good as a boy.... Go on."

The hand upon his forehead quitted its hold.

"I can't," said the Gentleman.

The arm about the boy relaxed.

Kit stood up.

"Thank you," he said, and readjusted his collar.

The Gentleman rippled off into laughter.

CHAPTER XXVII

THE HOLLOW IN THE COOMBE

For the first time Kit glanced round him.

On the top of the cliff, they were by no means on the top of the Downs. A great dun wave of earth, patched with gorse, surged up into the sky before him.

It flopped and flowed down to the edge of the cliff, swelling up round and steep towards the brow, a quarter of a mile back from the sea. He was standing at the foot of a prominent shoulder, curving away above him. On the right was a deep coombe, the hill at the blind-end of it sheer-seeming. On his left the jagged edge of the cliff ran up and up and out of sight. Beneath him the sea was a sparkling plain.

The Gentleman was kneeling beside his dead. He closed her eyes, and kissed the cold muzzle.

"Adieu, ma mie," he whispered. *"L'Irlande n'oubliera jamais."*

Then he put on his hat, and braved the sunshine.

"Take my arm, Little Chap."

Alfred Ollivant

So the two faced the hill.

A question bubbled to the lad's lips. At last it blurted out.

"How did they catch you, sir?"

"They didn't catch me. They murdered her."

The arm within the boy's trembled, but the voice continued quietly.

"Yesterday I had words with some old friends of mine in the Gap yonder. We parted in a hurry, and I rode up to the Head to watch the fight - your fight."

He flashed his grey eyes on the boy.

"You were in it, weren't you?"

"Yes - a bit."

The other drew a sighing breath.

"I'd have given all I had to have been there....

"From noon to sundown I watched the fight, and never stirred. My body was asleep. I was aware of nothing but those three black dots, miles beneath me on that plain of silver, spurting flame at each other. Bonnet Rouge grazed beside me. And when she heard the guns, she neighed, shaking her bridle. For she loved brave men and War, and knew it too. Yes, she led the Green Brigade at Marengo."

He came to a halt.

"When they came right under the cliff, I couldn't see from the top. So I came down here."

He lifted his face to the sun.

"And that was how they caught me - cornered me here - while I was watching - the sea on all sides but one - and they on that."

His face was dusky now.

"Her whinny was the first thing that woke me. I turned to see her coming towards me at a stumbling canter - like a hurt child running to its mother."

His eyes were shut, his voice strangely still.

"They'd run her through - a lady - who thought them friends."

A great vein stood out blue on his temple.

"I wouldn't have believed it of an Englishman."

He sighed profoundly.

"But they paid for it."

Slanting off the shoulder, he led down towards the coombe on his right.

The boy on his arm was trembling.

In the deep bosom of the coombe was a green hollow.

On the brink they paused. Above them a lark sang.

Alfred Ollivant

A little circle of men lay round the saucer in the sun, the flies upon their faces. In front of the others a big man sprawled across a great black horse.

He flung forward over the saddle-bow, face down. One fat hand was crumpled on the turf. His bob-wig had slipped awry.

There was no mistaking that bald red neck with the crease across it. It was Big Jerry Ram, the riding-officer.

The Gentleman toed the body.

"It was this carrion. 'Got you this time, sir,' said he, grinning his fat beef-steak British grin. 'Clipped your wings at last, I guess.'

"I said nothing. I was mad....

"He was a brave man - an extraordinarily brave man. You English, you are brave. But he was no soldier. He rode at me alone, handling that sabre of his like a flail. We'd hardly crossed blades before he knew his fate. 'You've got me, sir,' said he, splashing about with his sword. I said nothing. 'Maybe I hadn't ought to ha stuck her,' he gasped. He wasn't whining. He wasn't that sort. He knew he had to have it. 'It was tit for tat: your blood-mare - my old Robin. 'Tain't Christian, but 'tis sweet.' Then as he saw it coming - in a kind of scream - 'Through the heart if you're a gentleman, sir.'... So much I permitted him. You see he was brave."

Kit's brow was dank. The man's calm terrified him.

"The others gave little trouble. They'd sabres; but only one had a pistol, and it wouldn't go off - English-like....

"Then they formed a rallying group. Yes, they formed a rallying group. You see they were afraid....

"It was no good. I walked round them with my pistols."

Shuddering, the boy saw it all: the group of ghastly men, back to back in the hollow; silence, butterflies, and Death in breeches and boots stalking round.

"Then they broke. They couldn't run: I could. I would have spared them, mud that they were - but for her.

"You see," his voice was still again, "I loved her."

He dreamed, his eyes upon the hills.

"Yes," he said, "I was terrible."

Alfred Ollivant

CHAPTER XXVIII

ON THE TOP OF THE WORLD

I

The Gentleman led up the shoulder of the hill, the tails of his long riding-coat flapping about his legs.

Kit, panting behind, admired him as he had never admired even Uncle Jacko. The man seemed to know no fear, striding rapidly on, his enemy behind him.

True, the boy's dirk still flashed in the other's hand; but the lad had his jack-knife; and his eyes dwelt on the place where he could plant it home and home in that black back - there by the seam, where it was a little worn.

And the man had the scent-bottle!

Surely a fellow would be justified....

"Now's your chance, Little Chap!" came the gay voice.

Kit, betrayed to his own soul, sniggered and put the dark thought away with shuddering disgust.

The man was a gentleman, the man trusted him. Once he had saved his life; and once spared it. Should he pay his debt with the jack-knife?

The long-striding figure went up the hill as though on wings.

Kit clambered at his spurs.

Escape he knew was vain. As well might a canary attempt to escape a hawk.

The scabbard of the other's sword poking and peeping between his tails caught the boy's eye and fascinated it. It had seen plenty that sword, he would bet! What tales it could tell!

How he should like to know!...

"Have you ever fought a duel?" he blurted out.

"Used to a bit. Not now."

"Why? - d'you think it wrong?"

The other flung back a merry laugh.

"No, my little Puritan. I gave it up, because it gave me up. You see, I never quite met my match with the small-sword. Or rather I did meet my match once, but the beggar wouldn't fight."

"Do tell," panted Kit, scenting a story.

"It was in Egypt - during the occupation. He was said to be the finest sword in the British Army -

Abercromby's Black Cock, they called him. He'd a standing challenge out against any man of ours who'd take it up. Killed seven of our fellows in seven days, a man a morning, in single combat, between the outpost lines - all fair and square and according to Cocker, and the staffs of both Armies looking on. Sounds like a legend, don't it? - The eighth day I appeared to do battle with him. I was twenty-one at the time, and looked seventeen. It was to have been the great day of my life - and was the bitterest. Directly he saw me - 'I don't fight with children,' says he, high and mighty as a turkey-cock, and turned on his heel. I wept." He laughed joyously at the reminiscence.

"Curious how small the world is," he continued. "Five years passed - five years full of things. Then one fine day, a few weeks back, I was over yonder at Birling Gap, waiting for a friend, when who should come strolling round the corner, smelling of roast beef and Old England, but my old friend of the curly pate and ruddy cheeks. I'd a minute or two to spare. So I introduced myself, and we adjourned to the beach at once."

"What happened that time?" asked the boy keenly.

"Why, Fat George!" replied the other. "And deuced lucky for Master Black Cock too. You see, he was fat and scant o breath."

II

They had climbed to the top of the world.

It lay spread before them, wide and wonderful; head in the heavens, feet in the sea miles beneath on every side.

On the brow beside them the blackened skeleton of a building stood up stark against the light.

The charred stump of a flag-staff pricked up out of the turf. On the scorched grass lay a singed red flag and tattered pendant.

"What's this?" whispered Kit.

The ghastly desolation of the ruins amid the sea of light and living green appalled him. Moreover he smelt death.

"Signal-station," said the Gentleman, hurrying by. "Black Diamond stormed it at dusk on Saturday night - just before I came along. They took it and burnt the men inside. Black Diamond did the storming - Fat George the burning, he and old Toadie."

"Brutes!" hissed Kit.

"I don't much care for Fat George and old Toadie myself," replied the Gentleman, rather white. "They seem to me scarcely - what shall I say? - *spirituels....* Black Diamond was quite a different pair of shoes. A curious nature - three parts sheer devil, one part pure gentleman. I could tell you some strange tales about him."

III

They had turned their backs on the dark scene.

Before them the land rolled away, fold upon fold, the sea encircling it.

Big Jerry's coombe lay vast and vault-like beneath them on the right, certain dark specks in the centre of it.

They were not sheep, those specks: Kit knew what they were.

Over the shoulder of the coombe, a great flat bay, the sea white along the brown edge of it, swept away scimitar-wise into the mist.

The Gentleman stopped, his hand on the boy's shoulder.

"Pevensey Bay! That is where the first Frenchman who ever conquered England landed. Hastings yonder! Battle Abbey over there! - my name on its Roll. Such a wonderful old Church!"

He stopped abruptly.

A ship, lying inshore beneath him, tiny on the plain of sea, had caught his eye.

He flashed round on the boy.

"What nationality?" fiercely, and with pointing finger.

Kit knew at a glance. Even at that distance the ship had something of the dishevelled appearance of a virago after a street-fight. She was the privateer.

"Double Dutchman."

A hand clutched his throat. Eyes of steel pierced him to the heart.

"Frenchman or English? tell, or take the consequences!"

"I couldn't tell you that," choking.

A python arm swept about him.

A face smiled into his.

"I knew you wouldn't. And I wouldn't have liked you if you had. But -"

The boy snapped his eyes. After all he couldn't blame the man!

It was no quick stab that he felt, no maddening darkness that drowned him; but a swift forward thrust that shot him down the slope of the coombe.

It was steep as the roof of a house. Down he pelted, headlong, his legs attempting to catch up his falling body. In vain: head over heels, rolling, bumping, tumbling, a ripple of mocking laughter pursuing him.

There was no danger, he knew. The bottom of the coombe was flat as a floor, the cliff running athwart it a quarter of a mile away.

Alfred Ollivant

At last he fetched up, battered and breathless.

Above him he could see the figure of the Gentleman tiny against the sky.

"Forgive me, Little Chap," came a far voice. "I am in a hole, and have to get out as best I can. *Il faut que je file*. Here is your little prodder."

His arm swung. Something flashed in the sky, fell, always flashing, and stuck in the hillside above him, quivering there.

It was the boy's dirk.

III - ABERCROMBY'S BLACK COCK

CHAPTER XXIX

THE FLAG OF HIS COUNTRY

I

The Gentleman had gone, and the scent-bottle with him.

The boy stood on a track that ran among the gorse, and looked about him.

The wind was at his back, and the sun on his cheek. Above him the brow, rough with gorse, swelled up against the light.

He rushed up the hill into the sky.

On the top, he hunted the landscape with anxious eyes. There was nothing to be seen; no round but the zig-a-zig of the heartless grasshoppers, merry all about him, and the thunder of his own heart.

He swung round. About him, above him, below him, dumb earth, blind sea, deaf heaven.

Alfred Ollivant

What was his agony to them?

His hopes died, and he with them. Here was the end of his mission and the end of him.

Old Ding-dong had trusted him - and now!

Mother believed in him - and now!

There would be no Lewes before breakfast; no London before night; no Nelson to-morrow morning.

A jackdaw chuckled overhead; a far sheep bleated; a great beetle, with black wing-cases flung back, roared by.

For the rest, all was silence and despair.

He had hoped greatly; he had tried hard; and failed utterly.

Above all he had not eaten for twenty-four hours.

The boy sat down and wept.

II

About him in the turf the grasshoppers kept up their accursed zig-a-zig. Little cads! At least they might be gentlemen enough not to crack their jokes just now.

The thought tickled him. He began to smile. Plucking a grass-blade, he smote one of his annoyers across the tail. It hopped gloriously. The boy laughed, and rose to his feet, his heart rising with him.

After all he had done his best. Now he must get to Lewes and make his report.

He started.

About him the turf was bare and brown. Here a patch of tall thistles, hoary-crowned, stood out among grey bents. There a clump of gorse and bramble darkened the turf.

Before him a sea of long smooth hills, billow behind billow, rolled in on him out of Infinity. It seemed to him that a giant wind had crept beneath the carpet of green and lifted it. Smooth as water it flowed down to the sea on every side. There were no trees, no hedges, no habitations. It was the loneliest land he had ever seen, and one of the loveliest. Here Earth, the Woman, rounded and beautiful, reclined at her ease before him, naked as God had made her. How different she was from that savagely shaggy man-land in the North whence he sprang! But for a haystack like a hive on a far ridge, a fold in a hollow, and the hillsides patched here and there with plough, it might have been an uninhabited land.

Here he was alone with the Eternal.

A poet to the heart, the boy's soul rose within him. For the moment he forgot his troubles. He was walking on the back of the world, his head in heaven. Beneath him rose the sea, sheer as a wall. The sight of it, dropped from heaven, as it seemed, filled him with awe. It was so near, and yet so far.

The breeze had fallen; all was still. He could hear the rustle of the tide, and the chuckle of jackdaws. Overhead a raven flapped by with slow-skewing head.

Horror of loneliness swept upon the boy. He shrank into his body. The windows of his spirit shut with a bang. Night came down.

All was darkness, mortality, and fear.

Somewhere at the bottom of the coombe beneath lay that ring of still things. Behind rose the blackened skeleton of the signal-station - and heaven knew what inside! He glanced back fearfully. They weren't after him - yet.

He took to his heels, and ran, screaming.

A familiar face greeted him. In a flash he recognised it - a meadow-brown come all the way from Northumberland to comfort him. That was beautiful of the meadow-brown, it was Christian of the meadow-brown, seeing the war to the death that he and Gwen had waged against it at home.

The butterfly gave its message to the boy's heart and settling on a blue flower, began to sip leisurely. Dash it! - the meadow-brown wasn't afraid. Need he be?

His soul took charge again with a smile.

III

Over there on the left that sheer white bluff, thrusting out into the sea, would be Seaford Head.

Beyond it lay Newhaven; behind it somewhere Lewes. To get there he had only to keep along the highlands.

He held on at a steady jog-trot. The grass sparkled with dew; mushroom bulbs shoved through the turf at his toes; above him and beneath all was blaze.

He crossed a shoulder, threading the gorse; skirted the edge of another huge coombe, troughed out beneath him; passed an ancient withered elder, squatting crone-like on the brow, and climbed a knoll that rose up bald out of the gorse.

He topped the crest, and stopped suddenly. A little dewy-eyed pond, blue as the sky, was staring at him out of a saucer of green.

In a moment he was on his knees at the edge of it, and drinking greedily. Then he took off his coat and laid it on the edge of the saucer to dry.

That done he flung himself on his back to think.

After all there was no hurry. Young as he was, he knew his England well enough to know the reception that awaited him at Lewes. He could see them about him, that cluster of Army officers, as he told his story - stonily incredulous, grimly silent, some sniggering, others jeering openly. The boy's head had been turned by his first brush! - You'd only to look at him to see his

Alfred Ollivant

sort - the romantic sort, commonly called liars! Great eyes like a girl! What did a chap with eyes like that want in the Service? - Scent-bottle - loss of the *Tremendous* - kidnapping Nelson! Lorlumme, what a yarn!

A clamour of feet close by startled his heart. He leapt up, expecting cavalry.

But no: it was a patter-footed multitude of sheep, who welled in staring yellow flood over the edge of the saucer and down to the pond. Behind them stalked Abraham, a black and white bobtail at heel.

The patriarch wore a slouch-hat and old cloak, loose as a cloud. A wild beard flamed all about him; and in his hand was a long crook. He stood on the rim of the saucer and looked down at his drinking flock.

Kit expected him to raise his hands and bless somebody. Instead he spat luxuriously, and addressed his dog in gibberish.

"Ge ou tha go!" he growled, and only the dog knew he was being desired to get out of that gorse.

Kit watched the man placidly. Instinct, which is inherited experience, reassured him. There was nothing to be feared from this chap, and nothing to be got from him. Abraham was shaggy, he was unintelligible, he was harmless.

In his few days' experience of life, the boy had already learned one great truth: that every man is exactly what he *looks*. The face always reveals or betrays. And in this face, wild with the wildness of storms and skies, there was nothing but the stupid innocence of one of his own sheep.

The man threw at the boy one shy glance of a woodland creature, and then ignored him. Another moment and he was stalking on his way, with floating cloak, tall crook, dog at heel, a mass of yellow backs rippling along in front of him.

IV

The boy stood on the rim of the saucer and looked down.

Dim green lowlands lay beneath him, spurs of the Downs thrusting out into them.

Beyond, the bay swept away saucer-wise, the sea white along its brown edge. From his feet a shoulder, dark with gorse, plunged seaward. Beneath the swell of it, a level plain ran away to the shore, heaving up there in a little hillock that stood out from the beach as a bump of green.

Off the hillock lay the privateer hove-to. Another boat hung at her stern. The boy recognised it at once. It was the lugger *Kite*.

Behind the hillock, upon the plain, stood a solitary cottage.

At that cottage, lonely in a sea of turf, the boy stared long and earnestly.

Alfred Ollivant

It was flying a flag out of the chimney.

And that flag - yes - no - yes - was the Union Jack.

CHAPTER XXX

AN OLD SONG

I

He was off the rim and rushing down through the gorse with thumping heart.

True, Ding-dong had ordered him with his last breath to steer clear of human habitation - "They're all in it," the old man had said. But then he possessed the scent-bottle. Now he had nothing but his skin to lose, and as things were he could afford to lose that. Here at any rate was a straw to catch at. Moreover he was in no hurry to get to Lewes to be called a liar.

Of course it might only prove to be some loyal old lady, flying her colours dauntlessly in the face of the Frenchman. Just such a thing his mother might do; and there were thousands of her like up and down the country - thank heaven for it!

On the other hand it might be a temporary signal-station. After the sacking of the station on Beachy Head, what more likely than that this cottage should be seized for Government purposes and garrisoned? - his own chaps too, sailors - not those swaggering snobs in red coats.

If so, he saw his course clear as day.

There was the privateer. Somewhere among these huge smooth hills lurked the Gentleman, primed with his fatal message. Between the two was one boat, and so far as he knew one only - the long-boat of the smugglers.

If his surmise were correct, and this should prove a blockade-house, he would take the garrison, though it consisted of only half-a-dozen men, attack the Gang, and smash the boat at all costs.

II

The boy plunged down the hill.

The sun beat fiercely on his head, but he hardly felt it.

Along a track that snaked through the gorse, he pushed his way, flies buzzing about him. A shining gossamer lay across his path, bosom-high. From it a web swung in the wind. At the centre, where the threads met, a black and yellow spider, marked like a man of war, waited its prey. The lad brushed through it with a pang. The spider's work fell about him in ruins: he rushed for the gorse, and hung there topsy-turvy, as though heart-broken. Hard lines certainly! He had upset the spider's apple-cart, as the Almighty had upset his. But he had *had* to - and so no doubt had the Almighty.

He turned as he ran.

"Cheer up, old chap!" he hollaed back to his friend, crouching among the ruins of his home. "It'll all come out in the washing."

III

Fluffy thistle-heads, reminding him of Gwen's young chickens, stood up out of the gorse all about him. The bunched blackberries were ripening now: he almost expected to see Gwen's face, purple-mouthed, peering at him from a bramble. All about him the silver-downed gorse-pods were snapping like pistols. A stone-chat with ruddy breast spurted out of the gorse, and flirted upwards.

The path broadened; the gorse grew scantier. His feet crushed sweetness out of the thyme. Here and there a young ash thrust up feathery.

Of a sudden he found himself again at the top of one of those almost sheer descents to which he was becoming used.

At its foot grew a hanger of beeches, already bronzing to autumn.

Down he went, slithering on hands and tail, picked himself up towards the bottom, and ran away into the shade of the wood to find himself among silver-grey beech-stems.

Alfred Ollivant

How refreshing it was after the glare, how rich, how dark!

Till he was out of it, he had not known how hot it had been on the bare hill-side. Now he was aware of the sweat on his forehead, and a dripping shirt.

Beech-stems rose in stately columns all about him. The floor was red and brown mosaic, the roof a tracery of leaves intertwined with light. Eastward the sun flashed as through a window. Close by a wood-pigeon was praying.

Out of the aisle once again into the glare.

Now the Downs lay behind him, barren and dun. On his left-front the rounded bosom of another beech-wood rose, in its midst a single chestnut already rusting. Across the valley, behind a ridge, a blunt church-tower and yellow-lichened roofs peeped. On the hill beyond, a windmill cocked up against the sky.

He paid little attention, making straight for the flag of his country.

The cottage stood about a quarter of a mile away, conspicuously solitary in the greensward, the Union Jack brave above it.

The boy approached, wary but swift. Out here on the open plain there was no cover. He was exposed as a fly on a sheet of paper. Still things couldn't be worse - he comforted himself with that most comfortable of thoughts.

Some two hundred yards from the cottage a ruined

wall ran across the greensward. Behind it the boy took cover and spied.

The cottage was very small; yet, small as it was it was grim to a degree. The flint in rows, tier upon tier, grinned at him fiercely, reminding him of a dog showing its teeth. The colour of steel, the rows of set teeth, the shaggy roof of thatch, the flag ruffling it from the chimney, all bespoke the same sturdy fighting character. Indeed it was so small, and yet so truculent, that Kit laughed to see it.

Chained there a dumb watch-dog on the threshold of its country, it seemed to be saying as it crouched -

"You can all go to sleep: I'm watching."

Kit crossed the wall, and almost expected to hear the cottage growl.

Warily he approached. As he did so, the warrior aspect of the cottage grew upon him. It was less a cottage than a tiny fort. There were only three windows, one on each side the door, and a dormer. The lower windows though latticed were cross-barred; and the door of massive oak, iron-studded, was heavy enough for a castle. Through it, ajar, he caught the gleam of arms.

Certainly this was no peasant's cottage. What was it then? - a signal-station? -

There was no flag-staff, no signal-tackle.

Some lonely smuggler's hold? - not likely: for there was the flag.

Alfred Ollivant

Could the flag be a decoy?

There was nothing for it but to go and see.

He stole forward with noisy heart.

The cottage crouched; the sycamores behind it rustled; and the wind that stirred the sycamores brought to him the sound of a voice.

He stopped, fingering his dirk.

Friend or enemy?

The voice was that of a man, deeply melodious without being exactly musical, and came from beyond the cottage somewhere by the clump of sycamores behind.

It was humming a tune, and a tune the boy knew well. Holding his breath, and listening with his heart, the boy could distinguish the words -

Jesu, Lover of my Soul.

CHAPTER XXXI

THE MAN WITH THE SWORD

I

Those familiar words, so unexpected in that strange place, smote the boy's heart.

A thousand memories surged in on him.

His lips trembled. A very little, and he would have fallen on his knees.

It was as though an Angel had come to him walking through the Valley of the Shadow, to tell him all was well, and to go forward.

And forward he went with thankful heart.

The sea of turf ran right up to the wall, and broke against it. The windows, seen close, were less windows than loop-holes, barred across. On the sill of one was a pot of musk, newly watered, and very fragrant. Within upon the wall shimmered a ship's cutlass, and a brace of pistols.

The boy peered in.

Alfred Ollivant

A kitchen-parlour, raftered and paved with stone, formed the ground-floor. At one end was a huge fire-place; in the opposite corner a bed, piled high with clothes. A ladder led to a trap-door in the low ceiling. The sun flooded into the room through the one window in the other wall. The door on that side was half open; and behind it sat a man.

II

He was all in black, and very neat: an Englishman, a gentleman, and a parson, Kit would have sworn.

His back was turned. The boy could see nothing but a black coat, a pair of solid shoulders, and a curly head.

This was not the hymn-singer to be sure. He was otherwise engaged. There was something across his knees, and he was tending to it, and talking as he worked.

From his actions and his words, Kit would have sworn that he was bathing a child. For the man was talking as women talk to babies, and some men to the women they love - that little talk, half tender, half mocking, such nonsense, and so sweet.

Then something flashed and sparkled against the dark of the door; and Kit saw it was no babe that lay across the man's knees, but a naked blade.

He was furbishing it with a chamois leather, and caressing it with words.

Now he lifted the blade on flat hands, and kissed the point reverently.

Then he leaned forward, and peered round the half open door with extraordinary stealth.

Comic as the action was, there was yet something terrible about it.

Kit choked with laughter and fear.

The man was half child playing peep-bo! and half spider waiting for a fly.

That vision of the Eternal Child, which he had surprised in the eyes of old Ding-dong sailing into action, was manifest in this man too.

Were men only children? - Yes, surely! - the good ones, at least. Only sinners grew old. Christian never ages.

The man's head turned a trifle. There was a smile flickering about his lips; and in the smile was something of the ogre, and something of the boy.

It was clear that he meant to kill; equally clear that he took joy in his purpose.

He sat down again; and as he did so held up a finger, hushing himself.

He was playing a game, unaware that he was being watched, and enjoying it intensely.

Behind the door he sat now, blade in hand, spider-still.

Plainly he was waiting for somebody.

But for whom? - and what would happen when that somebody came?

The door opened another inch or two, and through it, Kit saw the privateer, black on the white water.

In a flash he understood.

The man was waiting for the French.

III

The humour of the thing - this lonely swordsman lying in wait behind the door for the crew of the privateer - seized the boy by the throat. The laughter poured out of him headlong.

The man leapt round, dark-faced and terrible. In a twinkle he was across the floor, wary as a panther.

The door opened.

Out he came, thrusting stealthily, his blade leading him. His flanks were covered, himself almost unseen in the dark of the door.

Whatever else the man might be, he was a soldier born.

Then he saw the boy and halted on the threshold.

A man more aggressively English Kit thought he had

never seen.

Forty or thereabouts, five feet ten high, and perfectly compact: he wore no wig, and his hair broke in crisp grey curls all about his head: a ruddy face, fighting jowl, and blue eyes, kindled with equal ease to savagery or smiles.

The boy's heart leapt to those eyes, as it leapt to the first blossom starring the black-thorn after winter's desolation. There was hope in them, the hope of Spring.

The man smelt of roast beef and Old England.

Kit loved him at a glance. And was he a stranger? - Had he not fought with this man, hunted with him, died with him a thousand times of old? Had they not stood shoulder to shoulder, and back to back, in many a desperate venture in the past that haunted him? Had he not tried him time and again on the anvil of hard experience, always to find that he rang true? Would he fail him now at his need, this old comrade, who had never failed him before? No. That old sense of the familiarity of all experience swept in on him with staggering force.

Drawn as in a dream, he stepped forward and took the other's hand.

"Friend," he said.

The man lowered his point. His eyes drank in the boy's face.

"So be it," he answered, twinkling.

The blue eyes lived in the brown ones; the hands gripped.

CHAPTER XXXII

THE BROKEN SQUARE

"My name is Caryll - Christopher Caryll."

The other nodded over him.

"Christopher Caryll, called by his mother Kit: an officer of the Sea Service, eh?"

The boy's eyes brightened.

"Yes, sir. How did you know?"

"I remember a Kit Caryll by name in the Mediterranean in the nineties. And I ought to know the King's uniform, seeing I was a King's officer myself before I took orders."

"A sailor?"

"Sailor be d'd!" cried the Parson, heartily. "I'd sooner be a cod-fish. No, sir, no: I hate the sea like I hate the French. D'you think if the Almighty had meant me for the water, He'd have troubled to give me that?" He thrust forth his right leg, and dwelt fondly on the calf, contracting and relaxing it.

Alfred Ollivant

"But I forget my manners."

He bent over his blade with tenderest chivalry.

"Will you allow me," with a sweep, "to introduce to your ladyship a young gentleman of the sister Service? Mr. Caryll - Lady Polly Kiss-me-quick."

He averted the sword, and shielding his mouth, whispered confidentially -

"The sweetest of her sex, Mr. Caryll, but that hot after the men you wouldn't believe."

Kit threw back his head and gurgled. Only fifteen, and man enough not to be ashamed to be a boy, he still loved make-believe. And his heart went out to this man, who was after all a brother-boy.

"No, I wasn't a sailor. I had my company in the King's Black Borderers," continued the Parson - "the old Blackguards, as they call us, of whom you may have heard."

The boy's eyes flashed.

"I should think I had!" he cried. "It was a brute in the Borderers nearly killed my Uncle Jacko in a duel - in Corsica - in '94. A chap called Joy. He was a notorious bully - a cursing swearing fellow. After-wards he died of drink, mother says. Uncle Jacko was her favourite brother."

The other's face had chilled.

"And what was mother's favourite brother's name - if

I may ask?"

"Gordon, sir - Jacko Gordon."

"Jacko Gordon - the Horse-Gunner!" laughed the Parson. "Ha! ha! ha!"

"Did you know him, sir?"

The Parson tossed his Polly in the air, and caught her deftly.

"Did we know him? did we not? You remember Jacko Gordon, my lady? - and the sands of Calvi?"

"That was where the bully fought him!" cried Kit. "Ran him through the fore-arm when he wasn't ready."

A dark breeze swept across the other's face.

"He was ready; and it was not the fore-arm," he replied with icy chilliness. "It was the wrist; was it not, my own?" bending over his blade.... "Yes; he had a lovely wrist - until she kissed it...." He shrugged. "But what would you? - 'Calves!' says he; and it was before the mess-tent -' d'you call those things? yours calves?' - 'And what d'you call em yourself?' says I, mighty polite. 'Why, *cows in calf!'* says he, and swaggers off with a silly guffaw.

"After that there was nothing for it but the usual of course. I ran him through the wrist. He dropped his blade....

"'D'you withdraw?' says I, she straining for his heart.

"'What I have said, I have said,' he answered, white as silver and steady as the firmament.

"Then little man Nelson knocked up my sword -

"'That'll do, Black Cock,' says he. 'A joke's a joke; but a brave man's death's a mighty bad joke. She's a little blood-sucker that lady o yours.' And nobody but Nelson'd ha dared to say it."

II

The boy was staring hard.

"Did they call you Black Cock, sir? Abercromby's Black Cock?"

"That's me, sir, at your service," replied the Parson - "Joy of Battle in the Regiment, Abercromby's Black Cock in the Army. What of it?"

"I met a man who knew you this morning."

The other's eyes leapt.

"Chap with a beak on a chestnut! - handsome young scoundrel! - Frenchified, theatrical, bit o red riband stuck on his stomach."

"That's the man, sir."

"Well, what of him? - Quick!"

Kit repeated the tale of Egypt, as the Gentleman had told it.

The other listened with rapt interest.

"It's all true," he said, "true as the Bible."

He was pacing up and down, his hands behind him.

"There was a time in my life," he began at last "when I had - er - the regrettable habit of - er - using foul language, as your Uncle Jacko may have told you. Never filthy language! never that. I always swore like a gentleman. Chucked the d's and b's and g's about a bit too merry. Well, one day - it was in Egypt - I was carrying on a bit, when a pious sort of ass I knew at home, who was standing by, said - 'I wonder what your mother'd think if she heard you now, Harry Joy.' So after I'd given him some for imself, I went back to my tent and thought a bit.

"You see I'd just heard from home that poor old mother was failing. And I couldn't help thinking - Now supposing she dies, and first thing she hears when she gets to heaven is her boy loosing off on earth!...

"So I took an oath Samson-style, and I prayed I and I said - 'Look here, Lord, if you'll look over what's past, and help me keep a clean tongue in future, I'll kill you a Frenchman a day for seven days....'

"So I sent a challenge into their lines. There was nothing stirring just then, and they took the thing up very readily. The business took place before reveille out in the desert, between the out-post lines at a place they got to call the cock-pit. All the bloods and bucks on both sides used to come out to see the fun. It was the regular thing - to see Black Cock breakfast....

"Well, on the seventh morning as they were carting their chap away, and I was wiping my sword, a swaggering great Cuirassier turned round and shouted,

"'To-morrow we bring David to slay your Goliath!'

"'D'you hear that, Black Cock?' says Olifant, the Guardsman. 'Are you game?' - 'I'm not tired, if they ain't,' says I."

His blue eyes began to twinkle.

"Next dawn, when I got to the Cock-pit, and saw their champion, why, he was a boy! - a boy like a girl! - one of these pretty pink and white things, all eyes and legs and a silly smile. 'I am David,' says he. 'Then go back to Jesse,' says I, pretty short. 'I don't fight with kids.'... And that afternoon I sent him a bottle of milk with my compliments."

The Parson stopped his pacing, and looked the boy in the eyes.

"Next day they broke us, sir, - broke the Black Borderers in square."

"Who did?"

The Parson was breathing deep, and his eyes were smouldering.

"The Legion d'Irlande. No other regiment in the world could have got in; and once in, no other regiment in the world but ours could have got em out, though I say it as shouldn't."

Voice and eyes burst into thunder and flame.

"And who led em? Why, my boy-girl friend storming along on an old white Arab, and laughing like the devil. 'Here, they come!' yells the Colonel. *'Prepare for - Cavalree!'* I jumped on to the big drum, and had a squint over the men's heads. Lor! I can see the dust of em now - like a mighty great wave sweeping across the desert, and the boy on the white Arab coming along like an earthquake six lengths before the lot. It sent me screaming mad to see em. 'Come on, ye dirty black-a-mouths!' I screeched. 'Irish stew for the rebel brigade!' 'Hullo, Black Cock!' he cried, and I saw him grinning through the dust. 'I'm going to cut your comb.' And he took the old horse by head, and rammed him at us - slap-bang, like riding at a bull-finch; and the whole blanky lot after him."

The Parson was stamping up and down, roaring out his story, his eyes laughing and battle-lusty.

"Such a hell of a hugger-mugger you never saw! They rolled in on us like the sea. Rough and tumble every man for himself - stab somebody - don't matter who!" He paused to pant. "It was the day of my life. The Colonel was down; the Majors were dead; the Captains heaven-knows-where. Our old Raven banner, that we took from their Black Horse at Dettingen was in the dust, the Junior Ensign tumbled up in it all anyhow. 'Got it, Miss B.?' I cried. 'Here!' squeals the poor little chap. 'Heave her up!' Then a horse jumped on him, and put him out of his pain.

"I got the old rag up somehow. 'Round this, men!' I yelled, jumping on the Colonel's dead charger. Get round, ye blanky blanks!' Then I saw this boy-girl chap grinning above me. 'Slash away!' I roared. 'Here's one for yourself!' and I jabbed the staff in his mug. 'No,' says he, as jolly as you like, 'I don't fight with poultry!' And dam-my-soul! - if he don't sneak his hand under the rag and tweak my nose! - this nose!" the Parson squeaked, tapping it - "this nose upon this face! this nose I'm talking to you out o now! And he jumped that wallopin old white out the way he came. 'Come along, children,' says he. 'You've had quite enough for one meal.' And away he goes, laughing like the devil, his blessed pathriots after him."

CHAPTER XXXIII

FIGHTING FITZ

The tempest in the Parson's wrathful blue eyes subsided.

"Yes, that was my first real meeting with Fighting Fitz."

"Was that Fighting Fitz?" cried the boy, ablaze.

He had heard, as who had not, of the brilliant young Irishman whom Napoleon had called the first light cavalryman in Europe after Marengo.

"That was Fighting Fitz of Green Brigade fame," said the Parson, mopping his forehead. "We knew him as the Boy Sabreur in Egypt. Even then it was said that no woman could resist him, and no man stand up against him. He went out with young de Beauharnais, Boney's step-son, and ran him through the body; and he carried on an intrigue with ... but there! there!... When he was First Consul, Boney decorated him before the Army, and disgraced him within the year. They said the little Corporal began to be jealous: the men worshipped Fitz....Anyway I know it'll be the regret of my life that I missed my chance when I first met him." He sighed profoundly.

"But you met him again, didn't you, sir?"

The Parson nodded.

"Last month. I was up on Beachy Head with the spy-glass, when I saw the *Kite* beating up for Cuckmere Haven. So I ran down to Birling Gap thinking - thinking -" he coughed - "she might a - a - be bringing me a little present from France - a bit o bacca, or dallop o tea, or what not, ye know.... What ye say?"

He turned on the boy savagely.

"I didn't say anything," replied Kit, astonished.

The Parson scowled.

"Well, as I swung round into the cutting I nearly ran into a chap on a chestnut - quite the Corinthian, with a bit o red riband stuck on his stomach. I brought up sharp on my heels.

"'Well, my fine fellow,' thinks I, 'what you posing here for? - and why's that mare in a lather?' But before I could say anything -

"'Hullo!' says he, 'I think I should know that nose.'

"'What ye mean?' says I, pretty sharp.

"'Why,' says he, 'I once had the pleasure of pulling it.'

"Then he laughed. And directly he laughed of course I knew.

"I put my hand upon my sword.

"'And what you doing attitudinising in *my* land, my lord?' says I, the bristles at the back of my neck rising. 'Play-acting your Caesar about to conquer Britain by the look o you!'

"'Why, your Majesty,' says he, 'I'm out for a ride on *your* land.'

"I gave him a look.

"'Shall we adjourn to the beach?' says I.

"'Charmed,' says he - 'if I'm not too young.'

"And he cocked his leg over the mare's withers, and slid down. 'Now, old lady!' says he. 'You know your own way.' And he gave her a spank; and off she went with a make-believe kick at him, up the hillside and out of sight.

"We went down to the beach, and took our coats off."

The Parson's eyes began to twinkle.

"Yes: the bully had met his match for once - and a bit more. After a very few minutes that was clear. 'How d'you feel?' says he. 'Why, right as rain,' I panted. But I knew he had me. And I knew by the look in his eyes he knew it too. 'True 'tis pity,' says he, running his eye over my shirt.

"'Get on with it,' I says, pretty gruff. 'I must play pussy-cat with my fat mouse,' says he. 'Where'd you like it?' and I must say he was mighty courteous about it. Well, I was just going to tell him, when somebody banged me over the head from behind.... I fell on my face, and a mountain seemed to fall on top of me. 'Shall I knife him, my lord?' comes a voice like a girl's. Then - 'Get off, you dung! or I'll make muck o you!' - 'I ony thought, my lord -' - 'Think, swine! *you* think!' And smack - smack goes his sword! The mountain got off. The lord was kneeling by my side.

"'I hope to the deuce you're not hurt, sir,' says he, very concerned.

"I got to my knees.

"'Thanks to you, my lord, I'm not.'

"'It was Big Belly there,' says he, helping me to my feet.... 'These fellows don't understand our ways.'

"'That's the worst of dabbling in dirty water,' says I.

"'Ah, it's not the water - it's the fish you meet in it I mind,' he says.

"He picked up my sword, and gave it me.

"I was trying to walk.

"'Here, take my arm,' says he. 'You've had about two ton o bad man upset on top o you.' And he walked me up and down that beach, tender as a lady - pon my soul he did.

"Just then I heard a holloa.

"'No time to cut to waste, my lord,' sings out someone. 'We've a clear run now, but only knows how long we shall have.'

"Then I saw the *Kite's* long-boat beached close by, and Diamond and a couple of his chaps standing by.

"The lord took me to a rock, and made me sit down.

"I wonder if you'll excuse me,' says he. 'I'm due to dine with little Boney tonight at eight sharp, and I must be up to time. Truth is I'm not in the Little Corporal's best books just now. He caught Josephine and me amusing ourselves in the rose-walk at Malmaison last week; and he wasn't best pleased.'

"And he took off his hat in his theatrical Frenchified way and went down to the boat.

"I sat on the rock, brushing my knees.

"Diamond shoved her off.

"'Good-day, Parson,' says he, grinning.

"'So this is your smuggling, Diamond!' I roared, shaking my fist at him.

"'Yes,' says he, 'I'm about as good a smuggler as you are Parson.'

"That made me mad.

"'I'm an Englishman anyway and not a blanky traitor!' I roared. 'Here's something to remember me by!' and I snatched the pistol out o my tail-pocket, and snapped it at him.

"The ball went through the full of his shirt.

Alfred Ollivant

"'Ah,' says he, mighty nasty, 'I'll drop a return card on you one o' these days, Mr. Clergyman. And don't you forget it.'

"Then the lord stood up and waved.

"'Thank you for a very pleasant afternoon, Mr. Joy,' he called. 'May I say *au revoir?*'

"'The same to you, my lord,' I answered. 'And the sooner the better.'

"And that's the last I saw of him.... And now what I want to know is *where is he?* - for I'm after him."

CHAPTER XXXIV

THE FACE ON THE WALL

"It's a long story," said Kit.

The Parson took him by the arm, and led the way into the kitchen.

It was more like a guard-room than a parlour. Clearly no woman reigned here. All was wood, or stone, or steel, clean as a ship, and as comfortless. Arms on the wall; iron-barred windows; no carpets, no curtains, no fal-lals.

The only soft thing in the room was the bed in the corner, piled high with clothes; the only ornament a print above the chimney-piece.

"It looks more like a fort than a kitchen," whispered Kit, awed.

"Ah, thereby hangs a tale!" replied the Parson.

He drew up before the face on the wall.

"You know who that is?" he asked, one hand on the boy's shoulder.

Kit laughed.

It was the face that had hung in old Ding-dong's cabin, that was hanging at that hour in thousands of English homes.

"A Colonel of Marines," continued the Parson - "Nelson by name." [Footnote: In 1795 Nelson was appointed Honorary Colonel of Marines in recognition of his services in the Mediterranean.]

"Indeed," said the boy ironically. "I'd a notion he was a sailor."

The other made no answer. Indeed he did not hear. He stood before the print, worshipping it.

"Every night and morning I say my prayers before that picture," he continued quietly, all the laughter out of his voice. And there was something profoundly stirring about the solemnity with which he added,

"If it's God's will that our country shall be saved, there is the man will save it!"

The boy looked up at him.

"Sir," he said, "Nelson will save the country, if we can save Nelson."

IV - THE GARRISON

CHAPTER XXXV

THE SOLDIER'S MOTHER

Kit told his tale.

The Parson listened without a word, his hands folded, and face inscrutable.

His silence chilled the boy.

"D'you believe me, sir?" he flashed out at last.

"Believe the boy!" cried the Parson fiercely. "Why, I *saw* the fight. I was dancing mad at the foot of the cliff. Great heavens, sir! - didn't you hear me holloa? I should have thought they'd have heard me in France. Why, for the first and last time in my life, I wanted to be a sailor myself!"

Kit finished with a free heart, withholding nothing: the death of Black Diamond; the fight with the privateers; the end of old Ding-dong; and the scene with the Gentleman on the cliff.

The Parson drank in the lad's words. His eyes were grave; his brow furrowed. So stern he seemed, his face

Alfred Ollivant

so smileless under those laughing curls, that Kit hardly recognised in him the boy-hearted swordsman of a few minutes since.

The story finished, he sat long unmoving; his mouth set, and eyes inward.

Then he began to pace up and down again.

"My prayer is heard," he said at last, and stopping turned to the boy.

"Kit Caryll, d'you know what I am?"

"You look like a - kind of a clergyman, sir."

"And that is what I am," replied the other a touch defiantly. "I am in Holy Orders in my own humble way."

He began pacing once more.

"We all have our weaknesses, sir.... My mother was mine.... She should have been the mother of saints rather than of a - ' bully swordsman!' - I think that was the phrase?" cocking a blue eye at the boy.

"After Egypt I came home to find her dying.... Well, she entreated me to forsake my profession and become a Christian - 'for my sake, Harry,' says she.... I argued it with her. I told her it was good work, God's work, to kill the French. I said I looked on myself as a Crusader fighting the Moors, as indeed I did. But she wouldn't hear of it. She said the Moors were black and the French white, and that made just all the difference.... And she begged so hard - and - and -"

His back was to the boy, and he was looking out of the window.

It was some time before he went on.

"I couldn't say her no then. So I told her I'd do as she wished and take Orders. But I made one condition. 'I won't go to the French; but if the French come to me, then,' I said, 'surely, mother, I may up and smite!' She gave me that. You see, she never thought they would come."

He cleared his throat.

"Well, the Bishop wouldn't give me a cure, because I didn't know the Catechism. So I kicked my heels till the Peace was broken, and things looked up a bit. And when little Boney began to get his Army of England together on the cliffs yonder, I cheered up, and came and pitched my tent on the nearest spot I could find to be ready. And here I've been ever since.

"On calm summer evenings I've seen the cliffs of France from Beachy Head, and with the spy-glass I've thought I've made out the tents of Lannes' camp. That's been bread and meat to me these two years past. Then a month ago I had that little affair with my lord. That knocked ten years off my life. I've been in training ever since. Today I think I'm a better man than I've ever been." He inhaled a deep breath, swelling his chest.

"And this morning, when I woke and saw that ship hove-to off the Wish, and old Piper told me she was a Frenchman, I just went down on my two knees and thanked God for His great mercies."

Alfred Ollivant

He blew his nose boisterously.

"Then I ran up my colours to tempt em ashore. And I've been waiting in hope ever since."

CHAPTER XXXVI

THE FIGHTING MAN

He clapped on his hat.

"And now the first thing to be done is to hold a Council of War with old Piper."

The boy looked up shyly.

"Could I have something to eat first, sir? I haven't tasted food for twenty-four hours."

The Parson fussed off to the cupboard.

"Just like me. Just like a man. No thought - no consideration. All comes of there being no woman about the place."

He brought out a knuckle of ham, a loaf, a pot of jam, and a jug of milk.

As he did so there came a groaning gurgle from the corner.

The Parson whirled round and shot a denouncing finger at the piled bed.

"You dare!" he roared.

"I was ony sniffin, sir," whimpered a cockney voice.

Then for the first time Kit saw that in the bed lay a man. A shaven head, pert and pug-like, and a face shining with sweat protruded. All the rest was lost beneath that mountain of clothes.

As Kit stared, the man winked a merry brown eye at him.

The boy approached.

"Isn't it rather stuffy under all those clothes?" he asked compassionately.

"It's like a h'oven, sir - that ot!" chirped the little man.

"You'll go to a much hotter place when you die, if you so much as stir a finger out," called the Parson with firm cheerfulness. "I'm a Parson, mind you. I know what I'm talkin about."

"Ah, I know you wouldn't go for to put a pore bloke away for fetchin his thumb to mop a drop o sweat off his conk," whined the other.

"Ha! you sweat, Knapp?"

"I spouts pushpiration, sir!"

"Capital, capital!" The Parson hopped across the room and bent his ear to the bed. "I can almost hear him simmer!" He twinkled up at Kit. "It's the very weather for him. He's in a sweet muck-sweat. Lying between two feather-beds, ain't you, me boy?"

He sat down on the table beside the eating lad.

"That's Nipper Knapp. He was my batman in the Borderers. I brought him down here to train, while I was waiting for the French. Such a pretty little bit o stuff! Arms like legs, and legs like bodies. I'll strip him for you one day. Only thing is I have to sweat the meat off him so. Get a belly on him in a day, little pig, if I'd let him."

He spoke of the man much as a farmer speaks of his beasts. The boy's sensitive soul recoiled.

"He can hear every word," he whispered.

"I don't mind," replied the Parson cheerfully.

"Nor don't I," chirped the voice from the bed.

"And what are you training him for?" asked Kit - "the Church, like yourself?"

"No, sir!" retorted the Parson shortly. "I'm training him to make the best use he can of the gifts God has given him - that's his hands and his feet. He can rattle his dukes, and chuck his trotters, as I never saw man yet. Strips ten six. All good, too; all guts. You can't glut him.... I'm backing him to run ten miles in the hour against any man in England, and fight him to a finish in a 24-ft. ring at the end."

The boy shoved back his plate.

"And have you any other spiritual duties, sir?"

he asked.

"I stand over Blob while Piper teaches him his prayers," replied the Parson sullenly.

"Who is Piper?"

The Parson was staring out of the window.

It was some time before he answered.

"I once asked Nelson who was the bravest man he'd ever met. He answered like a flash, 'My captain of the foretop aboard the *Agamemnon* - Ralph Piper. The bravest man,' said Nelson, 'because the best. He's my hero!' And I remember the voice in which he said it now."

Kit had risen to his feet.

All his life Nelson had been his hero; and now he was within touch of his hero's hero.

"Where is he?" with glowing eyes.

"Out there - under the sycamores."

Kit recalled the voice humming the hymn that had welcomed him.

CHAPTER XXXVII

THE SAINT

They passed out of the cottage.

A heavy-browed jasmine, the flowers fading now, hung about the door.

The greensward ran smoothly away to a shingle bank that rose, long-backed and brown, some three hundred yards away. The bank crossed the horizon like a low breast-work, sweeping away eastward in long roan curve. On the right it ran into a little blunt hill, green-brown and bare. Beyond the bank the sea leapt to the eye.

The Parson was walking reverently.

There was about him something of the subdued air of the schoolboy going to interview a respected master.

"Step quietly," he murmured. "We are going into the presence of a saint."

In front of the cottage, about two hundred yards from it, a little knoll, shaded with sycamores, humped up out of the greensward.

At the foot of it, in the shadow of a tree, a tall old man was sitting bolt upright in a wooden chair with wheels. A brown book had fallen open beside him; and a musket, propped against the chair, threw a black shadow across the page.

"Loaded!" muttered the Parson, pointing. "He can draw a cork from a bottle at a hundred yards."

"More than most saints could," whispered the boy.

"He's a common-sense saint, not the ordinary run," replied the Parson with a grin.

The old man's back was towards them. He was gazing intently through a long glass at the privateer. Kit could see nothing but a straight back and moon-silvered head.

"Piper, I've brought a young gentleman of your Service to see you," said the Parson in the quiet tone in which a man addresses a woman or a superior.

The old sailor dropped the glass. His great hands fumbled with the wheels of his chair, and he slewed himself about.

Kit's heart gave a jerk.

The old man ended abruptly at the thighs!

Irresistibly the boy recalled a doll of Gwen's whose china legs he had once plucked off in passion, leaving saw-dust stumps.

The Parson saw the look on the boy's face.

"Ah, I should have told you. Lost both legs in the action with the *Ca Ira*, wasn't it, Piper?"

The doll spoke.

"Not lost, sir - gone before."

Kit glanced at him sharply.

Was he joking?

No; in that grave face lurked no laughter. The old man had said the thing that he believed in simplest faith. And what a face it was! nobly large, worn as the earth, and as full of quiet dignity. Pale, too, but not with the pallor of ill-health. Indeed the old man looked hard and wholesome as a forest tree. Rather the boy was reminded of a cathedral seen in February sunshine.

The great upper lip was bare and stiff as clay. The wide mouth curled up at the corners, as though it often smiled. Friendly eyes, the colour of forget-me-nots, dwelt on the boy. A stiff white fringe framed all.

And the note of the whole was calm - calm invincible.

Then the boy's eyes fell on those blue bags thrusting out over the edge of the chair. A question leapt to his lips. It was out before he could stop it.

"Dud - dud - does it hurt?"

The old man's face broke up and shone. He chuckled.

A saint could laugh, then! the boy felt himself relieved.

"No, sir, thank you, ne'er a bit. And not nigh as much at the time as you might fancy - a tidy jar like to be sure.... One thing, I don't suffer from no bunions." He went off again into his deep chuckle; and again the boy felt comfort at heart.

The saint could joke!

"Tell him about it, Piper," said the Parson; "you and Nelson."

"Why, sir," said the old man, frank as a child, "the Captain were standin by my gun in the waist, where he'd no business to ha been reelly by rights. Flop I goes on the broad o my back, when it took me. He was down on his knees beside me in a second, dabbin with his little handkercher. 'Don't kneel in that, sir,' says I, 'your white breeches and all.' 'Ah, dear fellow!' says he, taking my hand, 'dear fellow! dear fellow!...' Then they carried me off to the cock-pit."

That was the whole story, but it was so simply told that the boy saw and felt it all.

"Yes, sir. There warn't a man aboard the *Agamemnon* but'd ha died for Captain Nelson and proud too."

He put the spy-glass to his eye to hide the fact that he was blinking.

"She's had a rare mauling, surely. I'd just like to know her story."

"Here's the young gentleman can tell you, Piper," chimed in the Parson.

There was a faint glow in the hollow of the old man's cheeks as he listened to the boy's tale, and he was rubbing his huge hands together slowly.

"Seems the powder's laid, but the match lies yet in the pocket of this here Gentleman," he said, as Kit concluded. "One thing's clear, sir! We want that boat!... Now if so be I might make so bold, if you and the young gentleman'd take the glass, and step across to the Wish there, you could see all along the shore past Cow Gap to the Head, and make out what they're up to."

"That's a good notion for a sailor!" cried the Parson briskly. "Come on, Kit."

"And I'll make my course for the cottage and see all's snug there," said the old man. "You never know what's comin next in this world. It's the wise man as is ready for the worst."

He trundled himself across the grass.

"Here's your book!" cried Kit, and bending picked it from the ground.

As he did so he saw the name.

It was Law's *Serious Call.*

CHAPTER XXXVIII

THE SIMPLETON

They passed out of the shadow of the sycamore into the sun-glare.

The greensward ran away into shallow creek lying between them and the little hill beyond. Crossing it, they began the ascent.

"This is the Wish," explained the Parson, climbing; "the Wash really, because the sea washed round it in old days. It's gone back along these parts. Old Piper says, when he was a boy, the creek used to fill at spring-tides."

At the top of the hill Kit looked about him.

The Wish thrust out into the brown beach, a natural watch-tower, some hundred feet high. This was no doubt the bump of green he had seen from the dew-pond.

Eastward a long sweep of shingle embraced Pevensey Bay. Westward, Beachy Head shouldered out into the sea.

It was nearly low tide. Barriers of black rocks bound

the sea.

On the edge of it a boy in a blue jersey danced. In his hand was a sea-weed scourge; and as the sea toppled in tiny ripples at his feet, he spanked it, leaping back to avoid the touch of the water. As he leapt he yelled; and in the stillness his pure treble rose to them.

"Hod back, ye saucy thing! hod back, I say!"

The Parson put his hand to his mouth.

"Blob!" he holloaed.

The boy looked up, and with a parting spank came towards them.

"Who's that?" asked Kit, "and what's he doing?"

"Blob - blobbing'," replied the Parson laconically.

"Who's Blob?"

The Parson took up his tale.

"You remember I told you Black Diamond promised to look me up some time. Well, I knew he'd be as good as his word. So very next day I had the windows barred, a brace of bullet-proof doors slung, got in a barrel of powder, and made all snug....

"And just as well I did, too. A couple of days later, just about the time the bats begin to twitter, I heard the thud of feet on the grass, and a laugh. They thought they'd taken on an easy job - just walk into the house, and cop me at my supper. We let em up to within twenty yards. Then we let em have it, the three of us - Piper, Knapp, and I....

"Such a panic! 'It's a trap!' screams one. 'Block-ademen!' yells a second. Diamond was the only one of the lot to keep his head. "Bout ship, boys!' he shouts. 'Call again another day.' And off they scuttled, quicker than they came....

"'Come on, Knapp!' says I, and bundles out after them, holloaing like a regiment. One or two turned, and there was a bit of a barney. I stuck one chap, and was just going to stick another - a fellow in blue jumping around in a queer kind of way - when all of a sudden he gave a jab in the back to one of his own chaps.

"Then he turned, and I saw he was a boy about your age, with a face like a pink moon.

"He came at me like a man, flashing his knife.

"'Here! who are you for?' says I.

"'Whoy, mesalf!' says he.

"'But what you at?' says I.

"'Whoy, foightin!' says he.

"'Who?' says I.

"'Whoy, the nearest!' says he, and smacks at me.

"Then Knapp tripped him from behind, and he was our prisoner....

"He's been with us ever since. Piper's been tryin to make a Christian of him."

"What's his story?"

"I don't know, and he can't tell us. He knows nothing - not even fear. I call him Blob, because blob's his nature. Piper found the name Hoad on his shirt. I daresay his people sold him to the Gap Gang; and they kept him."

"To be cruel to?" shuddered Kit.

"Not they," laughed the Parson. "He was plump as a little pig. They'd be kind to him because he wasn't right - superstition, you see. Kept him to bring em luck, probably. A kind of idol."

The boy in the blue jersey was coming up the hill towards them, slobbering at the mouth. His hands were in his pockets, and he lolloped along on his toes.

"Oi druv her back," he announced with complacent cunning. "She was creepin in on us, sloy-loike."

His face was that of a babe. Clearer eyes Kit had never seen, nor a more perfect mouth. But for the ears, large and flap, it might have been the face of a cherub, poised on the gawky body of fifteen. The expression, by no means vacant, was of slow and staring interest. Certainly this was no congenital idiot. Probably some chance blow on the head in infancy had arrested mental growth. The flesh had gone on; the mind had stopped. A baby-soul was sheathed in the body of a boy.

The two lads were much of a height, and much of an age. But what a difference between them!

The one was limp as a lolling flower, the other alert as a sword, and as keen. Experience had written nothing on the face of the simpleton. All there was blank as the moon. The haggard cheeks and anxious eyes of the other told that he had already drunk deep of the bitter waters of life.

Blob was staring at Kit with the solemn interest of a babe.

Then he pointed a finger.

"Boy!" he bleated.

"Call me 'sir'!" ordered Kit imperiously. "And take your hands out of your pockets when you talk to me."

"Go home, Blob!" said the Parson, patting him. "Home!" pointing, "Home! and stop making a blob o yourself for the present, there's a good boy. Mr. Piper wants you to help him."

Blob shook a slow head.

"Nay," he said in musical Sussex. "Oi'll boide with Maaster Sir."

Here was another boy in a land of men. In a dim way he felt their kinship.

CHAPTER XXXIX

THE FLAP OF A FLAG

The Parson was staring through the spy-glass at Beachy Head.

A mile and a half away, it lay in misty splendour, not unlike a lion sleeping.

At the foot of it a few tiny black figures moved among the rocks.

"I make out about a score of em," he said. "The boat's beached, and a man over it. I can catch the glint on his gun-barrel. We can't get at em except along the shore, hang it! They'd see us coming a mile off."

"If we can't get at the boat," said Kit, "neither can the Gentleman."

"That's truth," mused the Parson, dropping the glass.

"He'll prowl about till night-fall probably. Then he'll have a chance - if they've got liquor. The boat's his one hope. He's in a tightish place, mind! - enemy's country; wings clipped; his old friends his best enemies."

"And he doesn't know whether the privateer's a

252   Alfred Ollivant

Frenchman or not," said Kit. "Though, of course, he might come down to the shore and signal her - on chance."

"Not while it's light," replied the Parson grimly; "If he signalled from anywhere it'd be from here. And here I squat till dark. After dark he can signal till he's black in the face - he hasn't got a lantern."

The boy's anxious eyes were sea-ward.

The old pain of heart, forgotten for the moment in the cottage, had returned, the old sickening sense of failure. After all, the responsibility was *his*, and his alone. It was in *him* old Ding-dong had trusted; it was to *him* the scent-bottle had been bequeathed; the fate of Nelson rested on *his* shoulders.

Hither and thither his mind darted, seeking a way of escape from the net of circumstance.

"If we could only make sure of his thinking her an Englishman!" he fretted.

"She's flying no colours," said the Parson, "that's one good thing."

"I wish she'd fly the Union Jack," replied the boy.

The remark annoyed the Parson, practical or nothing.

"What's the good of wishing what can't be?" he snarled. "You might leave that to the women."

"Why can't it be?" retorted the boy hotly.

A sound behind him caught his ears. He turned to see the flag in the cottage chimney ruffling it behind the sycamores.

It flashed a message to his heart.

"By Jove, sir!" he panted. "I've got it."

The blood had rushed to his face, and ebbed as suddenly.

"Lend me your flag, and I'll swim out with it after dark!"

The Parson stared.

"To the privateer?"

"Why not? It can't be more than a few hundred yards. I've often done more."

"Well, what if you did get there?" curt and sarcastic. "Summon her to surrender, else you'd take her by storm and put the lot to the sword, I suppose?"

"Why, board her, sir, and run the flag up! She's not a man-of-war. They'll be keeping no watch, likely as not."

The boy was in a white blaze.

"They won't see it till broad daylight!" he panted, pressing. "And by that time the Gentleman, if he's hanging about, will see it too. If they haul it down then and run up the tricolour, he'll think it's a decoy."

There was something contagious about the lad's white-hot enthusiasm.

The light was coming and going in the Parson's eyes.

The scheme was as mad as you like. Still, there was a chance of success, a fighting chance. And was it not the only one?

Himself he no more doubted the lad's story than he doubted that a month since he had crossed swords with Fighting Fitz. But who else would believe?

Of course he must send Knapp over to Lewes at once to report to Beau Beauchamp, the Commandant there; but what would come of that?

Loving his old Service with passionate jealousy, he was not blind to the weakness of its traditional logic: it was not probable; therefore it was not true; and so to sleep again, dear boys!

And Beau Beauchamp, of all men!

The Parson had not yet forgotten the reception that heavy sensualist had given to his report that Fighting Fitz was riding up and down the land just outside his lines.

"*May I, sir?*"

The boy was burning at his side. Perforce the Parson began to smoulder too.

The adventure had just that smack of romance about it that tickled this man of prose. Could he have run the risk himself, he who could hardly swim to the bottom, he would have ventured it with laughing heart. Was he justified in staying the sailor-boy?

No, no, no! his heart thundered the answer at him.

There must always be a risk. And was ever risk better worth running than this one? But what a boy!

He was flaming merrily now.

"May I, sir?"

He turned to the lad, pale beside him, and smacked a hand into his.

"Kit!" he cried with gusty laughter, "you should have been a soldier!"

CHAPTER XL

THE SWIM IN THE DARK

Kit awoke with the horrors.

All was black about him, and a great hand lay on his breast.

He gripped it, gurgling.

A calm voice, already strangely familiar, reassured him.

"By your leave, sir, it's about time for you to rouse and bitt."

It was Nelson's old foretop-man. The moon, slanting through the window, shone on his white head and those tranquil, big-dog eyes of his.

Kit relaxed his hold.

"That you, Piper?" he sighed. "I was dreaming of Fat George. What's the time?"

"It's a little better'n two o'clock, sir; you've had a tidy sleep. The tide's pretty near down, and the moon's a-nigh off the water. By than you get alongside there'll likely be a bit o' mist on the water crep up from the eastud with the sun."

The boy slipped off his clothes, shivering.

"Where's Mr. Joy?"

"He came in from the Wish just on midnight. 'No Knapp yet?' says he. 'Then I shall make a reconnaissance in force myself.' 'Beggin your pardon, sir,' says he, don't see the force - one man agin a score.' 'Ah,' says he, 'you forget my lady.' And he whips up his Polly, and off he pops over the grass like a lad a-courtin." The old man chuckled as he told.

"What's Knapp up to?" trembled the boy.

"Why, sir, gone over to Lewes for the soldiers, and should ha been back hours sen."

"Wonder why he's not?"

"Got fightin and foolin on the road, sir, I'll lay," chuckled the old man. "Like a lamb with the heart of a lion is Knapp, sir. Frisks into trouble, and then fights out again. This is first time he's been let out of hissalf since he went into training. So he's all of a bubble like. Bubble or bust - that's how Knapp feels."

Stripped, the boy stood up in the darkness.

"Got the flag, Piper?"

"Here it be, sir. How'll you carry it?"

"So." He wound it up in a coil and tied it about his

Alfred Ollivant

neck, scarf-like.

"Now I'm ready."

II

The old man wheeled out to the edge of the shadow of the house.

All about was black and silver in the moon. A faint breeze ruffled the sycamores upon the knoll. Stars strewed the heavens. Beyond the shingle-bank the sea glistened like satin.

It was very still, very cold, very lonely.

Kit set his teeth to prevent them chattering. The night air kissed him coldly, and the moon, white above the inky Downs, glistened on his shoulders.

"There she lays, in the Channel off the Boulder Bank," whispered the old man, pointing to the privateer, dull-black against the glitter. "And it's my belieft there's not a sober man aboard of her. All stow'd away dead drunk under hatches - that's my belieft, sir. They kep it up from dark till midnight - dancin, drummin, fightin, and all manner. More like a cage full? wild beasties from Bedlam than a Christian ship. And for the last hour she might ha been a hulk full o corpuses."

He dropped his voice still further.

"He's in it, sure!" jerking his thumb starward. "Made

em blind to the world for His own good purpose - which is as you should lay em aboard unbeknownst and knife the blessed lot if so be it was your fancy."

The boy choked a laugh brimming on the edge of being. The old man's solemnity, his profound simplicity, touched the springs of mirth within him.

"Perhaps," he panted. "I hope so."

"Ah! I'm certain sure," replied the other with firm confidence.

Faith, the most infectious quality in the world because the truest, seized the boy's heart and lifted it.

"Good-bye, Piper."

"Good luck, sir."

The lad plunged into the moonlight.

III

A moon-clad wisp, he flitted across the greensward, the fringe of the flag-scarf fluttering behind him. It was a fine thing to do, but he wished devoutly somebody else had the doing of it. On the Wish in the sunshine, the Parson at his side, when the idea first struck him, it had seemed splendid. Now, alone in the dark, with the idea to translate into reality, he saw it very differently. It gave him no thrill of glory. He felt exactly as he had felt last March on the way to the dentist to have a tooth out - a mean sense of his own mortality, and an earnest desire to run away.

The turf shaded off into long bents growing out of sand; and that again ran away into shingle. As he breasted the bank, his hands succouring his feet, he heard steps behind him.

"Who's that?" he snarled, crouching.

Blob was standing at gaze a little way behind him.

"What ye want?"

The boy made no answer, staring with round moon-eyes.

"He's noiked," came a musing voice. "Oi dew loike to see un."

He shot out a finger, and, flinging back his head, gurgled laughter.

"Here, boy!" called Kit. "As you are there, you can carry me over these pebbles."

He leapt on the other's back, and Blob, sturdy as he looked limp, crashed down the shingle and across the stretch of wet sand at a loose-jointed canter.

"That'll do, my boy, thank you," said Kit, slipping down at the edge of the tide. "I'd give you a penny, only I've not got one. No, you can't come any further. It's too dangerous. This is a job for officers."

He began to paddle out, the ripples playing about

his ankles.

Blob's presence braced him to his task. It called to his spirit of a gentleman. He would just show this lout what blood meant.

Blob followed him with awed eyes.

"She's aloive," he warned his brother-boy. "She'll swallow ee."

"No, she won't," Kit replied. "She's an old friend of mine."

IV

The boy could swim at an age when to most lads walking is still an accomplishment. Now he waded quietly down a sandy reach between black rocks.

The water was warmer than the air. When it clasped his waist, he trusted himself to it faithfully.

The sea was his mother, and the mother of his race. Her arms were about him; her spirit entered into his. How pure she was, how strong, how good! He kissed her cool brow and dropped his head upon her bosom. Turning on his back, he saw the wall of the Downs, black beneath glorious stars. On the top of the wall poised the moon, peeping over the brim of the world at him. He waved to her, laughing: she too was a friend. And the moon, wise as innocent, smiled back.

He swam leisurely, without splash, almost without ripple, quiet as the tide.

He had the world to himself, and loved the loneliness.

Out here, the sea about him, the night above, he could feel the slow tides of God pushing onwards through the dark of Time.

Wars and tumults and all the tiny irritations and griefs of life, what were they to that immense-moving flood? And he was one with that flood. Stealing through the water with cleaving arms, he was assured of it.

V

Something rose shadowy and gaunt before him. It was the privateer.

The sight tumbled him out of Eternity into Time. His heart began to clamour, as though it would force its way out of his body.

No longer one with God, seeing all things with His large eyes, and loving them - he was a little boy, mortally afraid, alone in the vast and callous night.

In his flurry be began to splash about: then recollected himself, and trod water quietly.

The moon was deserting him, the sardonic moon he had thought of as a friend. Her silver rim glimmered behind the Downs and was gone. He missed her. Cold she was, still she had been company. He thought she might have stayed - just this one night! He felt aggrieved, and very much alone. And those stars strewing the night above him were so far, and had such hard little eyes.

The water grew dull and dark about him, and of a sudden greatly colder. The flag hung like a clammy halter about his neck. Verdun was not far, and death very near. But for the cold he would have cried. He wished he'd never come.

It flashed in upon him to hail the ship, and ask them for a cup of coffee. The thought amused him and saved the situation. He began to chuckle.

Squeezing the fear out of his mind, he set himself to the accomplishment of his task.

The thought of old Piper, calm invincibly, confirmed him in his purpose.

Yet he couldn't help reminding himself with a snigger, that old Piper was safe in an arm-chair on land, while he was out there in the water with the work to do.

Still, now if ever was his time. The moon was gone. In another hour the dawn would begin to glimmer. Between the two his chance lay.

Treading water a cable's-length away, he observed the ship intently.

She lay upon the water like a dead thing. The great dark hull, seen against the living night, appeared carcass-like. Her stillness was almost terrible.

Alfred Ollivant

Not a spar creaked, not a match glowed. She was dark as death, and as silent.

As he watched, a humming noise, rising and falling, came to him across the water. He held his breath. Then he recognised it, with a gasp of relief.

Somebody was snoring.

That domestic sound cheered him amazingly.

At least the ship was not a sepulchre. Her crew were neither dead nor devils. They were human. They snored.

He swam round the ship, stealthy as an otter in the Coquet.

So far as he could see there was not a soul on deck.

Then, as he came under her stern, he noticed for the first time that another vessel lay alongside.

A thought, swift as a dagger, struck at his heart.

Could it be that the Gentleman had somehow picked up a lugger, and so won aboard? Was he too late?

Then with a gasp of thankfulness he remembered.

It was the *Kite*, of course.

The tide had set her alongside; and now she lay scraping the side of the privateer. A handier stepping-stone he could not have asked.

CHAPTER XLI

PIGGY, THE PRIVATEERSMAN

I

In a minute he had clambered aboard the lugger.

The privateer had dropped a hawser over her side as buffer. The boy was up it in a moment, and on to the deck, his heart beating high.

The deck was empty.

No! a figure was leaning over the side, his back to Kit. No sailor, obviously. He was wearing a great bearskin, and Kit caught the glimmer of a bayonet. A sentinel, and not asleep, nor drunk; for he was humming *Ça Ira*.

La Coquette too then carried soldiers!

Stealthy as a cat, the boy drew away along the deck. Piper, weather-wise old man, had told him truth. Thin wisps of mists were sweeping over the sea, veiling the stars.

How God helps His little children who help Him!

Up the shrouds of the foremast. The ratlines seared his feet. A little wind licked his body. The mist was chill as a winding-sheet.

There was no danger of being seen. He was nearer the stars than the deck. Between him and it now lay a blanket of mist.

But what was that in the East?

It was the whitening of the dawn.

There was no time to be lost.

He swarmed up the top-gallant mast, unwound the flag, and made it fast.

How it fluttered! - what a rollicking tow-row! - had ever flag rampaged so boisterously!

The man below stopped humming. Kit could not see him; so he could not see the flag.

Down he slid, the mast scraping his knees as he went; but he scarcely felt the pain. His heart was swelling. The privateer was flying British colours. She was his. Single-handed he had taken a French ship. He was half in tears, half laughing. It seemed so dream-like, so ridiculous.

Down the shrouds, and back to the deck.

II

Not a soul stirred. Forward somewhere a man shouted in his sleep. Aft the sentinel was whistling now.

Swift as an eel, the boy flashed to the side, and poised for his plunge.

No! the splash would be heard.

Swiftly along the deck, making for his steppingstone, the lugger.

His work done, his heart brimming, the boy was ripe for mischief as a happy girl.

As he stole along the deck, his eyes never left the soldier's back. The fellow was leaning over the bulwark, his trousers tight, and their contents rounded and tempting. Should he, should he spank him?

A moment the boy struggled with his imp-self, and prevailed.

Nelson! Duty!

He slipped over into the lugger. The tide had shifted her position. Now she bumped under the stern of the privateer.

The port of the stern-cabin was open, and light poured from it. Standing on the weather-boarding, Kit peeped in.

A little fat man was sitting at a table, dead asleep, and

snoring stertorously. His arms were on the table, and his head on his arms. He was quite bald, and very red. His lips pouted, and the under one thrust up towards his nose. The little round body rose and fell, bladder-like. His nose was a snout, short and cocked. A more pig-like little person Kit thought he had never seen.

A great bottle stood on the table before him, and beside it a scratch-wig and guttering candle. On the table a pistol pinned down a chart, and under the sleeper's head was a sheet of paper and a pen.

Piggy had fallen asleep writing.

Flung into a corner was a cocked hat. Beside it lay a much-mounted sword, and on a chair a blue frock-coat, with tawdry epaulettes.

The boy lifted his eyes. An obscene print decorated the bulk-head. It smote him in the face like a handful of filth. He snatched his eyes away. They fell upon a tarpaulin-bag hung on the door. On the bag was an eagle, beneath it a large

N.

That settled it.

The boy meant to have that bag.

III

He was through the port in a twinkling.

The man was sleeping like the dead, his head askew on his hands, and lips compressed in pouting content. For the time being the body had mastered invincibly any soul there might be within. The man was so much slow-heaving earth.

The naked boy leaned over the sleeper. The pen had fallen from Piggy's hand, and left a little scrawl across the letter he had been writing.

The character was flourishing, self-complacent, and, above all, easy to read.

It was written in French, and ran, translated,

Sire,

I have to inform your Majesty that Sunday dawn I was lying off Seaford Head, waiting to escort the lugger Kite, *according to your Majesty's instructions. As I was on my knees inviting the good God to shower blessings on the sacred head of you, His so faithful servant, a sail was seen.*

I bore up for her immediately. She was an English ship of the line.

I engaged her at once, fearless of the odds, knowing that the good God is always on your Majesty's side. Desperate valour was displayed by your Majesty's seamen. We were out-numbered four to one.

She carried 120 guns in three tiers and was alive with men - all sent by me to answer before the Great Judge for being in arms against your anointed Majesty. May He deal with them as they deserve!

The Englishman was towing the lugger Kite. Knowing the vital importance of the mission on which she was engaged, I cut her out from under the enemy's stern, leading the boat attack myself, under a terrific fire from her stern-galleries.

The Kite had two dead men aboard, one of them, helas! the brave Monsieur de Diamond, so devoted to your Majesty's interests. He was sitting upon the despatch-bag, which thus had escaped the vigilance of his murderers.

My lord the General was not on board. I am lying off Beachy Head waiting for him. Should he not appear by tomorrow noon, I shall not dare to wait longer, but shall make all sail with the despatches I have captured.

I permit myself to congratulate your Majesty upon my victory, and sign myself with effusion,

Your Majesty's humble and adoring servant,

EGALITE LAGLOIRE.

P.S. - I have prepared, and now send, the chart for which your Majesty asked. As your Majesty's eye will see at a glance all is in order. We do but wait the last word from my lord the General. The red crosses mark the stations....

Here the pen had dropped from the writer's hand.

IV

The boy turned with beating heart: he had struck gold indeed.

Unshipping the despatch bag, he slung it about his shoulders.

Lifting the pistol, he snatched the chart, and thrust it under the flap of the locked bag.

The action set the candle swaling. It shot out a snake-like flame that licked the bald pate of the sleeping privateersman.

He awoke with a start and a *sacre*, clapping his hand to his singed head.

Then through drink-and-sleep-blurred eyes, he saw the naked figure by the door.

He half rose, little fat man, so pleased.

"*Mon ange!*" he cried, and fluttered both arms, much as Gwen's young canaries fluttered their wings when seeking food from their mother.

In a flash the boy had turned the key in the lock behind him, and flung it through the open port.

Then he swung the despatch-bag.

Many a pillow-fight with Gwen up and down the twisting passages of their attic nursery had made him expert. Crash it came down on Piggy's bald skull.

"One from your *ange!*" cried the lad, and followed up with a left-hander between the eyes.

Down crashed the amorous gentleman, spluttering.

A foot, planted fair on his mouth, stifled his cry.

Before he could recover, the boy was through the port, on to the lugger, and had slipped into the sea, quiet as a water-rat.

Behind him a dreadful scream woke the ship.

"*Les depeches! Les depeches!*"

CHAPTER XLII

THE MAN IN THE BOAT

I

The ship awoke suddenly from her swoon.

An appalling clamour boiled up from the still waters.

Bugle-calls split the air; drums rolled furiously; a carronade went off with a shattering roar; there was a rush of feet and tumult of voices. Above the confusion could be heard Piggy thumping at the door and squealing,

"*Les depeches! Les depeches!*"

Kit, sliding through the water, was thankful for the flash of insight that had made him lock the door, and throw away the key. That action meant minutes gained; these minutes might mean life.

The tide was with him now. But for that, and this merciful mist, his chances would be *nil*.

His ears behind him, he swam like a hunted otter.

Alfred Ollivant

Aboard the privateer things were moving fast. The confusion abated; order began to reign; with it the danger grew. Somebody was at work with an axe on the door. It came down with a crash. There was a shrill command and the scamper of feet.

Piggy was on deck.

"*Feu, imbecile! par la! dans le brouillard!*"

A bullet plopped into the water wide on the boy's right.

"*Au bateau!*"

Again that scamper of feet: then the rattle of blocks and creak of pulleys. Besides all was swiftness, and fierce silence; and that silence terrified the lad far more than the preceding tumult.

"*Depechez vous donc, gredins!*"

They were lowering a boat; and he was getting done.

The despatch-bag was heavy between his shoulders. His hold upon himself was relaxing: dissolution was setting in. The firm mind, which at all times and in all places means salvation, was dissipating. He tried not to think. All there was of him he needed for his swimming. Thought was waste; so was fear. And swim he did, and swim, through endless water, with sickening brain and failing arms.

Behind him he heard a splash, as the privateer's boat took the sea.

They'd be coming soon now. He didn't mind much: he

was too tired. And they couldn't hurt him: he was too far away.

He heard the splash of oars, and thumping rowlocks.

Here they came - straight towards him!

Then with a start he recollected: the privateer's boat would be pursuing; this was coming to meet him.

Had he been swimming round and round like a drowning dog?

No. Behind him he could hear shouts and orders on the privateer as the crew jumped into the boat.

This must be some other craft.

It was coming from the land, and a landsman was rowing it. He could tell by the uneven splash of the oars, the slish along the surface as a crab was caught, and the muffled curse as the man recovered himself.

Could it be the Parson come to his assistance?

The question answered itself.

The bows of a boat thrust on him through the mist. He saw a man's back, giving to his stroke.

"Hi!" he gasped, the boat's nose hard on top of him.

The rower glanced round.

There was no mistaking that falcon-face.

It was the Gentleman.

II

"Who's there?" peering suspiciously.

"Boy Hoad, powder-monkey o the *Dreadnought*."

"Is that the *Dreadnought*?" sharply.

"*Dreadnought*, forty-four. Oi'm drownin, sir. Take us in."

His hand was on the boat's gunwale.

"What the deuce you doing here?"

"Desartin, sir. They was for floggin me at sun-up."

"What for?"

"For - for fun."

"*For what*?"

"For funk, sir," panted the boy, recovering. "Oi don't care for being shotted. So when the guns begins to bang, Oi goos to bed."

The Gentleman threw back his head and ran off into laughter.

"You're the right sort, Mr. Toad. Come on board by all

means. But for you and your likes the world'd be a dull place."

Kit clambered in.

"What's that bag?" asked the Gentleman, swift as a sword.

"Duds," replied the boy as swift.

The Gentleman, sitting still as death, stared. It was an appalling moment. The boy could not face those eyes. He looked behind him. As he did so, the mist above drifted away, and the Union Jack at the foretop of the privateer floated out.

"There's her colours!" he panted.

"By Jove, you're right," cried the Gentleman, and began to row the boat clumsily about. "Stop that hole in the bottom with your foot, will you?"

The boat was water-logged and filling fast. The water was already over the Gentleman's spurs.

Down on his knees the boy baled for his life.

Behind him he heard a word of command: then the splash of oars, and the regular thump of rowlocks. The privateer's boat was away - a ten-oared galley from the sound of her, and they were driving her.

"Row, sir, row!" urged the boy. "They're after us!"

The Gentleman flung back into his oars.

Kit could not but admire him. He was rowing, as he believed, against death. The boat was sodden; he could not row; and the pursuers were coming up hand over hand. Yet his eyes danced, as he gasped,

"This is life."

The boy was looking behind him. He could not see the pursuing boat, but he could hear the sizzle of foam under her keel as she slipped through the water, and the rhythmical sweep of oars.

There was a terrible beauty about it - this swooping of Death on them out of the fog. He could hear the wings he could not see. She was close now, the Angel of the Swarthy Pinions.

On the thwart lay a pistol. He snatched it.

"Good boy!" panted the Gentleman.

Kit glanced forward.

He could see the loom of the land.

"There's the shore, sir!" he cried.

"And here are they!" gasped the other. "Pretty thing, by Jove!"

A boat's bows shot up behind them. A figure was standing in the stern.

"*Les voila*!" screamed a voice.

The Gentleman threw up his oars.

"French!"

Kit clapped the pistol to his head.

"Row!" he screamed. "Row!"

The other tumbled back into his oars. Up sprang his foot. The pistol was kicked out of the boy's hand, and the Gentleman was on him.

"O, you are a villain, Little Chap!" chuckled a voice in the lad's ear.

For a moment they hugged, the boat rocking beneath them.

"Can you swim?" came the voice at his ear.

"Yes," gurgled the lad, and as he felt the boat going sucked in a breath.

"Then shift for yourself. I can't."

As the waters closed about them the arms of the Gentleman loosed their hold.

CHAPTER XLIII

A BLACK BORDERER TO THE RESCUE

I

A boy was wading shoreward dizzily. As he surged through the water, his body made long rippling waves. He watched them with dull fascination, pointing.

Then he began to whimper peevishly. He was tired, he was cold. The shore waved up and down before his eyes. He knew he couldn't do it.

From behind him a yell penetrated his dying mind.

It stopped him dead.

He was a little child, nightmare-bound.

Waving to and fro, the water to his knees, he stretched both arms shoreward.

"Mother!" he wailed.

A shout answered him.

Some one was crashing down the shingle, racing

across the sand, and plunging through the water towards him.

The boy began to titter.

"Come on, Kit! come on!" came a rousing voice. "Don't look behind you! That's the style! Come on!"

What was this black splashing figure, sword in hand? Was it the Angel of Death in full regimentals? Surely he recognised the face beneath the shako?

"You aren't mother," the boy giggled, swaying.

A strong arm was round him; a body, firm and full of life, was pressed against his dying one; a voice, quickening as the Spring, was in his ear.

"Splendid, Kit! Well done indeed! Lean on me. Lots o time."

"Have the soldiers come?" sobbed the boy, struggling forward.

"One has," came the sturdy voice - "a Black Borderer."

They waded through the shallows, the ripples breaking prettily about them.

Behind them a fierce voice sang out an order.

The galley, which had brought up with a bump against the submerged longboat, had hoisted the Gentleman on board, and was swooping in pursuit.

The boy heard the beat of the oars, and sank on his

knees at the edge of the sea.

"I can't, sir. Take the bag. O go on!"

Two strong arms clutched him, and he was hoisted up.

All things were swimming away from him.

The last thing he knew was that he was in somebody's arms, and the somebody was running.

II

The boat swept shoreward.

A man with a musket, standing in the bows, was about to fire at the fugitives.

A sharp voice stayed him.

"*Ne tirez point! Nous les prendrons vivants. Ce n'est qu'un seul homme et le gosse.*"

A bugle from the shingle-bank retorted defiantly.

"*Halte!*"

The boat stopped short.

The crew looked over their shoulders.

"*Les soldats!*"

Upon the ridge a shako bobbed up.

A figure in uniform rose and ran at it

"Keep your eads down there all along the line!" it shouted. "Wait till I give the word, Royal Stand-backs."

The Gentleman sprang up in the boat.

"Ramez toujours, mes enfants!" he cried. *"C'est une ruse!"*

The men hung on their oars.

"*Laches!*" cried the Gentleman, smote the man on the foremost thwart a buffet, and leaping overboard floundered through the water.

The man in the bows fired.

There was no reply from the shingle-bank.

The men of the galley took courage. The boat swished through the shallows, and bumped ashore.

Out tumbled her crew, and stormed across the sand at the heels of the Gentleman.

The Parson was staggering up the shingle-bank, the boy in his arms.

At the top he paused, heaving like an earthquake, and looked back on his scampering pursuers.

"Yes, my beauties," he panted. "You just won't do it."

Knapp, keen as a terrier, bobbed up at his side.

"Shall I charge em, sir?" his little brown eyes bursting with desire - "me and the boy. Down the ill and into em plippety-plumpety-plop! O for God's sake, sir!" whimpering, dancing. "Ave mercy as you ope for it. Let me ave me smack if it's only for the glory of the old rigiment."

"Certainly not," said the Parson sternly. "This is war, not tomfoolery."

The little man collapsed sullenly.

"*From the right - retire by companies - on your supports!*" shouted the Parson in measured regimental voice.

From his manner he might have been addressing a Brigade and not merely Blob, disguised in an ancient shako, lying on his stomach, and armed with a hay-rake.

III

He plunged down the bank.

As he reached the greensward a warning shout from the cottage reached him.

"Ha! what's this?" joggled the Parson sharply. "Flank attack! who the pest? Oh, Gap Gang - I forgot."

A stream of fierce dark figures with running legs poured down the Wish and across the greensward at him.

"Hold tight round my neck, Kit!" he panted, taut to meet the new attack. "I want my sword-arm free. What! the boy's fainted!" He gave the limp body a hoist on his shoulder. "Now, Knapp! Let's see these guts o yours!"

Knapp shot by him, his arms working like piston-rods.

"Come on, Blob, me boy. Slaughder for somebody!" He pranced into action, throwing his legs like a hackney trotter. "Pray, duckie darlins, pray!" he called. "I'm a-comin! I'm a-comin! I'm a-comin!"

The life was bursting out of him. It made him laughing-mad. He was lusty as a young lion.

"Here they come!" muttered the Parson, labouring behind.

And come they did at a hound-slink, bunched together, and babbling. It was clear they were uncertain of each other and of success. Sin, the mighty Disintegrator, was at work upon their spirits. A more half-hearted crew of blackguards never attempted murder. They needed Black Diamond. He, and he alone, might have held them and swung them, as a fine horseman holds and swings a refuser at a fence.

And what dark faces! what dreadful eyes! what voices popping up like foul bubbles from a sewage pond!

"Them three all?"

"Enough too, ain't it?"

"I'm for gain back. Look at the face on that buster with the sword!"

"H'into em!" came a shrill treble from the rear. *"Cheerily, chaps, cheerily!"*

A crack from the cottage, the crack of doom.

The leading ruffian, a lumbering great horse-faced fellow, clapped his hand to his side.

"What's that?" he snapped.

"That's death!" came a solemn voice from across the green.

The man bowed his head as though in acknowledgement.

"I got it," he said, and fell like a falling tower.

His fellows wavered. This sudden arrow from the quiver of the Great Bowman, so unexpected expected, pierced the hearts of all.

Into them, toppling, bowled Knapp like a cannon-ball.

"Ow, dear! *Ow's* that? *Ow,* my pore face!"

The chirpy Cockney voice popped out from the thick of them like a cork from a bottle, and a smack from a sledge-hammer fist punctuated each ow.

Blob, at a lurching gallop, plunged into the opening his

leader had made, flashing his knife with a gurgling "Ho! ho!"

Last came the Parson with terrific sword.

It was all over before it had begun: a scuffle, a squeak, the flicker and tinkle of steel; and the cloud burst and scattered into its component drops.

The smugglers scampered away.

The Parson was wiping the point of his sword on a man.

"Dirty skunks!" he panted. "Had their bellyful before I'd begun."

Blob was laughing to himself.

"Oi loike killin," he gurgled. "It goos in so plop-loike."

A figure, tall and black as a winter tree, shot up against the light on the shingle-bank, and hung a second there.

The Parson waved.

"Too late, Monsieur le Poseur," he called mockingly. "Better luck next time."

The little party trotted across to the cottage, and entered.

Piper, awaiting them, slammed the door, and made all fast.

"Near thing, sir," chuckled the old man.

"Would have been but for that shot of yours," said the Parson, laying his burthen on the bed.

He leaned up against the wall, and panted, his good red face dripping.

"First round to England - eh?" he grinned.

BOOK III

FORT FLINT

I - BESIEGED

CHAPTER XLIV

THE ENGLISHMAN

All was dark within the kitchen of the cottage.

Spears of white light piercing the gloom told of day without.

The cottage was fast as a fortress. Stout planks were nailed across either door. Heavy shutters darkened the windows. Through a loop-hole a stream of light poured in on Nelson's old foretop-man.

Horn spectacles hung on his nose. His eyes were down, the silver head erect and drawn back. At arm's length beneath him he held a great Book in a splash of light.

He was reading aloud, spelling out the words, as does a child, and following with huge finger.

Outside a musket cracked; a bullet wanged against the

Alfred Ollivant

wall; there was the crisp trickle of dislodged mortar.

Still muttering, the old man closed his Book, and removed his spectacles. Then he slewed his chair round to the loop-hole, and felt for his musket.

The light poured in upon the moon-washed head, the noble brow, and calm eyes peering forth.

Deliberately the old man moved his head to and fro, searching the offender. Then the musket went to his shoulder, cheek hugged stock, the face grew set. The mystic had turned man of action.

There was a flash in the darkness, a smother of white in the room, and outside a sudden sobbing cry.

A hand waved in the cloud, and out of it a still voice said,

"He wun't trouble no more."

The old man leant his reeking musket against the wall, and took up his Book tranquilly.

CHAPTER XLV

THE PARSON AT HOME

I

A clap of thunder, followed by a monstrous hissing overhead, awoke Kit from dreams of blackberrying with Gwen in the dew-white dawn.

He started up.

"What's that?" he cried, seeking his mind.

"The privateer barking good-bye, sir," came old Piper's voice from across the room. "She's stood in with the tide, and had a slap with her bow-chaser. Now she's going about."

The memories swooped back on Kit; Nelson, the despatches, the swim in the dark.

In a moment he was at the loop-hole, peering over the old man's shoulder.

On these in the sunshine he saw the brown-patched sails of the privateer lifted ladder-like from behind the shingle-bank, and strangely close. Then her bows slid

Alfred Ollivant

into view, and he realised that she was standing out to sea:

The boy's heart soared.

They were free!

A great hand pulled him gently back from the loop-hole.

"By your leave, sir. They've a marksman on the knoll keeps on a-peckin at us."

The boy's heart sank.

"Then we *aren't* free?"

"Oh, no, sir. All round us, sir - a cord on em, Muster Joy calls it, soldier-fashion."

From above the Parson's cheery voice rang out.

"So she's left you in the lurch, my lord. That comes o trusting to a Frenchman."

Piper chuckled.

"Muster Joy and the Gentleman! Must keep on a-chaffin. At it all day yesterday they was, atween scrimmages."

A gay voice came sailing back from the open.

"Ah, Reverend Father, good morning! Yes, you must excuse her for the moment. She has an engagement to keep round the corner to-morrow."

"To-morrow!" echoed Kit, aghast. "Piper! how long have I been asleep?"

"Why, sir, you've slept round the clock and a bit more. It's nigh noon of what was to-morrow when you turned in."

No wonder he was hungry; no wonder he was fresh; no wonder that sound of hammering, which had disturbed him as he passed from a half-swoon into sleep, seemed so far off.

"Wednesday! Then to-morrow's Thursday!" he cried, rushing into his clothes. "O Nelson!" and he raced up the ladder.

The loft was full of light, dazzling after the twilight of the kitchen.

II

A mattress, stuffed clumsily in the seaward window, half blocked it. In the dormer looking towards the Downs, two biscuit-boxes crammed with earth sat on the sill, forming a rough head-cover.

Behind these Knapp sprawled on his stomach. Beside him was a wooden porringer full of bullets, and a basin of black powder; in his hand a musket.

In a cobweb corner by a barrel, Blob crouched covetously; while beside the mattress-curtain sat the Parson in his shirt-sleeves, furbishing Polly, and pausing every now and then to spy out through the bulges.

As Kit clambered on to the floor, the Parson turned, his blue eyes merry, and curls a-ripple.

"Ah, Kit, my boy, how are you?"

"Alive and well, sir, thanks to you. And you, sir?"

"I!" laughed the Parson. "I'm another man." A bullet whizzed by. The Parson listened sentimentally. "That's the music!" raising his face with a rapt smile. "Always makes me think of angels' wings."

He seemed to have grown, body and soul. His eyes shone, his cheeks glowed; he was crisp as a rimy apple.

Kit felt the change.

Responsibility, the searcher out of souls, had exhilarated and sobered the man. He was graver yet gayer, inspiring and inspired.

"Duck up aloft!" came a sudden roar from beneath.

The Parson smote Kit a blow on the chest that sent him staggering back against the wall.

A bullet whistled in at one window and out at the other.

The Parson crawled across to Knapp, lying on his face, and dealt him a tremendous buffet.

"Dog!" he thundered. "Why don't you shout?"

The little man's body leapt to the blow, but he made no answer.

"Go below!" ordered the Parson savagely. "What's the good of you? I set you there to warn us and all you can do is to grovel on your stomach and snivel."

The little Cockney rose without a word and crept away, his tail between his legs. Kit saw his face. One eye was black; and his face was so woebegone that but for the misery in it Kit would have smiled.

"Their shooting is exquisite," said the Parson with professional delight. "You can't show a finger.... They've nearly had Blob already - ain't they, Blob?"

Blob, cuddling in the corner, shook his head cunningly.

"Oi've had them," he said. "Three pennorth of em," pointing to the little pile of coppers at his side.

"I'm giving him a penny apiece for each Gang-er he gets, and twice the money for a Frenchman," the Parson explained. "It stimulates effort," he added, prim as a pedagogue, but with twinkling eye. "And now, Kit, your story."

CHAPTER XLVI

THE PARSON'S STORY

Swiftly the boy told his tale.

"But for you and the soldiers," he ended....

"There were no soldiers," answered the Parson curtly.

"What, sir! - I thought! - some men in shakos behind the bank - the men Knapp brought."

The Parson ground his teeth.

"Knapp brought no men. He got as far as the Lamb in Eastbourne on the hill yonder, and there he got playing the fool, and sneaked back here about twenty minutes after you were gone with a pair of black eyes and a pack of lies and nothing else."

All the ruddiness had left his face. It was grey as steel and dark.

"I tried him by drum-head court-martial then and there, for misconduct in the presence of the enemy. I was the President, Piper the Court. The Court found him guilty and sentenced him to be shot. I confirmed the sentence, and proceeded to carry it out."

He rapped the words out clean and clear. Kit felt himself seeing this man with new eyes, the eyes of a great respect. The fellow schoolboy of yesterday had turned into the man of war, stern and terrible. Kit was afraid of him.

"There was nothing to wait for," continued the Parson. "So I had him out and made him dig his own grave against the wall.

"'It's blanky ard,' said he.

"'You're a soldier; and this is war,' I answered. 'I'm going to count two - then fire. Make your peace with your Maker.'

"I hadn't got to two, when I heard a hubbub on the privateer, and knew you were either caught or in difficulties.

"'This can wait,' I said. 'I'll use you first, and shoot you afterwards!'"

The blood stole back to the Parson's face. His eyes lifted, twinkling now.

"It's resource that makes the soldier, you know, Kit. I slipped into my old regimentals, gave Knapp his bugle, clapped a shako on Blob's head, and put the two of them behind the shingle-bank to act as a skeleton-force.... And you know the rest."

Kit gazed at the square-set figure before him with respectful admiration.

"It must have been a close thing, sir."

The Parson shrugged.

"It would have been a mere bagatelle but for the Gap Gang cutting in on our line of retreat. That added interest, and made a bright little affair of what would otherwise have been a dull retirement."

"And how did the Gap Gang come to cut in?"

"Oh, that's easily explained....

"At midnight I went out to beat em up - crept along under the cliff past Holy Well. When I got to Cow Gap, there were my friends lying on their backs in a bunch, snoring like so many sows, and the boat beached beneath em. I believe I could have killed the lot then and there, and nobody the wiser; but I wasn't going to soil my hands with the cold blood of those swine. So I just jumped into the boat, and got to work at once - put my heel through her bottom, and was just tearing up a plank, when the noise wakes old Red Beard.

"'Who the blank's that?' he growled, sitting up in the moonlight.

"'Why,' says I, tearing away, 'the gentleman you're good enough to call the blankety Parson.'

"'Then guess we've got you, sir,' says he, and comes down the beach at me at the double.

"'Think so?' says I, jumping out to meet him.

"'Twenty to one, sir!' says he. 'Chuck it up.'

"'Pardon,' says I, 'nineteen to one, I think,' and downs him with my left. O, such a beauty! flop in the mug.

"They were all awake by this of course; and there was a little bit of trouble. I wasn't going to ask my sweet lady to soil her lips on those mucky blackguards, so I kept dodging away before them, just doing enough with my dukes to keep them amused. They were no more good than a mob of cattle, you see - drunk with sleep and liquor, the lot of em.

"'Out knives, boys, and finish the blank!' says old Toadie.

"And pon my soul they came on so hot I don't know what mightn't have happened, when all of a sudden,

"'The boat!' screams Fat George from behind. 'Some blankety blank's at the boat.'

"And sure enough there was a long-legged chap launching the boat. In he jumped, shoved her off, and lay on his oars, lookin at em, as they came running along the edge of the sea."

The Parson threw back his jolly head.

"Laugh, Kit! - I never saw a fellow laugh as he did. I roared to see him. And all the while those chaps were skipping about on the shore, howling like lunatics. You never heard such a row. Then Fat George, when he saw it was all up, tried the leary lay.

"'I know it's just a joke o the Genelman's,' says he in that greasy-wheazy voice of his.

"'That's just it, George,' the other calls across the water, 'and the best joke I've enjoyed since I saw Black Diamond brand you with the hot iron you'd just branded the lugger's kitten with.'

"'What I mean,' whines Fat George, 'you wouldn't go for to leave a lot o pore blokes on a dead foul lee-shore - what got there through trying to sarve you.'

"'Sarve me!' says the Gentleman. 'Yes, Garge, my faithful friend - sarve me in the back with two fut o carvin-knife, while I was chattin with Garge's pals.'

"At that Fat George snatches the musket and pulls.

"I heard the click of the hammer, but there was never so much as a flash in a pan.

"'Thank you, thank you, Fatty, my friend,' says the French feller. 'But you know you'd make better shooting, if I hadn't wetted your priming.'

"Then he struck his oars in the water. 'And now good-night all,' says he. 'Black Diamond was a man, if he was a devil. As to the rest of you, the best I can wish you is a long drop, and a rope that runs free. And as for you, Fat George, I won't forget you in t his world, and God won't forget you in the next.'

"Then he came rowing along inside the barrier of rocks to me.

"'I don't know who you are, sir,' says he, taking off his hat in his dandified French way, 'but I'm sure I owe you my best thanks. If it hadn't been for you, I hardly know how I should have managed.'

"Well, of course I knew very well who he was, and what he was after. But I knew the boat was sinking, and I saw he couldn't row. So I never thought he'd reach the ship. Still the longer I kept him talking, the better your chance. So -

"'You're very welcome, sir,' says I. 'Won't you step ashore and thank me in person?'

"'I'm grieved to the heart,' says he, 'but I must postpone that pleasure till another day. Perhaps we shall meet again. I hope to return in a few weeks - not alone next time.'

"'Quite so,' thinks I, 'at the head of the Army of England. No you don't, my fine fellow, not if I can keep you messing about there a few minutes longer.'

"'And perhaps we have met before,' says I, taking off my hat.

"He peered at me in the moonlight.

"'What!' he cries - 'not my old friend, Black Cock, again?'

"'The same at your service,' says I, 'still waiting to have his comb cut.'

"'This is a great happiness,' says he, very earnest, and paddles in a bit.

"'It's mutual,' says I. 'And if you've quite done posing won't you step ashore and let us consummate our joy? A sweet stretch of sand, and a lovely light.'

"Pon my soul for a moment I thought he would. Then,

"'I can't to-day, bad cess to it,' says he. 'Tell you the truth I'm in the devil's own hurry. Got an interview with his Sacred Majesty, our noble Emperor, whom may Heaven preserve, at twelve noon to-morrow. And if I don't keep it, I stand to lose a lot o little things - my head among em. I'm in disgrace, you see - always have been from a child!'

"He lifts his sword to his lips, quite the play-actor.

"'But here's to our next merry meeting, sir.'

"'And may it be soon, Monsieur le Poseur,' says I, answering his salute.

"And it's proved sooner than either of us expected. There's he: here'm I. One side this wall the first light cavalryman in Europe, 'tother - Harry Joy, ex-Captain of British infantry. Now we've g ot to see which is the better man."

He squared his shoulders.

Whoever else might find the situation unsatisfactory it was not Parson Joy.

CHAPTER XLVII

THE DESPATCH-BAG

I

"That is the first part of the story, and the least," said the Parson. "And while I'm telling you the rest you'd better have some grub."

He reached up to a rafter.

"I keep the tackle up here out of Blob's way. The boy's all belly - ain't you, you young shark?"

Blob stroked his waist feelingly.

"She kips on a-talkin," he purred. "She dawn't get much answer though."

"Well, don't eat that candle anyway, you little glutton!"

"Oi warn't eatin it," said Blob, aggrieved. "Oi were suckin it."

The Parson arranged what food there was on the floor.

"'Honour and salt-beef - campaigners' fare!' as Nelson

used to say in Corsica....

"And while you're at that, I'll get on with my story."

II

He went to the gable-end and took down a tarpaulin bag hanging on a staple.

"Kit, that was a great haul you made."

He took a packet from the bag.

"What d'you think this contains?" stripping the india-rubber from it.

There crept into his eyes again that steely look.

"It contains," he continued in the still voice of the man so moved that he dare hardly trust himself, "a list of all those gentlemen of Kent and Sussex who are *à nous*, as the paper says."

The boy dropped his knife.

"Traitors in fact!"

"That's the ugly word," said the Parson between set teeth. "And may God have mercy on them as they deserve!... When I read that list," he continued, breathing hard, "for the first time in my life I was sick, *sick* to call myself an Englishman.... There are men down there I've dined with, gamed with, chaffed with, may heaven forgive me for it! true men as I honestly believed, men I've seen drink the King's health and damnation to the French with three times three, as a Christian and a gentleman should. There are magistrates, squires, a peer or two, one sheriff, a deputy-lieutenant, and small fry - publicans, carriers, smugglers, and the like - by the score."

He spread squares of paper on the floor, piecing them.

"And here's a map in sections of the whole country from Pevensey to Westminster - farms, inns, cottages, all put down, see! - where guides can be got; the wells marked, bakers' shops, mills; roads, metalled and unmetalled; and in the margin here and there a Church or what-not drawn out pretty as you please for a sign-post."

The boy looked. Yes, it was the hand that had written the scent-bottle note.

"There's enough in that bag to hang some of the best names in England," continued the Parson with gloating delight. "And I hope to have that bag in Pitt's hands before many hours are out."

The colour stole back to his cheeks, and he began to rub his hands together.

"Kit, my boy, we'll have such a hanging as was never before seen in England - God helping us.... That's what we're here for."

The boy's eyes were raised to his.

"No, sir, please. What we're here for is to save Nelson."

III

The Parson staggered.

"Nelson!" he cried, ghastly.

His mind clutched in the dark at something it had lost.

"The plot, sir.... Beachy Head."

"My *God*!" cried the Parson, and died against the wall.

The despatch-bag and its contents had so possessed him that Nelson's need had for the moment slipped his mind.

"And I call myself a soldier!"

He leapt to life again.

"What's to-day?" savagely.

"Wednesday, sir."

"Is it to-morrow?"

"Yes, sir."

The life faded out of his blue eyes.

Till that moment he had been hugging the comfortable belief that Time, the soldier's best ally and worst enemy, was on his side. Sooner or later relief must come. Cosy in their tiny fortress, they could afford to wait for it. The Gentleman could not. Now for the first time the Parson learned that his anticipated ally was his foeman's.

"Talk of Knapp! - I'm the one ought to be shot."

"How soon shall we be relieved, sir?" asked the boy feverishly at his side. "When may we expect the soldiers?"

The words revived the Parson like a whip-lash. Knapp, a soldier, had betrayed his trust. He, a soldier, had let slip thirty golden hours. He was bitterly jealous for his dear Service.

"We shan't be relieved," he snarled. "How can the soldiers relieve us when they don't know we want relief? Knapp didn't get through - told you so already once."

"But the country-folk, sir! Surely they'll report."

"No, they won't," stonily. "This is Sussex. We aren't alive in Sussex: we're dead-alive.... If they did see anything was up they'd only think it was one of the ordinary rows between the blockade-men and the gentlemen, as they call the smugglers."

He looked out of the Downward window. There was little comfort. Tall men in French uniforms swaggered about England's greensward as though already it was theirs. He could catch their beastly foreign lingo. The sight and sound made him mad. Grim old watchdog that he was, he felt the bristles at the back of his neck rising. What right had these strange folk in his back-yard? - O to make his teeth meet in their gaitered legs!

Besides the Frenchmen, not a soul stirring.

English rooks cawing over English green, and an English sheepdog answering them.

A lonely land at the best of times, it was a desert now.

Westward in a cloud of beeches, a grey house glim-mered - George Cavendish's - empty. The Seahouses over by Splash Point - empty too. So was every house of any size for ten miles inland from Fair-light to Selsea Bill. Everybody bolted who could afford it. The old lady of Hailsham quite a proverb for pluck in these parts; and they said she looked under her bed every night to see if the French had come.

And the luck! where was the luck?

Ten days since this uttermost corner of England had stirred to the strange music of men making ready for battle: bugle-calling Cavalry in the new barracks in Eastbourne on the hill; thundering Artillery in the Circular Redoubt at Langney Point; Sea-Fencibles in the martello-towers along Pevensey Levels. Now all was still and dead again. A concentration in force had taken place at Lewes. The Cavalry had been withdrawn to the camp there. A case of cholera had emptied Langney Fort. The Sea-Fencibles had run away. Black Diamond had swept up the blockademen.

Darkness, darkness, everywhere.

Kit stole to his side.

"We *must* get a message through to Nelson," he chattered. "We *must*."

The boy felt himself at war with destiny, and crushed by it. He recalled the Man of Despair in the Iron Cage in Pilgrim's Progress. The fate of the country was in his hands. He alone had the knowledge that could save her, and he could not use it. He was a dumb thing, possessed of a vast world-secret, which he could not impart for lack of voice.

"If there's no other way, we must cut our way through."

The Parson met him with a rough,

"Nonsense."

"Why?" hotly.

"Impossible - that's why."

It was the first time he had thrown that dead-wall word across the lad's path, and it maddened the boy.

After all, *he* was responsible, not this beefy soldier.

"That's a word we don't know in *our* Service, sir," he cried with scornful nostrils.

The taunt touched the Parson on the raw.

He swung round savagely.

Alfred Ollivant

"*Your* Service!" he stormed. "At a time such as this, there is only one Service for loyal hearts, and that's the Service of his country."

The lad quailed before the thunder-and-lightning of the man's wrath.

"Why can't we sally?" sullenly.

The Parson shot a hand toward the window.

The boy followed his pointing finger.

In the open, behind the wall, was a camp-fire, a group of soldiers squatting round it, arms piled. To right and left, embracing the cottage, a chain of sentries ran, tall men all in tall-plumed bear-skins.

Old Piper was right. A cordon indeed!

"Grenadiers of the Guard!" rumbled the Parson in the boy's ear, rolling his r's like a *feu de joie*. "Marksmen to a man; veterans all; and half of them decorated."

Grenadiers of the Guard! the men of the Bridge of Lodi, of the Battle of the Pyramids and Mount Tabor, of Hochstadt and Hohenlinden.

Kit recalled the tops of the *Cocotie* swarming with riflemen, and old Ding-dong's surprised disgust.

Now he understood.

On the success of this venture hung Napoleon's world-projects. *Coûte que coûte*, he had told Mouche, he must bring off this coup. So he was employing on it the pick of the first Army the world had ever seen.

As he thought of the issues at stake, the boy's soul fainted within him.

How could he, Kit Caryll, aged fifteen, and hovering on the brink of tears, stand up against the Victor of Marengo?

CHAPTER XLVIII

THE DOXIE'S DAUGHTER

I

The boy's long face, anxious before, grew haggard now.

It wore the look of one with the enthusiasms of a saint across whose path Sin, the Insurmountable, has fallen suddenly.

"We're done," he said, husky and white.

His words revived the other. True man that he was, despair in the boy's heart quickened the courage in his own.

"Never say die till you're dead," he cried, squaring his shoulders - "that's the Englishman's motto."

His spirit rose to meet the occasion.

"Our theatrical friend outside there's no fool. But - but - but! there's just one element he's not reckoned with."

"What?" cried Kit, hanging on his words.

The Parson dropped head and voice.

"Who saved you from the *Tremendous*?" he whispered. "Who handed you up a cliff a goat couldn't climb? - who brought you to this house? - who put the flag-idea into your head, and brought it off?"

The Parson's words made sudden confusion in the lad's mind. It came to him with a shock of surprise to find such triumphant faith in this ruddy fighting-man.

"And why d'you think of all the houses in the world He sent you to this one?" the other continued.

"Because of you, sir."

The Parson frowned, and approached his lips to the lad's ear.

"Because it's got a secret passage!"

This most matter-of-fact explanation flashed the laughter to the boy's eyes.

"I mean it," said the other earnestly. "Ain't you noticed anything about the floor of the kitchen?"

"It sounds hollow."

"It is hollow. It's built over an old decoy-pond."

In a few words the Parson outlined the history of the secret passage.

A water-way had led from decoy-pond to sea. The sea had gone back and left the water-way and pond high and dry. Sixty years back a sly old sea-dog had built this lonely cottage over the pond. He had covered the water-way and made a drain of it. Thus he had secured a secret passage to the sea, and the cottage had become the receiving depôt of Ruxley's crew.

"Where does it lead to?" asked the boy, all eyes.

"Out into the creek we crossed on the way to the Wish."

"And how many people know about it?"

"Three. One's you; one's me; one's the son of the man who built the cottage - and that's old Piper down below there.... It's not been used for forty years. The sea went back and back, and the creek's been dry these years past."

Kit's knees invited him to prayer. This was not chance; it was not coincidence.

"You're right, sir," said the boy chokily. "He's in it."

"And what's more He's going to get us out," replied the Parson, cheerfully matter-of-fact.

The boy was slipping off his coat.

"I'd better start at once. There's not a second to lose. Nelson may sail this evening."

The Parson laid a kind hand on the lad's shoulder.

"The boy's as greedy for glory as Nelson himself," he laughed. "But the Navy can't do it *all*, you know. Give *us* a chance....When we've got the best pair of legs South of Thames trained to a tick, and fighting mad for their chance, we may as well use em."

Kit gasped.

"Nipper Knapp!" and added in a flash, "May I go with him, sir?"

"To the mouth of the drain," said the Parson. "No further."

II

He turned about.

"Blob, come here. Keep a sharp look-out at this window, and give a holloa if anything stirs. You can sing em a little song, if you know one to keep em quiet."

He slid down into the twilight of the kitchen. There only the old foretop-man was to be seen, patient at his post of watch.

"Where's Knapp, Piper?"

"Why, sir, in the cellar. Wanted to be alone with his trouble, I reck'n. Tarrabul down-earted, the poor lad be."

"I'll cheer him up," cried the Parson, and disappeared through an open trap-door into the night beneath.

"Nipper Knapp! Nipper Knapp, my boy!"

In two minutes he was back.

Knapp was at his heel, sparring playfully at the back of the other's head.

True, for the broken heart there is no such cure as action or the hope of it.

As they emerged into the twilight of the kitchen a voice, pure as a rivulet's, poured down in song upon them from above.

From outside came a gust of laughter, and then a roaring chorus.

"By the Lord!" thundered the Parson. "It's The Doxie's Daughter."

"And the Gap Gang singing choir!" said Piper grimly. "Likely it'll be the only hymn they knaw."

"One moment, Master Blob!" muttered the Parson between clenched teeth. "I'll swab that boy's soul clean if I have to do it with a scrubbing-brush.... Now, Knapp, ready yourself, while I write a note to the Commandant."

Knapp tore off his coat, and began to fight an exhibition battle with a ghost in the corner.

"Will ye fight the lot then, Jack?" chuckled old Piper.

"Ay, and wop em, too!" cried the little man, dodging, ducking. "Ave a slap at em first, and then go through -

that's my idee."

"It's not mine, though!" roared the Parson, catching him a rousing kick. "Get on with your undressing, d your eyes!"

He finished his note and folded it.

"And now for the sweet little cherub that sits up aloft."

III

He ran nimbly up the ladder, Kit at his heels.

The chorister had ceased his song.

Through the half-stuffed dormer, light streamed in on the white-washed wall, the cobwebs, rafters, and Polly in the corner, shining demure.

"Now where the dooce has that boy got?" muttered the Parson, looking round.

Kit pointed.

In the darkest corner, under the slope of the roof, stood an apple-barrel. Out of it two frog-like legs thrust and kicked with the action of one swimming. A protu- berance crowned the rim of the barrel. Body, head, and arms were lost.

The Parson whipped up Polly.

"One for yourself!" he roared, prodding the boy's bad eminence, "and one for The Doxie's Daughter!"

"Hoi! that's Blo-ub!" yelled a muffled voice. Two hands shot out and plastered themselves over the stimulated part. There was a wriggle. Then Blob stood before them, touzled, pink, his ears wide, an apple tight between his teeth.

"D'you call that keeping a look-out?" thundered the Parson.

"Oi wur lookin out," said Blob, dogged and sullen.

"Then you keep your eyes where few of us do."

"Oi thart oi yerd a Frenchie in the bar'l," said Blob in the slow and undulating voice of Sussex. "Oi went fur to fetch un out, when a tarrabul great oarse-fly settled on ma butt-end and stung her."

"It was no horse-fly," replied the Parson. "It was my dear lady. Now, don't bother to think of any more lies, my lad, but just take that lantern from the wall, and go below. We'll join you in a minute."

IV

The Parson pulled aside the hanging mattress, and peeped seaward.

"Come here, boy. I want to show you the lie of the land. D'you see that chap in blue knickers in the shade of the sycamores? - he's the Gap Gang sentry. They're camped somewhere behind the knoll, the main of them. That's their smoke you see among the trees."

That roaring chorus still rang in the boy's ear.

"The drain runs to the right of the knoll, and out into the creek bang opposite the Wish. Half-way down it there's a man-hole."

An icy pang pierced Kit's heart.

"It's quite small, and a bush grows over it. It's a million to one they know nothing of it. Still you should - er - watch it."

The Parson was gnawing his under-lip.

"I'll watch it," said the boy, the waves breaking white about his face.

It must be somewhere just about the man-hole that Fat George and Co. were camped. Still he wasn't going to let this soldier know he was afraid.

But the soldier knew.

Outwardly calm, his own heart was a whirlpool of doubts. How could he stop behind a wall and send this lad out into the open to face heaven knew what? Yet here surely his obvious duty lay. Should the enemy storm, what could a legless old sailor and a brace of boys do against them? And unless he was mistaken mischief was brewing. Where was the Gentleman all this time? Yesterday he had been everywhere all the time. To-day the Parson had caught but one fleeting glimpse of him. The old soldier preferred his enemy's activity to his quiet. Was this the lull before the storm?

"I only want you to go to the mouth of the drain, and see him off," he said with calm cheerfulness. "Once away, you'd only hamper him."

That was truth at all events. Once away, Knapp's chance lay in his feet. With luck the little man'd be in Lewes in an hour and a half. With luck a good man on a good horse'd be in Chatham before night, another at the Admiralty, a third at Merton, - that was, if Beau Beauchamp would leave his actress for the moment to play the man. With luck Nelson wouldn't have sailed.

Lots of luck, true! still, who was it was on their side?

The fog of his doubts cleared away.

He turned to the boy with glowing eyes.

"Kit," he whispered, hugging the lad's arm, "we'll have a Gazette to ourselves yet."

II - THE SALLY

CHAPTER XLIX

MAKING READY

The kitchen was dim as a sick-room, and strangely hushed. No one spoke but the Parson and he in whispers, lecturing Knapp, undressing in the corner.

The gravity of the enterprise, its certain perils, the issues at stake, oppressed the room. Death was there already; as yet indeed only a ghost at each man's elbow, in a few moments maybe to become incarnate.

Kit felt it and sickened.

Perched upon the table, his back to the boarded window, he whetted his dirk upon his shoe, and wondered if those others, those men, Knapp most of all, felt as he did.

Privately he thanked heaven that the dusk hid his face.

Through chinks and splintered bullet-holes, the light stole in, making daggers across the darkness.

It splashed the walls, the great stone-flags, the black mouth of the cellar, and the dresser in the corner.

Alfred Ollivant

There sat Knapp, a grey ghost spotted here and there with light. The little rifleman was naked now, save for a pair of fighting drawers. A heap of clothes sprawled at his feet.

The little rifleman was like a child. Broken-hearted a minute back, now he was as a lion in leash.

There was an adventure forward, and the off chance of a fight: he brimmed at the thought of it. Without imagination, he knew no fear; with little experience of pain, he didn't much believe in it. They wouldn't catch *him*; they wouldn't hit *him*!

Before him knelt the Parson with low head, swathing his feet with strips of torn towel, absorbed as a surgeon, careful as a mother.

"Is that easy? - now how's that? - try your foot down! Another turn round the ankle? - Remember, it'll be rough going till you strike the grass."

At the loop-hole Nelson's old foretop-man watched and waited. A gleam smote his silver hair and prophetic forehead. Kit watched him wondering.

The old man, so tranquil amid the stir and whisper of death, affected the boy as One years ago had affected other seamen tempest-tossed.

His chattering heart hushed as a sparrow hushes in the quiet of a great cathedral.

Then the world rushed in on him with a shout.

Again that gust of laughter outside, that roaring chorus.

The Gap Gang were making merry.

The contrast revolted the lad.

The table on which he sat began to rattle.

Quietly he slipped off it. But the old foretop-man had heard.

Leaving his post, he came rumbling across the uneven flags.

"The waitin time's generally always the worst time, sir," he whispered. "Sooner farty actions than wait for one - I've hard Lard Nelson say it himsalf."

"I am a bit - quaky," replied the boy, and would have admitted as much to no other man, and to few women.

"And none the worse for that, sir. It's a poor heart that can't feel fear. If a man's not a bit timersome about facin his Maker, then he ought to be. Pluck's doin your duty although you are afear'd. You'll be right enough once you're in it, surely.... And if you're not above a hint from a man before the mast, sir, you'll take them shoes off. Boardin-parties bare-fut - that was ollus the word aboard the *Agamemnon*.... Ah, Knapp, feelin slap?"

"Ay, fit to run for me life or fight for it," bubbled the little rifleman, prancing out of his corner.

The Parson beckoned Kit.

"You see his sort," he whispered. "The chap's as full of meat and mischief as a lion-cub." He turned again.

"Knapp," he said solemnly, "this is your officer. He's coming with you to see you off. He carries the King's commission as truly as I do. You'll obey him as you would me, and no nonsense, d'you see?"

"Very good, sir," said the little man, jigging and bobbing. "I'm all of a pop like. Seems I might go off any moment."

"Any tomfoolery and you will go off," replied the Parson sternly - "out of this world into the next - pop! as you say yourself. You've only one chance against the finest marksmen in the world, and that's to show em a clean pair of heels. If you don't, you've fought your last fight, my lad! Ginger Jake's cock of the South."

The last words went home. The little rifleman became very grave. He swung round to Piper in his swift bird-like way.

"Mr. Piper, pop off a prayer for us."

The common-sense saint lifted his head.

"God elp and strengthen your legs, Nipper Knapp," he prayed.

"That's the point, O Lord! - his legs!" punctuated the Parson.

"Sometimes," continued the old foretop-man solemnly, "I have wondered why the Lard saw good to take my legs to Himsalf. Rack'n I knaw now." He reached out a huge hand, gripped the little rifleman and pulled him closer. "There's nawthin cut to waste in this world," he whispered huskily. "And it's my belieft He's been savin of em up this ten year past agin this day - to put the strength of em into your'n, Jack Knapp. May you make good use o both pairs - your own o the flesh, and mine o the sperrit! - that's my best prayer for you."

The little rifleman, as simple as the old sailor, was profoundly touched.

"I'll do me best, Mr. Piper, struth I will!" he sniffed. "Never do to mess it a'ter all His trouble."

"Give us your hand on it!" said the old man. "And you too, sir, if so be a common sailor might make so bold."

The old sailor and the young shook hands feelingly: the two soldiers followed suit.

"Don't forget you're a Black Borderer, my boy," said the Parson, one hand on the rifleman's shoulder.

"That I'll never, sir!" replied the little man, almost in tears.

Parson and Kit gripped hands: neither spoke.

Then the Parson ran up the ladder.

Alfred Ollivant

CHAPTER L

IN THE DRAIN

The little party of adventurers filed down into the dark.

Blob's lantern shone on the rusty iron door, streaked with damp, which barred the mouth of the drain.

It was very chill down there. Knapp was shivering as he played with the bolts. Blob, impassive as a jellyfish, was still sucking at his apple.

Quick and clear Kit gave his orders.

"Knapp, stop tinkering those bolts about, and stand back till I give the word! Now, Blob, listen here! - Knapp and I are going through this door down the drain. You'll stand here with the lantern, and light us, d'you see?"

"Ah!" said Blob.

"You're not to stir, d'you see, boy?"

"Aw!" said Blob.

Kit gripped his arm, and looked into his round and dewy eyes.

"Half-way down the drain there's a hole, where the light comes in." He was articulating his words with the slow precision of one addressing a deaf man. *Now if, after we've passed that hole, anybody should get down through it into the drain, then you're to slam the door - and bolt!...*

"Now repeat my instructions."

Blob mooned and mowed, his eyes roaming the cellar.

"Repate moi ructions," he mumbled at last.

"Ass!" snapped Kit. "Here! - stand so! - the lantern between your feet. That's right. Now don't stir. Ready, Knapp?"

"On the boil, sir," bobbing and blowing on his fists.

"Then come on."

Kit drew the wheezing bolts, and flung back the door. A chill breeze entered.

Before the boy could stop him, the little rifleman was through the door and away down the drain.

"Come back!" ordered Kit in a fierce whisper.

The man, stooping in the drain, turned and grinned.

"In *my* Service, sir, Borderers lead."

"In *my* Service, officers do.... Come back!"

The boy had nothing but his dirk; but that he pointed

Alfred Ollivant

resolutely; and the lantern-light glimmered in the darkness as on a steel-barrel.

Knapp crawled back, delighted.

"You're the sort," he chuckled, patting the lad on the back. "Quite the little man o war."

"Get to heel," snarled Kit. "Hold your tongue. Keep your paws to yourself. And address me respectfully and properly."

The drain ran away before them, a long black tunnel, focussing in a remote jewel of light. It was like the Alley of Life, cramped and dark, and at the far end of it a little door opening on heaven. And across the door the boy seemed to see written the one word *Nelson*.

He advanced into the breathing darkness, his eye on that guiding light. Half-way down the drain a dim patch brightened the black floor. There was the man-hole; there was the danger-point.

He crept forward with groping hands. The bricks were cold and sweating, the atmosphere that of the grave. It seemed to smell of dead men. The boy felt as though a mountain was smothering him. He found himself breathing deep as though in difficulties.

Even Knapp, crawling at his heels, appeared affected.

The man was humming something in a dirge-like monotone. At first Kit thought it was some sort of a Litany; then he caught the words:

"Two little corpseses goes for a walk

In a church-yard under the sea,
Says the one to the other -
'I'll squeak if you'll squawk
To keep me company.'"

The humming ceased, and Kit missed it.

"Are you there, Knapp?"

"Yes, sir. Smotherified feelin, ain't it?"

"Do you hear anything?"

"Only me own teeth chatter."

"Hush, then."

They were drawing near the man-hole.

The boy was sweating, shivering. He was living in death.

A very little, and he would have had one of his old screaming panics of the night-nursery. Then that tiny diamond of light, hanging in the blackness before him, the one word written across it, steadied him. It was a star, his star. It sang to him the Song of Faith.

Besides, how could he run away? - he, an officer, a gentleman, a sailor, run away before a private soldier? No. It is easier to lead somebody who believes you to be brave than to let him know you are a coward - especially if he's a soldier. The thought tickled him, and his heart surged upward.

They were very near the man-hole now.

Alfred Ollivant

Kit turned and pointed.

Knapp put out his tongue in reply.

The patch of light on the floor was dim and chequered. The old bush then was in its place. The boy thanked heaven for it, and stopped dead.

Above the tumult of his heart he could hear a voice: so close too that had he prodded upwards through the thin crust of earth he would have stabbed the speaker.

And how well he knew that ghastly treble!

CHAPTER LI

VOICES OF THE LOST

"Where's Bandy?"

"Where we'll all be afore we're much older - in ell this alf our."

"What ye mean?"

"Ave a peep in the creek yonder. You'll see sharp enough what I mean."

Another voice, dark and brooding, joined in:

"Who stuck him?"

"The Genelman."

"What for?"

"Back-answerin him."

A fourth voice, very black and bitter, flared up:

"That's im! - bangs you up in the firin line, then sticks you if you look at him. If it's storm, we got to do it. If it's sally, we got to meet it. If it's neether, we got to set

round and take Piper's pot-luck, while he and his chaps lay safe out o range and, shoots us if we bolt."

"Where's the good in boltin?" came the brooding voice. "Nowhere to bolt to. Jack Ketch's our only friend this side the water."

There was a stony silence.

"How long's this - game goin to last? - that's what I want to know," came the black and bitter voice at last.

The ghastly treble chimed in:

"That's what I says to im last night when e come his rounds. 'We're only poor chaps, my lord,' says I. 'We've lost alf the number of our mess in your service. And now I'd make bold to ask how long you're goin to keep us here?'

"'Why,' says he, suckin his hanky, 'that depends on your sweet selves. You may go as soon as you've took the cottage.'

"'And what if the sogers come first?' I says. 'There's a camp at Lewes, you know, my lord.'

"'Why then,' says he, and I lay he thought he was funny, 'I'll leave you to the hands of your beloved compatriots. And what can a good man want more'n that?'

"'We're the Gap Gang, my lord,' says I.

"'Well,' says he, 'if that don't suit you, hurry up and take the cottage and have done with it. I'm gettin tired *o this messin about business.'*

"'Beg pardon, my lord,' says I, 'but what are we to ave for our trouble, when we ave took it?'

"'Why,' says he, very pleasant, 'if you're good, Friend George, when the job's done, per-raps,' says he, 'per-raps I'll give you a lift back to France in my lugger layin on the beach there.'

"'Our lugger, sure-ly, my lord,' says I.

"'No, my friend,' says he, 'it was the late lamented Diamond's. Now it's our noble Emperor's, Gorblessim! - a derelict picked up on the igh seas by one of His Majesty's frigates.'"

The treble ceased.

"Pretty position for the genelmen o the Gap Gang, ain't it?" came the black and bitter voice. *"Shot takin the place, or hung if you don't."*

"Ah," came the treble again, *"it wouldn't take me long to do somethin to him. See. Sow!"*

"Only you'd ave to get somebury to old is ands first," grumbled Red Beard.

"Scream!" said the fat man, unheeding. *"I'd make his soul talk."*

The brutal Toadie rumbled off into laughter.

CHAPTER LII

HARE AND HOUND

I

Brutes!

But - they knew nothing of the man-hole they were clustered round.

The boy's heart soared.

He passed on, as quiet as a mole.

Burrowing beneath the lowest hell, he had heard the voices of those in torment within hand's touch of him.

Now heaven opened its far door. He crawled towards the light. It was no longer a star; it was an eye, the eye of a soul, the Soul of Souls. And it was loving him.

The boy crawled on.

The great earth, warm and dark about him, gave him strength. She was a friendly great beast, breathing and blowing all round him. He could hear her, and feel her. On Beachy Head he had been a fly crawling on her hide; now he was the same fly swallowed. He was creeping along her gullet towards her mouth. Motherly old thing, she covered him well, and he was grateful to her. That good thick flesh of hers stood between him and that which he did not care to contemplate. As he crawled he kicked her in the ribs to show he recognized that she meant well.

The light was growing on him now. The wind blew on his damp forehead. He could see the round of sky, blue against the black arch of brick.

Warily he peeped through the screen of tamarisk that veiled the opening.

The creek lay a few feet below. Across it, the smooth side of the Wish flowed upward.

A sentinel crowned the little hill, but his face was seaward.

Otherwise the coast was clear.

No!

On the slope of the Wish, facing him, a man was lying.

II

The man was lying on his back half-way up the slope, reading a little brown book.

Kit could not see his face; but he had no need.

Well he knew those buck-skin breeches, those mud-spattered tops, those tall knees.

"Who's that bloke?" whispered a voice at his ear.

"The officer commanding the French. Hush!"

"Crikey!" whispered Knapp, much impressed, and peering through the tamarisk. "Ain't he got a pair o legs on him neether?"

Before Kit could stop him, he had brushed past and dropped into the creek, light as a feather.

For a moment he squatted there, monkey-fashion, blinking after the darkness.

The sun shone on his naked back, ridged and rippling. A little man, he was solid as a boulder: thighs tremendous, shin-bones great and bowed. Such fists too! such feet!

Kit leaned out. For better or worse, the thing was done now. No good calling him back, no good cursing him. Better make the best of it.

"You've got a clear run," whispered the boy. "Hug the far bank, so the sentry on the Wish can't see you; stick to the creek as far as you can; and when you leave the shore, take a wide sweep towards the Downs, to avoid their sentries; and then *run*, man! - *run* as you never ran before!"

"I'll run, man, run fast enough soon as you done talkin," replied the Cockney cheekily, hopping across the creek to the shelter of the far bank. "Be in Lewes afore you're back to the guv'nor, I'll lay. Ta-ta."

He was away down the creek, running like a monkey, finger-tips touching the ground.

Kit, thankful to tears, watched the sun on the man's ridged back, as he stole away.

Surely, he was through now.

A sound made him look up.

III

The Gentleman had not stirred. He was reading aloud, and loving what he read.

> "Little lamb, who made thee?
> Dost thou know who made thee?"

Heaven send Knapp had not heard; but he had.

Up bobbed the black shaven pate out of the creek, much as Kit had often seen the head of a coot bob up in one of the moorland tarns of his own Northumberland.

The little man stood listening, the sun on his shoulders, careless of discovery.

The voice on the hill, loving and laughing, drew him like a syren's.

Was the man mad?

He was climbing up out of the creek on to the grass.

Kit swept the tamarisk aside, and waved at him furiously. The little man soothed him with mocking hand, and crept on.

Kit dared not shout; he could not catch the other. What could he do? Watch and pray, with sickening heart.

"Little lamb, I'll tell thee,
Little lamb, I'll tell thee:
He is called by thy name."

Beautiful as it was, the boy could not listen. His soul was in his eyes, and his eyes on Knapp.

The little man was now behind the reader, and stalking him on hands and knees.

What on earth was he up to?

A horrible thought wrenched the boy's heart.

Would Knapp stab the other as he lay?

If so, could he stand by and see that little baboon-thing with the hairy bosom and leg-of-mutton fists murder in cold blood a noble gentleman to whom he owed his life?

Then he remembered thankfully that Knapp had no weapons.

"Little Lamb, God bless thee!

Little Lamb, God bless thee!"

Knapp had stopped now, and seemed bending over the other. Then he deliberately thrust his hand into the face beneath him.

The Gentleman sat up, snatching for his sword.

"Tweak his conk!" popped a Cockney voice - "the conk of a lord!" And he was up and away, and down the slope with the merriest spurt of laughter.

The Gentleman was on his feet in a second, pursuing, a smear of blood at his nose.

Knapp heard him.

"Chise me!" he called, and came swinging down the slope at his ease, a smug grin on his face.

He was the fastest man but one South of Thames that day, and how was he to know that one was after him?

If he was not aware of it, Kit, watching with all his eyes, was.

The Gentleman was hounding at the other's heels, swift, silent, terrible.

"Run!" screamed the boy.

The rifleman glanced over his shoulder.

"God A'mighty!" he yelled. "E's catchin me."

The light went out of his face. Fists and knees woke to

sudden life and began to hammer furiously. The long easy swing became a terrific pitter-patter. Flinging back his head, he set himself to run the race of his life.

IV

Knapp was naked, and trained to a tick.

The Gentleman was the faster, and the slope helped his long legs; but he was booted and spurred.

Kit watched the smooth swoop of the one, and the terrific bob-a-bob-bob of the other. He was reminded of an eagle he had once seen stooping at a rabbit on the Cheviots.

Each was running for his all, and each knew it; but the Gentleman was having the best of it.

Knapp, running with his head as well as with his heels, was making straight for the creek.

On the flat, among the boulders, he, naked-nimble, would be on better terms with the booted Gentleman.

But - he would never get there. Kit saw it at a glance.

Down the hill he came with pounding fists, and great knees going. His head was flung back, his face screwed tight.

He had the lion's heart, this naughty little man. Death, swift and terrible, cast the shadow of its wings over him. He could not see it, but he could feel it overhead, swooping, swooping. He would not look back. His mistake made, he would do his desperate best to retrieve it. At least he would show the world how a Borderer can die.

Behind him the Gentleman, the wind in his hair, was feeling for his throat.

Another moment and that hub-bub of beating heart and running legs would stop for ever - skewered.

Kit could not bear it. Casting disguise aside, he leapt into the creek, and snatched a pebble.

"Chuck!" screamed the rifleman, and jinked like a hare.

Kit saw the gleam of a white waistcoat, and flung with all his might.

The pebble sped true as that which slew Goliath.

It took effect between the fourth and fifth button. Down went the Gentleman with a windy groan, as though the soul was being sucked out of his body.

Knapp, the pressure relieved, was his Cockney self again in a second. He swung on at a leisurely trot with the flick of heel, and swagger of elbow, peculiar to the crack taking his ease.

"Thank-ye!" he called, pert and patronising. "Lucky shot!"

"Run, fool, run!" yelled Kit. "The sentry!"

On the crest of the hill, against the sky-line, the sentry was kneeling as he took aim.

"What! - eh! - oh! - im? - blime!" and Knapp buckled to again in earnest.

The sentinel fired.

It was a long shot; but the man was a Grenadier of the Guard, and picked at that.

Up went Knapp's arms, and down into the creek he stumbled, there to fall on his face. Up again to run a little further; down once more; turned head over heels; up again and out of sight.

Kit's heart rose and fell with the little man.

What to make of it? - was he hard hit? - or was he at his eternal fooling once more?

CHAPTER LII

OLD TOADIE

I

He had no time for further questions. He must see to his own line of retreat.

The Gentleman was winded, and nothing more. The opening of the drain was discovered. No matter. It had done its work, or would have when once it had seen him home.

He clambered up the bank, brushed through the tamarisk, back into the comfortable darkness.

Thank heaven! Blob, the faithful, was still there.

He marked the cheerful gleam of the lantern, a tiny red spark in the darkness.

As he shuffled rapidly along he saw the patch of light on the floor beneath the man-hole.

But - was he mistaken? - or was not that patch, dim and dappled before, bright now as the moon?

He stopped. His heart was thumping so that he almost expected the covering drain to crack, and reveal him to the world.

Suddenly the patch vanished. All was darkness save the red eye of Blob's lantern far away.

Then that too went out.

The blackness was stifling, horrible. He opened his mouth to draw breath.

Then the light at the man-hole appeared again, shining now no longer on the floor, but on a man's head, bristling, and with huge ears.

Some one was squatting in the drain.

His heart that had been racing brought up bump.

"Any one there, Toadie?" came a voice through the man-hole.

"Only the boy," rumbled the man in the drain.

The words woke Kit to his position. With a ghastly effort he confirmed his mind and faced the situation.

There was one thing for it - to make for the opening, and trust his heels.

Better to be shot down in the open, anyway, than killed in the drain like a rabbit.

He turned round.

As he did so, a hand appeared at the opening, and swept back the tamarisk. A smiling face showed at the mouth of the drain.

"Tiger, Tiger, burning bright
In the forest of the night,"

came the voice of a playful ogre. "Did you ever hear of a man called Blake, Little Chap? One of God's own."

As he said it, a door slammed violently; a great gust of wind rushed past the boy down the drain.

Blob, the faithful, had obeyed his orders.

The boy was alone in Hell, and the Devil was stalking him.

II

Kit turned round.

Under the man-hole squatted old Toadie. The light bathed his hunched shoulders, his receding forehead, his projecting teeth.

The horror of it, the darkness, here in the bowels of the earth, hidden from sun and wind and light of heaven, undid the boy.

He tried to scream and could not. He battered madly at the bricks, caging him like an iron destiny, and only hurt his hands.

Surely, surely God would hear him!

Toadie began to hop towards him - hop - hop - hop.

The boy was breathing stertorously through his nose, almost snorting. The saliva was dribbling down his chin. He sank in a heap against the bricks and said,

"Hullo!"

"Ello!" came a deep voice. *"Feel sick?"*

"I don't know," giggled the boy, crouching limp on the brick-floor.

He knew now what those rabbits he and Gwen had ferreted with glee felt, old Yellow Jack worming down the burrow after them.

Yes: it was nicer to ferret than to be ferreted.

Nicest of all perhaps to be the ferret and suck blood, suck blood, suck blood, glued between the eyes of your victim.

Again the boy giggled.

The horror was passing. It was only a nightmare now, too terrible to be true, and a familiar nightmare. To be hemmed in thus in darkness, an ogre creeping in upon him, he just a throbbing heart and breathing nostrils.... Often before ... in life, in death, in dreams.... He didn't know, and didn't greatly care.... Time to wake soon.... Mother or old Nan would knock in a minute.... This sort of dream always ended in that knock.

He beckoned to the hopping toad, smiling. They might just as well be friends. Mother's knock would disturb them soon enough.

A noise roused him from his waking death.

It was the shuffling of feet.

Old Toadie heard it too, and snarled across his shoulder.

"Who the hell's that?"

In the darkness there was a falling flash.

It was Blob; Blob, the brave, who had fulfilled his orders and more. Loyal to his brother-boy, he had slammed the door as bidden, and, himself, the wrong side of it, had come to Kit's assistance.

After all he was a boy, and was not the young gentleman a boy? - and is not all the world against boys? - Boys that must hold together, or they will surely all be lost. Kit heard and lived anew.

III

Before him in the darkness was a muffled tumult. Out of it came Blob's plaintive squeak,

"Give over squeegin"

And the bass reply,

"I'll squeege your eart out !"

"Hullo! hullo! hullo! - what's forrad there?" came the Gentleman's echoing voice, as he crept towards them.

Kit scuffled down the drain, and tripped over a tumbling mass. It writhed; it stank; it was hot; it had two voices that growled and squeaked.

"Well done, Blob!" he panted. "Which is you?"

"Oi'm me," came a smothered treble from the heart of the tumble.

The boy's hand felt a shirt, warm and wet.

"Is that you?" prodding with his dirk.

"G-r-r, you young -"

Kit slid the dirk home. He was surprised to find how smoothly the steel ran in. It was not hard, then, to kill a man, and it was strangely pleasing.

The man shivered and relaxed.

"Is that old Toadie you've got there?" called the Gentleman, crawling leisurely along.

"It was."

"What you doing to him?"

"Killing him."

"Ah, well," said the Gentleman, *"I never cared much*

for old. Toadie. We weren't simpatico. If you care to wait a minute I'll -"

"Can't," gasped Kit. "No time. Now, boy, hurry!"

Blob crawled out from beneath the dead man.

"Anudder pennorth for Blo-ub!" he gurgled, and added jealously, one hand on the corpse, "He's moine. Oi killed un first."

"Never mind about that! This way."

There was one chance and one only. The door blocked one end; the Gentleman the other; the only exit was the man-hole. They must risk it.

"Here, Blob! - up here! - quick now! - give us a leg!"

Blob gave him a heave. Up he went into the light, like a cork from a bottle. Staying himself on his elbows, he hung, half in the hole, half out of it, the light dazzling him.

A roar of laughter smote him in the heart.

Blinking, he looked about him.

Above waved the sycamores, breeze-stirred and dark, and walling him round, the Gap Gang.

Kit's first thought was to drop.

Two soft arms seized him from behind; a sickening breath was on his cheek; a smooth face pressed his; and a fawning treble was saying in his ear with appalling tenderness,

"Let ole George elp you, Lovey."

CHAPTER LIV

THE PARSON'S AGONY

I

The Parson stamped up and down the loft, gnawing his thumb.

Those long shots from the rear had ceased half an hour ago. A tall Grenadier drooped across the wall. How should he have known there was one in the cottage could reach out a fatal finger and tap him on the forehead at two hundred yards?

The Parson's jolly face was haggard.

Now and then he peered out of the seaward window, listening. On the knoll all was still. He could see nothing, could hear nothing. Blue Knickers had withdrawn; he could mark no prowling figures. Only among the tree-trunks a pale wisp of smoke meandered upwards, telling of a camp-fire behind.

About him was the drowsy buzz-z-z of an August noon. A cabbage butterfly sailed by. The creature's insufferable airs annoyed him. The fate of Nelson, the life of a noble lad, these were nothing to it, curse it for its callousness!

The minutes passed. The silence was so oppressive that he could hear it. It stifled him.

What an age the boy was! Good heavens! - he could have got to the mouth of the drain and back half-a-hundred times by now! What was the delay? - Things must have gone awry! Yet how could they? - It was always the way! There was no trusting any living soul but yourself! Why the devil couldn't he be in two places at once? - It was *damnable!*

He pulled himself together with a jerk.

Here he was becoming unjust, irritable, womanish; everything he had always most despised in a man of action.

A shout came to him from seaward.

A shot followed.

The perspiration started to his forehead. He ran to the ladder-head.

In the dimness below he could see the old foretop-man sitting alert beside the black square of the open trap.

Piper was stooping forward, one great hand curved at his ear, listening intently.

"Piper!"

"Sir."

"All well below there?"

"Well, sir, I'm not justly sure. A minute back I seemed to feel like a gush o wind -"

"Then hail the boy, man!"

"Boy Hoad! below there!" in stentorian tones.

The only answer was a rush of air through the open trap, and the muffled slam of a door, house-shaking.

II

The Parson ran down into the cellar.

Blob's lantern glimmered on the floor, but there was no Blob.

He felt the door, cold to his hands as a corpse. It was shut fast as death. The catch had snapped; but the bolts were not home.

His first impulse was to open; his second to refrain. A man with a musket anywhere in the drain could not miss him. And he once down, the door open, all was over! - the cottage stormed, the despatches taken, old man Piper slain, and Nelson lost.

His ear against the clammy iron, he listened. Yes; outside the door he could detect the sound of faint breathing.

A distance away, he could hear the scuffling of feet.

He saw it all. They had shot Blob, who lay without, breathing his last. The door, left unguarded, had slammed, and they were nabbing Kit and Knapp in the drain.

His hand was upon the catch once more. Should he go? - dared he stay?

His spirit wrought within him.

Strong man though he was, he was whimpering in the darkness.

To slink behind that iron door was eternal shame; to go was inevitable ruin. Could he save his own old skin at the cost of that boy's? And yet he could not get away from the remorseless fact that to save his own skin might be to save his country.

His agony was short but terrible. The patriot prevailed over the man. The discipline of twenty years' soldiering had taught him life's hardest lesson - to sacrifice his feelings to his duty. He made his choice, and chose the path that has always seemed best to Englishmen in such case.

He slammed the bolts home.

He was up the ramp in a moment, and had banged the trap-door behind him.

Old Piper turned from the loop-hole.

"Seems there's summat up yonder behind the trees, sir.

I yeard - Ah! what'll that be?"

From behind the knoll came a sudden holloa, then an uproarious burst of laughter.

"They've got em, by God!" The old man swung his chair about with lion-like eyes. "By your leave, sir, you must go to them lads."

The Parson was tearing off coat and cravat.

"I'm going.... I'll slip out of the dormer-window so as to leave the door shut."

He sped up the ladder, and down again in a twinkling.

"Here are the despatches! If I go down, it'll take em ten minutes to rush the place and give you time to burn the papers. Here are my pistols! one for the first French-man, and t'other - well, you're a better man than I am, Piper, you know what's right, but -"

"I'll trust my Maker before the Gap Gang," said the old man. "He'll understand.... Good-bye, sir. God help you."

"He will," cried the Parson. "It's His battle. Good-bye, Piper. I'm cut to the heart to leave you. But -"

He was up the ladder and out of the window in a moment, stealing across the greensward, Polly in one hand, and Knapp's bugle in the other.

No spatter of fire greeted him from the knoll; no flitting figures retreated before him. All was peace, and the fair breeze ruffling the sycamores.

The Gap Gang were at some bloody business behind the trees.

CHAPTER LV

PRETTY POLLY-KISS-ME-QUICK

Kit's life stopped short.

"That's one on em. Where's t'other?" growled Beardie.

"Oi'm here," said Blob, and thrust up, pink and impassive, in his cheek an obvious slice of apple.

"That's right," said Fat George in sleek, caressing voice. "Give the genelman your and, my dear. He'll elp you out. There you are! There's no call for *you* to be scared. *You're* among old friends."

The Gang had gathered round the hole.

Beardie on his hands and knees was peering down into the drain.

Then he threw up his head with a savage roar.

"My God! they've done old Toadie."

He burst through the crowd at the boy, eyes and beard ablaze.

Kit, tight-clutched in Fat George's arms, shut his eyes.

There flashed before his mind a lonely figure, bound and buffeted in the palace of a high-priest eighteen hundred years ago. He saw it, patient among its persecutors, with the eyes of perfect vision, and grew strangely calm and comforted.

These evil men appeared to him in a clearer, a purer light. For one splendid second he was sorry for them.

"Father, forgive them," he prayed, and added aloud, "Good-bye, Blob."

The voice at his ear brought him back from heaven.

"Stidy, Beardie! - You're spiling sport. Ave the Mossoos twigged anything up?"

"Nay," said Dingy Joe. "They're a'ter the naked chap."

"Then we've got this little bit o business all to ourselves, the Genelmen o the Gap Gang ave. Let's take im up among the trees, and gag im first."

Was God in heaven? would He allow it?

As though in answer, close at hand a bugle sounded.

The boy had a vision of a winged figure, sword in hand, swooping wrathfully down upon them.

Surely he knew it - that swoop, that sword, that splendid rage.

It was St. Michael, the Archangel, in the famous picture by Guido Reni, a copy of which hung in the drawing-room at home.

"Remember the crew o the Curlew, men!" roared a mighty voice.

The arms about the boy loosened.

"The sogers!" shrilled Fat George, and bolted with a scream.

The rest followed in cataract rout. They pelted past the lad, bellowing, bleating: a tumult of arms, legs, aweful eyes in aweful faces. Only Beardie had the strength of mind to aim a smashing blow at the boy's head as he fled, and he missed.

"Make for the cottage, boys!" thundered the Parson, storming by. "Oh, Polly, my love and my lady!" and his sword flashed and sang and swept against the sky.

"Grenadiers!" rang an imperious voice from out of the ground.

Kit jumped round.

The Gentleman's head was thrust through the manhole; his eyes sweeping the greensward.

Fighting Fitz had seized the situation in a glance. Could he thrust his Grenadiers between the boys and the cottage, victory was his.

Lifting himself on his hands, his head thrown back, he sent the singing voice that the veterans of the Prussian Guard had heard at Marengo out of the cloud as Kellerman's Green Brigade roared down on them - he sent it swinging over grass and knoll,

"À la maison, mes enfants!"

Kit did not hesitate. Dirk in hand, he leapt at the head flashing in the sun. Here, in the heat and hell of battle, he had no thought of mercy.

The Gentleman heard the patter of his coming, and swept about.

"Sold again, Little Chap!" he laughed, and bobbed underground.

The chance was gone. There was not a second to be lost.

"This way, Blob!" yelled the boy, and dashed up the knoll, making for the cottage.

CHAPTER LVI

THE RACE FOR THE COTTAGE

I

And it was full time.

As he stormed up the knoll, he heard upon his right the clink of arms, and the sound of a Frenchman shouting.

Down through the sheltering sycamores he plunged, and burst out into the open.

A tall Grenadier, who had been sentry upon the shingle-bank, was racing up on his right across the greensward, screaming as he ran.

His yells were of effect. Half a dozen ragged ruffians bobbed up from behind the broken wall in the rear, and seeing only the boys, made fiercely for them.

It was a race for the cottage; and the door of the cottage was shut.

That dead mask of wood stared at Kit blankly. Had it no eyes? no soul? no understanding? was it not English, heart of oak, its life sucked these centuries

Alfred Ollivant

from the breast of the same mother? could it not *feel* his agony?

"Piper! Piper! the door's shut!"

"*Ay, sir, but it wun't be drackly-minute,*" came a straining voice from within; and the boy could hear the rending of torn boards, and the splintering of terrific hatchet-work.

The Grenadier with set teeth and blue-black muzzle was launching forward with huge strides.

Kit could hear the rattle of his cartridge-pouch flopping as he ran.

Would the door open? if so, which would reach it first?

"Faster, Blob, faster!"

"Oi'd run faaster, if ma legs would," panted Blob, lumbering behind.

He was doing his best; but he was no match for the fawn-footed gentleman, who led him. Lumps of ghostly clay, inherited from a long line of furrow-following ancestors, clung to his heels, impeding him.

Kit gripped his dirk and ran.

His eyes were on the Grenadier, a black and yellow fellow, with a wart between the brows. That wart held Kit's imagination. It sickened him. It was just his luck to have to deal with a warted man, when he had always loathed warts! But for the wart he felt he could have been heroic.

At the thought the tide of his humour welled within him; and the Grenadier was amazed to see a smile in the eyes of this boy with the long face, ghastly-pale, racing against him.

Taken off his guard, he smiled too.

So each ran towards the other, whom he meant to kill, with smiling eyes.

II

The cottage door began to open slowly, so slowly.

The boy could see the old foretop-man in the darkened passage. A hatchet was in his mouth; he was handling the door with one hand, and his chair with the other.

So easy for a whole man to open the door, so hard for the disabled seaman!

The Grenadier, hounding with huge strides, was already almost there.

"Man on your left, Piper!" the boy screamed.

"All right, sir!" mumbled the old seaman. "Give me cutlass room - all I ask!"

He put both hands to the wheels of his chair, and spun out into the open, hatchet in mouth.

As he did so, round the corner of the cottage swooped

Alfred Ollivant

half a dozen yelling cut-throats.

"Take the Frenchman, sir!" roared the old man. "I'll tackle these -"

With a wrench, he slewed his chair, spun the wheels furiously, and shocked into the cloud of them.

The Grenadier launched at his back, bayonet at the charge.

"Coward!" gasped Kit, still five yards away, and flung his dirk.

It stuck in the ground at the man's feet, and tripped him. He plunged forward on hands and knees, and gathered himself as a wave about to break.

As he rose, Kit leapt on him, naked-handed.

The man was hurled through the open door, and brought up against the inner wall with an appalling shock.

For a moment man and boy hugged cheek to cheek.

Kit's legs were round the other's hips, his arms about the other's neck.

"Beast! don't bite!" he gurgled, as the man munched his shoulder; and the image of Gwen, who when hard-driven used her teeth effectively, rose before him.

The image faded. The man had the under-grip, and was squeezing his soul out. Another moment, and his ribs must go.

"Blob!" he choked.

A dark something shot through the door and shocked against the Frenchman.

"Where'll Oi kill him?" asked a voice.

"Where you like," muttered Kit, swooning.

A hand rose and fell.

The man relaxed his grip. Kit could feel him fading and fading away, as the life oozed out of him. He was a-horse on Death.

"Assez," muttered the Frenchman sleepily, swayed and fell.

Dazed and dizzy, Kit staggered to his feet.

A shadow darkened the door; a strange voice cried in horrible triumph:

"*Our'n!*"

Two pistols lay on the table. Blindly the boy snatched both.

"Now!" he said, as one in a dream, and, shoving a pistol against the man's bare and shaggy bosom, fired.

Blindly he stepped over the fellow's body, and out into the open.

A man, on hands and knees, was crawling away round the corner of the cottage; another lay dead on his face across the way.

Before him he saw a little cloud of men, and the gleam of a silver head thrusting out moon-like from among them.

Blindly he fired into the brown, and blindly followed up.

One man fell; others slunk away, snarling.

III

The whole thing was over.

Buzzing August prevailed again.

"Are you hurt?" sobbed Kit.

"No, sir, I'm bravely, thank you. Properly shook up, though." The old man was heaving like the sea. "They'd no knives nor nothin, only one on em, and Boy Hoad stuck him as he passed. They hurt emselves more'n me. I bluv I'm a better man above the waist nor ever I were. All the juice like goes to my arms now I've no legs - that's how I reck'n it be."

"We must get in before they come again. Quick!"

"Ah, they won't come again, sir. Easy satisfied, the Gap Gang. Got no guts because they got no God.... Ah, here's Mr. Joy!"

The Parson was coming across the greensward, high and mighty as a turkey-cock.

The Gentleman was standing among the sycamores, laughing.

He waved his hand to the boy.

"Congratulations, Little Chap," he called.

"Don't accept em," snarled the Parson. "Posing impostor! - coxcomb! - cad!"

"What! has he wounded you, sir?" asked old Piper.

"Pinked me in the calf, the coward!" snapped the Parson. "He's not a gentleman. I always knew he wasn't! - Frenchified feller!"

He looked round with grim satisfaction.

"So you've been busy, too. I reckon they're half a dozen short o what they were before the sally. And we've got our man through, too!"

He pointed across the plain.

From the foot of the Downs a string of Grenadiers were coming back at the double.

They had no prisoner.

III - THE SHADOW OF THE WOMAN

CHAPTER LVII

THE PARLEY

I

The door was shut, and all once again darkness in the cottage of the kitchen.

Something slithering along the floor caught Kit's ear.

Then he saw that Blob had by the collar the Grenadier he had killed, and with groanings and pantings and strange animal noises, was hauling his victim towards the dark mouth of the cellar.

"Leave him alone," called Kit sternly. "D'you call that a respectable way to treat the dead?" He laid a piece of sacking over the corpse, adding - "That'll do to cover him up till we can bury him properly."

"But Oi don't want un buried," whined Blob. "Oi be goin to keep un agin the fifth o Novambur - guy for Bloub!"

"You're going to do no such thing, you disgusting little

beast. You'll get your tuppence, and you don't deserve that."

"Ah," said Blob cunningly, "this un'll be worth a little better'n tuppence surely. You knaw who he be, Maaster Sir?"

"Who then?"

Blob dropped his voice to a mysterious whisper.

"Squoire Nabowlin. Mus. Poiper tall me."

"Who?"

"Squoire Nabowlin," reiterated the boy. "Nabowlin Bounabaardie - the top Frenchie. See the legs on him! red and gold and buttons and all."

II

The Gentleman was sauntering across the grass towards the cottage, his hands behind him.

The Parson brushed aside the mattress, and thrust out, snarling.

"Keep your distance, sir, or take the consequences."

The Gentleman strolled forward.

"Ah, there you are, Padre. I came to have a little chat."

Alfred Ollivant

"Stand fast then, and state your business! - This is war, not play-acting. I hate your silly swagger."

"Well, in the first place I thought you might care to know that your man's through."

"Thank you for nothing. Knew that already."

"But you know - there's always a little but in this world - hateful word, isn't it? - but, but, but - he's too late."

"What ye mean?"

"I mean that Nelson reached Dover last night, and sails this afternoon. The *Medusa*'ll be off here at dawn if this breeze holds."

Dover!

The Parson had forgotten Dover. Chatham, the Admiralty, Merton! in his note he had urged Beauchamp to send messengers post-haste to all three; but Dover!

"That's all right," he called calmly. "I've a galloping express half-way there by now, thank ye."

The other shook his head with a grave smile.

"It's sixty miles in a bee-line from Lewes to Dover, and plenty of public-houses on the road. No Englishman could do it under eight hours on a hot day. If your romance-man gets there by midnight, he'll do well - and still be hours too late."

The Parson remained unmoved.

"It makes no odds," he called loftily. "If you want to know, Nelson's not in England."

"Is he not? where is he then?"

"Why, where he ought to be - hammering the Combined Squadron somewhere St. Vincent way."

"How d'you know?"

"He's my cousin on my father's side. I heard from his mother only - only -"

"By last night's mail!" suggested the Gentleman. "May I ask then why you trouble to send a galloping express to Dover to stop him?"

The Parson's face darkened. He thrust forward.

"And may I ask how *you* know Nelson got to Dover last night?"

The other shrugged.

"I have agents."

The Parson nodded grimly.

"Yes; I've a list of em."

"*Your* countrymen, *my* friends" - with a malicious little bow - "the Friends of Freedom."

The Parson leaned out, black as night.

"Friends of Freedom be d -d!" he thundered -

"bloody traitors!"

The other raised a shocked hand.

"Holy Padre! Reverend Father! *Virginibus puerisque*, if you please."

The Parson turned to find Kit at his elbow.

"I'm only a deacon," he grumbled. And it's only what you French gentry call a *fashion de polly*."

"I am not French - or only on my mother's side," replied the other gently.

"Well, Frenchified then - it's all the same, ain't it? - all that bowin and scrapin and humbuggin business - you know what I mean."

"Yes, yes, I know, my polished friend.... And as to these same *couleur-de-rose* gentry I understand your feelings entirely, and for the very good reason that I share them. And I don't mind telling you in confidence that as to the bulk of them your description is not too highly-coloured."

"And if *they're* that, what are *you*, I'd like to know?" shouted the Parson.

"I am an Irishman. I serve my country - I do not sell her."

"And are all Irishmen traitors?"

A gleam came into the other's eyes. He smiled frostily.

"All who are worthy of the name," he said....

"But to return to our sheep. They have served me, these sanguinary gentlemen, so I can't stand by and see them hanged, when I can save em. And to put it shortly - I want that despatch-bag, please!"

He came forward like a child, hand outstretched, and smiling charmingly.

The Parson flung out a finger and volleyed laughter.

"And he thinks he's going to get it! Ask pretty; don't forget to say please; and he shall have everything he wants, he shall, he shall. There's a lambkin! there's a little lovey!" He leaned out again. "And what you going to give us for it?"

"Why, a free pass-out, with all the honours of war."

"Thank you for nothing. Seems to me I can have a free pass-out whenever I like. I've just free-passed out a man. And I'm only a minute or two back myself from a little stroll with a lady."

III

The Gentleman sauntered forward.

"I am sorry to be so importunate," he said gravely, "but I *must* have those despatches and I mean to have them."

Alfred Ollivant

He stopped.

"The position is this: Nelson is *mine*." He brought down his right fist on his left. "*Nothing* can save him now - *nothing*. This time to-morrow, so sure as that sun will rise, he will be dead or on the way to Verdun. That has been arranged."

"*How?*" thundered the Parson. "*How* has it been arranged?"

The Gentleman was pacing to and fro before the window; and his eyes were down.

"It's enough for you to know," he said at last, "that I - I have influence with a lady, who - who has influence with Nelson."

"What *does* he mean?" whispered Kit.

The Parson had turned very white.

He knew that woman, by nature so noble; and he knew something of her history - the history of the shame of man.

"D'you mean to tell me *She's* going to sell *her* Nelson to that organ-grinder's monkey from Corsica?" he roared. "Because if you'll tell me that, I'll tell you you're a liar."

The Gentleman still paced before the window.

"I'll tell you nothing of the sort," he said. "She believes herself to be serving her country." He was speaking very slowly, almost mincing his words. "She has - has come into possession of information...."

The man, usually so self-possessed, stuttered and stopped dead.

"And how did she come into possession of that information, I wonder?" asked the Parson, slow and white.

The Gentleman flashed his face up.

"I'll put it in brutal English so that even *you* can understand. *I made a fool of a woman who thought she was making a fool of me.*"

There was a lengthy silence.

"And they call him the Gentleman!" came the Parson's voice at last - "the *Gentleman!*"

The other had resumed his pacing.

"He sneaks himself into the confidence of a lady," continued the Parson quietly. "He conceals his identity -"

Again the other flashed his eyes up.

"I did not!" he shouted, hammering with his hand. "The first words I ever spoke to her in the drawing-room at Merton were to tell her who I was. That night she told Pitt over his port. And Pitt told her - but there! - I needn't go into that.... And when she asked me what brought me to Merton, I answered truthfully - 'Love of adventure and the fairest face in Europe.'"

Alfred Ollivant

The Parson leaned out.

"I understand you now. You take advantage of that face of yours; you worm yourself into the confidence of a woman, a noble woman; and you -"

The Gentleman blazed appalling eyes up at him.

"And *you* have not seen my Ireland suffer!"

The Parson quailed before the white blast of the other's anger. It was as though a hail of lightnings had struck him.

"*His* Ireland! ass!" was the only retort he could think of.

"Nelson then let us put aside," continued the other, cold again. "There remain - you and the despatches. I want the despatches. You want yourselves. Shall we exchange?"

"No, we shan't," snapped the Parson.

"I know your straits," continued the other. "You're short of provisions -"

"Short of provisions!" guffawed the Parson. "Why, step this way, and I'll show you a boy with the bellyache."

"And short of men," the other continued, quite himself again. "What does your garrison consist of? - one holy padre, one half an old sailor, Monsieur Mooncalf, and Little Chap."

"And what's your own lot?" bellowed the Parson - "one dozen of sweepings of France, one dozen of the picked scum of our country, and one conceited young whipper-snapper, who swaggers about in breeches and boots all day *and was never on a horse in his life to my certain knowledge!*"

The Gentleman waved his hand.

"Take the consequences then," he said. "A rivederci."

"Take the consequences yourself!" roared the Parson - "you and your river dirties. I'll see your friends hung high as Haman yet."

The other shook his head.

"You won't live to see that, dear man," he said quietly, and turned away.

CHAPTER LVIII

THE PLANK CAPONIER

Kit was in the cellar stripping his belt and cartridge-pouch from Blob's Grenadier.

As he rose from his knees Piper hailed him.

"Mr. Joy callin you, sir."

The boy ran up the ramp. The old man, handling his musket, was peering through the Northward loop-hole.

"What is it?"

"Summat up yonder, sir."

The boy raced up the ladder.

The Parson was at the dormer looking towards the Downs, shimmering now in the fair evening.

"What's the meaning of this?" he said, pointing.

A great Sussex wain, top-heavy with hay, was drawing out of a farmyard among trees, a quarter of a mile away. A white horse was in the shafts, and a black in the lead. Two Grenadiers were at the head of the black leader, who was giving trouble. Others in shirt-sleeves were mounting to the top of the load.

"Old Gander's wain," said the Parson. "That's old mare Jenny in the shafts, and her three-year-old daughter in the lead. Ha, Miss Blossom! - That's your sort! - Knock em sprawling! - Teach the Mossoos to handle an English lady!"

A tall man ran out of the farmyard, a snow-storm of white-frocked children pursuing him; and even at that distance Parson and boy could hear them screaming laughter. The tall man snatched up one and kissed her. Then he took off his hat with an enormous sweep to the others, and turned.

"Humph! posing rather prettily this time!" muttered the Parson, watching kind-eyed.

On the top of the wain, clear against the sky, a tall figure now rose, and gathered the rope-reins in his hand.

The men at the leader's head jumped aside.

Up she went, sky-high.

The coachman handled her as a mother handles a wilful child. The wind was towards them, and they could hear him singing to her.

"Hum! he can handle the ribands a bit," muttered the Parson, watching intently. "Miss Blossom's never tasted a bit before."

The filly dropped, and flung forward with the shock of

a breaking wave.

The slope was with them. The old mare, with snarling head and backward ears, broke into a lumbering trot, snatching at her daug hter's tail.The wain began to gather weigh, creaking, jolting, jerking along.

The filly was tearing into her collar; the old mare, swept along by the pursuing wain, broke into a heavy gallop. The Gentleman, holding them hard, was singing to them as they came.

"Mean mischief, sir," called Piper from below.

"Jove, they do!" muttered the Parson, chin forward, and eyes flaming as he watched. "Like a Horse Artillery battery coming into action."

The wain leapt and swung and bounced along like a live thing.

"Ah, I thought so.... Pace too good.... He's dropping his load....Ah! - there goes another!"

A Grenadier was seen to fall with flapping tails, and another, and another; till the track of the thundering wain was strewn with men, who picked themselves up and pursued.

Only the intrepid coachman, his feet set deep, held his place, swaying to the swing of the wain.

The Parson gnawed his lip as he watched.

"What's it all mean, Piper?"

"Don't justly know what to make of it, sir."

"You can't get a line on him?"

"No, sir. He's slewed aside out o my range."

And indeed the Gentleman had swung his team to the left, as though to avoid the old man's fire. They were lurching along at a thundering gallop. It seemed as though the horses were fleeing from the wain.

The Parson was leaning far out of the window to watch.

"Round he comes!"

As he spoke, the Gentleman flung back with all his strength, and wrenched to the right.

Round came the leader; the wheeler, slithering, jerking, almost swept off her legs, as the wain came on top of her. Then the whole came thundering across the greensward at the gable-end of the cottage.

"Ca'ant be going to ram us, sir, surely?" shouted Piper.

The old man could see nothing now, but he could hear the roar of the approaching wain.

"I believe he is!" cried the Parson.

It was the boy's swift mind that first leapt to the Gentleman's plan.

"No, sir!" he screamed. "Don't you see? - He'll bring the waggon alongside at a gallop, jam it against the wall, and then -"

And then! the Parson saw it in a flash: - axemen at work on the door beneath the wain, and stormers through the dormer-window over the top.

"By God, you've got it!"

It must be stopped at all costs.

But how?

The wain was coming at the cottage from the flank. A shot from the left shoulder at an impossible angle at a galloping target - was that their only hope?

The Parson glanced wildly round.

The thunder of the wain and the singing voice of the coachman was in his ears.

An old plank was lying in the loft.

"Plank Caponier!" he yelled, pounced on it, and thrust it out of the window. "Now, Kit! - You're lightest! - There's your musket - loaded! - Blob, sit on this end with me!"

Kit, musket in hand, ran out on the plank.

He was standing on air.

"Steady!" hoarsed the Parson, blue eyes gleaming through the window. "Don't look down! Aim at her chest! Wait till you can see the roll of her eye!"

Kit heard nothing, saw nothing, but a foam-splashed breast, a nodding head, racing knees, and reaching feet.

All the world for him was in that black and shining bosom. It grew upon him as he looked. It was no more a chest. It was a cloud, about to burst on the world. He fired into the heart of it, sure he could not miss.

Up went the filly, fighting the air.

The boy saw her belly, her thighs, and the swish of her tail between her hocks.

Down she came in roaring ruin, the old mare an avalanche of snow burying her.

"In, Kit!" screamed the Parson.

"No, sir!" yelled the boy.

In a blinding light he saw the thing to do, and flashed to do it.

"The lynch-pins!"

Down he jumped, and dirk in hand raced for the tangle of horseflesh, black and white and heaving like an angry sea.

Swift as he was, the Gentleman was swifter.

Before the boy had touched ground, he was down from his perch, slashing at the tackle with his sword. Now he leapt to the mare's head, hurling her back into her breeching.

While Kit was yet twenty yards away, he was up again, standing on the shafts, reins in hand.

"Now, my lady!" came the high singing voice.

The brave old thing answered to it as though to a lover. She flung forward with a sob.

"I'll take the mare and the man!" panted the Parson, racing up behind, his curls almost cracking. "You go for the lynch-pins!"

He swept past, Polly in hand.

"Forgive me, Jenny!" he cried; and thrust home.

A spout of blood seemed to darken the sky, and deluge all. The wain brought up with a dreadful jerk.

"Home, sir, if you can!" shouted Piper from his loop-hole. "Here's the Grannydears!"

"Kit!" bawled the Parson. "Where are you?"

The lad crept out from under the wain.

"Got the lynch-pins?"

"Yes."

"Then come on!"

Under the fore-wheel the Gentleman was lying on his back, with closed eyes.

The boy stopped.

"Are you hurt, sir?"

The other shook a smiling head.

"Only shocked. Jerked off my box. Run, Little Chap, run! - or they'll bottle you."

"Kit, damn you!" stormed the Parson. "*Will* you run?"

Across the greensward half a dozen Grenadiers were hurling. The nearest dropped on his knee, and took deliberate aim at the boy.

The loop-hole clouded suddenly.

Out of it Death spoke.

The Grenadier toppled over on to his back with flapping hands. A moment he sat bolt-erect, a foolish-familiar look on his face - Kit somehow expected him to put his tongue out - then collapsed ghastly.

The boy made for the cottage.

Blob, leaning out of the dormer, chewing an apple, watched him with spiteful amusement.

"Say, Maaster Sir," he cried, as he spat and slobbered, "reck'n they'll catch you."

"Shall I unbolt the door, sir?" shouted Piper.

"You do, by God!" roared the wrathful Parson. "They're on our heels, fool!"

"How'll you manage then, sir?"

"Leave that to me, and stick to your shooting!"

A great water-butt stood at the corner, empty now.

The Parson, man of myriad resource, had trundled it beneath the dormer, and turned it upside down in a second.

"Up, boy!"

Kit was on it, and in through the window in a twinkle. The Parson followed.

The leading Grenadier came at him, bayonet at the charge. The Parson put the steel aside with his blade, and met the man fair in the face with his heel.

"Good punch!" he cried cheerily, and kicking the butt away from under him, scrambled into the loft.

He stood awhile both hands on his knees, heaving. Then he looked up, his blue eyes good and grinning.

"Prettiest thing I ever saw in my life!" he panted. "But, you young scaramouch! what the deuce d'you mean by stopping to chatter to that chap?"

"I thought he was hurt," gasped the boy panting against the wall. "He's my friend."

CHAPTER LIX

MISS BLOSSOM

"Pistol, please."

The Gentleman was standing beneath the dormer, one hand uplifted.

The Parson looked down at him.

"Well, you're a calm chap," he said with slow delight.

Better than anything in the world he loved a brave man.

"I know my man," replied the other in the same still voice.

He was far away in April twilight-land.

The fine face, gay as the morning a few minutes since, had now a wistful evening look. The shadows had fallen on it: rain was not far.

Even the Parson, blind-eyed Englishman that he was, noticed it, and was touched. After all the man was a boy, and a beaten boy.

"Are you hurt?" he gruffed.

"No - not hurt."

The Parson thought he understood.

"It was the pluckiest attempt I ever saw!" he cried with the generosity of the victor. "That black filly had never known the feel of a collar, till twenty minutes since.... I was to have broken her this autumn."

"She was the least bit awkward at the start," mused the other. "But she handled sweetly all the same."

"We had all the luck," continued the Parson. "But for that plank, you'd have brought it off. It'll be your turn next time!"

The other lifted his face swiftly.

"Ah, no," he cried, "you mistake. *That's* nothing! It's *this!*"

He pointed.

Fifty yards away the wain lay wrecked on the greensward, the old white mare crumpled in the shafts. She was stone-dead, and her muzzle, with its coarse long hairs, was resting on the quarters of her daughter.

"That's the worst of war," said the Gentleman in that remote voice of his. "*We* know; *they* don't."

"I expect it's all fairer than it seems," said the Parson huskily.

The other nodded.

"Have you a pistol?"

The filly was not dead. Lying on her side, she was lifting her head and craning back to gaze at her dead dam.

Something clutched the Parson by the throat. A veil was rent. For a moment he seemed to see the tragedy as the man beneath him saw it - the passion, the pathos of that blind suffering in the cause of another.

"Here!" he said hoarsely, handing down a pistol.

The Gentleman took it, and seeing a pale face peering behind the other's shoulder,

"She's not suffering, I think. Don't look, Little Chap."

He walked back to the filly.

Lying still now, her head along the greensward, she watched him coming; snorting through full-blown nostrils.

He knelt at her head, pulling her ear, and caressing her.

"There, then, there! - It's all over now, little woman. I've come to comfort you."

CHAPTER LX

THE TWO PRAYERS

I

The Gentleman was walking away into the sunset.

The Parson turned from the dormer, and his eyes were wet.

"And, now, my boy," he cried, "you know what a gentleman is."

The words loosed the fountains of laughter in the lad's heart.

"I thought, sir, that you said -"

"You thought wrong," snapped the Parson. "I said nothing of the sort."

He swung round on Blob and kicked him.

"What fur why?" whimpered Blob.

"Teach you!" cried the Parson. "Want some more, eh? Then behave yourself. I'm sick o your nonsense."

He reached up to the rafter.

"Eat and sleep - that's the whole duty of man just at present. Blob, take Piper his rations, and ask him to forgive an old soldier who's a bit short in the temper in action - and do the same yourself, my boy. Here, Kit."

They snatched a hasty meal.

Outside the dusk was falling.

The Parson brushed the crumbs off his cravat.

"And now will you take first watch, or shall I?"

"I will, sir. I don't feel like sleep."

"Very well. Wake me when the moon dips behind the Downs, or earlier if there's a sign of the soldiers."

Kit took his post at the dormer. The other slipped off his coat.

"I'm not much of a Parson as you may have found out," he muttered, "still I am an Englishman." And he plumped down on his knees defiantly.

His was a very short and simple prayer; the prayer tens of thousands of Englishmen were praying from their hearts at that time.

Kneeling in his shirt, Polly shining before him against the wall, he repeated it most earnestly.

The whispered words, so simple and heart-felt, reached the ears of the boy at the dormer.

"God bless our dear country; and God d - the French."

The waters of laughter came roaring up the boy's throat, and surged over, irresistible.

The Parson rose from his knees, and scowled at the lad's shaking shoulders.

"I suppose they're too proud to pray in *his* Service," he sneered. "Pack o pirates!" He took off his coat and folded it with thumps. "Yet I know one sailor who's not above paying his respects to his Maker - and that's Lord Nelson, of whom you may have heard. Seen him myself in the trenches at Calvi. I remember a great buck of a Dragoon Guardsman asking him,

"'Why d'you pray, little man?' 'Why,' says Nelson, simple as a child, 'because mother taught me.' Yes, sir," fiercely, "and that's why I pray - and jolly good reason too."

"Did she teach you that prayer?" asked Kit demurely.

"Bah! blurry young tarry-breeks!" muttered the other; and curling on the floor, his rolled jacket beneath his head, the old campaigner was off to sleep, Polly fair and faithful beside him.

II

The boy had the house to himself, and the world too. At last he could retire once more upon the Love within him.

He could pray - without words.

The sea was a plain shining beneath the moon. Against the light, inky sycamores ruffled, stars entangled in their leaves. On the shingle-bank the bear-skinn'd sentinel showed black against white waters.

The plain beauty of the night stole upon his mind. All was jewelled silence, save for the jar-r-r of the familiar goat-sucker from the foot of the hills, and the wash of the sea.

How calm it was, how strong, how radiant!

He had been far away. Now he was drawing near again. It was his once more. He possessed it all, all, all, and loved it as his own.

All day he had been the prisoner of his own distraught senses. And how comfortable it was, after the darkness of that life which is death, to resume the large love-liness of Life Unending.

Space and Time had no more meaning for him. He was again eternal and infinite. All this beauty of earth and sky and moon-wan water, it was not outside him, it was himself. He reached out a hand to pluck a handful of stars, and could not - because they were too close. You cannot pluck the jewels of your own heart.

Yet however deep he plunged into Eternity, the ache of Time was still present to his mind, remote indeed, on the farthest shores of memory, but always there, an ache that would not still. He felt the pain of it, and still more the pettiness. To him, sitting at the heart of things, drinking in the great night, they seemed

Alfred Ollivant

strangely mean and tawdry now, the excitements of the past day.

Let not your heart be troubled, came the voice of the Poet of Truth down the ages.

Was it worthy of a Son of God so to vex himself with the trivialities of this world?

What was war? what victory? what defeat?

True he must do his best for conscience' sake, but God would swing the stars across the heaven whether Napoleon landed or not. He would still march on His great way, though Nelson were lost.

Smiling to himself, the lad was wondering whether to the Maker of those stars, this earth, that sea, the issue of this business might be more than the issue of a squabble between two sparrows would be to him.

III

He crossed to the northward window.

The Downs surged before him like a wave, dull against the brilliant darkness. Overhead the slow stars trailed by, dipping, one after one, behind the dark curtain of hills. The moon climbed above the sycamores. Out on the plain something sparkled frostily. It was the bayonet of a sentinel, lonely-pacing in the moonlight.

The sight brought the lad back to earth.

How would it all end? Were these few bearskinn'd trespassers only the spray of seas to follow?

In a little while would England be flooded with them? Aghast, he peered seaward: and seemed to behold a black tide of men sweeping across the moon-drift. They deluged England. The fringe of them lapped about his own northern home. A man in a tree was shooting at Gwen running for her life, her hair behind her, screaming, "Kit!"

Something fell on the floor with a sharp tap, and stopped the shriek on the verge of his lips.

What was it?

Another tap. Something was bobbing briskly across the floor. He picked it up. It was a pebble, and must have come through the window.

Cocking his pistol, he rose.

"Down't shoot," said a low voice.

Alfred Ollivant

CHAPTER LXI

KNAPP'S RETURN

Beneath the window stood the little rifleman, white in the shadow of the house, and grinning up at him.

"How did you get through?"

"Slip through em, sir - h'easy as a h'eel."

"Don't talk so loud," whispered the boy. "Just hop on to the sill of the lower window. I'll see if I can haul you in."

"No, sir. I won't come in. I may be more usefuller outside. Keep em on the Key Whiff as the sayin is."

"Then keep still! don't jig! hug in here in the shadow of the house! I'll call Mr. Joy."

The Parson was at the window in a minute and listening to the man's story.

According to his own account Knapp had done the twelve miles to Lewes under the hour.

"Went slap away, as your orders was, sir, no foolin nor nothin, just slap bang through em - you ask

Mr. Caryll."

"Never mind about your feats," said the Parson shortly. "Did you see the Commandant?"

"O yes, sir. Ran straight away through the camp to his tent, where the flag were flyin, never bothered about no sentries nor nothin. Just as I trot up, a little bit of a butterfly lady like bob out o the tent, and when she see me - 'Beau, boy!' she squeals. 'Beau, boy! ere's a niked man! *Do* come and see!' And she jig up and down and tiddle her fingers at me, please as Punch.... Out come ole Whiskers, sword and all. 'You something something!' says he, and knocks her back into the tent. Then he run at me, roarin."

The little man was sniggering.

"I see by his eyes he meant it all, so -

"'Here, sir,' says I, 'somethin for yourself!' and chucks the note in his mug."

The Parson was breathing deep.

"And what then?"

"Why, sir, I'd nothin on me ony the dooks me God give me. So I up and I skip it."

The Parson leaned out, and smote at the man's shaven skull with the butt-end of his pistol.

"Ain't I done right, sir?" squeaked the little man, dodging back.

"You've sold us!" cursed the Parson, and he was white even in the moon.

"Hush, sir! hush!" cried Kit. "For goodness' sake, hush! They'll hear you."

"Hullo! hullo! what's all this?" came a voice from across the sward.

"Excuse me, sir!" whispered Knapp, unabashed. "I'd best be steppin it. Here are your papers, sir." He flung a packet through the window and flashed away.

The Gentleman sat on the wall in the moonlight.

"So your chap's back," he called in his friendly voice.

"Yes, sir," replied the Parson harshly, "and the soldiers on his heels two thousand strong, with a couple of Horse Batteries, and a company of Sappers to rig up a gallows for conceited young coxcombs who pose on walls in the moonlight."

"Very glad to see any friends of yours any time," replied the Gentleman. "But unless they come soon I'm afraid we shall miss. I'm off at dawn. But I'll see you again before going. Good-night."

He sauntered away.

The Parson turned, grinding his teeth.

Then he saw the boy's face, and laid a hand on his shoulder.

"Turn in, boy, and try to get a snooze. What tomorrow

brings Heaven knows, but we do know we shall want all our strength to meet it."

CHAPTER LXII

THE PARSON MUSES

The Parson opened his packet.

It contained a batch of newspapers dropped for him daily at Lewes by the coach, and not called for since last Saturday.

Ah, here we are!

The Times, Monday, August 19 - that was the day before yesterday.

Lord Nelson is arrived at Portsmouth.

Then the Gentleman was right!

He was here, the man his country had believed barring the passage of the Combined Squadron Vigo way.

Why had the watch-dog left his post?

We may infer from the circumstance of his Lordship's coming home, that information had reached him of the Combined Squadron having got into Ferrol.

He dared say they had. Where was the man should

have stopped them?

The Times, August 20.

Lord Nelson arrived at his seat at Merton in Surrey yesterday....

O, the Gentleman! the Gentleman! It was all true then!...

and will most probably attend at the Admiralty this day.

Probably attend!

And this was Nelson! his Nelson!

Victory, Spithead, August 18, 1805.

The Victory, with the fleet under my command, left Gibraltar twenty-seven days ago....

Nelson and Bronté.

That's right. Do the thing thoroughly if you're going to do it at all. Come home yourself, and bring your fleet with you. It might get in the way of the Combined Squadron if it stopped off Cadiz. Pity to be rude, you know!

As soon as Lord Nelson's flag was descried at Spithead, the ramparts, and every place which could command a view of the entrance of the harbour, were crowded with spectators. As he approached the shore, he was saluted with loud and reiterated huzzas, as enthusiastic and sincere as if he had returned crowned with a third great naval victory.

That third great victory, where was it now?

Poor little chap! poor little Nelson!

And what was this? The *Moniteur, Paris, August 12.* Boo-woo-woo.... Bob Calder's battle. [Footnote: Sir Robert Calder had fought an indecisive action with Villeneuve in July.] Bob Calder ought to be shot. Had em and then wouldn't hammer em. Call emselves sailors!

Vice-Admiral Calder stood off with thirteen ships, and left the Combined Squadron masters of the sea.

Masters of the Sea!

O good God! good God!

And what was Nelson doing?

The sudden arrival of Lord Nelson in the Metropolis, after so long an absence, and such arduous service, is a circumstance peculiarly interesting to the inhabitants, who were yesterday waiting in thousands about the Admiralty to give him a truly British reception. Many, of course, were disappointed in their object, and can only wait for another opportunity; but that, we have reason to believe, will occur this evening, as it is reported in the Naval circles, that his Lordship intends to pay a visit to Vauxhall Gardens, in honour of the birthday of the Duke of Clarence. The report is, in many points of view, entitled to consideration, for there is no other Gala in the season which affords such an infinite degree of nautical attraction.

Gala with a big G!

No other Gala in the season which affords such an infinite degree of nautical attraction.

Poor England! poor Nelson!

Alfred Ollivant

IV - THE GENTLEMAN'S LAST CARD

CHAPTER LXIII

NELSON'S TOPSAILS

Kit awoke with a start.

The dormer made a patch of diamond light in the dead of the wall, and the chill of dawn sharpened the air.

Blob was bending over him.

"Nelson's a-comin," he announced, much as he might have said breakfast was in.

Kit looked up into the round pink face, fresh as a daisy, and dewy-eyed above him.

"No!" he cried, and started to his elbow.

"He is though, lad," said the Parson at the window, very quiet.

Kit was beside him in a minute.

The mattress was down, and the Parson, leaning out into the blue, both hands on the sill, munched his thoughts.

"There's his tops'ls," said he, nodding east to where far across the waters a glimmer as of an iceberg hung in the dawn. "Take the glass and have a peep at her."

Mists still swathed the waters. Through them the sun peered ghostly, twinkling on the intripping tide beyond the shingle-bank.

And - there again! far away, poised between sky and sea, that glimmer of pearls.

It was some tall ship standing across the bay, the sun making glory on her royals.

"Make her out?"

"Yes, sir. She's a frigate right enough - can't be anything else with that height of canvas."

For in those dark days there was little business on the narrow seas other than the business of war. For weeks together the Channel waters were virgin of merchant-men. Trading bottoms dared not venture. Majestic three-deckers and tall frigates paced the seas alone. Anon a privateer swooped. Then a black smuggler scuttled from shore to shore between twilights. Rarely a vast convoy, herded like sheep, drove by, the dogs of war barking at the laggards. For the rest naked waters, ship-forsaken.

"It's the *Medusa*" said the Parson deliberately. "How soon'll she be off here, think you, sailor-boy?"

"I hardly know, sir. With this breeze I should think she might be abreast of us in two hours, and round the Head in four."

"And into the trap in five," mused the Parson.

"And Nelson bandaged, his back to the wall, facing a French firing party - all at about six o'clock of a sweet summer evening, August 22nd, the year of Our Lord, 1805."

He began to whistle meditatively.

The fine head, a-ripple with curls, was outlined against the sky. The face was keener than a few days back; the jolly laughing look was there no more. The blue eyes were touched to steel; and nose and jowl thrust forth with ominous grimness. It was the face of the determined fighter, hard-set and terrible.

He leaned out into the morning, whistling quietly, as fair a mark as any sharp-shooter on the knoll might wish, so Kit suddenly recalled, and plucked at him.

The other's arm was iron against him. The Parson made no move, seeming neither to feel, nor understand. A man of marble, he dwelt in the mind; brooding on that glimmer of pearls in the east.

Yet after a minute, as though the message had taken just that time to reach his remote brain, he answered the boy's thought.

"That's all right, Kit," he said, deliberate as in a dream. "The Gentleman has changed his dispositions. He's withdrawn from the knoll. Where the Gang are I don't know, but he has got the main of his Grenadiers on the landside still."

Kit peeped out of the Downs-ward window.

The old picquet on the plain, the old cordon of pacing Grenadiers, the old camp-fire with the drifting smoke and arms piled beside it; and further North, from beneath a thorn, the flash of a bayonet told of an outlying sentry posted there to watch for the relieving force no doubt.

Sick at heart, the lad turned and looked out over the Parson's shoulder.

On his right front humped the knoll, an islet set in a sea of turf, now only tenanted by dark sycamores, ruffling it in the dawn-wind.

Beneath him the greensward ran away to the shingle-bank. Beyond the crest of it, the mast of the lugger pricked up black against the sparkling water.

There was neither stir nor sound, save for the ripple of the tide, and overhead the eternal chirp of the sparrows, careless that history was being made about them.

All was still, all deserted.

As he looked, the lad's mind flamed to a thought.

"I say!" he whispered, clutching the Parson's arm. "What about the lugger?"

"Well! what about the lugger?"

"Rush her now! Here's our chance!"

The Parson turned calm eyes upon the other's splendid ones.

"Aye, lad, aye," he said, with the crushing calm a man wields so mightily. "But give the Gentleman his due, he's not quite such a fool as you'd make him out. He knows our aim as well as he knows his own. We've got to get to Nelson. There's only one way left - the lugger. If he's left that way open it's as plain as the nose on your face it's because he wants us to take it."

Ugh, these men! the boy worshipped the man's courage and scorned his caution. He throbbed for the relief of action. Only let him be doing! anything, anything in the world was better than standing here to watch Nelson sweep doom-wards.

"And suppose," he flashed, "suppose the Gentleman makes away in his lugger now! what shall we do? Twiddle our thumbs and whistle, till the soldiers come, I suppose! And then," with the crude irony of fifteen, "then perhaps, if we're very brave, and the Gentleman has got *well* away to sea, we'll take a little stroll with a strong escort to the top of Beachy Head to see Nelson strung up to his own yard-arm!"

The boy's fiery insults left the other cold.

"You're young, my boy, offensively young," he said. "A bad fault, but one you may hope to grow out of. One thing I'm sure of. You do your friend a great injustice. He won't leave that despatch-bag in our hands till he's forced to at the point of the steel."

"But what can we *do*?" blazed the boy - "do, do, do! There's Nelson!" with flashing forefinger. "Here are we. He won't come to us. We *must* get to him. There's only one way - the lugger. It may be a poor chance, still if it's the only one! O, sir, sir! surely it's better to die attempting something, than stand and *rot* to death here!"

The words poured forth in a white-hot torrent, shaking him.

Anybody in the world but the practical Englishman would have been moved.

He only grunted.

"I wish I knew what was going on behind that shingle-bank," he grumbled, half to himself.

The boy's soul quenched, only to flame forth again.

"I'll be your eyes, sir!"

The Parson shook a dubious head.

"Oh let me! O do! sir! sir!"

He was hopping, trembling at the other's side.

The Parson with his slow and chewing mind was digesting the situation.

Beneath his calm, he was mad to know what was going on behind the shingle-bank. If he went himself, who would be left in garrison? - the old story.

Yet if he sent Kit?

Twice already he had let the boy go forth alone, and each time had barely plucked him from the jaws of death. Could he send him forth a third time to face

Alfred Ollivant

what God should send?

Could he?

He locked his jaws.

Duty, duty, duty! a hard mistress for those who serve her, but the only one for an Englishman.

His mind made up, true man that he was, he wasted no time in excusing himself to himself or to others.

Somewhat grey about the jaws, he swung about.

"Very well," shortly. "Just a peep - no more, mind!"

CHAPTER LXIV

RUMBLINGS OF THUNDER

The boy slid down the ladder into the gloom of the kitchen.

There was no familiar silver head at its wonted place of watch by the loop-hole.

"Piper!"

"Sir!"

The old foretop-man was sitting beside the trapdoor, peering down into the blackness of the cellar, and listening intently.

"That you, Master Kit? Would you step this way, sir? There keeps on a kind of a rumbling like in the drain - a'most as though the gentlemen be running a cargo. I ca'ant justly make it out."

The boy came to his side and listened. True, there was a muffled noise of rolling in the drain, and dull banging against the door. Well, they might bang till they were blue: they would make as much impression on that door as the breeze on Beachy Head.

Alfred Ollivant

The old man looked up and saw the lad beside him in shirt-sleeves.

"Hullo, sir! what's forrad then?"

"I'm going to take a little trot over to the shingle-bank to have a look round," said the boy, shivering. "I want you to stand by the door to let me out and in."

The old man rolled up his sleeves, snatched his cutlass from the corner, whetted it with the easy grace of a bird whetting its beak, and spat on his hands.

"Then it's stand by to repel boarders! Rithe away, sir, when you are."

The Parson peered down.

"All's quiet," he whispered. "Ready, Kit?"

"Yes, sir."

The boy stood up pale in the gloom.

"Then ease those bolts away. Gently, Piper!"

The old man opened quietly.

A sweet wind stole in, and with it a flood of light.

Kit peeped out.

How naked it looked, how terrible!

"One moment."

He bent, untied his shoe-lace, and tied it up again.

Upstairs it had seemed such an easy thing to dare this deed, so full of the poetry and romance of war. Down here, face to face with the bare fact, it was a different matter. A plank, as it were, had been thrust out from solid earth over Eternity; it was his to walk that plank; and he didn't like the job.

Piper held the door, waiting respectfully. The old man's sleeves were rolled to the arm-pit. On one hairy fore-arm a dancing-girl was tattooed, record of the days, now forty years since, before, in his own simple phrase, he had larned Christ.

He knew no fear himself: for he knew that he was impregnable. But his heart went out to this slip of a lad, who had to face Eternity alone, and found it terrible.

The twilight of love, always in all faces the same, which comes when at a call the Christ rises from the deeps of the heart, darkened his eyes.

He gave a shy little cough.

"There's one bower-anchor'll weather any storm, by your leave, sir," he said, the sailor and the Christian quaintly commingled.

The boy felt the other's strength flow into his.

"I know," he panted, and plunged.

CHAPTER LXV

THE DOINGS IN THE CREEK

I

As he ran he seemed to himself to be a body of lead borne on watery dream-legs.

In the sally of yesterday at least he had Knapp with him. Now he was alone. And to dare alone is to be revealed to yourself, naked as you are.

A visible danger would have strengthened him. It was the horror of he-knew-not-what coming from he-knew-not-where that made his heart hammer.

The boy's body screamed to go back. His will thrust it forward. The shock and struggle of the two charged him as with electricity. A touch, he felt, and he might go off in a flash of lightning.

As he held on, and nothing happened, mind began to ride body more masterfully. The flesh, beaten, gave and gave; till in despair, abandoning its backward pull, it threw forward into the work.

What was death? was it what the parsons seemed to

think - a foreign land, millions of miles away, with an old man in a temper waiting somewhere in the middle to be nasty to him?

Heaven and earth, this world and the next! Were there indeed two? a great gulf between them. Or were both one and everlasting? Was he, believing himself in Time, dwelling in Eternity now? Was he immortal now?

His heart answered, *Now or never.*

What then to fear?

The thought whirled him forward.

The grass felt goodly beneath his feet. The sun, still pale in mist, blessed him. A fresh wind flowed about him, flustering hair and shirt. His heart eased.

After all his rear was fairly safe, and his flank unthreatened. As to his front - well, he had his eyes and his dirk.

Gripping himself together, every hair alert, he ran.

He was nearly across the sward now. Tall grass-blades pricked sparsely through the sand. The shingle-bank, roan against the sparkle of the sea, surged before him, and behind it - what?

He was living in his eyes.

The knoll lay now to his right rear. Behind it, across the creek, rose the Wish; and on the crest a Grenadier gazing seawards.

Opposite the little hill, standing on the bank somewhere just above the entrance to the sluice, stood the Gentleman.

II

Kit dropped to his hands and knees.

The other had not seen him: for he was standing, back turned, and a short black-snouted pistol in the hand behind him; directing operations in the creek.

What did it all mean? what was that banging and business in the creek?

It was to find this out that he had come.

A sound close at hand drew his mind to his ears.

The crest of the shingle-bank was some twenty yards away. From the reverse slope came the crunch and scream of disturbed pebbles.

Somebody was scrambling up the bank towards him, the pebbles pouring noisily away beneath his feet.

What to do? - turn and bolt? He could be back across the grass before the slow-foot Frenchman had sworn himself to the crest. Lie there out in the open, to be made prisoner, or potted at thirty yards?

No, no, no! To retreat was shame: to stay death. But one course remained - the riskiest, which, as he had heard the Parson say, in a tight place is often the safest. That course was forward. Take the man unawares as he crested the rise; dirk him; one swift glimpse at the lugger and the doings in the creek; and then pelting home before the enemy had realised the situation and begun to shout.

"*François! François!*" came an irritable voice.

The climber stopped.

"*Qu'as-tu donc, mon Caporal?*"

"*Nom d'un chien!*" snapped the other. "*Faut il me faire matelot? Aidez moi un peu avec ces satanées cordes!*"

The climber slithered down on his heels, a cataract of shingle streaming behind him.

Swift to seize his chance, Kit rushed the crest, the crash of the Frenchman's retreat drowning his approach.

There, flat on his face, he peeped.

Beneath him, on the run of the shingle, lay the lugger. Her jib was flapping; the mainsail set for the hoisting; every stick and stay in place. Half a dozen burly Grenadiers, black-muzzled with a week's beard, were busy about her, stowing their kits, laughing and chattering.

A sprightly little Corporal, balancing on the stern, was spitting forth orders.

The foreign language, there on his native shore, made a

Alfred Ollivant

discord in the boy's heart.

"*Quand partirons-nous?*" asked François, wading down the shingle, pack on back.

"*Aussitôt que tout sera prêt la-bas,_*" answered the corporal, casting a glance over his shoulder. "*_Bah! ces gueux d'Anglais! Monsieur le Général en a par dessus les yeux.*"

Kit followed the man's eyes.

III

A track of feet led from the lugger to the creek across the wet sand. Along it a tail of smugglers were trundling barrels gingerly. At the entrance to the sluice others were hoisting and heaving. Above them stood that slight figure against the sky-line, the ominous pistol lurking behind him.

And it was clear the ruffians were smouldering to mutiny. Their heads were over their shoulders as they worked, and their eyes on the lugger. The soldiers were coming! they felt the halter tightening round their necks; and they were mad to be away.

Only one man in the world could have held them there at all, Kit felt, and he had all his work cut out. That slight figure against the sky-line, so calm, so terrible, seemed compact of power.

Kit had seen his friend in many moods; now he saw

him in another. And the boy thought he loved him in this last rôle best, because in it he feared him most. This was not the man of poetry, charming as April, gay-hearted as a boy; this was the remorseless leader, iron for his cause, brutal, if you will, as a man who deals with brutes must be.

There was a sultry silence - the silence and horror before the storm breaks. Kit felt it and was appalled. He could almost hear the flames of mutiny roaring in those dull and darkened hearts.

For one moment the boy forgot himself and his cause. He was a play-goer, watching a drama. This man was the hero, valiant, lonely, a miracle of strength. The boy felt for him a passionate sympathy. Could he hold them? - Would they break?

Even as he watched, a man shot out of the ruck and away, scampering furiously with the shrugged shoulders and ducked head of one expecting a blow.

It came sure as fate, and as deliberate.

Out shot the Gentleman's pistol hand.

A crack, a stab of flame, and the man was flopping on the sand like a landed fish.

As the Gentleman fired, another from below stormed up the bank at him. A flash of lightning darted at him, and struck him in the chest. The fellow collapsed in a heap.

The boy had half risen to his elbow.

"Well done!" he cried with blazing enthusiasm. Then he remembered where he was, and dropped.

No man had heard. The Grenadiers like himself were busy watching the doings in the creek. A murmur of applause rose from among them.

"Bravo, Monsieur le Général! Hein! Canaille!"

In the creek all was quiet again now. The flame of mutiny was quenched; the Gang had resumed their work; and the Gentleman was wiping his blade upon his sleeve.

CHAPTER LXVI

BUGLES

I

In the loft the Parson was patting the shoulder of the lad now panting beside him.

"Another notch to the Navy," he said.... "What news, boy?"

Kit told of the lugger, ready to sail; of the business of the barrels in the creek; of the rumbling in the drain.

The Parson listened with nodding head.

"I feel like a mouse that knows it's going to have a cat jump on its back, but don't know quite when or just how," he muttered.

"Meantime there's Nelson, sir!" cried the boy, great-eyed and anxious.

"I know, my boy, I know. But while there's the lugger, there's hope."

He leaned out of the window. A sentry was now on the

Alfred Ollivant

shingle-bank; and he could see the tall-plumed bearskins of the Grenadiers busy about the lugger.

The boy took up the telescope.

The mists were lifting, and the sun shone white upon the water. He could see the frigate, faint indeed and far, stately-pacing towards her doom; he could see the mast of the lugger, Grenadier-guarded, and those leagues of shining waste between the two.

Where was help?

An awful darkness drowned his heart.

He shut the telescope with a snap.

"We're beat," he sobbed.

The other gripped his arm.

"If we're beat, England's beat. If England's beat, the Devil's won, and the world's lost - which is absurd."

The man's stern enthusiasm fired the boy afresh.

"If you'll tell me what to do I'll do it," he said a little tremulously. "But I don't see the way."

"There is a way, Kit. There must be. And we shall find it."

The man was indomitable. There seemed no ghost of a chance; still no shadow of despair clouded that clear spirit. As the sea of difficulties rose about him, his soul rose to meet it on triumphant wings.

Yet the problem before him seemed insoluble.

Nelson there: they here: one boat between, and that boat guarded by the pick of the Army of England.

He turned those good blue eyes of his upon the boy with a drolling baffled look.

"How's it to be done? - what says the Commodore?"

The light had fled from the boy's face. Pale and still, he looked like a young saint about to be martyred.

"There's only one way I can think of, sir."

"What's that?"

The lad lifted the eyes of a woman.

"Pray."

A darkness drove across the Parson's face.

"You pray," he growled. "I'll sharpen my sword."

Turning to the corner he bowed to Polly shining among the cobwebs.

"A sweet morning, my lady," he cried. "And promise of a fair day's work."

The boy turned his face to the wall.

II

"Mr. Joy, sir!"

"Well, Piper."

"There's a man on a horse."

"Where?"

"Rithe away oop a-top o th' hill over Willingdon - on the old drove-road from Lewes."

The Parson sprang to his feet.

"Sharp work!" he said with a grin at Kit's back.

"Well done you, boy!"

Kit leapt to the window.

"Theer!" said Blob, pointing.

Far away on the rim of the world stood a tiny horseman.

What was he, that little speck of blackness on the horse without legs? - ploughboy or dragoon? - alone or the leader of a troop?

"Wave!" cried the Parson at his elbow.

Sobbing and frantic, the lad fluttered his handkerchief.

As though in answer a bugle-call rang echoing down

to them.

"The soldiers!" gasped Kit, his knees fainting beneath him. "O, thank God!"

Close at hand another bugle rang out merrily.

"Nipper Knapp!" cried Piper. "Butter my wig, if it ain't!"

A shoal of silver minnows flashed and twinkled above the crest.

"Bayonets, by God!" roared the Parson. "Here they come, the little darlings!" as a black trickle of figures poured over the crest.

Others too had seen and heard.

A shot rang out in the stillness: the Grenadier under the thorn came back on his picquet at the double. The shot was answered ironically from the hill-side by the English Last Post. Here in the dawn France and England challenged each other tauntingly.

It was splendid. Kit's blood danced to it. He thought of old-time tournays, the champion riding into the ring at the last moment. He was half sob, half song. The wine of glory flushed his veins as at the moment when he stormed with the crew of the *Tremendous* at the heels of Lushy. His eyes ran; his voice broke. Now it was a shrill treble, now a hoarse bass.

The Parson was chewing his lip.

"Horse or foot, I wonder?"

"Foot," cried Kit, stamping up and down.

"Damnation!" grumbled the Parson. "Are they doubling?"

"Not they!" cried Kit, mad to insolence - "doing the goose-step by numbers so far as I can see. Good old leather-stocks!"

Knapp might have heard him: for the bugle close at hand blew the charge furiously.

"Now they've broken into a double. Come on, you chaps! come on!"

"Well done, Knapp!" muttered the Parson, swallowing his excitement. "Good little boy! Good little b-o-y! If he lives through this, he shall have a pint o beer to his breakfast to-morrow, by God he shall. Piper! how long'll they take getting here?"

"Why, sir, a little better'n half an hour, I reckon. Drop down by Motcombe, through Upperton, and down along Water Lane."

The Parson turned to Kit.

"How long will it be before the tide will float the lugger, think you?"

"Twenty minutes, sir."

The Parson grunted.

"Pot begins to boil," he said, and took off his coat.

"O, if they're too late!" cried Kit in swift agony, and turned to glance at the far frigate.

"God's never too late, my boy," answered the Parson, folding his coat carefully.

III

Rolling up his sleeves, he was looking through the seaward window.

The Gang were streaming across the greensward, and round the cottage, pointing, shouting.

Behind them came the Gentleman. He was swinging his sword, and chopping at the daisies. Whoever else was disturbed, it was not he.

Last the Grenadiers who formed the lugger-guard came toppling over the shingle-bank.

The Gentleman stayed them with imperious hand.

The Parson saw it and grinned. The chap, for all his high-faluting ways, was a soldier through and through. He missed no point, not the smallest. The Parson respected him.

The other, crossing the sward, raised his head and saw the man at the window. The eyes of the two met. Each smiled. Each knew the other's heart.

"No, no," cried the Gentleman with a little wave. "I

give nothing away. I can't afford to. I know my opponent."

The Parson bowed, tightening his belt. And after all it was a pretty compliment from the first light cavalryman in Europe.

The Gentleman passed round the cottage and out of sight.

"What shall you do?" asked Kit hoarsely at the Parson's elbow.

"Why, the only thing there is to be done - and that's nothing."

He sat down on a broken box, took out a handkerchief and began to furbish his blade with the delicate tenderness of a woman bathing a child.

Kit, fretted almost to tears, watched him with angry admiration. The crisis had come, and this curly greyhead sat, calm as a village Solomon in his door of summer evenings, and talked baby to his sword.

"I don't see *that* helps much," sneered the boy - "cleaning the plate!"

"Nor does fussing for that matter," retorted the other tranquilly. "In war, as in the world, you must do as you're done by. That mayn't be parson's truth; but it is soldier's. And I'm a soldier for the time being. The cards lie with the Gentleman. We shall have to follow suit - or trump. If he's got a card up his sleeve he must play it - now or never."

The boy turned to the window.

The Gentleman was standing upon the broken wall, hand over his eyes, taking in the situation.

He flung a finger here, an order there.

The Grenadiers threw forward across the plain in skirmishing order.

"Looks like business," muttered the Parson, tucking in his shirt. "What's it going to be?"

He had not long to wait.

The Gentleman vaulted the wall, and came swiftly across the grass towards them.

CHAPTER LXVII

THE ACE OF TRUMPS

I

He came rapidly across the lawn, the sun upon him.

Kit thought him the fairest figure of a man he had ever seen.

The Parson was comely with the comeliness of an apple, this man was beautiful with the beauty of sun and sword in one.

But the boy noticed that there was more of the sword and less of the sun than of old about him.

Was the strain telling on him too?

"Forgive me for disturbing you so early," called the gay voice. "The Reverend Father was at his devotions doubtless!"

"No, sir," retorted the Parson. "The Reverend Father was watching the Horse, Foot, and Artillery, pelting down the hill on top o you."

"I've been watching em too," replied the other. "And sorry I am I shan't be here to entertain em - I've a soft place for the soldiers myself. But I'm just off for a day on the water. A pretty morning!"

"Yes; as pretty a morning to hang a play-actor on as ever I saw."

The other waved a hand.

"Ah, but I'm not going to hang you, dear Padre. I have other views for you."

He was fascinating, but somehow he was fearful too. He was the python: they were the rabbits. He had power: and that power was none the less terrible because it was mysterious.

The Parson leaned out, bold and bluffing.

"I take you. The game's up. And you've come to surrender, eh?"

The other shook his head.

"No. I just stepped across to say good-bye, and see if I couldn't perhaps persuade you to come with me."

"No, sir, thank you all the same. I'm a land-animal myself. Besides I'm too cosy here."

The other stood silent a full minute, nodding a slow head.

"Alas, poor ghost!" he said at length half to himself, and made as though to turn.

The Parson was staggered.

Had he no card then? was he merely bluffing?

"What's it mean?" he whispered fiercely to Kit.

"It means he's going - and Nelson's last chance with him!" panted the boy. "O, *make* him stay!"

The Parson leaned out again.

"I hope you'll come back to see your friends hung, my lord!" he bawled.

The Gentleman turned again.

"Friends?"

"Well, aren't they your friends? - Lord Alfiriston, Sir Harry Dene, and the rest. I gathered they were from the despatch-bag you're so good as to leave in my hands."

"I'm leaving no despatch-bag in your hands."

The Parson jumped round.

What did the fellow mean? Had he somehow?...

No, there it was on the staple, the tarpaulin bag stamped with the Imperial Eagle.

He took it down.

"This is the boy I meant. Won't you leave this with us?"

The Gentleman shook his head.

"What you going to do with it?" mockingly.

"What I'm going to do with you."

Man and boy, hugging close in the window, each felt the other tauten.

"What's that?"

The other rolled his eyes heavenward.

The Parson was breathing through his nose.

"What ye mean?"

A tiny smile broke about the Gentleman's lips. He raised a finger, and drew nearer on his toes, stealthy as a child about to rev eal a secretto its mother; and there was a horror about him.

"*Hush, and I'll whisper you!*"

The horror grew upon the man. The Parson shivered.

The very air was listening.

"*Powder-mine.*"

"*A what?*"

"*A powder-mine.*"

The laughter bubbled up in his eyes, and rippled about his face. He was a child, a cruel child, who springs a carefully-prepared surprise on a comrade, and dwells wantonly on the effect.

"Not vairy nice, is it?" he bantered. "I *do* feel for you."

He stood beneath the window, hands clasped before him, chin down, the little maiden, demure yet malicious: the little maiden and yet – the Devil.

"So sorray. But I do not want those despatches to fall into the hands of bad men. You forgive?" winningly.

The Parson drew a great breath. It was so sudden, so aweful, so utter.

It was Piper who broke the silence from below.

"We're settin on a powder-mine, sir. Is that it?"

"That's it."

"Ah, well," came the philosophic voice. "Short and sweet - bless God. Better'n lingerin on it out."

Kit panted,

"Nelson!" and swooned.

II

When he came round the Gentleman was approaching slowly across the grass.

He bantered no more. Maiden and Devil were dead. He was man, and grey as dew.

"Captain Joy," he was saying quietly. "Let us face facts. Samson is bound. Over there," pointing to Beachy Head, "are the liers in wait. That frigate's the *Medusa*. Nelson's aboard of her. She can't escape."

The words stung Kit to new life.

"She can't escape perhaps," he shouted. "But can't she fight?"

The other shook his head.

"Why?" persisted Kit, hot for the honour of his Service. "Why can't she fight?"

"She can't fight," said the Gentleman slowly, "because her powder's wet."

"What!" bellowed the Parson - "more traitors!"

"The Gunner is mine," replied the Gentleman briefly.

"Oh, the Navy! the Navy!" cried the Parson, rocking.

"But, I don't believe it!" screamed Kit. "Let him prove it! Let him tell us how he's worked it."

The Gentleman walked slowly up and down before the window.

"We needn't enter into that," he said, cold as death.

The Parson launched a slow laughing sneer, terrible

Alfred Ollivant

to hear.

"What! more gentlemanliness from our Gentleman!"

The words whipped the other's face white.

He stopped in his walk, and lifted slow eyes.

"It may be that I have loved my country better than my God," he said. A smile flashed across his face -"*But what a country to be damned for!*"

Slowly he came towards the cottage.

"To return to the point. Nelson is lost. No power on earth can save him now."

"I do not look to any power on earth for help," replied the Parson solemnly.

"Let us talk as men," answered the other as solemn. "You have nothing to gain by holding out, and everything to lose. All that an honourable soldier could do you have done. Is it not now the part of true courage to accept the inevitable? For the last time, will you surrender?"

The great veins started on the Parson's forehead.

"Never!" he bawled. "Do your d'dest!"

The Gentleman turned and turned again.

"The blood of those boys be on your head, Mr. Joy!"

"Let the boys answer for themselves," retorted the

Parson, short and sullen.

The Gentleman paused.

"Little Chap," he called, "will you come? - France is a fair country. You shall have Monsieur Moon-calf there for squire. Myself I will see to it that you are happy."

"I would rather be dead in England than alive in France," the boy answered passionately. "What about you, Blob?"

"Here Oi be and here Oi boide," replied Blob doggedly, and dulled the romance of the statement by adding - "Oi aren't got ma money yet."

"Think twice, Little Chap!" called the Gentleman. "You are young. You are happy. The day is before you. The night is not yet. It is early to draw down the blinds."

The Parson had turned his back to the window.

"Ask the ass for time," he whispered. "We must have time."

The boy leaned out.

"May I have ten minutes to think it over, sir?"

"Two, my boy."

"Oh, sir!" pitiful, appealing.

The Gentleman glanced across his shoulder, and turned again.

Alfred Ollivant

"Ah, well! five be it."

He took out his watch, and sat on the wall with dangling legs.

CHAPTER LXVIII

THE BLESSING

I

"I must have a word with Piper."

The Parson was down the ladder in a flash.

The old foretop-man, humming his hymn in the eternal twilight, turned.

"Well, sir?"

"You've heard, Piper?"

"I've hard, sir. And if so be a common seaman might make so bold, there's but one thing for it, and that's the cold steel."

He laid his Bible aside and took up his cutlass.

"It's a forlorn hope, Piper."

"It's the only one, sir."

The Parson swung round.

Alfred Ollivant

"And there's another thing," he cried in terrible agony. "What about you, Piper? We shall take it in the open; but *you*, you'll have to wait for it. I *can't* leave you to fall alive into the hands of those - those - O my God! my God!" stamping up and down.

There was quiet thrill in the voice that answered,

"They ca'an't touch me, sir. I'm safe in Jesus." The old man seemed to shine in the darkness.

"It's not death I fear for you!" cried the Parson. "No Christian fears that for his friend. It's - it's the old game - the Gap Gang."

"Ah, they won't have no time for no larks," interposed the other with a comfortable chuckle. "They can do their muckiest. It won't last long. The soldiers'll stop that."

The words, and the way of saying them, quickened the Parson to tremendous life.

"You're right, old friend," he cried, his voice naming in the gloom. "Death to face, but nothing to fear."

"Death to face," echoed the old man, "and Christ to follow."

II

"I'm distressed to disturb you," came a cold voice from without. "But time's nearly up."

"You said five minutes, sir!" called Kit.

"You've had three, my boy. You've got two."

"And we'll make good use of em," gasped the Parson, and raced up the ladder.

Snatching the despatch-bag from the staple, he tumbled the contents on the floor, and set the whole ablaze. The papers curled and crackled; and their dreadful secret escaped joyfully in merry little flames.

"May God deal so with all traitors in his own good time!" prayed the Parson.

He trod out the flames, and turned to the boys.

"I'm goin for em."

"So'm I, sir - and Blob."

"So be it!" said the Parson, short and fierce. "Out knives. Off coats. Tighten belly-bands."

He was on his knees, stuffing his coat into the empty despatch-bag, working in a white fury.

"Now ask no questions, but listen, and obey! I'm going to undo the back door *noisily*. You'll undo the front door *quietly*. I shall sally, the despatch-bag slung across my shoulders - so - see? - Give me a good start. Choose your moment. Then follow."

The words came swift as hail. The Parson was at his best - the Englishman in action, back to the door, face to Eternity. The shock and storm of circumstance made lightning in the dark of his mind. He saw all before him clear as a landscape at night in the flashes of a thunderstorm.

"Directly they begin to close on you, you'll get a panic - a screaming panic. Bolt back for the cottage; slam the door; lock and bar; through the house, out at the front, and make for the lugger! You may not be seen - the cottage'll cover you: and I'll keep em occupied as long as I can. If all goes as I hope, you'll find the lugger unguarded. The rest I must leave to you and the Almighty. It's a poor chance, but the only one."

"Gentlemen, gentlemen!" came the warning voice from without.

III

The Parson slid down into the darkness.

"Piper," he cried, hoarse and dry. "I believe - I believe these lads will win through. It's God's battle. He *must* help."

"He will, sir," replied the old man, firm as faith.

"I'm a clergyman. You're a good man. This is a desperate business. Will you give us your blessing?"

He was down on his knees, in his white shirt, his sword a gleam of silver on the slabs before him.

"Kit."

The boy, swift to grasp his meaning, knelt beside him, pulling Blob after him.

An arm stole round him; his stole round Blob.

So they knelt in the twilight, hugging close in that aweful sense of loneliness that comes to men when the Gates of Death are seen to swing back to let them through.

Kit thought of his Confirmation six months ago.

Now the end was come - so soon.

Well, well, he had often died before. And how clearly it all came back to him, this final stage in the little pilgrimage, these last few steps, solemn, beautiful, and slow, up to the familiar threshold; then the old door, the old smile, and - the old forgetfulness.

He had no regrets, and was strangely calm, strangely uplifted. He could look back without shame, and forward without fear. Now he was thankful that in these days of his ordeal he had been true to himself and to his trust. He had done his best. There was little more to do. That little should be done as became the son of his father.

IV

In the gloom they knelt before this unanointed Priest of Jehovah.

Alfred Ollivant

His office sat upon that white old man, native to him as his soul.

He spread his great-knuckled hands above them, a patriarch, a prophet, an apostle of Jesus Christ by the will of God.

"God bless you, sir - and you, Master Kit - and you, Boy Hoad." He drew his hand across his mouth.

"So be. Amen," he added solemnly.

"Amen," said they all.

The Parson rose.

He gripped the old man's hand.

Blob he patted on the back.

"Kit," he said, and, drawing the boy towards him, kissed him.

CHAPTER LXIX

THE PARSON'S SORTIE

I

"Time!" came the stern voice from without.

The Parson slammed back the last bolt with a clang, and whipped up his sword.

"*Ready?*"

The man was in a white flame, roaring for battle.

"*Yes.*"

Time had stopped: Eternity was there.

"*Then God help us all to die!*"

He flung back the door and plunged.

It was a venture of despair; but there was no despair in that heart of oak.

Swift as a flood, and as silent, he made for the wall, the despatch-bag flopping in the small of his back. And his silence added to the terror of his coming.

The white-hearted crew huddling behind the wall felt it. Here and there a scared head dodged up only to duck again.

One man alone left cover and went out to meet the solitary swordsman.

The Gentleman vaulted the wall, and came across the sward with steady eyes, twisting his sword-knot about his wrist.

There was a rimy look about his face, and a snarl in the voice that shouted to the crew behind him,

"Come! close in there! You've got to finish this job before you go. The soldiers are on your heels, remember."

Close at hand a sudden drum rolled.

It smote the guilty hearts of the Gang like a summons to the Last Judgment.

"What's that?"

They rose up like dead men and looked behind them. It was not much they saw, but it was sufficient.

Close in their rear, on a rise of the ground, a man stood against the sky, thundering fatally on a monster drum.

He wore a red coat; he was a soldier.

And as they gazed, he beat a furious rat-a-tan-tan

and charged.

That was enough. The Gang broke.

II

The Gentleman flashed round to meet the new danger.

He saw a pair of twinkling legs, a huge drum, belly-borne, and two drum-sticks, brandished vaingloriously, driving a rout of men before them.

The humour of the thing seized him.

"Well done, Soldier!" he laughed, and was back over the wall in a trice, attempting to stop the rout.

He might as well have attempted to stay the tide. A torrent of men tumbled past him in howling tumult.

He stood like a lighthouse in the tide-way.

"What! one man lick the lot o you!" came the whipping voice. "O, good God!" with a passion of scorn - "you sweeps! you swine!"

His blade flashed and fell.

"Pretty stroke!" shouted the Parson, flying the wall. "At em again, sir!" He cut in fiercely on the flank. "Come on, Knapp! - That's the style! Bellyful for once! Bellyful for the boy!"

"I'm there, sir!" cried Knapp, very brisk and bright.

He had flung aside his drum, and was tearing up, wielding his drum-sticks like battle-axes.

"Into em!" bellowed the Parson. "Give em the glory o God! Give em the Lord's own delight!"

He was hounding at the heels of the last smuggler, and the Gentleman was hounding at his.

"Ow's that-a-tat-tat? ow's that?" cried Knapp, racing up from behind, and came down with a flourish and a thump on the swordsman's head as he thrust.

Down went the Gentleman in sprawling ruin.

"That's a little bit o better, ain't it?" chirped the Cockney, and skipping over the fallen man, he was at the Parson's side, in the thick and fury of it, bringing down his drum-sticks to the battle-cry of,

"Ow's that-a-tat-tat? ow's that?"

III

The old man and the boys watched from the cottage. The door was ajar. They huddled behind it, peering. Beside them lay the table, a musket across it. In the silence they could hear each other's hearts.

"Say, Maaster Sir!" whispered Blob. "Be you fear'd?"

"Ask no questions, and you'll be told no lies," replied Kit. "Be you?"

"Oi dun knaw," replied the cautious lad. "Moi insoide seems koind o swimmy loike."

"Then stand by to lend a hand with this table when I give the word," was all Kit's answer.

He was watching with all his eyes.

Parson and Gentleman were about to clash.

Then a little figure rose out of the earth, and sullen thunder smote on the silence.

Piper drew a deep breath.

"I thart so," he said, comfortably.

"Who is it?" asked Kit.

"Jack Knapp, sir," said the old man, picking his teeth. "Sneaked a drum from a travellin showman by the look on it, and tow-rowin like a rigiment. See him thump it. Ho! ho! That's joy to Jack, I knaw. Now he's for chargin em, drum and all. Ha! ha!"

Whoever else might escape there was no hope for that wingless old man. His fate was certain, his end was already come. Within five minutes at most the great doors would have slammed on him for ever. And here he sat chuckling like a boy at a fair.

It is something to be a saint, thought Kit, something to be as sure as that. This old man had built his house upon the Rock indeed.

They watched the stampede, and the Gentleman's vain attempt to stay it. Their hearts surged to the Parson's battle-cry, and sank to the Gentleman's thrust, to surge again as Knapp felled his man.

"Knapp'd him a nice un," chuckled the old man, not above a pun at death's door. "Reglar revellin in it is Knapp, I knaw."

"Our time's coming!" panted Kit. "Stand by, Blob!"

The Gentleman was down, the Gang upon the run. "Now, sir!" cried Piper. "Now's your chance."

IV

"Now, Blob! - nippy with the table there!"

Out they rushed, and dumped the table down on the left of the door.

"That'll do, sir, thank you," said the old man, trundling out after them. "That'll cover my flank nicely.... Butter-my-wig!" with kindling eyes on the battle, "but Mr. Joy's busy."

"Come on, Blob!" yelled Kit.

"Come along, boys!" roared the Parson. "Pretty work forrad, and plenty for all!"

The Gentleman rose white-faced from his knees.

"A moil a moil" he shouted, waving.

Behind him Kit heard a yell, and the crash and scatter of men storming down the shingle-bank.

Then silence as they took the grass.

He flung his head across his shoulder as he ran.

The lugger-guard, loosed at last, were hurling across the greensward at him, bayonets at the charge.

Such tall and terrible men! - and how they strode along, bearskins a-bob, savage eyes smouldering, snapping fierce phrases at each other as they came!

Kit loosed his soul in a ghastly scream.

"Back, Blob!"

It was well done, and not difficult to do. He had but to utter the horror that was in him.

"O, Kit!" came the Parson's resentful bellow.

"I'm afraid!" screamed the lad. "I can't help it. O-o-o-h!"

He ran with huddled head, clutching at the boy before him.

"*Attrapez ces gaillards! Ne tirez pas!*" shouted the Gentleman. "*Un deux d'entre vous leur coupent le chemin! Les autres, par ici!*"

"*Ah, oui, mon Général!*" panted the Corporal. "*Francois! Albert!*"

Two men sprang away from the rest and raced to intercept the boys.

What a pace they ran! Their black-gaitered legs seemed to skim the ground.

The boy had not allowed for such speed.

"*Toi de l'autre côté de la chaumière. Moi ici!*" called the swifter of the two.

He flashed behind the cottage, and flashed up again round the gable-end.

Kit recognised him. It was François, his friend of the dawn.

"Tiens! c'est toi, mon gars!" cried the man, with a quick smile.

A simple countryman, this François, he was a soldier because he had to be. That business beyond the wall, where the swords and shouts were, was little to his liking. This was a job after his own heart. He was a boy playing prisoner's base with another boy. Neither would be hurt.

So as he slewed round the gable-end he smiled.

Kit saw the smile and resented it. It angered him that this fellow did not take him seriously. He had not to resent it for long.

The smile died a swift and terrible death on François' face.

"*Dâme!*" he screamed, and slithered back on his heels. A musket barrel was thrusting into his flank.

"*Pray!*" said a solemn voice.

There was a horrible plop as the man collapsed, coughing.

CHAPTER LXX

THE LAST OF OLD FAITHFUL

The old man clapped his smoking musket down, and snatched his cutlass.

"Any more for me, sir?"

"Another on your right, Piper!"

"Very good, sir."

The old man spun himself to the corner, and waited behind the wall.

The boy, running with all his might, watched fascinated.

Round the corner the doomed man whirled with a grin. The cutlass swooped. The fellow sprawled over his slayer, the shock of the onset rolling the chair back. The old man shook off the body, as he might have shaken off a cloak, and backed himself, cutlass bloody in his mouth.

"In with you, Master Kit!"

"You too!" panted Kit, thrusting the chair before him.

"No, sir, no!" fiercely. "I can do a bit o business here yet." He was loading swiftly, eyes on the battle. "Starn agin the door, larboard in the loo'th, and cutlass-room all round - what better can a seaman want?"

"But -"

"Sharp, sir! - No time to waste. Here they come."

The Gentleman had gathered his Grenadiers in his hand, and was swinging them back at the cottage.

"In with you, sir!" urged the old man, ablaze. "Bolt and bar."

"O Piper!" whimpering.

"Nelson, sir!"

The word went home. The boy shot in, and slammed the door. All again was darkness, and Blob breathing heavily at his side.

"I'm through! I'm through!" came a triumphant yell.

Kit's eye was at a crack.

The Parson had broken away from the rout, and was making for the hills, the despatch-bag flopping in his back.

The Gentleman, leading the charge at the cottage, turned.

"*Abattez moi eel homme là!*" he sang.

Alfred Ollivant

A Grenadier dropped to his knee.

Outside the door a musket cracked.

The Grenadier leapt to his feet, whirled round with floating tails, bowed to his executioner in absurdest doll-fashion, and subsided languidly into death.

The Parson was away, the Gentleman after him with sleuth-hound strides.

The bunch of Grenadiers stormed on for the cottage.

Kit shot the bolts.

He was banging the door of life on that maimed old man, and he would as soon have slammed the gate of heaven in his mother's face.

"Good-bye, *dear* old Piper!" he whispered.

"Good-bye, sir," cheerily. "And if I might make so bold my sarvice to Lard Nelson - Ralph Piper, old *Agamemnon*."

There was silence: then the patter of feet and deep breathing of men racing to kill.

Kit could see the back of the old man's head on a level with his eye, and just beyond, growing hugely on his gaze, the face of the leading Grenadier, livid beneath his bearskin.

Kit shut his eyes as he rammed the last bolt home. Close to his ear, he heard a voice, low as the sea and as deep. It was humming Soldiers of Christ arise.

That too ceased.

Old Faithful was spitting on his hands.

Alfred Ollivant

CHAPTER LXXI

ON THE SHINGLE-BANK

A crash and grunt covered the noise of the front door opening.

Kit peeped out. The way was clear.

"Now, Blob! for your life."

Out the boys sped.

How still it was on this side after the other!

There was a fury of fighting in the distance and a dreadful smothered worry against the back door; here a tranquil sward, trees bowing, and the shingle-bank a roan breast-work against a background of silver.

"Run quietly, boy! On your toes like me. You run like a walrus."

"Tidn't me," gasped Blob. "It's ma legs. They keep on a-creakin."

Swiftly they fled across the grass.

Was there anybody at the lugger? - were they free?

The boy was sick with hope.

Behind him he could hear far yells and the occasional clash of steel. Kit guessed what had happened. The Parson, wary old man of war, his ruse successful, the enemy drawn off, had flung back into the fight.

So far his plan had worked to a miracle.

The boy recalled Piper's last words.

His sarvice to Lard Nelson!

Piper never doubted then. Piper had been sure.

And Piper was right. The Lord was on their side. He felt it, and his spirit began to sing.

Then the song died, and his soul with it.

He could hear voices behind the shingle-bank. A double-sentry at the least had been left over the lugger.

Well, they must go through with it now.

"Knife ready?" he croaked.

"Ye'."

The grass was growing sparse about them. He began to hear his feet. So did the men beyond the bank. There was the click of a cocking musket. The fellow was ready: the fellow would pot them at twenty yards as they came over the crest.

Thought was lost in lightning action.

"Holà, l'ami!" he yelled.

"*Qui vive?*" came the unseen voice.

"Ami! à moi!"

Feet crashed up the shingle. As he topped the crest, a Grenadier, all eyes and bayonet and bristling chin, was plunging up the steep, another at his heels. The first flashed his eyes up in the boy's.

"*Sapristi!*" he cried, and tried to come down to the ready. The shingle roared away beneath his feet. Back he slithered. And as he did so, Kit launched down on him.

"*Sacré nom!*" the fellow screamed, and toppled back on the bayonet of his mate.

Kit ran over his falling body into the arms of the other.

"Take the man behind!" he yelled back.

Arms wound about him: a stertorous breathing was at his ear: for a moment the two rocked, then fell.

The boy was buried alive. A stifling carcase blotted out the sun. His arms were pinioned, but his hands remained free.

Short-handling his dirk, he turned it in.

"*Assassin!*" muttered the man, in his ear.

Kit pressed and slowly pressed. The man writhed and tried to rise. The boy's lithe young arms, though they could not squeeze to death, could hold; and hold they did. The man saw it, ceased to struggle, and hugged.

Thank God the boy had the under-grip. His arms protected him. Else he must have burst.

A groan was squeezed out of him.

"*Quittez donc!*" in his ear.

"Jamais," faintly.

He pressed and pressed. The man hugged and hugged. One must give. Which should it be? Not he, not he, not he, though he fainted. Piper had been *sure*.

A warm gush spouted out upon his fingers, and trickled down his fore-arm.

It was horrible. He felt it to be murder, not war. Yet that python-embrace was squeezing the heart out of his mouth.

Great heavens! - was the man made of iron? - would he never have enough?

Then he felt a prick in his own flesh. Perforce he stayed his hand.

Well, he had done his best. And even at that moment, his brain swimming to a death-swoon, his humour flashed out of the darkness to his succour.

If that didn't stop the chap, hang it! he deserved victory.

But it did.

Gently, very gently, the arms relaxed. He could feel the man fading away and away in his embrace. All that power and stress of life was pouring out into infinity. The man was dying at his ear. Lying his length upon the boy, he shuddered from head to heel.

"*Marie*," he sighed.

There was a last ripple of life, and the boy knew he was holding earth.

He wriggled out into the light with throbbing temples.

His hand and shirt-cuff caught his eye. He started back. They followed him. He tried to fling his hand away. It would not be flung. He stared, breathing like a frightened horse.

His jaw dropping, he looked at his handiwork.

The fellow was lying on his face, long legs wide. But for the hilt of the dirk sticking out of his loins, he looked much as other men. Yet - he was not. Think! A minute ago - and now! How wonderful it all was, and how terrible! The mystery of it made chaos in his brain.

He was frightened at himself, even more than at the dead man, or his deed.

Leaning back on his hands, the man he had killed at his feet, those instant questions which oppress us all in the rare moments when we stand still and are compelled by the shock of circumstance to look inward on ourselves, drummed at his brain.

What was he? - where was he? - why was he?

He staggered to his feet, pressing his hands to his eyes, to try to recollect his meaning.

He failed, only recalling his mission of the moment.

Shutting his eyes, he grasped the dirk.

"Awful sorry," he whispered hoarsely. "I must," and plucked it forth with a shudder.

Then he looked up.

The first Grenadier lay spread-eagled on the slope above him.

Blob was crawling out from beneath him, his pink muzzle thrust up with an air of grave and innocent amazement.

Kit pointed a finger.

"Ha! ha! you do look funny!" he laughed madly. "You're like one of Magic's puppies poking out to have a first peep at the world."

"Oi loike killin better'n bein kill'd," Blob announced solemnly, and crept out on hands and knees, a tip of pink tongue travelling about his lips. Then he turned to his dead.

Kit wound up again.

"Never mind about him," he said, staggering to his feet. "He'll keep. This way. Bring his musket along. Quick!"

He picked up the musket of his own dead, and swayed blindly down towards the lugger.

Blob followed at first reluctantly. Then some memory amused him, and he began to brim slow mirth.

"Er says - 'Dear! dear!' and Oi says - 'Theer! theer!' and plops it in, and plops it in."

Still adrift on the sea of his emotions, Kit paid no heed.

He was swimming down the shingle-bank, aware of nothing but the tip of his nose and vague bad dreams at the back of his heart.

The lugger was lying on the steep of the shingle, poised as though for launching.

The swarthy jib was bellying seaward. She was yearning for the water.

Kit rallied.

The slope was with them; the wind was with them; the very boat was with them. And the tide, running in with a splash, already flopped about her keel.

How soon would she float?

Two minutes might do it - or twenty.

CHAPTER LXXII

THE RACE FOR THE LUGGER

I

There was not a moment to be lost.

"Throw your musket aboard her!" cried Kit, bringing up against the lugger. "Now put your shoulder to and heave with a will! heave!"

They might as well have tried to move a mountain. Yet even as the boy strained, a wave shot up and sluiced his feet. And how that cold clasp warmed his heart!

The tide was tumbling in, the Lord God thrusting it. A minute, a little minute, and they would be away.

"Aboard her, Blob!" he panted. "That's right, clumsy! Noisy does it! Now chuck every single thing you can lay hands on, overboard - except the muskets, idiot!"

Fiercely the boys set to work. Kits and cans, ballast and blocks, spare spars and tackle, higgledy-piggledy overboard they went, some on the shingle, some splashing into the tide, to be snatched and tumbled and ducked.

Alfred Ollivant

As yet they were not discovered. Kit working madly in the belly of the boat could see nothing; but afar he could hear the Parson's terrible roar, and Knapp's crisp,

"*Ow's that-a-tat, ow's that?*"

Somehow, only the Lord knew how, those two inspired warriors still kept the ring.

It was great, but it could not last. The end must come, and it must come soon.

Anxiously the boy peeped over the side. The tide seemed to mock them. With what a swoop it rushed to their rescue, and with what a scream of derision it withdrew again! Kit compared it unconsciously to the to and fro of the emotions in his heart, now surging him heaven-high, now leaving him stranded.

Then he spied a greased bat for launching lying on the slope. In a trice he was overboard, had seized it, and racing down the streaming shingle as a wave withdrew, thrust the bat beneath the keel. The wave curled, stemmed by the advancing water, and swept about him to the knee.

As it clasped the lugger, a puff of wind leapt from the land, and skirmished across the sea.

The jib filled to it, and strained seaward.

Was he wrong? - or did she stir and tremble, like a girl to her lover?

How to help her?

If they could hoist the main-sail!

He was back over the side in a moment.

The boat was clean-swept now of everything but the muskets and a mess of shingle for ballast at the bottom. The anchor had gone over the stern and trailed on the slope. Even Blob had disappeared.

Kit pushed at the boom to thrust it over.

"Blob! Blob! where are you?"

"Here Oi be!" panted a voice forward.

Kit turned to see Blob, his shoulders rounded, and arms taut, heaving at the main-mast.

"She wun't budge!" he cried, his face crimson with honest effort. "Seems she's grow'd in loike."

"Fool!" he cried. "Lend a hand with the boom here! Shove, boy, shove! - Now on to the main-brace! No, fool, no! - Here - on to this! Now all together - heave! heave! heave!"

The great sail rose, groaning terribly.

Heaven send the smugglers hadn't heard!

But they had.

II

So much a far scream told them.

"We're seen!" panted Kit. "Now whistle for the wind, my boy, and hand me that musket."

The water was slopping all about the lugger. Empty as a barrel she began to rock to the rocking of the tide. A puff would launch her.

The boy glanced seaward.

Over there was that white glimmer, clearer now. It was like the arm of a drowning woman flinging up for help. The glimpse of it inspired the boy.

"I'm coming, sir," he called across the waters. "One more fight first."

He hitched his belt. Now he had no doubt of the issue. Here his friend, the sea, was beside him, whispering to him, loving him, taunting him. She was his hope, his heart, his strength. And for the first time it flashed upon the lad what the fight was really for. It was for her, the World's Woman. She went to the Victor, and she was on his side: for he was England, and England had won her first, and, true woman that she was, she clove to her first conqueror.

III

They were coming.

He thrilled to them.

"Now, Blob! you take that side. I'll take this. Pick off a man as he comes over the crest. Then out knives, and do your best!"

He leapt on to the taffrail, balancing by the mizzen. Tiptoeing so, he could just see over the crest of the shingle-bank.

And he was never to forget the sight he then saw. ·

Towards him across the greensward, a torrent of men streamed like a tide-race, silent all.

A huge Grenadier led them. Behind in a bunch came the smugglers, Fat George shambling along in the midst with a fury of arm-work. As his swifter comrades passed him, he clutched at them covetously.

"*Ands off!*" screamed a lanky lad.

The fat man's knife flashed. The lad fell.

The others raced on. What was it to them?

As they came, they tossed up tormented faces. Their eyes were peep-holes. Through them he stared into the bottomless pit, and there beheld things not meant for human vision.

Alfred Ollivant

His eyes passed with relief to the wholesome ugliness of the little Englishman pounding at the smugglers' heels.

Knapp had dropped his drumsticks, and was limping along now naked-fisted. His eyes were shut, and his running drawers red in patches as his tunic. He was merry no more, his head on one shoulder, labouring painfully in his stride. It was clear that he was hard-hit, and just as clear that he meant going through to the finish.

Behind him three Grenadiers, one behind the other, strung out across the green. The Parson coursed the last of them; the Gentleman coursed the Parson.

They were all running swiftly, but the last two were the swiftest.

The Parson was gaining on the Grenadier, and the Gentleman on the Parson.

It was such a race as Kit had never seen before.

Which would reach his man first?

On that, it seemed to his prophetic vision, hung all.

He tried to yell,

"Come on, sir!"

But his voice stuck as in a nightmare, and seemed to suffocate him.

A blade soared and swooped.

"*One!*" came the Parson's voice, clear across the green, as he took the falling man in his stride.

The Gentleman, hard at his heels, tripped over the dead man.

Collected as always, he snatched the fellow's musket, and sprawling on his face, fired at the Parson's back.

A smuggler fell.

"*Thank ye!*" gasped the Parson. "*Two!*" as the second Grenadier went down.

Then the flight of men, pursuer and pursued, dipped out of sight; but Kit could hear the stampede of feet behind the bank racing towards him, then a hiss and stumbling fall.

"*Three!*" panted the Parson's voice, and in a dying roar, "*Mind yourselves, boys! They're on you.*"

IV

"Ready, Blob!"

The boy was white as steel.

He had no body. He was not afraid.

Nelson was calling him, and he should not call in vain.

Over the crest stormed the leading Grenadier,

Alfred Ollivant

monstrous-seeming against the sky.

Kit fired at the man's cross-belts.

Down the shingle the fellow sprawled, whether dead or alive, wounded or whole, Kit knew not till he splashed into the water, and lay still in the flop of the tide.

Behind him came the smugglers.

As they topped the crest a star hung above their heads, then fell, flashing.

"*Four - and - five!*" came the Parson's voice.

"He's on us!" screamed Dingy Joe. "Sword and all!"

They broke away to right and left along the ridge like a covey of partridges when the hawk swoops.

Anything to get away from that avenging voice roaring out of a whirlwind of lightnings!

"After em, Knapp!"

Slung along by his own impetus, the Parson hurled down the steep.

"Warm work!" he panted, grinning luridly at the boy, and he brought up with a bang against the lugger.

As he shocked against the boat, the great tan sail filled. Shock and wind together gave the necessary impulse. The lugger, light as a bubble, swayed, slithered, crunched down the shingle, felt the greased bat, and took the water with a dip and lovely curtsey.

"We're through!" roared the Parson, sprawling upon the side.

Alfred Ollivant

CHAPTER LXXIII

NOBLESSE OBLIGE

I

The anchor was trailing down the shingle-bank after them.

The Gentleman had picked it up, and came walking down the slope, leaning back a little as he came.

He was smiling the brave man's wistful smile.

He had lost and he knew it.

Blob snatched a musket and aimed at his waistcoat.

The Parson struck up the barrel.

"Your friends are safe, sir," he called, hoarse and quiet. "I've burnt the despatches."

"They don't deserve to be, but thank you all the same," replied the other as quiet.

He let the anchor go. It fell with a splash into the water.

"I salute a gallant soldier, a gallant sailor, and my friend Monsieur Moon-calf!" he said, and stood, the water to his ankles, and hilt to his lips.

II

On the ridge the man-pack was at the worry.

Suddenly a face gleamed up through the thick of them.

"*Sir!*" screamed a voice.

The Parson started round.

"Knapp!" he cried, with sickening face. "Put back!"

A hand was on his shoulder. It was Kit.

The boy did not speak; he did not weep; he pointed seaward to where a topsail flashed white on the horizon.

The Parson looked at the green waters swinging by.

"And I can't swim!" he groaned. "God forgive me!"

An inspiration seized him.

He leapt on to the taffrail.

"Sir," he shouted, pointing, "that's a brave man!"

The Gentleman turned and saw the bloody business

Alfred Ollivant

going on behind him.

"I am the servant of the brave," he cried, and stormed back.

The Parson sat down, and broke into tears.

BOOK IV

NELSON

I - H.M.S. *MEDUSA*

CHAPTER LXXIV

NATURE, THE COMFORTER

I

The crash of the waves on the shingle grew faint behind.

The lugger began to prattle, as she took the water bobbingly. Overhead the sky was blue, with wisps of snow. Kit hugged the tiller, shivering in spasms.

On his right Beachy Head, rusty of hide, waded white-footed into the deep. Before him opened the sea, a plain of palest blue, blurred with wind and patched here and there with silver. Eastward a road of twinkling light ran across the water. Pevensey Levels lay behind him, brown beyond the shingle. At back of them a range of dim hills rose and launched into the sea; and Northward a vague gloom in the sky told of man's great camping-place by the Thames.

　　　　Alfred Ollivant

The great sea lolled about the boy, breathing in sleep.

How soothing was the slow large life of the waters after the hubbub and horror of those last few minutes, already so remote!

Above him a kittiwake dreamed. The boy let himself drift, his mind rocking to the rock of the sea.

The waters swung by, singing to themselves. They poured peace upon his troubled spirit. Their strong life entered into his, a resistless tide. Feebly he tried to stay it. He wanted to go back to his distress, to dwell upon it, to worry it, as a young dog frets to go back to the kill.

Nature, the Comforter, would have none of it. She loved her ailing little one over well to let him have his way. She had him in her arms, and would not let him go. She sang in his ear; she rocked his spirit to sleep. The floodgates were open; and that tide of healing stole in upon his being. In his mind it made religious music. He could not resist it. Half reluctant he let himself drift on those sweet waters.

The sea roamed blindly by. He watched her as a sick child watches his mother. Sense was alive; self was dead. His body was the eye of his soul, the avenue of spirit. It had no life of its own to cloud his clear vision.

The tide of healing swept forward, smoothing the rough surfaces, washing away the jagged edges of pain. As it flowed on, that squabble on the beach a few minutes back receded, ultimately to be lost to view. It had been drowned by the incoming waters.

He was walking backwards on himself towards the centre that some call Christ; withdrawing from the Circumference, where the winds of the World moan always. And in that Centre, always for all men the same, there was Peace and Love and Life Eternal, as on that Circumference there had been War and Darkness and Discord.

Lying on the bosom of the mother-deep, watching her breathe, the boy smiled.

II

The Parson at his side was stroking his calves.

The boy watched him with dreamy eyes.

"Are you hurt, sir?" he asked in a far-away voice.

It came from the depths of no-where. It seemed no longer his. He listened to it with awe.

"Nothing that matters," replied the Parson. "Thank God for His great mercies, and my dear lady here."

Lifting his sword, he kissed the hilt.

"She was inspired," he said in reverent whisper. "I never saw the like and never shall again." He wiped the blade upon his knee-breeches. "Their beastly hairs stick yet - see!"

The boy heard no word. He sat quite still, his eyes on

Alfred Ollivant

that twinkling waste beneath the boom. The sun, which had been shining through mist, now blazed hot upon his face. He eased the boat away, and the shadow of the great brown lug fell upon him comfortably.

"It's all very wonderful," he said, his eyes on the musing waters.

"It's a miracle - nothing less," replied the Parson, unslinging the despatch-bag. "This bag did me yeoman service. Look!" It was slashed to ribands, the rolled coat within gashed through and through; and as he shook it a bullet fell out of the folds. "I owe my life to it and Piper's shooting. The old man dropped a chap dead at two hundred yards as he was braining me."

The boy woke at last.

"What of him - old Piper?"

"Ah, what?" said the Parson, grey and grave beneath the sweat.

Neither spoke again.

III

Beyond the Boulder Bank the wind freshened. The lugger began to breast the water merrily, plumping into the swells with a delicious shock, shooting the water aside in spurts of foam, and ploughing a furrow white behind her.

The Parson stared about him with startled eyes.

"Good Lord!" he said, breathing deep, as one just awaking to a new and terrible danger.

Kit looked at him, and was shocked at the change that had come over him. He could scarcely recognise in this grey-green spectre the roaring swordsman of the shingle-bank.

"I'm tired," said the Parson suddenly, "very tired."

He flopped forward on his knees.

"My sins have found me out," he moaned. "May mother forgive me!"

His courage had faded with his colour.

Collapsing, he lay like a dead thing in a slop of sand and water at the bottom of the boat.

Kit heard his voice as in a dream.

The boy was sitting quite still, the smell of the sea in his nostrils, the wind in his hair, the hiss and flop of the waters in his ears.

The life of the body was coming back to him. The good salt breeze flushed his veins. The tiller began to pull at his hand. The lugger swung and curtseyed, graceful as a dancing girl. She was alive. She was careering over the swells, snatching for her head. She knew her mission, and revelled in it.

Nelson, Nelson, Nelson! she whispered, hissed, and

sang the word.

The boy began to hand her over the seas, as a man hands his lady down a ball-room. She was so swift so strong: throbbing-full of life. He loved her, and began to live again.

Blob was sitting cocked up in the bows, pink as ever and as impassive.

At the sight of the boy Kit felt a certain resentment, and, with the swift self-knowledge peculiar to him, was glad to feel it, for it told him he was coming round. He wished the boy to collapse alongside the Parson. Why didn't he, the silly little land-lubber? Kit, the one sailor aboard, here on his own element, wished to lord it out alone.

"How d'you feel, Blob?" he called, hoping for the best.

"Whoy," said Blob, the breeze in his teeth, "Oi'm that empty Oi can hear me innuds rollin. Oi could just fancy a loomp o porruk - fatty-loike."

The Parson raised himself.

"Swine," he moaned, "have you no soul?"

He turned on his elbow.

"Can't you take her where it's flatter?" he snarled.

"I like a bit of a bobble myself, sir," answered Kit.

"Calls himself a sailor!" sneered the other, and collapsed again.

IV

The frigate was drawing near, the lily flag of a Vice-Admiral of the White at her foretop-gallant mast-head.

A tide of delicious tears surged up in the lad's heart as he beheld her. She was England; she was his own. He possessed her, and was she not beautiful?

Stately lady, she walked the waters, swaying them, her breasts splendid in the sunshine. Her head was in the heavens, a stir of snow at her feet. She was mistress of the seas, and mother of them. And with what noble mirth she lorded it in this her nursery! The turbulent little folks swarmed to clutch her skirts as she swept by. She moved among them, their play-fellow and yet their sovereign lady: here a mocking bow, there a laughing curtsey; anon a stoop, a swift kiss, and she rose, an armful of blossom-babies smothering her.

The boy's heart went out to her in a passion of worship.

She was a tall Princess, stone-blind and beautiful, walking to her doom; and he a boy-knight bucketing across the moor on his pony to save her and the burthen she bore so preciously in her arms - her little son.

And he *would* save her. Nay, he *had* saved her.

He was so proud he could have shouted; he was so moved he could almost have wept.

The lugger thumped through the seas, tugging at her tiller, eager as himself. She reminded him of the scuttling haste with which old Trumps, his pony, bustled along, head set for home; and he laughed merrily. The fuss and fury of the little thing contrasted so ludicrously with the majestic calm of the swan-lady sweeping towards him.

The frigate was close on him now.

As the lugger topped the ridges, Kit, peering beneath the boom, could see the black and yellow of the Nelson chequer on her sides.

Clouds of canvas, tier on tier, towered above him.

He could see the shine of her bows as she lifted, dripping. The water spurted from her foot in foaming cataracts as she plunged.

He steered as though to cross her bows. When he heard the swish of the green waters cleaving before her keel, he put his helm hard down.

"Hail them, Blob!" he screamed, and scrambling forward brought the lug-sail down with a rattle.

"*Boat ahoy*" a voice from the frigate "*who are you?*"

Blob stood in the bows, one hand on the flapping jib. "Oi'm Blob Oad what killed Nabowlin Bownabaardie," he yelled.

The frigate, standing stately on, swung up alongside. Kit, rushing to the side, fended her off, as she slid past, huge above him.

"Heave to!" he screamed, bumping against the sliding

side. "Heave to!"

A deep voice above him spoke.

Kit looked up. A man, leaning over the side, was watching him bump stern-wards with a sardonic grin.

"Bye-bye," he murmured deeply. "My love to the little gurls."

Was he mad? was he mocking?

Kit thought he had never seen so striking a face. The man was a giant with moon-splendid eyes. There was a power about the face, the power of darkness. The sun never shone upon it - only the moon, the moon. But for her wan glimmer it was without light. Kit thought of a wild night at sea, the moon gleaming fitfully on savage waters. The moon, always the moon!

"Despatches for Nelson!" screamed the boy - "for Nelson, Nelson, Nelson!"

The moon went out. There was one flash of lightning, then horror of darkness. The man's life had shocked to a halt. He did not stir, he did not wink, he did not breathe.

Then the blackness lifted, and the moon shone out once more between dark scuds.

"Nelson ain't a-board," he said.

Alfred Ollivant

CHAPTER LXXV

ON THE DECK OF THE *MEDUSA*

I

The man folded his arms and gazed down at the boy, mildly amused.

"Not on board?" gasped Kit faintly. "Where is he, then?"

The moon was out again and shining serenely.

"Why, where I'd like to be - with his best gurl."

He took out a tooth-pick, and began to clean his teeth with gusto.

Kit hardly heard. Desperately he clutched the sliding side. It seemed to him as though the world was slipping away from him. If he let go all was lost.

"Mr. Dark!" twanged a nasal voice from the deck.

The giant leapt round.

"My lord."

"What's that boat doing under my quarter?"

"A Deal hovel, my lord, asking for brandy."

Feet came towards the side.

"First time I ever heard of a hovel stopping a King's ship to ask for brandy."

"That's what I told him, my lord," came the firm reply.

"You didn't!" screamed Kit from far below. "You didn't. Heave to! Heave to! or -"

"You'll sink me, I suppose, young gentleman!"

Kit looked up.

A one-eyed little man was twinkling down at him.

II

The boy came over the side.

He was without hat and in his shirt, a pale stripling, gaunt of cheek, and with flaming eyes.

"Liar!" he cried, and transfixed the giant with a finger.

The one-eyed little man, one-armed too, four stars on his breast, turned on the boy in a cold blaze.

"Remember in whose presence you stand!" he said. "I

Alfred Ollivant

am Lord Nelson."

"He said you weren't on board, sir," cried the boy stubbornly.

"I said nothing of the sort, my lord," replied the giant calmly. "I said I wasn't going to stop the way of your lordship's frigate to let a smuggler's brat liquor up."

"And quite right too," said Nelson. "What is it the boy wants?"

"I understood him to ask for brandy, my lord - for the corpse in the boat."

"What! is there a corpse in the boat?"

"O yes, my lord - a nice little bit of a corpse. But whether the two young gents killed him and are bringing him off to your lordship for a present, as I ave known done in the Caribbees, or whether they dug him up and took him aboard for ballast, only the young gents know."

Those strange eyes dwelt upon the lad sardonically. One thing was plain. Mr. Dark was amusing himself.

Nelson seemed not to hear him.

"Who are you?" rounding on the boy.

"I'm of the same Service as yourself, my lord," replied Kit, white as ice. "A midshipman. My name is Caryll."

"What ship?"

"The *Tremendous*, my lord."

"The *Tremendous*! let's see. What do I know of the *Tremendous*?"

"Gone where we've all got to go some day, my lord - down, down, down," said the giant. "Posted missing Tuesday night." He had folded his arms and was leaning up against the side, moody as the devil. "For some it makes a change; for others it don't. I'm one of the last sort. It's all stale to me. I live there - down, down, down." He yawned with creaking jaws.

Nelson stared at him, then turned to the boy.

"And may I ask what you're doing here, Mr. Carvell?"

"He said he had despatches for you, my lord," interrupted the giant languidly. "Don't see em myself."

Kit's swift mind leapt at the fellow's mistake.

Swift as he was, there was one present swifter - the man who in a flashing moment had won the day at St. Vincent.

Nelson swept round on the giant.

"He said - he had - despatches - for me? You just told me he wanted brandy. How d'you account for that?"

The stillness before the storm was never so appalling as that calm. In all the world only the giant's slow eyelids seemed to stir. The boy felt lightning in the air: he felt it in his heart.

Alfred Ollivant

Dark remained unmoved. He lolled against the bulwark, legs crossed. It was scarcely respectful to the great seaman who stood before him; but the man seemed a law to himself. His chin dropped, his arms folded, those glimmering eyes of his never lifted from his feet.

"I don't account for it, my lord," came the deep voice. "I can't account for myself - much less for my lies."

Far down in those strange eyes Kit caught a gleam. Was it humour? - was it anguish? - what was it? He did not know. The man baffled him. He was groping in the dark and finding - darkness. He was at war with this man, war to the death; and yet, yet, yet, he felt they had something in common. What was it? - a kindred soul? - who should say?

For a long minute Nelson gazed gravely at the other.

"You're mighty strange, Mr. Dark," he said at last.

The man nodded and nodded.

"I'm mighty dark, Mr. Strange," he said - "mighty dark."

III

Nelson turned to the boy.

"Come below," he said.

"*My lord*," came a voice as out of a fog.

Nelson turned.

The giant was following them at a panther-prowl.

As Kit saw him a phrase from the Old Book flashed to his mind - *the Body of this Death.*

Only the eyes lived; abysms through which the boy gazed down to behold the last nicker of a drowning soul.

It was not quite out, that gallant little light. Down there in the tumult of dark waters it fought for life despairingly.

Without, the man was black and white and strangely still. Within, God and Devil were at battle. And the Devil was winning.

The giant prowled across the deck, kneading his hands.

"*Can I have a word with your lordship?*"

The voice was clogged and husky as the voice of one dead for centuries.

"By all means," briskly.

"*Alone, my lord?*"

"Certainly. Here?"

The man rolled his eyes up at Kit. The boy's knees gave. He almost fainted. The soul flickered its last

Alfred Ollivant

before his eyes. The man was dark forever.

"Over here, my lord. By the side, if you please."

His words came stifled as out of the grave.

Kit heard them remotely.

His voice tried to burst through iron blackness and failed.

His soul yelled,

"Murder!" but no sound came. Feet and tongue stuck fast. The Powers of Darkness had prevailed over him also.

The two were walking away across the deck, side by side, the big man and the little.

Nightmare-bound, the boy watched their backs, the one huge-shouldered, slouching, the other sprightly and slight as a lad's.

In the one there was no light. He was a vast black body, unlit now even by the moon. The other was radiant beside him. The Angel of Darkness was about to swallow the Child of Light. The boy saw what was going to happen and could not stay it.

Then he heard a sound.

The man was moaning as he walked.

Nelson stopped.

"Aren't you well, Dark?" he asked, so quietly, so kindly.

The giant swayed. Head and eyes were down, arms swinging. He was as a man asleep preparing for a plunge. And his light was out.

Nelson laid a hand upon his shoulder.

"Can I help you?" he asked, with the shy tenderness of a woman.

The groan sighed itself away. Just so must Lazarus have sighed when the life first began to trickle back along disused veins. Slowly the giant pulled himself together, squaring vast shoulders. Then he drew a tremendous breath. In the darkness a tiny star began to glow.

"You have helped me, my lord," he said, and his voice was clear again.

Then they turned and came back across the deck.

CHAPTER LXXVI

IN THE CABIN OF THE *MEDUSA*

I

Admiral and midshipman were alone in the cabin.

Kit was taking in his hero's face.

It was the face - the boy saw it with amazement - of a *disappointed* man!

The hero of St. Vincent, the victor of the Nile, the conqueror of Copenhagen, a disappointed man!

"Tell your story."

Standing by the door Kit told his tale.

By the port the great seaman listened in chill silence.

His face was turned away. Kit dwelt anxiously on the keen, pale profile, the ruined eye, the lopped arm. Was his listener incredulous? He could not say, and Nelson did not speak.

The boy stumbled on his way.

Alone in that quiet cabin, his own voice shrill and small the only sound, face to face with the man who had saved Europe once, and must again, a confused and silly story he made of it.

Out on the uncritical sea he had almost thought himself a hero: in here, eye to eye with Nelson, he knew himself just a pinch-beck boy.

The silence grew upon him. He found himself listening to his own voice, and half wondering whether he was not dreaming. This almighty little man, so careless, so terrible, chilled him to the core.

He stumbled, sought his mind like a schoolboy posed for a word, sought in vain, and stopped dead.

Nelson drummed upon the table.

"Is that all?"

"All, sir?"

The other strummed impatiently.

"I'm *Lord* Nelson."

The boy was dumb, his heart flaring.

And this was the man the nation worshipped!

Nelson turned his eye upon the boy. There was a sardonic droop about his lips.

"Mr. Carvell," he said slowly, "I have been a midshipman myself. Is this a joke?"

Kit flamed. He had given himself freely for this man, had died a hundred deaths for him - for this!

"If it's a joke, my lord," white-hot and thrilling, "it's a joke for which a good many men have died."

He saw once more the lower deck of the *Tremendous*. He recalled the man in the powder-magazine, and old Ding-dong dying beneath the cliff. He thought of Piper outside that door.

Nelson turned on the boy in a white blast.

"I am Admiral Lord Nelson. You're Mr. Midshipman Carvell. And I'll trouble you not to forget it."

He held out his hand.

"Your papers."

"There are none, sir - my lord. All burnt."

"Pah!" cried Nelson, and turned with a stamp.

On the table was a chart, a pistol at the corner of it acting as paper-weight.

He bent over it.

Kit, with bleeding heart, gazed at his back, blue-coated and white-breeched.

A darn in the seat of the breeches held his gaze. It seemed so odd somehow that Nelson's breeches should be darned. It was the last thing he should have suspected of the hero of Aboukir Bay. He longed to put out his finger and feel it, that darn in Nelson's breeches. Was it real? - or was it a dream-darn? It was real; he could swear it. And it helped him. There was something comfortably human about it. After all, then, a hero was only flesh and blood: he wore darned breeches.

Sometimes the boy wore darned breeches himself, his mother compelling him. There was something in common, then, between him and his hero.

Nelson turned suddenly to find the boy's eyes brimming with laughter.

Across his face swept a great white anger.

"This is scarcely a matter for giggling, Mr. Carvell," he cried terribly. "It seems to me that you by no means realise the *astounding* nature of the charge you bring. If it prove true, it means the hanging of a brother-officer before the Fleet. If not - His Majesty will have no further need of your services."

"The powder-magazine will tell its own story," replied Kit, curt as an insulted girl. "Ask it."

Nelson's eye flashed.

"I'm not in the habit of receiving suggestions from my midshipmen, Mr. Carvell."

"You doubt my word!" with a sob.

"I doubt your story, sir. And I've good reason to. My officers are not in the habit of selling me. But we can soon have the truth."

He opened the door.

"Desire Mr. Dark to be good enough to step this way," he called to the sentry outside, and shut the door again.

"Mr. Dark is my Gunner and the officer against whom you bring your charge - a charge of such a nature as *never*, never in all the years of my service, have I known one officer to bring against another."

He was pacing rapidly up and down the cabin, his stump flapping.

"I have tried to serve you, sir," said Kit in twilight voice, and said no more.

His face was a thought paler than before; his eyes a shade darker. He was bracing himself for a last fight.

Something about the boy, his twilight voice, his pallor, those dark and hunted eyes, struck Nelson.

He stopped his pacing.

"You've nothing to fear, Mr. Carvell," he said less sternly - "if your story prove true."

"It is true, my lord," replied the boy steadfastly.

"God forbid," shuddered the great seaman, and resumed his walk.

II

There was a knock.

Dark entered, sombrely magnificent.

He stood by the door, splendid with that strange splendour of moonlight.

His head, massive as a mountain, was splashed with silver; and from under great and gloomy brows those vast eyes gleamed, unfathomable.

Over by the port stood Nelson, high and white.

"Mr. Dark," he began in chill and formal voice, "I've sent for you upon the most unpleasant business it's ever been my lot to be mixed up in. Had I only to consider myself, what I have to say would be left unsaid. But I have to think of other and larger issues. If a mischance England might be lost."

The other listened immovable. He was like a smouldering volcano. Every moment Kit expected to see flames leap from his eyes.

Nelson cleared his throat, and continued.

"This young gentleman, Mr. Carvell, has been telling me a strange and terrible tale that affects you."

He turned his eye full-blaze upon the other.

"It is this, Mr. Dark - that you have been paid to sell me to the French."

The giant was stone. Not a muscle twitched. Then the tip of his tongue journeyed round his lips. The lips moved. Kit read the words on them, though no sound came.

They were,

"*Not paid.*"

Nelson waited, breathing deep. Receiving no answer, he went on,

"The story so far as I can make it out is this."

Calm and twanging, he stood by the port-hole, and outlined to his alleged murderer-to-be the story of his plot. That mighty man could have crumpled him in one hand, and tossed him through the port-hole. And the giant knew it - so much his eyes betrayed. And the boy, watching from his corner, knew it too. Only the little lopped man talking through his nose across the cabin seemed unaware of it.

The shrill voice ceased. There was silence in the cabin.

"That's the story, Mr. Dark. And I may say I don't believe *one* word of it."

"Thank you, my lord," came the other's voice, deep and rumbling.

"And if you'll give me your word that it's all moonshine," continued Nelson, "why, I'll ask you to shake my hand and forgive me. And that's an end of the dirtiest bit of business I ever had to handle."

The other's voice stuck in his throat. Out it came at last like muffled drums.

"My lord, you're a gentleman."

Nelson came to him with outstretched hand and a wonderful smile.

"Forgive me," he said.

The darkness drifted from the saint's face, leaving behind it evening calm, the stars beginning to shine.

Folding his arms, he bowed deliberately.

Nelson's hand dropped. He stopped short, and his smile died. In a flash the man of action, brisk and curt, had taken the place of the comrade chivalrously admitting a mistake.

"Then I must trouble you to fetch the key of the powder-magazine, and to follow me." He clapped on his cocked hat.

The great man turned swiftly.

"One moment, my lord," and he was gone.

III

There was a rush up the companion-ladder, and the noise of running feet on the deck overhead.

"Great God!" groaned Nelson, ghastly, and flung open the port.

A dark mass with straggling legs shot past.

There was the plump of a body striking the sea, and crash of showering waters.

"*Man overboard!*" roared a voice from the deck. "*Back tops'ls. Here, sir!*"

A rope coiled out and splashed the water.

Nelson's head was through the port.

The man came up beneath him, and turned to face the ship and his Admiral.

"O, Dark! Dark! Dark!" cried Nelson, and there was agony in his voice.

Dark looked up, the hair plastered about his forehead.

"Nelson," he shouted. "I ask your pardon."

"It's yours, Dark," choked the other. "But O! I thought - I thought you loved me! - every man of you."

"Often and often I could have killed you," gasped the other, bobbing to the seas.

"Rather that than this!" sobbed the great seaman. "Murder's the braver deed."

"I was mad!" groaned the other. "She was in my blood. She was my soul. She *is* my soul - the Christ be kind to her! O, if any man in the world can understand, that man should be Lord Nelson."

"No! no! no!" raved Nelson, tossing with his head, stamping with his feet, thumping the port with his fists. "Myself! my wife! my friend! - but *not* my country! *Not* that, Dark! *never* that!"

"*Lively there!*" roared the voice from the deck. "*Lower away.*"

There was the splash of a boat.

Dark flung aside the rope to which he had been holding.

There was silence in the cabin.

Through it came a despairing voice from the water.

"I can't sink! - My God, my God! - I can't sink!"

Nelson swept the pistol off the table and thrust through the port.

"Catch!" he gasped, and threw.

The man rose to it like a leaping fish, flung a high hand, and caught it. Then he sank back.

"Thank you, my lord," he cried, terrible joy in his voice. "May God forgive me as you have done."

Kit had a vision of a black mouth open, a thrusting barrel ringed with teeth, two screwed eyes, and then -

"Don't look, boy!" screamed Nelson, and plucked him away.

The slamming port drowned another sound.

CHAPTER LXXVII

THE *MEDUSA* GOES ABOUT

I

Nelson rocked on the table. His hands were to his eyes, pressing, pressing, as though he would blind himself.

"And this is what comes of it!" he moaned.

Then he rose, and crossed the cabin, walking uncertainly as a little child.

Kit thought he would have fallen, and stepped forward. The great captain waved him back with his stump. Then he passed out alone.

A minute later the boy heard a door open and shut, and peeped out.

Nelson was coming out of the powder-magazine.

Down the gangway he came pale and uplifted. He was quite calm, and about his face there was the rain-washed look the boy had seen on his mother's as she came out of the room where Uncle Jacko lay dead.

Alfred Ollivant

"You were right, Mr. Carvell," he said quietly. "Forgive me."

"Caryll, my lord," ventured the lad - "Kit Caryll."

Nelson's eye leapt.

"Kit Caryll!" he cried. "Kit Caryll! Kit Caryll!" He held the boy's hand, and a beautiful smile broke all about his face. "Have I been blind? You're your father over again."

He dwelt on the boy's face, flooding it with tenderness.

"D'you know," he continued quietly, "d'you know you come to me as a friend risen from the dead? - a friend of my best days, come back to remind me of the years - the happy years - before ... I won the Nile."

Kit heard him, amazed.

He was not happy, then, this man who had won all the world has to give!

He looked *back* for his best days.

They were not now: they were the days before fame had come; fame, the Betrayer, that like a roaring breaker lifts a man heavenwards, and before he can clutch his star, has smashed him on the beach.

The boy recalled his first indelible impression - that the hero was a *disappointed* man.

Disappointed of what? - he, young still, crowned with glory, queens at his feet, nations worshipping him.

Could it be of happiness?

"I have a message for you from another friend of those days, my lord."

"Who's that?"

"Commander Harding."

A darkness chilled the other's face.

"Well."

The boy gave old Ding-dong's dying message.

"I thank you," said Nelson coldly. "Commander Harding always did what he believed to be his duty."

Then the tenderness returned, and he put his hand on the boy's shoulder.

"Come on deck," he said.

II

The boy's throat was surging as he followed Nelson on deck. Now he would have died for the man whom twenty minutes before he could have knifed with joy.

Up there in the sunlight and wind all was noise and bustle.

A little lap-dog officer trotted up in a fuss.

Alfred Ollivant

"Mr. Dark gone mad, my lord, mad, and jumped overboard. We lowered a boat, but he shot himself, shot himself, before we could get to him."

"Call the boat away," said Nelson briefly. "And be so good as to make your course back for Dover."

"For Dover, my lord, Dover?" blankly.

"And don't let me have to repeat my orders."

"Very good indeed, my lord. Very good indeed." He trotted forward, barking fussily.

Nelson climbed on to the poop, Kit at his heels, and leaned over the side listlessly.

"What's that boat under my starn?"

"The boat I came off in, my lord."

"Ah, I forgot.... Is that a dead man in the starn-sheets?"

"No, my lord. That's Mr. Joy, who commanded us in the cottage. He used to know you, my lord. Joy, Captain in the Black Borderers."

A wave of colour swept across the other's white cheek. He flashed his eye on Kit.

"Joy!" he cried. "Old Peg-top Timbers! Hi! below there!" He leaned far over. "Joy! Joy of Battle!"

III

The Parson came up the side.

The crispness was out of his curls; his cheek was mottled; and the brave blue eyes seemed old, hollow, and faded. Even Polly hung somewhat limply from his wrist.

The two men, standing hand in hand, looked into each other's eyes.

"Old friend," said Nelson.

"Colonel," said the Parson, and with the word his life began to flow again.

Nelson's eye twinkled. He laid his hand on the other's shoulder.

"The same old Joy, I see," he said, and added gravely, "Harry, you've saved my life."

"Then I've saved England," replied the Parson, and dwelt upon his friend with the simple love of one brave man for another.

"Yes, yes," said Nelson, with that naive vanity of his so beautiful in its innocence. "England can trust her Nelson. And but for you, Harry, Nelson would be lost."

"You owe a little to me," answered the Parson, "more to Kit here, and most, if I may say so, to my sweet lady."

Alfred Ollivant

"Polly!" cried Nelson - "Pretty Miss Kiss-me-quick!"

"Ah," said the Parson, touched. "You don't forget old friends, Nelson. Nor does she. My love," he murmured, bending, "you remember Captain Nelson of the *Agamemnon*, who was good enough to second us in some of our little affairs in Corsica? Lord Nelson - Miss Kiss-me-quick. She says," he continued, drawing himself up, "that she'll permit the Victor of the Nile to salute her on the cheek."

He held the blade before him with a bow.

Nelson swept off his cocked hat.

"I am honoured indeed," he said, and, standing on the poop before them all, kissed the point.

Kit looked on with tender eyes. He was touched, and not at all surprised, to find that great men too loved solemn make-believe. The vision of the Eternal Child rose before his eyes once more: that Child who is never far in any of us, and least of all in the world's mighty ones.

Nelson turned to the Parson anxiously.

"But, Harry, are you wounded?"

"Mortally," the other answered - "by your beastly sea. But this is better," stamping the deck. "This is more like land."

"Come below," said the great captain. "Here, take my arm.... Only one now, you know."

"One's good enough for the French," laughed the Parson. "But, Nelson! what in the name of goodness are you doing here?"

"Why," said Nelson, stumping away, the other's arm tucked beneath his, "I heard from a - a private source -"

He brought up suddenly. A moment he stood with snoring nostrils, staring before him.

Hell had opened at his feet, and he was looking into it.

"She -"

It was the sigh of a dying soul.

"She -"

Each word was a gasp.

"She -"

He lifted his face, and a glimmer as of dawn broke over it.

"- can explain."

CHAPTER LXXVIII

NELSON'S HEART

In the quiet cabin they looked into each other's eyes, these two old friends.

It was ten years since they had met.

The one was now the world's hero, the other a retired Captain of the Line.

Nelson was thinking as his eyes dwelt upon his friend,

"Just the same."

The Parson,

"What a change!"

It was the old Nelson he saw, and yet only the wraith of the old Nelson. There was a grey and ghastly darkness about him that made the Parson afraid. It was the grey of snow at dusk, the darkness of a pool which was haunted.

The Parson knew the tale, as all Europe knew it. Once he had doubted: now he could doubt no longer. Nelson's story was graven on his face - the story of the man who has betrayed himself. It was writ large there - the struggle, the surrender, the quenching of his ideal in the cataract of passion. He had run away from his best self, as many a man has run. He had slammed a door behind him, hoping to shut out his soul. And now the door had burst open. The ghost of himself, his old self, that had haunted him so long, rapping at the door, refusing in God's name to be laid, had rushed in upon him with a shriek.

He was wrestling with it now.

No wonder he was changed.

The Parson, almost in tears, recalled the Nelson with whom he had chewed ships' biscuits and exchanged dreams in the trenches at Calvi - the Nelson of Corsican days with a face like the morning and a school-boy's heart, his eyes forward into the future. Now he had realised his dreams and more. The young post-captain had become Lord Nelson, Duke of Bronté: St. Vincent, the Nile, Copenhagen behind him.

And, and, and....

Suddenly, as though divining the thoughts of his old friend, Nelson fell forward.

"O Joy!" he cried, "I have sinned."

He clutched the Parson's shoulder, hugging it.

"Ten minutes since I saw it all." He lifted a dreadful eye. "It was *BLAZED* upon me in a flash of lightning." His voice had the hollow muffled sound of a man in a nightmare. "I saw myself: not the man the world is looking to, but plain Horatio Nelson - the sinner."

The confession, shuddering forth from the lips of the great seaman, sprang the horror in the other's heart.

"There, there!" he croaked. "There, there, Nelson!"

"Honours, Orders, Westminster Abbey, and the world's cheers are nothing," came the nightmare voice. "*That* remains."

The Parson collected himself and cleared his throat.

"We all make mistakes, Nelson," he said gruffly. "Everybody stumbles, but no man need lie in the mud."

"I must," cried the other hoarsely. "I must - in honour. Honour!" he cried, throwing back his head with terrible laughter. "Nelson's honour! - O, Joy, you knew me as I was: you see me as I am. *You* can judge. Is it not *hideous* that it should come to this? - that men should *snigger* when Nelson and honour are coupled together."

The tears rolled down the Parson's face.

"Ah, my dear fellow," he kept on saying, patting the other's back, "my dear, dear fellow."

"I have been hiding from my God all these years - and to-day He found me!" sobbed the voice upon his shoulder. "O, He is just - terribly just. He knows no mercy - none."

"None *here*" murmured the Parson. "*There* there's plenty for all."

Nelson lifted a blurred face.

"You think that?"

"I'm sure of it," sturdily. "And I know all about that sort of thing now, you know. I'm a parson."

Nelson held the other off.

"Are you a parson?"

"Yes, sir," a thought defiantly. "And why not?"

His heat brought no twinkle to the other's one wet eye.

The nightmare was passing: Nelson was drifting away into dreams.

"My father's a parson," he mused, as one talking to himself. "If I hadn't gone to sea at twelve, I think I should have been. Nelson and religion! - it sounds strange. Yet I always wished to give all to God."

"You have," cried the Parson fiercely. "Who dares say you've not?"

"I do," said Nelson, dreaming.

"And what would have come to God's world but for you?" shouted the Parson. "Why, swamped by a pack of rackety French atheists."

Nelson seemed not to hear.

"*What is a man advantaged if he gain the whole world, and lose himself?*" he whispered.

Alfred Ollivant

The Parson gathered the other in his arms.

"Nelson," he said with tender sternness, "if you've wronged the Almighty, you must make Him amends."

"How, Harry?" came the voice from his shoulder.

"Why," said the Parson with a grave smile, "you must arise and smite His enemies."

Slowly Nelson composed himself. A great calm swept over him.

"You're right," he said at last, the light breaking about his face. "I am England's David. It is for me to slay Goliath. Sinner as I am, He has chosen me to do this work for Him, and I will do it. Yes, I will do it."

He turned to the port and gazed out.

To the Parson it seemed an hour before he turned again.

The nightmare madness had passed. His face was altogether changed. It was that of a child who wakes from sleep in a panic. There was a startled little smile about it.

"Harry," he said in shy waking voice, "have I been dreaming? - or have I been talking a lot of nonsense?"

The Parson, for all his simplicity, was something of a man of the world.

"Why," he cried heartily, "you've been standing with your back to me, mumbling and grumbling, and being damned rude."

Nelson laughed.

Was the Parson wrong? - or was there in that laugh a note of almost hysterical relief?

"I'll make it up to you, Harry. I'll make it up to you, my boy." He thrust his hand into his bosom, and produced a miniature. "Look here!" in reverent voice - "my Guardian Angel."

CHAPTER LXXIX

IN THE CABIN AGAIN

Kit was in the gun-room, the centre of a group of rosy-faced lads, eagerly questioning.

He could not eat; he could not answer.

"Caryll, the Admiral wants you."

The boy rose and went, trembling.

In the door of the cabin stood the Parson, his blue eyes very kind.

He put a hand on the boy's shoulder, and drew him in.

"Lord Nelson," he said, "I believe this is the most gallant lad in either Service."

The great captain came towards him. The boy saw him through a mist.

"Kit," said Nelson, with that wonderful smile of his - "I may call you Kit? Your father was always Kit to me - will you shake the hand of a brother-officer, who's proud to call himself such?" He added, gazing into the boy's eyes - "Your father was my friend. I hope his son will be."

Kit's heart surged. His knees began to give. He felt himself fading away.

Then the arm that was wont to encircle another waist was round his. His head sank where another head, beloved of Romney, often cushioned.

He began to whimper.

They supported him to a chair, the white head and the curly dark one mingling over his. And no woman could have been more tender than those two men of war, each in his own way so great.

"That's all right, my boy," said the Parson, "my dear boy. Don't be afraid to cry. All men cry - only we don't let the ladies know it."

"We won't tell the midshipmen," murmured Nelson at the other ear. "I'm safe - I weep myself sometimes in confidence. You must just think of me as of a father."

"Paws off, if you please, my lord," replied the Parson. "I'm his adopted father and mother and all; aren't I, Kit? - old friends first, you know."

"Well," gasped Kit between sobs and laughter, "you see I've got a mother, thank you."

"Have you?" cried Nelson, rising from his knees. "Is she like mine, I wonder? If so, I love her already. But there! I love her for her son's sake. And I'm going to write to her to tell her she has a son she can be proud of."

He sat down at his desk.

"Ah, what would England be without her mothers?" he said, taking up a pen.

*　*　*　*　*

The quill pen ceased to squeak.

Nelson thumped the letter with characteristic zeal, rose and gave it to the boy.

Kit pocketed it, his eyes looking thanks through tears.

"Your father'd be proud of you," said Nelson. "He was a true seaman - as his son will be."

"He's thinking of turning soldier, ain't you, Kit?" cut in the Parson. "He's like me - got no use for the sea except as an emetic."

"No, no," said Nelson, smiling. "The Navy claims her cubs."

"Well, well," replied the other, "I won't dispute the point. But like another young seaman I used to know perhaps some day he'll rise to be Colonel of Marines, and win great victories at sea as the result of what we've taught him on land."

"Soldier and sailor too, eh?" said Nelson, and added in a stage-whisper to Kit - "He can never quite forgive us being the Senior Service."

A clock struck two.

"Come, Kit," said the Parson. "What d'you say? Shouldn't we be getting back?"

"I'm ready, sir."

"What!" cried Nelson. "You're never going back?"

"The soldier is," said the Parson. "The sailor can speak for himself. In *my* Service a job half done is a job not done. *We* like to see things through.... Besides, there's Knapp, and old Piper."

"Ah, yes," said Nelson gravely. "I was forgetting. Dear old Piper!"

"He sent a message to you, my lord," said Kit, and gave it.

"Thank you," said Nelson quietly. "Old Agamemnons never forget each other.... If by any mercy of God my old friend should be alive," he continued, "give him my love - Nelson's love; and say his old captain's proud to have sailed with such a man."

"We will indeed," said the Parson thickly. "Come, Kit."

"No, no," cried Nelson, staying him. "You'll leave me my midshipman. I want all my best men by me now."

The Parson turned.

"What say you, Kit?"

The boy looked at Nelson.

"Take your choice, my boy."

"I should like to see the thing through, my lord."

Nelson patted him on the shoulder.

"There spoke the seaman," he said. "Never be satisfied with nearly. Always go for quite."

CHAPTER LXXX

THE *MEDUSA* DIPS HER ENSIGN

I

The *MEDUSA* had gone about and was rocking lazily home, the land misty on her larboard.

Forward a knot of tars were gathered, Blob's cherub-face for centre-piece.

The lad was telling his tale in his slow, musical way.

A hoary old sea-dog with unlaughing eyes was putting leading questions. The men crowded round with grins and thrusting heads. They spat; they chewed; they nudged each other. Here and there a ripple rose to a roar. One man turned his back, and hands deep in his pockets, laughed silently in the face of heaven. Another was stuffing his pig-tail into his mouth to stifle his merriment.

Blob held on his ghastly way unheeding.

His eyes, fresh as dew, had the round and staring look of a new-born babe; the tulip face lolled forward on slender stalk; and a tip of pink tongue played about a

Alfred Ollivant

mouth, beautiful as a bud.

"And what did er say then?"

"Whoy," came the pure voice, "er said - 'Dear! dear!' and Oi says - Theer! theer!' and plops it in, and plops it in, and plops it in."

The Parson hailed him from the poop.

The little group broke up. Blob came through them, calm as the moon, and as unconscious.

"Who is the lad?" whispered Nelson, as the boy lolloped up in laceless boots, hands deep in his waistband.

"One of the garrison," replied the Parson. "Simple Sussex - with the face of a cherub and the soul of a stoat."

"Ah," said Nelson, "another of the heroes."

He took a step towards the advancing boy.

"I don't know your name," said the Victor of the Nile with grave courtesy. "But I may shake you by the hand?"

"Ye'," said Blob, mouth and eyes round.

"Thank you," said the hero, taking the other's limp paw. "I am Lord Nelson."

"Ah," said Blob. "O'im Blob Oad what killed Nabowlin Bownabaardie."

"You've saved me a lot o trouble," replied Nelson, grave but for his twinkling eye.

Blob stared, breathing like a beast.

"Don't you ave two arms on you?" he asked at last curiously.

"I get along very well with one, thank you."

"Mus. Poiper, he've got no legs - only ends loike," pursued Blob.

The Parson hailed him.

"Hi! are you coming ashore with us, or will you stay with this gentleman to fight the French?"

The boy wagged his head cunningly.

"Oi'll goo with Maaster Sir. Oi'm his lad."

"He's coming with me later," said Nelson. "Won't you too?"

"Maybe," said Blob. "When Oi got ma money."

"Plenty o killing, you know, Blob," said the Parson slyly.

Blob rippled off into roguish laughter.

"Oi'll coom," he said. "Mate, pudden and killin - that's what Oi loike."

II

Nelson stood at the gangway.

"Good-bye, Kit. I shall hope to have the pleasure of your company aboard the *Victory* when I sail."

Kit tried to thank him, failed, and went over the side.

"Good-bye, Harry."

The two old friends stood eye to eye, hand to hand, the great sea wide about them and the lugger bobbing beneath.

"Good-bye, Nelson," said the Parson, and added, "Good luck."

The other smiled.

"Trust Nelson," he said.

III

They cast off.

The slow and stately frigate began to draw away.

As she slid past, the boys fending her off, and the Parson already composing himself at the bottom of the boat, Nelson leaned over the side.

"Thank you," he said, and swept off his cocked hat.

Then he turned.

The boys could see him no more. But that shrill voice, so familiar now, twanged above them.

"Now, my lads! I'll ask you to give three cheers for the crew of the Kite. Hip! hip! -"

"Hooray!"

A roaring cheer leapt from the silence. In a moment the shrouds were black with waving men. The great hurrahing vessel drew away, curtseying as she went.

Even the Parson lifted a languid head and peered.

"He's dipping his ensign to you, Kit. Take the salute."

Kit looked through swimming eyes.

The old sense of experience renewed was strong on him - the battle won, the return home in the evening, the cheers of the saved, and his heart drowned in love and glory.

Could it be true?

Yes. The Victor of the Nile had dipped his flag to a ten days' midshipman.

"Ah," said the Parson, "there's Nelson! - God bless him!"

At the stern of the great ship, an empty sleeve pinned

to his breast, stood the greatest seaman of all time, one hand to his cocked hat.

II - KNAPP'S STORY

CHAPTER LXXXI

THE RETURN

I

A mile from shore, under the lee of the land, the wind fell away.

The lugger, with lolling mainsail, flowed down a path of gold. The shore was dark and still before them, and the sun poised above the Downs, blue at the back.

As they neared the land, the calm grew. Save for the lap of waters at the bow, all was hushed in the gracious evening.

Kit, steering, peered under the swaying boom at the shore.

The Parson, Polly in hand, stood in the bows, viking-like.

The lugger was about to beach at the very spot where they had started twelve hours since.

Alfred Ollivant

The tide was much as then; but otherwise what a change!

Then in the cold sunshine men had been busy with each other's lives; now all was sunset peace and waters kissing the shore.

But for one grim reminder of what had been, they might have been returning from a pleasure trip.

The Grenadier Kit had stabbed lay on the slope of the shingle, ghastly to greet them. Just out of reach of the tide he sprawled as he had fallen. No man had touched him. He lay then as now spread-eagled on his face, with wide gaitered legs, and hands flung before him. His chin dug into the shingle; and his shako had fallen askew over staring eyes. It was almost as though he was making faces at them.

Kit saw it and sickened.

Beside the dead man there was none to greet them.

A wood-pigeon crooned itself to sleep among the sycamores on the knoll; the sea fell with a lazy swish upon the shore; behind the orange-lichened roof of the cottage, the Downs loomed black in the glow of sunset The rest was silence and terror.

The lugger grounded, and crashed to a halt in the white fringe of the tide.

The Parson leaped ashore, Polly twinkling in his hand.

"Stand by the boat, Blob!" he ordered, feeling the land with his feet. "Kit, got your dirk? Then follow me."

II

Light and alert, he ran up the slope.

Kit followed with lagging feet.

Never a greedy fighter, for the time the lad had drunk his fill of battle. He tired of hearing his own heart; and that heart tired of its thumping. After twelve hours of the sea's large peace, here he was back again on the evil earth, where the soul is always sick, amid dangers and darkness, beastly men lurking to murder him.

Is it always so on land? he wondered. Is there no heaven on earth except at sea? - where God is because man is not.

He longed to have the waters wide about him again.

Not so the Parson. The feel of the land, firm beneath his feet, thrilled him to new life. He was on his element once more and in it: earth on earth, the warrior at war. A natural fighter, loving it whole-heartedly for its own sake, he was ready for a thousand, almost hoping for them.

Keen of eye, tight-curled, he took the slope at a brisk trot.

A path of stepping-stones led across the green towards the house; each stepping-stone a dead man sprawling face down in a swirl of green.

Kit saw it all as he had seen it then: the tail of Grenadiers, the pursuing Parson, the hounding Gentleman.

Alfred Ollivant

Then it had possessed him; now he only wanted to get away. Home, mother, Gwen, and an apple in the loft; soft cheeks, kind eyes, the voices of women loving him, chaffing him - these he longed for. He was tired of being a man for the time being: he wanted to be a little boy again, to be cuddled, to be loved.

And for him it was no new experience, this battle-sickness on the return to the field at evening. He had been there before. When? Where? He could not recall, yet somehow he remembered.

"One - two - three - four - five!" counted the Parson. "I thought I should never catch the last. How he ran! When I was on him he snarled back like a beaten wolf. Then he got it - whish-h-h!"

Kit trailed blindly at his heels.

That stink of dead men, would he never again get it out of his nostrils?

III

The cottage lay before them, just as they had left it. It was barricaded still, and curiously dark.

"Ha!" muttered the Parson. "I don't like the look of this. Left incline, Kit. Make for cover."

The old soldier, wary as a fox, sheered off for the sycamore knoll.

There was a touch of death and of autumn in the air. Already the leaves on the sycamores were shrivelled; and a rusting chestnut was hung with nuts prickly as sea-urchins. As they passed among the trees a robin lifted its winter-sweet song.

The Parson peered out.

The cottage faced them, grey and grinning. There was no sign or stir of life about it; but manifold evidence of death. On the greensward, all about dead men lay crumpled, faces downwards, killed clearly in flight.

Kit's heart turned white.

Dead men as dung upon the grass here in the holiness of evening, and a robin singing in the sycamores overhead.

Song and slaughter! God's work and man's! O, would the day never come when men would *understand*?

"Pretty work," said the Parson, with the zeal of a professional, as he stepped off the knoll. "Cavalry! See here! - a beautiful stroke. A big man on a big horse, I should say, and putting *lots* o beef into it Yes, yes, yes," with the gusto of an expert. "They've used the edge - see! Got em on the run, then cut em in collops - and all over my bowling-green, tool" treading at the offending horse-hooves.

Kit gave a little cough.

He had seen the lower deck of the *Tremendous* awash with blood; he had dirked men, and shot them. But this was different. That was death in battle: this was death in life.

The Parson looked up and saw the lad white as a woman in such circumstance. He remembered himself.

"I forgot," he muttered. "You're not used to it. War ain't beautiful as seen in the after-glow."

"It's the quiet," whispered Kit, ghastly. "Like a churchyard - the dead unburied."

"Shut your eyes," said the Parson in steadying voice. "Take my arm. Don't think. Repeat a hymn to yourself."

He walked delicately among the dead, Kit stumbling on his arm.

At the garden-gate they stayed.

The Parson hailed, and Kit started dreadfully.

A wood-pigeon with loud wings splashed out of the sycamores. The kitchen clock within ticked. Other answer there was none.

"I must try the door," whispered the Parson. "Will you come? - or stop here?"

"Come."

The Parson walked down the tiny path between trampled beds, Kit shivering on his arm, and Polly leading him.

The cottage was blind; the windows shuttered; the

glass in them shattered.

It seemed more like a mortuary than a human habitation.

The Parson tried the door - in vain.

He laid his ear to it, and listened.

"There's some one there, I'll swear," he whispered, and knocked.

A chair rolled and rolled.

"Piper!"

"No," muttered Kit, with his truer instincts.

Somebody groaned. Broken feet dragged to the door.

The Parson edged off along the wall, hugging it with his shoulder.

"This'll do," he whispered. "Keep behind me. If it's a trick we shall do very well here - flank covered, play for Polly, and the attack with us."

"I don't want any more fighting," whimpered Kit. "I - I want mother."

Bolts groaned, somebody groaning with them.

"Who's there?" husked a ghostly voice.

"Friend," called the Parson.

CHAPTER LXXXII

BACK TO THE DOOR

I

The lock creaked; the door opened.

A face of yellow clay, bandaged about, peered forth.

"That you, Mr. Joy?" came the ghostly voice, terrible in its remoteness.

The Parson dropped his point.

"Knapp?"

The little bandaged figure, in grey shirt and bloody drawers, wrapped about with an old horse-blanket, looked at him with stagnant eyes.

"What's left o me."

There was no gladness in his voice, no light of welcome in his eyes.

The merry little fighter of the morning, then cockiest of men, was now no more than a yellow shadow; dead, you would have said, but for that ghost of a voice, dribbling dreadfully out of his corpse.

The Parson went towards him.

"I never thought to see you alive again, Knapp."

"I'm a little alive," said the man wearily. "They done me - all but."

The Cockney snap was out of his voice. His words came like a drunkard's: he was slurring them, running them together, skipping hard consonants.

"I'll never be a man no more, I won't," he added with a dry sob.

The Parson gripped his hand.

A look of beastly rage darted into the other's eyes.

"Blast ye!" he screamed, and struck at the Parson's face with his elbow. "I'm one - great wownd, you -." He spewed out a torrent of hideous names. "And yet you must go for to wring my and!"

He lifted his foot to stamp it. His wounds twitched at him. He lowered it gingerly and with a groan.

"I ain't a man," he sobbed. "I'm one - great wownd."

"My poor chap," choked the Parson.

The other turned, body, legs, neck, and head moving all of a piece, and shuffled into the cottage on his heels.

The Parson followed.

"Don't touch me!" screamed the other, striking back with his elbows. "Don't come anigh me, my God! or I'll -"

He hobbled in, muffled to the feet in bandages.

II

He led into the parlour.

It was much the same, save that now a great clothes-horse, hung with soldiers' cloaks, made as it were a Sanctuary at one end of the room.

Piper's wheel-chair stood empty in the twilight Knapp let himself down in it with screwed face.

For a time he whimpered tearlessly. He was too weak to weep, and not strong enough to contain himself.

The Parson bent over him.

"Your heroism has not been in vain, my brave fellow," he said. "But for you Lord Nelson would be now in the hands of the French."

"Blast Nelson!" snarled the little rifleman. "What's Nelson to me? Blame fool that I were."

The heroic soul was quenched for the moment. He was flesh distraught - no more.

A flask of brandy was on the window-sill. The Parson poured from it into a glass and gave it him.

Knapp revived.

The Parson took down the shutters, and the evening light streamed in, calm and healing.

"Take your time," said the Parson gently. "Tell us what you can when you can."

Knapp sipped his brandy.

"It was the knives - when they closed. That done me up. Ow, my God!" He shuddered. "If it hadn't been for the Genelman."

"Yes?" said Kit eagerly.

A glow lit the man's eye. The yellow of his cheek flushed ever so faintly.

"I'd die for im," he said, "only he's died for me - what pull his nose and all."

"Is he dead then?" asked Kit.

"Who's tellin this tale? - you or me?"

He put down his glass.

"That there's a genelman."

His eyes were down, and his hands upon his knees. He began to tell the story over in his own mind, but only here and there his tongue took fire and flashed a light

Alfred Ollivant

upon the tale for the outsider to read by.

"Drew em off o me.... I couldn't tell you.... Cursin em and killin em.... Down on his knees, aside o me.... Give me his arm same as I might ha been a lady....

"So we goes back to the cottage, me no better nor dead meat on his arm.... I can't tell you.... I don't know.... I'll never forget it."

He drew the back of his hand across his eyes.

"They kep doggin on him - unduds on em.... Sich faces on em.... Ow, my God! - I sees em now." He shivered and glanced behind him. "And he talkin back at em, easy as you please, chaffin em like.... Seem they dursn't go for to touch him.... Round to the back door.... Old Piper."

Parson and boy were hanging over him.

"Slipp'd out of his chair ... layin on the ground ... all anyhow ... no legs and all.

"'Ullo, Sailor!' says the Genelman. 'Ow are ye?'

"'I'm done, sir,' says pore old Pipes, smotherified. He were layin on his face.

"'Done, be d'd!' says the Genelman, and whips round sudden with his sword.

"Course they run, - curs!

"Round he come again, quick as light, catches old Piper under the arm-pits, and pops him in his chair.

"'Run him in, Soldier!' says he. 'Sharp's the word. I'll keep em off.'

"So I run him in best I could. I weren't stiff yet, so every twitch tears you."

"'Don't bother about me,' says old Pipes. 'Back to the door, Knapp. They're all on to him.'

"Back I obbles all I knoo.... Ah, I'll never forget it."

He lifted his face to the Parson.

"They used to say in the rigimint you was the best sword in Europe, sir." He laid a finger on the other's arm. "This mornin you was the second-best."

"I'm sure of it," says the Parson quietly.

Knapp stumbled on.

"He stood just outside the door.... I did a bit behind him with the baynit, when they got inside his guard.... He kep on killin em.... It was like the Lord Amighty makin lightnins out of His eyes and blastin em.... I never see the like - blessed if I did!"

The long-lost tears poured down his cheek. He was living again.

"They couldn't make nothing of it, and drew back a bit.

"'What!' cries the Genelman, laughin. 'A round dozen of you, and wopp'd by one! I wonder what Black Diamond'd think o you?'

"At that Fat George truss Dingy Joe by the arms.

"'Ow's this?' he squeals, and runs him on the Genelman's blade, dodgin back himself into Red Beard's arms.

"'Good idee!' kughs old Red Beard, and he throws his arms round the fat chap.

"'This'll smother him!' he roars. 'Now, boys, follow up!'

"And down he charge on the Genelman, Fat George in his arms."

For a moment the ghost of the old Knapp walked.

"Fat George weren't for avin it, Fat George weren't," he sniggered, shaking his head. "And I don't blame Fat George neether. Talk! - talk o talkin! - and the face on him!"

He lifted one hand and tittered.

"Old Red Beard stagger in along - just his beard, and his eyes, and his legs beneath, and them hairy arms of is'n like ropes round the fat chap's belly.

"'Your turn now, ole pal,' says he. 'How d'ye like it yourself?' And somehow I fancies he and Fat George hadn't been best friends.

"Well, I see it was all up then, and the Genelman see it too.

"'Shut the door, Soldier,' says he, very calm, 'and

yourself inside of it.'

"'What, sir?' says I, 'and leave - '

"'Do what you're told!' says he, sharp-like."

The little rifleman looked up into the face of his old company commander.

"Well, sir, I'm a soldier. I know my officer. In I goes!"

III

The Parson was stamping up and down like a man in mortal pain.

"And I wasn't there," he moaned. "I left him to do my dirty work - and ran!"

Opening the back-door, he gazed out on the encircling Downs, the light white now behind their blackness.

Outside the door was a fairy circle - just such a circle as a long-armed man with a sweeping sword would make - and round it not twinkling fairies but dead men. It was as though this was a magic ring, fatal to all who crossed it.

In the centre of the ring he could detect heel-marks, where the Gentleman had stood.

Fitting his own heels to the dents, he stood with crouching knees, making play with Polly among the ghosts of the smugglers.

He saw it all: the swarming satyrs, the closing door, the white-faced rifleman at the crack, and the Gentleman, back to the door, face to the Downs, his blade leaping out to scorch intruders within the pale.

"O Polly!" he cried. "We three - we three could have held the door against ten thousand."

The tears flowed down his face. The thought of this young man spending himself for a legless sailor, and a wounded rifleman, his enemies, who half-an-hour before had stood between him and his life's success, touched him to the quick.

"What a man!" he cried.

CHAPTER LXXXIII

PIPER PRAYS

I

He turned back into the kitchen.

Knapp was continuing his tale.

"'Pull em off,' says one, black and bitter. 'Don't spoil your own sport.'

"'The sogers are comin,' says another.

"'It's only the foot,' says the first. 'We've ten minutes afore we need slip it. Roll him on his back,' says he."

The Parson turned to Kit listening with dreadful-eyed fascination.

"Kit, go and tell Blob to come here."

The boy went giddily.

"'Then Fat George chime in,

"'Let him be, boys,' says he, in a fainty kind of a voice.

'He only done what he ought.' And he goes off in a sort of a croak,

"'It ain't been all my fault, my God,' says he. 'You made me that way, only You knows why.'

"And Red Beard chime in usky from underneath somewhere,

"'That's it, ole pal,' he says. 'It's for Him as made, us to explain us.'

"And I reck'n he pop off and the fat chap too.'"

II

"Then he groan, does the Genelman."

The Parson groaned too.

Knapp lifted his face.

"Ah," said he. "And fancy me layin there listenin, just the thick of the door a-tween us."

He stared at the hands upon his knees.

"I made shift to get on my legs, but lor bless you! I couldn't stir. It was all, 'O my God, send a thunder-bolt and put him out of his pain!'

"Then he groan again.

"At that old Pipes - I'd thought he were gone - layin back in his chair, ead all anyhow: -

"'Jack,' he says usky, 'is that the Genelman?'

"'May the Lord ave mercy on im!' I cries. 'It's im. He's dyin for us, Mr. Piper - dyin slow.'

"'So did Jesus,' says he, calm as you please.

"'But can't we do nothin, my God?' I cries.

"'Nothin,' says he, sleepy-like. 'I'm dyin; you're done. God is our ope and strength.'

"'Can't you pray, Mr. Piper?' I begs him. 'You're a good un at that. Ave a go at em,' I says. 'Maybe they'd listen to you. Sure-ly they can't set by and see a genelman like that chaw'd up in cold blood.'

"He didn't answer. But I could see his head pitch forward a bit. And I hears a kind of a mutter.

"Then he stops, and I could see he were listenin,

"'Go it, Mr. Piper,' I says. 'Go it. Pitch it in. You're workin em. Pray! pray! pray!'

"'I ave prayed,' says he. 'Here's the answer.'

"Then I sat up. And well I might. I could hear it comin meself - low and far, and all the while a-growin like a mutter o thunder. It made me shake to hear it - not being brought up religious like.

"Then there was a rushin and a roarin, and the earth

Alfred Ollivant

shook, and h'all of a sudden h'out of the whirlwind a great voice ollaed: -

"'Tally-ho! forrad! - mush em up, boys, and no Woody quarter!'

"'Your prayer is eard, Mr. Piper,' says I. 'It's a Jedgement on em.'

"'My prayer is eard,' says pore old Pipea. 'It's the orse-dragoons.'

"Then his ead loll sideways, and he was h'off again."

CHAPTER LXXXIV

IN THE COTTAGE

I

Knapp was leaning forward, his chin on his hands.

"Yes, it was a sweet cop. They was expectin the foot, and they got the orse, and got em ot."

He chuckled faintly.

"I couldn't see much, but I eard enough to make my eart glad. Scream! - I tell ye.... It were better'n beer to me.

"Then I faints for loss o blood."

He paused, staring at the ground.

"When I come to, the foot - soldiers were carrying the Genelman through the door - them long legs of is'n and all."

His voice began to jerk.

"Just the same - only more paler-like."

Alfred Ollivant

He was jigging with his knees, and the words joggled as they came out.

"Then he see me.

"'Hullo, Soldier,' says he. 'No, no, don't get up,' me trying to rise to me officer. 'We're both a bit dicky, I expect. How are you?'

"'Nicely thank you, sir,' says I, choky. 'And you, sir?'

"He smiles that way of his.

"'I'll be better soon,' says he. But I knoo from the way of his voice he'd got his marchin orders all right; and I knoo e knoo'd it too."

The little man was sniffing; and the tears were flowing down his nose.

"'Take me to Sailor,' says he to the chaps.

"So they took him to where pore old Pipes lay in his chair, his head lollin back, somethin dreadful to see.

"The Genelman bends over him, and takes one of his hands.

"That stirs the old man.

"'That you, sir?' says he, usky-like.

"'Ah, friend,' says the Genelman, 'how goes it?'

"'Tarrabul ornary,' says pore old Pipes.

"'You'll be better soon,' says the Genelman, strokin his hand. 'It's a rough passage,' says he, 'but it's Ome right enough once you're there.'

"'Ome it is,' says Pipes, and back goes his head, and he was h'off again.

"Then the Genelman turn to one of the chaps.

"'Just spread your coat on that dresser, my man, will you?' he says. 'Now lift him gently. Don't wake him. He's set his course for the Old Country.... Now just lay me on the floor, and prop me up against the wall - same as Soldier there.'"

Knapp was sobbing now.

"'Same as Soldier there,' he repeated. 'There weren't to be no difference a-tween us. O no! 'Same as Soldier there,' he says - and me pull his nose only yesterday! And strike me dead!" - he lifted a streaming face - "if it didn't come over me all of a pop what Mr. Piper said about him and Jesus."

II

He pulled himself together and went on.

"Then up come the orse-captain, great black charger in a lather.

"'What luck?' says he.

Alfred Ollivant

"'Why none,' says the foot-captain, little black and red chap, plumpy. 'The Grenadier chaps in the farm-buildings surrendered at discretion. Plucky fine sports-men, these French beggars, ain't they?'

"'Well, you was about a thousand to one, Chollie, so I don't know as I blames em,' says the orse-captain, laughin.

"'All very well for *you*,' grumbles Plumpy, mighty bitter. 'I suppose you bagged all *your* lot.'

"'Every mother's son on em,' says t'other, chuckin himself off. 'Rare sport. Look there !' and he shows the edge of his sword.

"'Just your luck, Bill,' says Chollie. 'I sweats my soul out to get up in time, and just when I'm there, up you larrups on them blame ole camels o your'n, and dashes the cup from my lips. Who'd be a - foot-slogger?' says he; and he takes the other by the arm; 'Now tell us all about it.'

"'Why that's soon told,' says the orse-captain. 'Them we didn't cut up in the open, we run to earth in a drain, and pots em pretty from the mouth.'

"'Any prisoners?' says Plumpy, mighty keen.

"'There *was* two,' says, the orse-captain, sniggerin.

"Plumpy turns on his heel.

"'Damme you might ha left me the prisoners, Bill,' says he. 'Given my chaps a taste o the stuff after all their trouble.' And he says it so ot and uffy like that the

Genelman, leanin against the wall, laughs.

"The orse-captain heard him, and pokes in.

"'Who's that?' he says.

"Then when he saw the Genelman agin the wall, he offs his helmet - he knoo what was what did the orse-captain, I will say that.

"'Can we do anything for you, sir?' says he, hushed like.

"'Nothing for Sailor and me, thank you,' says the Genelman. 'I don't know about Soldier there.'

"'I'll send a man back to Lewes for a doctor at once,' says theorse-captain. 'We must be going on. There's a scare all over the country that Fighting Fitz has landed at Pevensey at the head of a Cavalry Division.'

"The Genelman laughed a bit.

"'A wild-goose chase, believe me,' says he.

"'I think so too, sir,' says the orse-captain. 'Still General Beauchamp got an express from Pitt to that effect last night. Some chap swore he'd seen him. And we all know if there's any man in the world'd do it, it's Fighting Fitz.'

"'I am Fighting Fitz,' says the Genelman. 'There's no landing except what has took place.'"

Knapp dried his eyes.

Alfred Ollivant

"Yes; he was a - General all right, and he give his life for Private Knapp."

III - THE WISH AT EVENING

CHAPTER LXXXV

THE SANCTUARY

I

"Where is Piper?" asked the Parson.

The little rifleman pointed to the tall clothes - horse hung about with cloaks, which made a Sanctuary of the far end of the kitchen.

"Is he dead?" whispering.

"I fancies so, sir. Lingered it out wunnerful, chattin to the Genelman, ummin an ymn and that. But he's not to say spoke these hours past."

The door opened and Kit entered on tip-toe.

The Parson beckoned him, and drawing aside the clothes-horse, entered the Sanctuary.

Kit followed reverently.

Within stood the kitchen dresser. On it, in the religious

Alfred Ollivant

light, lay the old foretop-man.

Somebody had flung a horse-blanket about his lower body that, lying so, the horror of what was not might be concealed.

Yet even so Kit found himself shuddering.

The terror of that lopped trunk, flat on its back, shocked his heart.

Childlike he felt in the dimness for the Parson's fingers, and was made glad by their grip.

"I think he's gone," whispered the Parson.

II

The old man's head, moon-white in the dusk, lay on a soldier's knapsack. An officer's short cloak, buttoned about his throat, was flung back from his body. The great hands, fingers so touching in their thick-jointed awkwardness, were folded on his bare and shaggy breast. His wounds were hidden, but tattooed upon his chest was something that Kit at first mistook for a cross. Then he saw it was an anchor.

And as he looked the anchor seemed to glow and grow. No longer a blue smudge on the skin, it was an anchor in the heart, shining through the flesh - the anchor on which this brave old battleship had ridden out the gale of life.

The old man lay calm as marble. The cheeks were hollowed, and the fringe of stiff white hair uplifted.

A more beautiful picture of an Englishman, faithful unto death, it was impossible to conceive.

Kit thought of Sir Geoffrey Blount, the old Crusader with chipped nose - mailed hands folded just so, casqued head tilted just so - asleep on the stone-slab in the lady-chapel at home.

But how far more beautiful than that broken-nosed old warrior was this Crusader of the Sea!

III

The Parson bent.

"Piper!" he called low. *"Piper!"* The old man stirred.

"D'you know who I am?"

One great forefinger uplifted and fell.

"We won through," choked the Parson. *"Nelson's safe."*

The old man's lips parted.

"Mr. Caryll's brought a message for you from Nelson," continued the Parson. "Kit!"

The boy bent his lips to the ear of the dying sailor.

"Piper!" he cried, his pure boy's voice ringing out fearlessly. *"Nelson - sent - his - love - to - you - his - love."*

"He can't hear," choked the Parson. "It's no good."

"Hush," said the boy.

He knew the message would take minutes travelling along the dying passages to the brain.

At last, at last it reached.

The old man's face broke into a smile, fair as a winter sunset.

"Love" he whispered, nodded deliberately, and died.

CHAPTER LXXXVI

TWILIGHT

I

The Parson turned to the window, weeping.

Kit crossed to comfort him.

"It's all right, sir," he said tenderly, taking the other by the arm.

A hand plucked at his ankle.

"Little Chap," whispered a voice.

The boy looked down.

At his feet, propped on a straw-stuffed haversack against the wall, lay the Gentleman.

Kit was kneeling beside him in an instant.

"O, sir!" he cried, with sobbing heart.

The other tweaked his nose with tender fingers.

"Cela ne fait rien."

"But are you hurt, sir?"

"Pas trop.... Not quite what I was at dawn; and not quite what I shall be at dark."

He was sitting strangely huddled.

"May I see?" begged Kit, fingers at his breast.

"Certainly not," the other replied with his faint chuckle.

"But have they made you comfortable?"

"Quite.... So kind, you English - once you've got your own way. I've been lying here, dreaming and drifting, while the flies buzzed and Sailor on the table there muttered about his Saviour."

The Parson bent over him.

"Sir," he said, "what you must think of me -"

His voice came in gusts.

The other lifted his face.

"Comfort yourself, my friend. In your place I should have done the same."

"I swear to you -" gasped the Parson, broken and blubbering.

The other took his fingers.

"Friend," he said, "you won; but I didn't lose."

The old flicker of swords was in his eyes.

"Defeat can't touch the man who won't admit it. Look at Sailor there! He was impregnable. So am I."

II

A robin sang outside.

The trill fell sweetly on the silence.

The Parson bent above the dying man.

"Is there anything we can do for you, sir?"

The other raised wistful eyes, mischievous a little.

"I should like to pose my last under the stars."

The Parson's mouth twitched. He gathered the other in his arms, easily as a reaper gathers his sheaves.

They left the Sanctuary.

"Come along, Little Chap."

He held out his finger for the boy.

Kit grasped it.

So they passed out into the holy evening.

Alfred Ollivant

The light streamed from behind dark hills in floods.

As he felt the evening sweet about him, the Gentleman drew a delicious breath.

"The peace of God that passeth all understanding," he murmured, and saluted with languid hand.

III

Blob was coming across the greensward towards them.

He was lolling along, both hands tucked in his waist-band, whistling.

Then he looked up, and saw the limp figure with the dangling legs being carried towards him.

He stopped dead, gaping.

The colour left his cheek; his face puckered like a child's making ready to cry.

That helpless man, borne as he had seen babies borne, flashed a light on his twilight mind. For one swift second he saw, as others see, the pathos of things human. A rumour of the world's tragedy pierced to his remote soul; and the pity of it staggered him.

Flinging back his head he thrust out a questioning finger.

"Why?" he wailed.

"That," said the Gentleman as he was carried by, "is the question which Life asks and Death answers. Good-night, Monsieur Moon-calf. Beautiful dreams."

Alfred Ollivant

CHAPTER LXXXVII

HIS CAUSE

Half-way up the Wish, in the hollow where yesterday Knapp had stolen upon him, the Parson laid him down.

He lay long-legged, gazing towards the hills, whence came the light.

Beneath him the flint cottage, against which he had broken his strength in vain, rose sturdily.

"A nice fight, eh, Parson?"

"I shall get no better - this side of heaven," replied the Parson simply.

"There's only one thing," continued the other. "I think you should have a peep at those powder-barrels in the sluice. Powder's a funny thing - especially when it don't go off."

"I will, sir," said the Parson. "Thank you. I ought to have thought of it myself."

He started down the slope.

A few steps away he paused and plucked a blade of

grass. Then he climbed slowly back, the square face very grave.

At the feet of the dying man he halted, and took the grass-blade from his mouth.

"Sir," he said, "are you a Christian?"

At that moment, in that light, sudden though it was, the question seemed beautifully fitting.

"All men are when they are dying," came the quiet reply. "They must be. As the world-tide ebbs, the Christ-tide flows. That is the Law."

"I ask," continued the Parson in labouring voice, "for this reason: I've no doubt you're a better man than I am. Still I'm a clergyman, though I'm not much good at it. And if you've got anything on your conscience - anything you care to tell me - I'll - I'll - in duty-bound I'll -"

Kit made a move to rise.

The dying fingers closed round his own.

"I forget nothing," said the Gentleman simply. "I regret nothing."

"Nothing?" asked the Parson, stubborn to do his duty.

The other closed his eyes.

"One thing perhaps."

"What?"

　　　　　Alfred Ollivant

There was a sighing silence.

"Ireland," came the quivering reply.

"Sir," cried Kit, with flashing intuition, "you are dying for her."

The other squeezed his fingers.

"Ah, thank you, thank you! how generous! How kind! how most un-English!"

"We mean well anyway," grunted the Parson.

"Yes," said the other slowly. "You did her to death: but you did it for the best. That's England to the core!"

The man's white bitterness struck like a sword. It was something new; it was something terrible.

"Drogheda in the name of God!"

"What's done can't be undone," growled the Parson, all the Englishman coming out in him. "I believe we're trying now."

He bent over his fading enemy.

A thousand dim emotions troubled his heart. Words surged up like waves in the fog of his mind and were gone again, unuttered.

"Good-bye," he said at last gruffly, and made a stiff little bob.

A hand sought his.

The Parson hugged it between both his own, and turned, dumb still.

Alfred Ollivant

CHAPTER LXXXVIII

THE ADVENTURER

The dusk began to shroud them.

Beneath them the Parson was climbing out of the creek, making for the mouth of the drain.

"That's a dear man," said the Gentleman. "He's so English - true as steel, and thick as mud."

He rolled his head round. Kit caught the ghost of the old gay twinkle in his eyes.

"Shall I tell you a secret?"

"Yes."

"What d'you think was in those powder-barrels?"

"Beer," flashed the boy.

"Sand, Little Chap - best Eastbourne sand."

The boy rippled off into low laughter.

The Parson, on hands and knees at the mouth of the drain, heard him and looked back. It was not quite his notion of how a dying should be conducted: still, they were both a bit mad, those two on the hill-side, both the poet-y kind, and so must be excused.

"Yes," said the Gentleman, "I think I had the best of you there."

"I think you had."

His comrade's courage warmed the boy's heart.

He had always associated a death-bed with drawn blinds, hushed voices, sniffling women on their knees and the like.

And here lay this long-limbed man on the grass in the evening, the night bending to kiss him, the sea hushed behind, making ready for the plunge with the high heart and twinkling humour of the lad running down the sands to bathe.

A little wind breathed on them chilly.

The Gentleman began to shudder.

The boy brooded over his dim outline.

A sudden burning curiosity kindled his heart.

"Is it - very aweful?" he ventured at last.

"Not a bit," whispered the other. "It's as easy as living, once you know how."

The boy rippled.

Alfred Ollivant

"Have you ever done it before?"

"Every hour of every day since the beginning."

The boy hugged his hand. He then too had the sense of reiterated life, eternal here on earth.

"Ah, you feel that," he said comfortably. "Then I know you're not afraid."

"Not a bit," sleepily. "I'm too interested - the undiscovered country, you know." His chest was sinking in upon his voice. "What's it going to be?"

Piper's last word leapt to the lad's tongue.

"Love," he said, before he knew that he had said it.

The Gentleman nodded.

"I believe you," he whispered. "Yes, yes, yes.

"*The face familiar smiling through His tears -*

"I can see it."

Kit was crying, he knew not why.

Unable now to see the other's face, he stretched a hand and stroked it.

"Are you there, sir?"

"Always there, Little Chap."

The voice was far, and getting further.

"How - how d'you feel?"

"Why, as I never felt before," chuckling still.

For long he lay still, the night gathering about him. Then the voice came again out of the darkness.

"Ah! there's the first star!"

He lay with hands folded, and face starward. He was drinking in the dark as it began to people, and humming to himself. Kit, listening with all his heart, heard as it were the voice of one singing in Eternity. And whether his ear heard words, or whether only his heart heard the song the other's heart was singing, he never knew.

"Hark to her, hark to the Voice of the Beautiful Spring,
Calling to come,
Calling to come,

Over the moon-whitened wave on a kittiwake's wing,
Over the foam,
Furrow and foam,

Leap to her, leap, O my heart, when thou hearest her sing,
Home to her, home,
Home to her, home."

The song ceased.

There was an age-long silence.

Alfred Ollivant

Then out of the darkness from millions of miles away a whisper,

"Kiss me, Little Chap."

CHAPTER LXXXIX

THE LAST POST

The Parson bore the dead man down the hill beneath the stars, Kit still holding the cold hand.

Here yesterday this same limp and lolling figure had chased Knapp with rousing limbs. Now not all the trumpets of his own Brigade could stir his little finger.

Over the greensward the Parson bore his burthen, past the hushed sycamores, into the kitchen.

They entered the Sanctuary.

One candle there showed a Union Jack shrouding a still something on the dresser.

Beside it the Parson laid his dead.

Knapp, bloody-bandaged, crept through the curtain and joined them, Blob at his heels.

So they gathered in the half-light: the garrison who had held the Fort, and the man who had stormed it.

It was but the kitchen of a cottage; yet no soul there but felt that he was standing upon hallowed ground.

Alfred Ollivant

Kit bent above the dead.

Beautiful as he had been in life, the Gentleman was yet lovelier in death.

Reverently Kit crossed the dead man's hands and laid his sword beside him.

As he raised his head, one standing at the foot of the dresser bent. It was Blob. Kit shot out a hand, fearing some irreverence. Then he saw and stayed.

Something in the spirit of the occasion, the stillness, the hallowed light, had waked in the boy some inherited memory of noble death-beds, brave as they were beautiful.

The soul of the past, quickening the dull present, stirred him to lovely action.

He kissed the dead man's feet, and withdrew weeping.

Across the dresser Knapp was blubbering.

"E were a genelman," he repeated over and over again. "E were a genelman."

From the head of the table the Parson echoed him.

"He was a soldier and a gentleman; and he lies beside the bravest man and truest Christian who ever trod a deck."

He paused and they could hear the flutter of his breath.

"And now I am going to honour him as never foreigner

was honoured yet."

He flung back the flag that shrouded the old fore-top-man, and spread it over both.

"In death we are all friends," he said, arranging it with tender fingers. "Let us pray."

And in the dusk the living knelt beside the dead.

It was high noon.

The *Victory's* barge lay on Southsea Beach.

A midshipman, with keen long face and anxious eyes, was standing by it, a curly-haired parson at his side.

"Listen here, Kit," the latter was saying, "this is the *Times* of a week ago: -

"*The intelligence which we announced yesterday, respecting the breaking up of the camp at Boulogne, has been confirmed by the crew of a gun-boat, which was captured on its way from that port to Havre.*"

He laid his hand on the boy's arm.

"Nap's given it up," he said. "And we know why."

"Hark!" cried Kit. "Here comes Nelson."

And come he did, the man for whom they had fought and conquered.

They could see nothing for the swell of the beach; but they could hear.

Alfred Ollivant

And what they heard was the Voice of England marching shorewards to see her hero off.

A roaring flood of sound made the stillness tremble. It was stupendous.

The vanguard of the mob trickled over the bank with tossing arms and backward faces. Behind them a vast black tide of people brimmed, welled over, and rippled down towards the watchers; and aloft on their shoulders was a figure, dark against the light.

How small he looked, that battered little man, shorn of an arm, and one eye bashed; yet riding the flood, and ruling it!

His cocked hat was in his hand, his white hair bare to heaven.

He looked what he was - the man on whom the world's eyes were set, and aware of it.

It was an inspiration to behold him.

Kit was moved to dumb madness. His heart was all tears and triumph. He was a flood in flames. A glory was looking through his eyes. The veil of flesh was fading.

Nelson was far the calmest there. He was radiant indeed, but with the radiance of the moon, steering its way amid droves of clouds. That high pale look hid the blazing heart.

So he came, shoulder-borne: here a hand to an old stumping sailor; there a smile to a woman; anon a wave to a familiar face.

Grimy navvies wept, roared, stamped, as they bore him. They fought for a grip of his hand. They jostled for a look. They sang hymns and bawdy ballads, the tears rolling down their faces. Women, drunk with ecstasy, screamed and tossed their babies. Urchins howled and tumbled. Young men lurched, laughed, and fought. In front a tiny boy in a blue jersey marched manfully, thumping a toy drum.

A grey virago, locks a-flutter, fell on her knees in the path of the mob.

"Save us, Lard Nelson, save us!" she screamed.

In a lull of the tempest, the clear voice, somewhat shrill, made answer,

"Yes, I'll save you."

There was a second's quiet, one of those tremendous seconds such as must have been before the world was: then a roar to shatter hearts.

A hand gripped Kit's.

The boy looked up into the Parson's blue and brimming eyes.

"It was worth it," those eyes said.

Then the crowd broke all about them. The boy was carried off his feet. It was like swimming amid breakers.

　　　　Alfred Ollivant

He caught a tumbling glimpse of Nelson stretching a hand over many heads to the Parson; and his eye read the words,

"But for you, old friend!"

Then dimly, as in a dream, he was butting his way towards the boat, he and the Parson, Nelson between them.

A hand touched his - a touch, no more; but it was the Nelson-touch.

Then he would have liked to die.

Earth contained no more for him; and he was sure of heaven.

[*I will answer no questions about this book* - A. O.]